William Smith, Theophilus D. Hall

Short Tales and Anecdotes from Ancient History

and passages from English authors for translation into latin prose

William Smith, Theophilus D. Hall

Short Tales and Anecdotes from Ancient History
and passages from English authors for translation into latin prose

ISBN/EAN: 9783337361112

Printed in Europe, USA, Canada, Australia, Japan

Cover: Foto ©Andreas Hilbeck / pixelio.de

More available books at **www.hansebooks.com**

PRINCIPIA LATINA.—Part V.

SHORT TALES AND ANECDOTES

FROM ANCIENT HISTORY

AND PASSAGES FROM ENGLISH AUTHORS

FOR TRANSLATION INTO LATIN PROSE.

WITH AN ENGLISH-LATIN VOCABULARY.

By WILLIAM SMITH, D.C.L., LL.D.

Tenth Edition, revised and considerably enlarged,

By T. D. HALL, M.A.

LONDON:
JOHN MURRAY, ALBEMARLE STREET.
1892.

DR. WM. SMITH'S LATIN AND GREEK COURSE.

LATIN COURSE.

THE YOUNG BEGINNER'S SERIES

(FOR CHILDREN).

A FIRST LATIN BOOK: Containing the Rudiments of Grammar, Easy Grammatical Questions and Exercises, with Vocabularies. 12mo. 2s.

A SECOND LATIN BOOK: Containing an Easy Latin Reading-Book: with Analysis of Sentences, Notes, and Vocabulary. 12mo. 2s.

A THIRD LATIN BOOK: Containing Easy Exercises on the Latin Syntax, with a Dictionary to the Exercises. 12mo. 2s.

A FOURTH LATIN BOOK: Containing a Latin-English Vocabulary for Beginners, arranged according to Subjects and Etymology. 12mo. 2s.

THE PRINCIPIA SERIES.

PRINCIPIA LATINA, PART I. A First Course. Containing a Grammar, Delectus, and Exercise-Book. With Vocabularies. With Accidence, adapted to 'Public School Latin Primer.' 12mo. 3s. 6d.

APPENDIX TO PRINCIPIA LATINA, PART I. Being Additional Exercises, with Examination Papers. 12mo. 2s. 6d.

PRINCIPIA LATINA, PART II. A First Reading-Book. Containing an Introduction to Ancient Mythology, Geography, Roman Antiquities, and History. With Notes and a Dictionary. 12mo. 3s. 6d.

PRINCIPIA LATINA, PART III. A Second Reading-Book. Containing Easy Hexameters and Pentameters; Eclogae Ovidianae; Prosody and Metre. 1st Verse Book. 12mo. 3s. 6d.

PRINCIPIA LATINA, PART IV. Prose Competition. Containing Rules of Syntax, with Examples, Explanations of Synonyms, and Exercises on the Syntax. 12mo. 3s. 6d.

PRINCIPIA LATINA, PART V. Short Tales and Anecdotes from Ancient History and Passages from English Authors for Translation into Latin Prose. 12mo. *New and Enlarged Edition.* 3s. 6d.

THE STUDENT'S LATIN GRAMMAR, for the Upper Forms. Post 8vo. 6s.

A SMALLER LATIN GRAMMAR, for the Middle and Lower Forms, abridged from the above. 12mo. 3s. 6d.

GREEK COURSE.

INITIA GRÆCA, PART I. An Introduction to Greek: comprehending Grammar, Delectus, and Exercise-Book. With Vocabularies. 12mo. 3s. 6d.

APPENDIX TO INITIA GRÆCA, PART I. Being Additional Exercises, with Examination Papers, and Easy Reading Lessons, with the Sentences analysed, serving as an Introduction to INITIA GRÆCA, PART II. 12mo. 2s. 6d.

INITIA GRÆCA, PART II. A Reading-Book. Containing Short Tales, Anecdotes, Fables, Mythology, and Grecian History. Arranged in a systematic Progression, with a Lexicon. 12mo. 3s. 6d.

INITIA GRÆCA, PART III. Greek Prose Composition. Containing the Rules of Syntax, with Copious Examples and Exercises. 12mo. 3s. 6d.

THE STUDENT'S GREEK GRAMMAR, for the Upper Forms. By Professor CURTIUS. Post 8vo. 6s.

A SMALLER GREEK GRAMMAR, for the Middle and Lower Forms; abridged from the above Work. 12mo. 3s. 6d.

THE ACCIDENCE OF THE GREEK LANGUAGE. Extracted from the above Work. 12mo. 2s. 6d.

JOHN MURRAY, ALBEMARLE STREET.

PREFACE TO THE NEW EDITION.

THIS work was originally drawn up at the suggestion of the Rev. F. E. Durnford, Master of the Lower School at Eton, who had been accustomed to give similar tales to his pupils for translation. The sale of nine editions proves that it has met an acknowledged want, and it is hoped that the improvements and additions which have been introduced into the present edition will make it still more generally useful.

The additions are the following :—

1. An Introduction; illustrating some of the differences of construction which Latin as compared with English idiom presents: especially in the connexion of clauses by means of Relative (i.e. Conjunctive) Pronouns and Adverbs, and in its larger use of Participles. A brief, but, it is hoped, sufficient, account is also given of what is so striking a feature of Latin narrative prose, the *oratio obliqua*, together with some examples for practice in it (pp. 8–18).

2. A short series of very easy paragraphs (Nos. i–xv); prefixed to the original 'Short Tales and Anecdotes,' and designed to facilitate the young student's first attempts in the way of connected Latin prose. These paragraphs have been taken from Bible story, substan-

tially as related in a very correctly written Scripture compendium of the fourth century A.D.

3. A complete Vocabulary of all the English words contained in these preliminary paragraphs and the series of 'Short Tales and Anecdotes'; excepting in a few cases where the Latin equivalent is immediately supplied in the Notes.

4. An Appendix, consisting of passages of moderate difficulty, selected from English authors, for translation into Latin. Here very little help has been supplied, and *the English words contained in these passages have not been indexed for the Vocabulary.* The student must learn, sooner or later, 'to swim without corks'; and the best time for him to make the effort is perhaps, when—after due preliminary practice and careful Latin reading—he begins to attack passages of original, idiomatic English. The very first thing he has then to learn, is so to phrase his matter, that it may naturally assume a Latin form; and the supplying of verbal equivalents might tend to lead in the wrong direction—namely, that of word for word translation. In cases where more verbal help is required than is here supplied, the student should have recourse to a good English-Latin Dictionary, in which a fuller treatment both of words and phrases may be expected than is compatible with the scope of such a work as the present.

5. Besides these distinct additions, the notes to the original 'Tales and Anecdotes' have been extended; with the object of supplying help in every case where the young student might reasonably be expected to

feel uncertainty or embarrassment. Some teachers may think the amount of help supplied excessive; but it must be borne in mind that the feeling for what is and what is not Latin, is not to be acquired by continual fumbling in the dark, but by gaining familiarity with good examples.

The practice of reading the paragraphs aloud into Latin, *after accuracy has been secured*, is strongly recommended both to teachers and private students.

CONTENTS.

I. INTRODUCTION.

COMPLEX SENTENCES.

THE present work assumes a knowledge of the structure and arrangement of Simple Sentences. Complex Sentences are built up from Simple Sentences and clauses by means of—

    1. Conjunctions.
    2. Relative (or Conjunctive) Pronouns.
    3. Participles.

1. CONNECTION BY MEANS OF CONJUNCTIONS.—Conjunctions show the relations of the parts of a Complex Sentence to each other. Being link-words, their natural position is at the commencement of the clauses which they serve to introduce; and there is little that is peculiar about their use in Latin as compared with English. A few points, however, may be noted.

Et . . . et.—When there are two co-ordinate clauses, both equally emphatic, **et** often introduces the first as well as the second. (Compare in Greek μέν . . . δέ.) Thus it may sometimes be desirable to use the introductory **et**, even though there is nothing to correspond to it in the English. See Ex. 53, l. 7 :*—

('The boy) repressed the pain without uttering a word, *and* held his arm quite still.'—Puer *et* dolorem pressit, *et* bracchium immotum tenuit.

ʏ   * All the references to Exercises are to those in this work.

So Ex. 28, l. 3 :—

'Cyrus was courteous and obliging to Lysander in other respects, *and* (iu particular) showed him a piece of ground fenced in and carefully planted.'—*Et* ceteris in rebus comis erga Lysandrum atque humanus fuit, *et* ei quendam conseptum agrum diligenter consitum ostendit.

Compare also the following period (Liv. xxii. 6), in which this construction occurs twice over :—

Eum *et* robora virorum sequebantur, *et* ipse quacunque iu parte premi ac laborare senserat suos, impigre ferebat opem ; insignemque armis *et* hostes summa vi petebant *et* tuebantur cives.

'He was followed by the very flower of his troops, *and*, in whatever part of the field he had remarked his men to be hard-pressed and put to it, energetically rendered assistance in person ; and being marked out by his armour, he was attacked by the enemy *and* defended by his fellow-citizens with the utmost energy.' See also St. L. G. § 562.

Cum (quum)*.—This is the ordinary connective between clauses related to each other in the order of time ; and is frequently found where an English writer would prefer detached sentences. It is used in narrative with the Imperfect and Pluperfect Tenses Subjunctive. For examples, see—

Ex. 1. Cum Porsena eum . . . terreret . . .
  „ 3. Qui cum Janiculum primo impetu cepisset . . .
  „ 5. Cum adversus Veientes . . .
    ib. cum saepe victores exstitissent . . .
  „ 6. Cum eos vidisset . . .

In English the relation of time is often left unmarked, being apparent from the thread of the narrative.

---

* The orthography of the classical period is *cum ;* in older writers, *quom.* The form *quum* (based on the archaic *quom*) has not been traced further back than the 4th century A.D., and has therefore been discarded by most modern editors. (See Dr. Smith's Lat. Dict., 21st ed., *Orthograph. Index.*)

See p. 7, where examples are given showing the characteristics both of Latinized and of idiomatic English narrative.

With the Imperfect Subjunctive, **cum** serves to represent the English Imperfect Participle both in the Active and the Passive Voice: as—

'*Perceiving* that things were well-nigh desperate,' cum intelligeret rem paene in extremo sitam esse.

'*Being praised* on account of his frugality,' cum ob frugalitatem laudaretur.

Autem, enim.—These two Conjunctions are unemphatic, and incapable of beginning a sentence or clause. When the Conjunctions *but, for,* are emphatic, the former must be represented by **sed** or **at**, and the latter by **nam** or **namque**. See St. L. G. §§ 572, 581.

2. CONNECTION BY MEANS OF THE RELATIVE.—The Relative Pronoun has two uses.

(1.) *Descriptive* or *Adjectival* : as—

Duae legiones quae proxime conscriptae erant, 'the two legions which had been last enlisted.'

Treviri, quorum inter Gallos virtutis opinio est singularis, 'the Treviri, whose reputation among the Gauls for valour is extraordinary.'

This is the ordinary use of the Relative both in English and in Latin, and needs no special illustration.

(2.) *Conjunctive.*—Very often the clause or sentence introduced by the Relative is not meant to be descriptive of the person or thing referred to, but contains quite new and independent matter, which is simply linked on by the Relative to what precedes. (See Sch. Man. E. Gr. § 233, 2.)

B 2

This use is rare in English, but very frequent in Latin. Thus new periods and paragraphs are continually met with beginning in this way—

> quo facto proelio . . .
> quibus rebus constitutis . . .
> cujus adventu spe illata militibus . . .
> quem protinus armis exuit . . .

Here the English idiom requires a Personal or Demonstrative Pronoun, either with or without a Conjunction :—

> 'No sooner was *this* battle fought ' . . .
> ' When *these* matters were settled ' . . .
> ' On *his* arrival fresh hope ' . . .
> ' He at once stripped *him* of his arms ' . . .

This use of the Relative gives continuity to the style, which otherwise might to a Latin ear seem abrupt and disconnected.

Examples for the application of this construction may be found in the following paragraphs : e.g.—

> Ex. ii. ' They were routed by them in the first encounter ' — a quibus cum primo proelio fusi essent . . .
> Ex. iv. ' When they saw their brother in the distance '—quem cum fratres conspicati essent . . .
> Ex. v. ' Now when Moses had grown up' — qui cum adolevisset . . .

See also Ex. 3, Notes 3 and 8 ; Ex. 4, Note 3 ; Ex. 5, Note 8, &c.

3. PARTICIPIAL CONSTRUCTION.—Latin writers make special use of the Perfect Participle Passive ; and to this more than anything else, the complexity and close structure of the Latin period are due.

Ablative Absolute.—In English the Case Absolute is rather rare ; in Latin it is of very frequent occurrence.

It may be used—

(1.) When two clauses containing different Subjects, the former of which has for its Predicate a Passive Verb, are connected by a Conjunction : as—

'The city was pillaged and the booty grante l to the soldiers.' —Urbe direpta praeda militibus concessa est.

'Hasdrubal was cut off and Rome saved.'—Hasdrubale perempto Roma servata esse videbatur.

This construction can only be used when the one predicate is in some way dependent on the other. If the two are wholly distinct, each must have its own finite Verb : as—

'In the same year Numantia was taken and Ti. Gracchus slain.' —Eodem anno Numantia capta et Ti. Gracchus occisus est.

Obs. The Ablative Absolute cannot be used when the Subject or the Object of the two verbs is the same. Thus, in the sentence 'Pompey was defeated and fled to Egypt,' if the predicate 'was defeated' is converted into a Participle, it becomes an adjunct of the Subject, and therefore must be in the Nominative :—

Victus Pompeius ad Aegyptum confugit.

The case in which the same Noun is the Direct Object of two Verbs is treated below.

(2.) When two predicates belonging to the same Subject, the former of which consists of a Transitive Verb and its Object, are connected by a Conjunction. This case is really identical with the former, since the first predicate has to be converted into the Passive voice, when it has no longer the same Subject with the second. Examples—

'They raised a shout and rushed into the river.' — Clamore sublato in amnem irruerunt.

[Here, clamore sublato is the participial form of the predicate, clamor sublatus est.]

'He invaded their territory, ravaged their lands through and through, and then proceeded to attack their city.'—Ingressus fines, pervastatis finibus, urbem aggreditur.

Perfect Participle in agreement with Direct Object.— When the same Noun is the Direct Object of two Transitive Verbs, the former is often expressed by a Perfect Participle Passive in agreement with the Direct Object : as—

'He forthwith slew him and stripped him of his arms.'—Quem protinus obtruncatum armis exuit. (Literally, he stripped him having been slain.)

'He thrust his hand into the fire and allowed it to be burned to a cinder.'—Dexteram injectam foculo exuri passus est.

'He recalled the cavalry, and covered them (covered their retreat) with infantry.' — Consul equites revocatos circumdedit peditibus.

'He asked them (the spies) if they had properly studied what they had been ordered to spy out, gave them and their beasts a meal, and dismissed them unharmed.'—Interrogatos an satis ea considerassent quae speculari jussi erant, prandio dato ipsis jumentisque eorum, incolumes dimisit.

Numerous examples which may be so treated occur in the following pages : e.g.—

Ex. ii. 'He recovered all the booty and restored it to the king.' —Omnem praedam receptam regi restituit.

Ex. v. 'The king's daughter finding a babe in the river, had it nurtured for her own.'—Regis filia parvulum in flumine inventum pro proprio nutriendum curavit.

Ex. vi. 'He slew the Egyptian and hid him in the sand.'— Occisum Aegyptium in arena celavit.

See also Ex. 8, l. 10 ; Ex. 15, l. 8 ; Ex. 29, fin. ; Ex. 44, l. 17 ; Ex. 56, fin.

Obs. In none of these instances could the Ablative Absolute be used. Thus it would be incorrect to write—' dexterā injectā foculo *eam* exuri passus est '—' praedā receptā *eam* regi restituit.'

PERIODIC STRUCTURE.

Latin is pre-eminently the language of complex periods. Most English writers, especially in narrative, prefer short sentences; aiming at brightness of style, and careful not to overtax the attention of the reader.* In Latin, on the contrary, many clauses are often brought into the compass of a single period, and the attention of the reader is kept on the stretch to its close. Take as an example the following passage :—

'Then being seized by the king's body-guard, and brought before the king, when Porsena sought to frighten him by having fires brought, he thrust his hand into the lighted altar, until it was consumed by the flames.'

This is a translation from a Latin author, and the Latin structure is purposely retained. A writer of English would naturally present the facts in very different fashion—somewhat as follows :—

'The assassin was immediately arrested by the royal body-guard and brought before Porsena. In order to intimidate him, the king ordered fire to be brought into the room. But the undaunted youth thrust his right hand into the lighted altar, and held it there until it was consumed by the flames.'

Here note :—

1. The single period, which in the former version moves heavily, has been lightened by being broken up into sentences of moderate length.

2. In the former version, certain important incidents of the story are in a manner suppressed, by being subordinated to the principal verb. In the more idiomatic English version, these points are brought out

* "Modern English is essentially a language of separate sentences." (Postgate, *Sermo Latinus*, p. 45.)

prominently, and put in the most direct and telling way :—'He was at once arrested'—'Porsena ordered fire to be brought.'

3. The link-word 'when' ('when Porsena,' &c.) is dispensed with; thus leaving the clause introduced by it to stand as an independent sentence.

Besides this, the simple pronoun 'he' is in the latter version replaced by a noun or noun-phrase descriptive of the Subject :—'the assassin'—'the undaunted youth.' This is in keeping with the ordinary character of English narrative, to which it adds point and emphasis; but less so with that of Latin.

The student is recommended to practise himself by translating other Latin paragraphs into what may be described as the 'vivid' style; afterwards turning them back again into Latin, and re-forming the periods by the combination of closely related detached sentences.

DIRECT AND INDIRECT SPEECH.

1. DIRECT SPEECH.—In direct speech, as a rule, the principal verbs are in the Indicative Mood; and when a speech or remark on the part of any of the persons named is introduced, it is given in the exact actual words of the speaker: thus,—

"A Persian said to the Spartans: 'The multitude of our arrows will darken the sun.' 'Then,' replied they, 'we shall fight in the shade.'"

In Latin :—

Quidam Persa Spartanis dixit: 'Sagittarum nostrarum multitudo solem obscurabit.'—'Tum,' responderunt, 'in umbra pugnabimus.'

Here the verbs dixit, responderunt, have no syntactical effect whatever upon the clauses following. The words of the speakers are given without any change at all. This method has a lively, dramatic effect, and is well adapted to animated narrative in which conversations are introduced.

2. INDIRECT SPEECH.—The preceding method is however but little used in historical narrative, its place being taken by what is called Indirect Speech or Oratio obliqua. In this scheme, all the clauses of a reported speech are made to depend upon some verb of 'saying' by which they are introduced. (This is done in English by means of the Conjunction 'that':—he said that ... they replied that ...)

Hence we no longer have the exact actual words spoken, but they undergo certain changes arising out of their syntactical dependence. Moreover, both 'speakers' (1st person) and persons 'spoken to' (2nd person) become persons 'spoken of,' and consequently the Third person takes the place of the First and Second throughout.

According to this construction, the foregoing example will read as follows :—

ENGLISH-INDIRECT.	LATIN-INDIRECT.
A Persian once said to the Spartans, *that* the multitude of *their* arrows would darken the sun. The Spartans replied that in that case *they* would fight in the shade.	Quidam Persa dixit Spartanis, multitudinem sagittarum *suarum* solem obscuraturam esse. Illi responderunt, ita se in umbra pugnaturos.

Here the construction of 'Accusative and Infinitive' takes the place of 'Nominative and Indicative'; and the 1st person plural 'nos' with its pronominal adjective noster is replaced by se, suus.

The following are the chief rules of Oratio obliqua :—

1. In all principal clauses, the construction of Accusative and Infinitive takes the place of Nominative and Indicative. (See foregoing example.)

2. In all subordinate clauses, the Subjunctive takes the place of the Indicative.

ENGLISH-DIRECT.	LATIN-DIRECT.	LATIN-INDIRECT.
'This,' he said, 'my brother, who took part in the fray, will prove to the satisfaction of you all.'	'Haec,' inquit, 'frater meus, qui rixae *interfuit*, vobis omnibus approbabit.'	Ea dixit fratrem suum, qui rixae *interfuerit*, iis omnibus approbaturum.
'These,' he said, 'are the things which I desire.'	'Haec sunt,' inquit, 'quae ego volo.'	(Dixit) haec esse quae *velit*.

As a general rule, a Present or Future Indicative is represented by a Present Subjunctive, and a Perfect Indicative by a Perfect Subjunctive; but the Imperfect and Pluperfect Subjunctive are also used.

3. Questions in Oratio obliqua take sometimes the Subjunctive and sometimes the Infinitive Mood. They always take the Subjunctive when closely following a verb of 'asking': as—

Interrogabat cur paucis centurionibus *obedirent*.—'He asked why they obeyed a mere handful of centurions?' (Direct form, cur obeditis . . .)

(This is strictly in accordance with the rule for Indirect Questions: St. L. G. § 433.) They also take the Subjunctive when asked in order to elicit a reply, even though no verb of asking be expressed: as—

Dictator litteras ad senatum misit, . . . Veios jam fore in potestate populi Romani : quid de praeda faciendum *censerent?*—' Veii (he said) would ere long be in the power of the Roman people ; what did they think should be done about the booty ? ' (Direct form, Quid censetis ?)

But when questions are neither closely connected with a verb of 'asking,' nor asked in order to elicit a reply, but only as a sort of rhetorical appeal, they are more frequently expressed by the Infinitive : as—

Postremo, quid esse turpius quam auctore hoste de summis rebus consilium capere?—' What could be more shameful than to form plans concerning the most important matters at the suggestion of the enemy ? ' (Direct form, quid est turpius . . .)

Quando *ausuros* (*esse*) exposcere remedia, nisi novum principem precibus vel armis adirent?—' When would they have the courage to demand redress, if they failed to approach the new sovereign with petitions or with arms?' (Direct form, quando audebitis . . .)

In neither of these examples is the question asked in order to obtain information. The questions, in fact, answer themselves; and the interrogative form is used solely for the sake of effect. The sense in the first is, '*Nothing* could be more shameful'; and in the second the obvious answer is, 'Never.' Hence the Infinitive is used as in a predicative sentence.

The Subjunctive is however found even in indirect questions of this kind, but much less frequently.*

4. Commands or requests are expressed by the Subjunctive; some such verb as imperavit or oravit being mentally supplied : as—

Si quid vellent, ad Idus Aprilis *reverterentur.*—'If they wanted

---

* Omitting those cases in which the interrogative sentence is introduced by a verb of 'asking,' examples of Interrogative Infinitive as compared with Interrogative Subjunctive are in Livy at least *four* to one, and in Tacitus at least *six* to one.

anything, they should come back again by the 13th of April.'
(Direct form, revertimini.)

Illos *repeterent* auimos quos recenti clade habuissent.—'They
should once more display that dauntless courage which they had
shown in the recent disaster.' (Direct form, repetite.)

5. In hypothetical sentences, the Subjunctive of the
second member ('apodŏsis,' St. L. G. § 424) becomes
the Future Infinitive. In such cases the Imperfect
Tenses of the Subjunctive are represented by the
Future Infinitive with *esse*, and the Perfect Tenses by
the Future Infinitive with *fuisse*. Examples:—

ENGLISH-DIRECT.	LATIN-DIRECT.	LATIN-INDIRECT.
If I were to say so, I should lie.	Si ita dicam [dicerem], mentiar [mentirer].	Dixit, si ita diceret, se mentiturum esse.
Ariovistus replied: 'If I had wanted anything of Caesar, I would have come to him.'	Ariovistus respondit: Si quid mihi a Caesare opus esset, ad eum *venissem.*	Ariovistus respondit, si quid ipsi a Caesare opus esset, sese ad eum *venturum fuisse.*

In all other cases, such Subjunctives as occur in
direct speech remain in oblique.

The following additional examples are given in
order to enable the student to trace out in detail the
principal changes which are rendered necessary by the
use of Oratio obliqua.

'Divico, a chief of the Helvetii, said':—Divico dux Helvetiorum
dixit:

ENGLISH-DIRECT.	LATIN-DIRECT.	LATIN-INDIRECT.
'If the Roman people will make peace with us, we will go into that part of the country where you fix and decide, and will remain there: but if	Si populus Romanus pacem *nobiscum fecerit*, in eam partem *ibimus* atque ibi *erimus*, ubi *tu nos constitueris* atque esse *volueris:* sin bello persequi per-	Si populus Romanus pacem *cum Helvetiis faceret*, in eam partem *ituros* atque ibi *futuros* Helvetios ubi *eos* Caesar *constituisset* atque esse *voluisset:*

ENGLISH-DIRECT.	LATIN-DIRECT.	LATIN-INDIRECT.

you persist on following us up with war, then (we say) remember the old disaster of the Roman people and the original prowess of the Helvetii. . . . We have learned from our fathers to fight rather with (open) courage than with guile, or in reliance on ambuscades. Wherefore do not so act that this ground on which we stand, should gain a name from (another) disaster of the Roman people and the destruction of its army.'

severaveris, reminiscere et veteris incommodi populi Romani et pristinae virtutis Helvetiorum. . . . *Nos* ita a patribus *nostris didicimus,* ut magis virtute quam dolo *contendamus,* aut insidiis *nitamur.* Quare ne *commiseris* ut *hic* locus ubi *constitimus,* ex calamitate populi Romani nomen *capiat* et internecione exercitus.

sin bello persequi *perseveraret, reminisceretur* et veteris incommodi populi Romani et pristinae virtutis Helvetiorum. . . . *Se* ita a patribus (*suis*) *didicisse,* ut magis virtute quam dolo *contenderent* aut insidiis *niterentur.* Quare ne *committeret* ut is locus ubi *constitissent* ex calamitate populi Romani nomen *caperet* et internecione exercitus.

' Caesar replied ' :—Caesar respondit :

'I feel the less hesitation [less hesitation is allowed me], just because I keep in memory those things which you (the Helvetian ambassadors) have mentioned ; and I resent them the more deeply in that they happened through no fault of the Roman people . . . Moreover, if I were willing to forget the old affront, how could I possibly banish the recollection of recent injuries?'

Eo *mihi* minus dubitationis *datur,* quod *has* res quas *vos* commemoravistis in memoria *teneo ;* atque eo gravius *fero,* quo minus merito populi Romani *acciderunt.* . . . Quod si veteris contumeliae oblivisci *vellem,* num etiam recentium injuriarum deponere *possem ?*

Eo *sibi* minus dubitationis *dari,* quod *eas* res quas legati Helvetii *commemorassent* in memoria *teneret,* atque eo gravius *ferre* quo minus merito populi Romani *accidissent.* . . . Quod si veteris contumeliae oblivisci *vellet,* num etiam recentium injuriarum memoriam deponere *posse ?*

EXAMPLES FOR PRACTICE IN

ORATIO OBLIQUA.

N.B.—The following Exercises in Oratio obliqua should be postponed till the pupil has attained some familiarity with ordinary narrative.

In the following paragraphs all speeches are given in the Direct form. Before executing the Indirect version, the student should prepare the passage by transferring them into the corresponding form in English. Take the following example from Ex. xvi. :—

"He said to his tutor : 'Why is no one found to cut down so cruel a tyrant ?' He replied : 'It is not the will that is wanting, but the opportunity' . . . . The boy then said : 'Give me a sword' . . . ."

INDIRECT ENGLISH FORM :—"He *asked* his tutor why no one *was found* to cut down (who would cut down). . . . . He replied *that* not the will but the opportunity *was wanting*. . . . The boy then *begged that he would* give him a sword . . . ."

(a) ANECDOTE OF CATO THE YOUNGER.

Cato (when) in-his-boyhood[1] called on[2] Sulla for the purpose of paying-his-respects-to[3] him. There he saw

---

[1] praetextatus ; i.e. *still wearing the purple-bordered toga*, hence = puer. This was the dress of well-born Roman boys, until they ex-

changed it for the plain toga (toga pura or virilis) of manhood.

[2] venio, 4 ; foll. by ad.

[3] salūto.

the heads of the proscribed (which had been) brought
into the atrium. Struck[4] by the brutality of the proceeding,[5] he said to his tutor,[6] Sarpedon by name:
"Why is no one found to[7] cut down so cruel a tyrant ?"
He replied: ("It is) not the will that is wanting to
men, but the opportunity[8]; because his life[9] is guarded
by a large body[10] of soldiers." The boy then said,[11]
"Give me a sword: I shall easily kill him, because
I am accustomed to sit down on his couch."

---

[4] commotus.
[5] res; which has a much wider
use than the corresponding English
word. [6] paedagōgus.
[7] rel. :—who should cut down.

[8] facultas. [9] salus.
[10] praesidium.
[11] In indirect form, obsecravit,
begged, besought.

(b) Anecdote of Alcibiades.

Alcibiades[1] (when) still in-his-boyhood[2] called-on
his uncle Pericles. Seeing him sitting sadly[3] by-
himself,[4] he said to him : "Why are you so sad ?" He
replied : "In-accordance-with-the-command[5] of the
Senate, I have built the Propylaea of Minerva, that[6]
is, the approach[7] to the Acropolis.[8] An immense
sum-of-money has been spent on that work; and I
cannot discover how to render[9] a (satisfactory) account
of the service (rendered). I am therefore[10] in diffi-

---

[1] Say, when Alcibiades . . . had
come to his uncle . . . and had seen
him . . .
[2] Compare preceding Ex., Note
1. Only here of course praetextatus cannot be used, being appli-

cable only to Roman youths.
[3] Say, sad. [4] secreto.
[5] abl.; alone or with ex.
[6] rel. pl. [7] januae, pl.
[8] arx (gen.).
[9] subj. [10] ideo.

culties."[11] "Well-then,"[12] said the boy, "try-to-find[13] rather how to avoid[14] giving an account (at all)." Pericles is said to have followed[15] the boy's advice, and made it his aim,[16] that the Athenians might be involved[17] in war with-their-neighbours,[18] *and so*[19] might not have leisure[20] for examining accounts.

---

[11] conflictor, *dep.*

[12] ergo : this sentence is best left in the Direct form.　[13] quaero.

[14] Expr. by non with reddo.

[15] utor, with *abl.*

[16] *to make anything one's aim,*

id agere, foll. by ut, ne.　[17] *part.*

[18] bellum finitimum‾ or finitimorum.

[19] Will these words stand after the participle ?

[20] *to have leisure,* vaco, 1.

(c) DEATH OF T. JUBELLIUS, THE CAMPANIAN.

When Fulvius Flaccus was (engaged in) inflicting capital punishment upon[1] the chief men of the state of-Cales,[2] he received a letter from the Senate, requiring[3] him to put[4] an end to his punishment of them. T. Jubellius, a Campanian, voluntarily offered himself to the Roman officer[5] (for execution), and with a loud voice said : "Since you are possessed by so intense[6] a desire for draining our blood, why do you not kill me also, that you may be able to boast that a man braver than you has been destroyed by your order ? " Fulvius

---

[1] supplicio afficere hominem, *to visit him with capital punishment.*

[2] Calēnus, *adj.*

[3] *Say, and, a letter having been received from the Senate, was compelled . . .*

[4] facio, statuo.

[5] Say, *to him* (is): see Introd. p. 8.

[6] tantus: in Lat., plain words like magnus, tantus, are preferred to such as might seem more vividly descriptive. So, tanta vis frigoris, *such intense severity of cold.*

replied : "I would cheerfully do it, were I not hindered by the will of the Senate." "But behold[7] me," replied the other, "to whom the Senate has given no instructions,[8] exhibiting[9] a feat gratifying indeed to your eyes, but beyond[10] the measure of your soul." Then immediately he slew[P] his wife and children and fell upon his sword.

---

[7] aspice.	[9] opus edere.
[8] Expr. by nihil praecipere.	[10] Say, *greater than your soul.*

(d) COLLATINUS IS BANISHED FROM ROME.

Brutus summons the people to an assembly. There first of all he rehearses the oath of the people: 'We will suffer no-man to reign nor to be in Rome from-whom[1] there may be danger to liberty.'—"That (point) (said he) must be most-jealously[2] guarded;[3] nor must anything be-made-light-of[4] which has-a-bearing[5] upon it. I speak reluctantly on account of the person (concerned); nor should I have spoken[6] did[7] not my affection for the commonwealth prevail[8] (over everything else). The Roman people believes that the very name of the royal race is-an-obstacle[9] to liberty." Then he called upon the other consul: "Lucius Tarquinius," he said, "remove this (ground of) fear of your own free-will. We remember, we acknowledge; you

---

[1] *from whom,* unde.	[6] For the tense, see Introd., p. 12.
[2] Say, *with utmost effort,* summa ope.	[7] nisi.
[3] tueor.	[8] vinco, used absolutely, i.e. without expressed object.
[4] *ger. part.* of contemno.	
[5] pertineo, foll. by ad.	[9] obsto, 1.

PR. LAT.—V.   C

expelled the kings. Complete your service.[10] Carry
hence the royal name. Your fellow-citizens will not
only restore to you your own property, with-my-
sanction;[11] but if aught is lacking will bountifully
increase it. Go away (as) a friend. Relieve the state
of perhaps a groundless fear." [12] Tarquinius reluctantly
abdicated [13] his office, transferred [14] all his property to
Lavinium, and retired from the city.

---

[10] beneficium.

[11] me auctore.   [12] *abl.*

[13] Say, *abdicated himself from the consulship.*   [14] *part.*

(e) Bocchus and Sulla.

Thereupon the king tells[1] him to return in ten days,
(saying): " I have decided[2] nothing yet, but will give
my answer[3] on that day." Then both depart to their
(respective) camps. But when night was well advanced,[4] Sulla was secretly sent-for by Bocchus; who
is said to have addressed him thus: "I never made
war upon the Roman people; I simply[5] defended my
territories by arms against armed men. That (course) I
abandon;[6] since such is your pleasure,[7] wage war with
Jugurtha as you wish. I will not pass[8] the river
Mulucha, which was (the boundary) between me and
Jugurtha, nor will I suffer Jugurtha to pass-within[9] it.
Further, whatever you ask worthy of myself and you,
you shall not experience[10] a rebuff."

---

[1] jubeo.   [2] decerno.

[3] Say, *would answer.*

[4] ubi plerumque noctis proces-
sit. Also, multa de nocte might
be used.

[5] i.e. *only.*   [6] omitto.

[7] Expr. by placet.

[8] egredior, with *acc.*   [9] intro, 1.

[10] Say, *you shall not go away re-
pulsed* (repello).

II. EASY STORIES

FROM BIBLE HISTORY.

N.B.—The letter P after a word indicates that a participial construction is to be used: thus, Ex. i., *on his return*, reversus; Ex. ii., *he recovered the prisoners*, receptis captivis.

(i.) ABRAHAM.

Abraham is said [1] to have been born in the thousand [2] (and) seventh year after the Deluge. His [3] wife was called Sarah, and their first abode was in the country of the Chaldeans, near [4] the river Euphrates. Afterwards he sojourned at Charrae, along with his father Terah, and-from-thence,[5] on the death of his father,[6] he set out for the land of the Canaanites : and settled first in a place which [7] has the name of Shechem. Shortly after, on account of a famine,[8] he removed into Egypt ; and on-his-return P dwelt near the Dead Sea.[9]

PROPER NAMES. — Abraham, Sichem (*Shechem*), indeclinable. Sara, Tera, 1 decl. *Chaldeans*, Chaldaei, orum ; Euphrātes, is, *m.*; Charrae, arum ; *Canaanites*, Cananaei, orum.

---

[1] fertur, to stand first.
[2] Say, thousand*th*.
[3] *dat.* of is.   [4] apud.
[5] unde, *whence* ; before which no Conj. is needed.
[6] *abl. abs.*, with *perf. part. of*

morior : (*his*) *father having died.*
[7] Say, *to which is the name* . . .
[8] Say, *dearth of corn*, annonae inopia.
[9] Say, *near the lake to which is the name* (*of*) *the Dead Sea.*

C 2

(ii.) ABRAHAM (*continued*).

At that time the neighbouring nations were in arms;
and the kings of the cities of-the-Plain[1] fought a battle [2]
with certain other kings who had invaded[3] their territories. They were routed by them in the first encounter; the city (of) Sodom, in which Lot Abraham's
brother's son lived, was taken[4] by the enemy, and Lot
himself was made-prisoner.[5]   When Abraham learned [p]
this,[6] he hastily armed [p][7] three hundred (and) eighteen
of his own servants, pursued the enemy, stripped [p][8]
them of booty and arms, and put them to flight.
He recovered [p] the prisoners, (and) among them Lot,
restored the booty which-had-been-recovered [p] to its
owners,[9] and [10] refused to accept anything for himself.

PROPER NAMES.—*Sodom*, Sodŏma, orum, *n. pl.*, and ae, *f.*; Lot,
indecl.

---

[1] campester, tris, tre.
[2] proelium committere.
[3] incurro, foll. by in and *acc.*
[4] expugno.
[5] capio.
[6] Say, *which things being learned*
(cognosco).   [7] *abl. abs.*

[8] Say, *put them to flight* (in
fugam conjicere), *stripped of booty
and arms* (*abl.*).
[9] Say, *to those from whom* (*dat.*)
it had been taken (eripio).
[10] Say, *nor was he willing to take
anything for himself.*

(iii.) BETHEL.

Jacob, fearing the anger of his brother, set out for Mesopotamia. While [1] journeying, he saw the Lord in a vision,[2] and on-that-account, holding [3] the place of his dream sacred, he called it the House of God; and vowed that, if he returned [4] in prosperity,[5] he would give the tenth part of all that should have been gained by him as an offering [6] to God. He then betook himself to his uncle Laban. Laban [7] recognized him (as) his kinsman and entertained him generously. He remained there about twenty years, and gained great wealth: moreover he took as his wives two daughters of Laban, and returned with them into his own native-land.

PROPER NAMES. — Jacob, Laban, *indecl.* (Jacŏbus = *James*). Mesopotamia, ae, *f.*

---

[1] Note that dum must never be used with a Participle. Say simply, *journeying*: or if dum be used, it must be with pres. indic. (St. L. G. § 393 *obs.* 2).

[2] per somnum.

[3] habens or quum haberet.

[4] Say, *should have returned.*

[5] prosperis rebus.

[6] dono : dative of Purpose.

[7] Say, *by whom being recognized* ... *he was generously entertained.*

(iv.) JACOB AND JOSEPH.

After the death[P] of his father, Jacob continued-to-dwell[1] in the same land. On-one-occasion,[2] his sons had gone away from him with their flocks, to seek pasture[3]; but Joseph and little Benjamin remained at home. Now[4] Joseph was a very great favourite[5] of his father, and on-account-of that was an-object-of-hatred[6] to his brothers : moreover from certain dreams which he had,[7] he seemed to be destined to greater things. He was now sent[P] by his father to bring him tidings about his brothers; (and so) became a ready subject for ill-treatment.[8] When they saw their brother[9] in-the-distance, they formed a plan for killing him. But on-account-of-the-opposition-of-Reuben,[10] they refrained from his death,[11] but sold him to some[12] merchants who carried[13] him into Egypt. There he at length gained[14] the favour of the king, and was set over the whole land.

PROPER NAMES.—Joseph, Benjamin, Reuben, *indecl.*

---

[1] Imperfect. This Tense has the following meanings : (1) *to be engaged in doing*; (2) *to be wont to do*; (3) *to begin to do*; (4) *to continue to do something.*   [2] aliquando.

[3] Say, *for the sake of* (causâ) *pasture.*

[4] autem, which must not stand first in the sentence. 'Now' is here a conjunction; used to carry on the story to another point.

[5] admodum carus, of course with *dat.*

[6] invīsus, with *dat.*

[7] Say, *of him* (is).

[8] opportunus injuriae—an expressive phrase.

[9] *rel.*, see p. 4: *to form a plan,* consilium inire.

[10] *abl. abs.*, Reuben opposing, obsisto.

[11] nex : which means always cruel or violent death.

[12] quidam.   [13] abduco.

[14] **Phr.**: magnam gratiam inire apud . . .

(v.) MOSES.

Afterwards the Hebrews were cruelly oppressed by the Egyptians. The severe labour of building cities was imposed on them; and since their overflowing numbers[1] were already feared—lest some day they should assert[2] their freedom by arms—they were ordered to destroy their new-born male children.[3] About[4] this time, the king's daughter, having found a babe in the river, had[5] it nurtured as[6] her own son, and gave the boy the name of Moses. Now Moses, when he-grew-up-to-manhood, seeing a Hebrew beaten[7] by an Egyptian, was moved[p] with anger, and, having rescued[8] him from oppression, slew[9] the Egyptian and hid him in the sand. Afterwards he became the leader of the Hebrews, and, after securing[10] their[11] liberty, ruled over them for forty years.

PROPER NAMES.—Moses or Moӱses, is; *a Hebrew*, Hebraeus.

---

[1] abundans multitudo.

[2] *to assert one's liberty*, se in libertatem vindicare : strictly a legal phrase ; hence the necessity here to add 'armis.'

[3] recens (*adv.*) editos liberos.

[4] per.

[5] '*to have a thing done*,' curare foll. by *ger. part.*: infantem in fluvio repertum nutriendum curavit.   [6] pro.

[7] pulso, *pres. inf. pass.*

. [8] vindico, foll. by ab. Expr. *having rescued* by cum with *plup. subj.*

[9] Say, *he hid him slain:* Introd. p. 6.

[10] comparo, 1.   [11] iis.

(vi.) JOSHUA.

On the death[p] of Moses, the chief command [1] fell [2] on Joshua. For Moses had appointed him as his successor on account of his high-qualities.[3] In the beginning of his government, sending [4] messengers through the camp, he ordered all the Israelites to prepare corn, and announced [5] a march (within) [6] the next three days. But the strong [7] current of the Jordan barred their passage; because neither was there a supply of ships for the emergency [8] nor could the river easily be forded, which was then flowing [9] with full channel.

Accordingly he ordered the ark to-be-carried-in-front by the priests, and (directed) them [10] to stand still in the middle of the river. This [11] done, the Jordan is said to have been divided by-divine-power [12]; and so the forces were led across on dry ground.[13]

PROPER NAMES.—*Joshua*, Josua, ae; *Jordan*, Jordānes, is, *m.*; *Israelites*, Israelītae, arum.

---

[1] summa imperii.

[2] Expr. by penes (which follows its noun) and esse.   [3] Say, *virtues*.

[4] di-mitto: the prefix signifies, *in different directions.* Constr. *abl. abs.*

[5] pronuntio, 1: *hist. pres.*

[6] *abl.* only: triduum, *space of three days.*   [7] Use Superlative.

[8] pro tempore.

[9] *pass.* of fero in middle sense, *to carry itself along.*   [10] idem.

[11] *rel.*   [12] divinĭtus, *adv.*

[13] per siccum.

(vii.) JEPHTHAH.

The Hebrews with-Jephthah-as-their-leader [1] waged [2] war with the Ammonites. Then Jephthah, before the signal for battle was given,[3] vowed that, if he were victorious,[4] he [5] would sacrifice to God whatever should meet [6] him first on his return [7] home. (Accordingly) having conquered his enemies, as he [8] was returning home, his daughter met him, who-had-set-out [P] joyfully with cymbals and companies-of-dancers to welcome [P] her victorious father. Jephthah, horror-struck,[9] rent [P] his clothes in-grief, and revealed to his daughter the inevitable-nature [10] of his vow. But the maiden, with fortitude beyond her sex,[11] not refusing [P] to die, (but) asked only for two months, that she might first visit [12] her companions [13]. When these [14] were spent,[15] she voluntarily returned to her father, and he [16] paid [17] his vow.

PROPER NAMES.—Jephthah, *indecl.*; *Ammonites*, Ammonītae, arum.

---

[1] *abl. abs.*   [2] *imperf.*

[3] *imperf. subj.*

[4] *to be victorious*, prospere pugnare : *plup. subj.*

[5] *acc.* and *fut. inf.*

[6] *pluperf. subj.*

[7] revertor, *dep. : pres. part.*, *to him returning*.

[8] Begin period with *rel.*, cui cum . . ., (*to*) *whom, as he was returning home,* &c.

[9] consternatus, from consterno, avi, atum, 1, *to dismay, strike with terror;* collateral form of consterno, stravi, stratum, 3, *to strew, cover the ground.*   [10] necessitas.

[11] constantia non feminea.

[12] video.

[13] aequales : strictly, *those of the same age.*   [14] *rel. : abl. abs.*

[15] *to spend* (of time), ago.

[16] isque.   [17] solvo, persolvo.

(viii.) SAMSON.

Afterwards Samson was-judge-over[1] the Hebrews, and the Philistines were subdued by the valour of a single (man). Accordingly[2] they lay-in-wait[3] for his life. They dared not to attack him openly, but[4] they bribed his wife with money to betray[5] the (secret of the) valour of her husband.

She assailed[P] him with feminine blandishments, and[6] at length prevailed-upon him to reveal[5] that his strength lay[7] in the hair[8] of his head. Then she cut-off[P] his hair while he was asleep,[9] (and so) delivered him up to the enemy. Then they put-out[10] his eyes, bound[11] him in fetters, and threw him into prison.

PROPER NAMES.—*Philistines,* Philistīni, orum ; Samson, *indecl.*

---

[1] praesum, *dat.*
[2] Combine this and following sentence into a period, and arrange thus : *as* (cum) *they did not dare to attack him* (rel.) *openly, they lay in wait for his life, and bribed,* &c.
[3] insidior, 1, foll. by *dat.*

[4] Say, *and.*
[5] ut and *subj.*
[6] no longer necessary after *part.*
[7] sitas esse.   [8] crines.
[9] to (*him*) *sleeping.*
[10] effodio, *abl. abs.*
[11] *perf. part. pass.* : Introd. p. 6.

(ix.) SAMSON (*continued*).

But soon his locks (began) to grow, and with them his prowess[1] began to return. And now Samson, conscious of recovered strength,[2] only waited for an opportunity of full revenge.[3] Once[4] the Philistines were celebrating-a-festival.[5] Samson was brought forth to make sport[6] for his enemies. Now the temple in which the chiefs of the Philistines were feasting, was supported[7] on two columns of immense size. Then Samson, standing between these, seized[8] his opportunity. He first called-on[9] God, (and then,) putting forth[9] all his strength, pulled[10] the columns down. The whole crowd was overwhelmed by the[11] downfall (of the temple), and he himself perished with his enemies, not unavenged, having-been-judge-over[12] the Hebrews forty years.

---

[1] virtus. [2] robur, oris, *n*.
[3] justae ultionis tempus (justus
=*proper, adequate*).
[4] Say, *once when the enemy were celebrating.* [5] festos dies agere.
[6] Say, *that he might be for sport* (ludibrium); *dat.* of Purpose: see St. L. G. § 297. [7] subnixus.
[8] occasione arrepta. This and foll. sentence are to be combined in

one period: *then Samson, having seized his opportunity, having first* (prius) *called on God,* &c. The words '*and then*' thus become unnecessary.
[9] conixus totis viribus.
[10] *pull down,* dejicio.
[11] *rel.,* quâ ruinâ; which must stand first.
[12] cum praefuisset.

(x.) ELI.

In the high-priesthood[1] of Eli, the Hebrews waged war with the Philistines. They were defeated[P] in-battle,[2] but they determined to renew the fight. They brought-forth[3] the ark of God into the battle, and the sons of Eli went forth with it. The High-priest himself was weighed down with years.[4] His eyes were dim,[5] and he was not able to discharge[6] the duties of the priesthood. When the ark came within[7] sight of the enemy, they were at first terrified[P] and prepared to flee.[8] Soon they recovered[P] their firmness; their feelings were changed;[P] and they joined-in-the-conflict[9] with their whole strength. The Hebrews were routed;[10] the ark was taken;[10] and the sons of the High-priest fell.[10] The tidings[11] of this disaster were brought to Eli, who was horror-struck and gave up the ghost. He had been High-priest[12] for forty years.

PROPER NAME.—Eli, *indecl.*

---

[1] sacerdos: *abl. abs.*

[2] acies.   [3] *hist. pres.*

[4] annis gravior.

[5] Say, *his eyes being covered* (obduco); after which of course no conjunction is needed.

[6] Say, *to satisfy* (satisfacio, with dat.) *the duty of priesthood.*

[7] in conspectum.

[8] Say, *prepared (imperf.) flight.*

[9] concurro.

[10] *hist. pres.*

[11] Say, *which disaster being reported* (nuntio, 1), *Eli horror-struck* (consternatus) *expired* (animam exspirare).

[12] Say, *had been over that priesthood*, praefuerat.

(xi.) THE ISRAELITES OPPRESSED BY THE PHILISTINES.

In the reign[1] of Saul, the Israelites were oppressed by the Philistines, who, having been victorious in war, had taken from them the liberty to carry arms[2]; so that, excepting[3] the king and Jonathan his son, and a few others, no one had either sword or spear. Under-these-circumstances[4] Jonathan, with his armour-bearer[5] only as his companion, entered[P] the enemy's camp, slew[P] about twenty of them, and struck[6] terror into the whole army. No sooner[7] did the king observe this than he hastily led[P] out his forces, pursued[P] the enemy, and gained[8] a splendid[9] victory.

PROPER NAMES.—Saûl, *indecl.*; Jonathan, *indecl.*, or Jonatha, ae.

---

[1] Say, *Saul being king,* Saul rege or regnante.

[2] Say, *had taken from them* (adimo, with *acc.* and *dat.*) *the use of arms.*

[3] Use plural, exceptis.

[4] hic, *adv.*

[5] injicio, 3; with *acc.* and *dat.*

[6] abl. abs.

[7] Say, *as soon as:* simul atque (ac) with *perf. indic.*

[8] potior, with *abl.*

[9] insignis.

(xii.) SAUL'S RASH IMPRECATION.

On that day the king is said to-have-issued-a-proclamation,[1] with a-solemn-curse,[2] that [3] no one should take food except after [4] the defeat of the enemy. Jonathan, ignorant of this prohibition, having found (some) honeycomb, dipped [p] the-point-of-a-javelin [5] (in it), and tasted the honey. No sooner [6] was this found out, than the king ordered his son to be put to death: [7] but he was rescued from destruction by the help of the people.

After this [8] Saul led his army against the Amale-kites; took (prisoner) their king and subdued the nation; but was himself overcome by the desire of booty to [9] his own destruction.

PROPER NAME.—*Amalekites*, Amalekītae, arum.

---

[1] edīco.   [2] detestatio.
[3] Say, *lest any one*, ne quis.
[4] Say, *unless the enemy being defeated* (*abl. abs.*).
[5] spiculum.

[6] See preceding Ex., Note 7.
[7] Use phr., supplicio afficere, *to visit with* (*capital*) *punishment.*
[8] Begin, deinde cum . . .
[9] in, with *acc.*

(xiii.) GOLIATH.

One of the Philistines, Goliath by name, was a man of gigantic[1] stature and strength.[2] He advanced[P] before the ranks of his (countrymen) and in proudly-defiant[3] words challenged anyone[4] of the Hebrews to single combat. Thereupon king Saul offered great rewards and the hand[5] of his daughter in marriage to the man[6] who should slay[7] the challenger[P] and bring back his spoils. No[8] one out of so great a host dared to attack him. Accordingly, David, still a boy, offered himself for the fight. He rejected[P] the usual arms, took[P] only (his) staff, a sling, and five stones, (and) advanced to the battle. At the first shot,[9] letting[10] fly a stone from the sling, he struck[P] the Philistine (and) slew him. He then carried off the head and spoils of the vanquished (giant), and afterwards laid-up[11] the sword in the temple.

PROPER NAMES.—Goliath, *indecl.*, or Golia, ae; David, *indecl.*

---

[1] Say, *of wonderful size.*
[2] robur.   [3] ferox.
[4] *anyone* here = *anyone you please;* quivis, quilibet.
[5] Say, *marriage,* nuptiae, arum.
[6] The regular antecedent to the Relative is the pron. is, ea, id. The Rel. clause then defines the antecedent.

[7] *Pluperf. subj.* This clause may be rendered, *who should bring back the spoils of him-challenging killed,* qui provocantis spolia occisi referret.
[8] Begin, cum nemo . . . Then *accordingly* may be omitted.
[9] ictus, ûs.
[10] mitto, *abl. abs.*   [11] pono.

(xiv.) DAVID SPARES SAUL.

To escape[1] the anger of Saul, David betook himself to the desert. (But) Saul pursued him hither also, vainly seeking means[2] to destroy him. In the desert there was an immense cave, into which David had retired. Not knowing this,[3] the king had entered the mouth[4] of the cave to rest,[5] and there had fallen asleep. When David observed this, although all (his followers) urged[P] him to use the opportunity, he refrained from slaying[6] the king, (and) only carried-off[P] his mantle. Then issuing (from the cave), he addressed the king from a safe place at a distance,[7] mentioning[8] his own acts-of-kindness towards him, how he had often exposed his life[9] in behalf of his kingdom, and how last (of all), when-he (Saul)-had-been-delivered-up[P] to him by God, he had been unwilling to destroy him.

In reply to this[10] Saul began to confess[11] his fault, to entreat[11] forgiveness, and to praise[11] the loyalty[12] of David, calling him king and son.

---

[1] Combine first two sentences :— '*when David, that he might escape ... Saul pursued him ...*'

[2] quomodo.

[3] cujus rei ignarus.

[4] aditus, ûs.

[5] reficiendi corporis causa.

[6] Say, *he abstained from the destruction* (exitio) *of the king.*

[7] tuto eminus loco.

[8] *pres. part.*

[9] caput objectare.

[10] ad haec.   [11] *hist. inf.*

[12] pietas.

(xv.) Death of Saul.

After this David fled-for-refuge to the Philistines, between whom and king Saul there was war. They[1] were about-to-join battle on the morrow,[2] (when) Saul was warned by a seer that he would fall in battle. David was not present[3] at the battle, being an-object-of-suspicion[4] to the chiefs of the enemy, and on this account having been sent-back[5] from the camp. The Hebrews were routed in battle, and Saul's sons slain; (and) he himself, to avoid falling alive into the hands[6] of the enemy, threw himself on[7] his sword. On the death[p] of Saul, David became king first of a part of the nation[8] and afterwards of the whole.

---

[1] Begin, qui cum . . .
[2] postero die.
[3] intersum, with *dat.*
[4] suspectus, with *dat.*
[5] relĕgo, 1.

[6] Say, *lest he should come into the hands of* . . .
[7] incumbo, 3, with *dat.*
[8] civitas.

III. SHORT TALES AND ANECDOTES.

1. SCAEVOLA.

King[1] Porsena was besieging the city of Rome. Quintus Mucius Scaevola, a youth of brave spirit, betook himself to the enemy, with the intention[2] of killing the king. But[3] there he killed the king's secretary instead of the king himself. He was then seized[p] by the king's body-guards, and brought[p 4] to the king: (but) when Porsena sought-to-frighten[5] him by (having) fire[6] brought (into the room), he thrust[7] his right hand into a lighted altar, until it was consumed[8] by the flames. The king, astonished-at[9] this feat, let[10] the young man go unharmed. Then he said that three hundred other young men had conspired against the king.[11] Porsena, terrified by this,[12] made peace with the Romans.

---

[1] Say, *when* King Porsena . . .
[2] eo consilio ut . . .
[3] at, which is stronger than sed.
[4] deduco.   [5] *imperf. subj.*
[6] *plur.*
[7] impono, with *acc.* and *dat.*

Note, this verb must come at the end of its own clause.
[8] *perf. indic.*   [9] miratus.
[10] *to let go,* dimitto.
[11] Say, against *him.*
[12] hac re *or* qua re.

2. CORIOLANUS.

In the nineteenth year after the expulsion [1] of the kings, C. Marcius, surnamed [2] Coriolanus from Corioli, a city of the Volscians, which [3] he had taken in-war, began to make-himself [4] obnoxious to the populace.[5] Whereupon, being banished from the city, he went-straight [6] to the Volscians, the most-determined [7] foes of the Romans; and being made by them commander of (their) army, he repeatedly [8] defeated the Romans (in battle). He had already approached within [9] five miles of the city, and [10] could not be induced [11] by any deputations of his fellow-citizens to [12] spare his native-place. At last (his) mother Veturia and (his) wife Volumnia came to him from the city, and by their [13] tears and entreaties he was prevailed-upon [14] to [12] withdraw (his) army. For this [15] he is said to have been put-to-death by the Volscians as [16] a traitor.

---

[1] Abstract verbal nouns such as *expulsion* must often be rendered in Latin by means of *perf. part. pass.*: post exactos reges.

[2] dictus.

[3] *fem.* to agree with urbe.

[4] fio.   [5] plebs, *the plebeian order.*

[6] contendo.   [7] *sup.* of acer.

[8] Say, *often.*

[9] Say, *as far as to the fifth mile-stone* (milliarium) *of the city.*

[10] and ... not=nec.   [11] flecto.

[12] ut and *subj.*   [13] *rel.*

[14] commoveo.   [15] quo facto.

[16] Express the 'as': it is not meant that he *was* a traitor.

D 2

3. HORATIUS COCLES.

Porsena, king of the Etruscans, was-making-an-attempt[1] to restore[2] the Tarquinii, who-had-been-banished[P] by the people of-Rome.[3] He captured[4] the Janiculum at the first assault, [when] Horatius Cocles, planting-himself[5] in-front-of the Sublician[6] Bridge, which unites the banks of the Tiber, withstood single-handed[7] the host[8] of the enemy, until the bridge in his rear was broken-asunder.[9] This[10] done, he immediately leaped-down into the Tiber, and swam-across armed (as he was) to his own (men).

---

[1] tento.   [2] restituo.
[3] *adj.*: and note that the clause 'banished . . . Rome' must come immediately after Tarquinios, to which it is adjectival.
[4] qui cum : see Introd. p. 4.
[5] stans.   [6] i.e. *built of piles.*

[7] Say, *alone.*   [8] acies.
[9] *imperf. subj.*; the use of the *subj.* implying that he *waited for it to be broken asunder.* (The indicative interruptus est would simply state the fact that *it was* so broken.)
[10] See Ex. 2, Note 15.

---

4. THE SCHOOLMASTER OF FALERII.

In[1] the war against-the-Veientines,[2] M. Furius Camillus was besieging the city of Veii. In the course of the siege,[3] a schoolmaster[4] had brought the sons of the chief men from the city to his camp; but[5] Camillus,

---

[1] The prep. *in* may be used, but is not indispensable.
[2] There are three ways of expressing this: (i) by *gen.*, bellum Veientum. (ii) by *adj.*, bellum Veiens. (iii) by *prep.*, bellum

adversus Veientes, cum Veientibus.
[3] Begin, in *qua* obsidione, cum . . . Introd. p. 4.
[4] ludi litterarii magister.
[5] Will this *conj.* now be needed ?

instead of accepting[6] this gift, handed over the scoundrel, with his hands bound behind his back, to the
boys, to be taken back[7] to Falerii ; and gave them
rods to whip[8] the traitor into the city.

---

[6] Expr. 'instead of accepting'
by negative : he did *not* accept . . .
but . . .

[7] *ger. part.* of reduco.
[8] Say, *with which they might
drive* (ago) . . .

---

5. THE FABII AT THE CREMERA.

When the Romans were carrying on war against the
Veientes, the family of the Fabii[1] demanded for itself
(the conduct of) this war, and they[2] set out (to the
number of) three hundred and six, under the command[3]
of Fabius the consul. After having been victorious
in several engagements,[4] they pitched their camp near[5]
the river Cremera. Thereupon the Veientes, having-
recourse[6] to stratagem, drove their flocks within[7] view
of the enemy;[8] and they, having gone forth to seize
them,[9] fell into the ambush (prepared for them) and all
perished to a man.[10] One of that family, who-had-
been-left[P] at home on account of his immature[11] age,
propagated his race.

---

[1] gens Fabia.
[2] Observe the change to the
plural. The subject gens would
require a singular verb.
[3] Expr. by *abl. absol.* with dux.
[4] Say, when they had *often
proved* (exsisto) *victors.*
[5] apud.

[6] convertor (*reflex. pass.*), foll.
by ad.   [7] in with *acc.*
[8] Say, of *them.*
[9] Expr. by *rel.*, which, being itself a connective, renders the 'and'
at the beginning of the clause in-
admissible:—ad quae rapienda . . .
[10] ad unum.   [11] impubes, eris.

6. Pyrrhus and the Roman Soldiers.

A battle was fought[1] (in which) Pyrrhus was-victorious[2] by the aid of his elephants. Night put[3] an end to the battle. Laevinus however escaped under-cover-of[4] night. Pyrrhus treated the Romans whom[5] he-had-made-prisoners (to the number of) eighteen hundred with the utmost consideration.[6] When he saw that those who had been killed in battle all lay with wounds received-in-front,[7] and with a fierce expression[8] even in-death,[9] he is said to have raised his hands towards[9] heaven, with this exclamation,[10] "Had[11] I such men, I would soon subdue the (whole) world."

[1] *abl. absol.*

[2] Say, *conquered.*

[3] Say, *gave* or *made* an end (finem facere or dare).   [4] per.

[5] Say, *whom, a thousand eight hundred, he had captured.*

[6] honor.   [7] adversus, a, um.

[8] vultus.   [9] ad.

[10] vox: — observe that both in this and foll. clause, the prep. *with* must be expressed; meaning *together with, along with.*

[11] Say, *I, with such men, would soon . . .*

7. PYRRHUS AND ROME.

Pyrrhus being[1]-already-possessed[2] with great admiration for-the-Romans,[3] sent Cineas, a most distinguished man, as[4] an ambassador to[5] sue-for peace, on[6] these terms, that Pyrrhus should retain under his dominion that part of Italy of which he had taken possession by arms.[7] The Romans answered that he could have no peace with them, unless he withdrew from[8] Italy. When Cineas had returned, Pyrrhus asked[9] him what[10] he thought of Rome. Cineas replied that he had seen the native-city of kings.

---

[1] There is no *pres. part. pass.* in Latin; but the sense of one may be expr. by cum with *subj.*

[2] *pass.* of teneo.

[3] *gen.* ; this case having a much wider range of meaning than Eng. ' of.' See Ex. 4, Note 2 (i).

[4] ' as ' must not be expr. here, since it simply indicates apposition. On the contrary in Ex. 2, *fin.*, it indicates comparison, and needed therefore to be expressed.

[5] *rel.* with *subj.* ;

[6] ea condicione ut.

[7] Since the clause ' of which ... arms ' is purely adjectival, it must follow the words to which it relates ; and the verb ' should retain ' (teneret) finishes the sentence.

[8] ex, because he was then *in* Italy.

[9] Say, *to Pyrrhus asking*.

[10] Say, *of-what-sort* (qualis) *Rome appeared to him*. Note that, according to the ordinary rule for indirect or reported questions, the verb for ' seemed ' must be *subj.*

8. MENENIUS AGRIPPA.

When the populace [1] had seceded from the senate [2] to the Sacred Mount, because [3] they could not endure the tribute and military service, and could not be induced-to-return, [4] Menenius Agrippa reasoned with them [5] as follows [6]. "Once-upon-a-time," said he, "the limbs of the human body, [7] seeing [8] the belly (as they thought) leading-an-idle-life, [9] fell-out [10] with it, and refused it their services. But-when-by-so-doing [11] they themselves too grew-weak, [12] they perceived that the belly distributed the food [13] which-it-received [p] through all the members, and (so) they became-reconciled [14] to it. In-like-manner, [15] the senate [2] and people, (who are) as-it-were one body, perish through-discord, (but) are-made-strong [16] by concord." Won-over [17] by this fable, the populace [1] returned to the city.

---

[1] plebs —*the plebeian order*. (The secession here referred to, however, proceeded 'not from those who resented their disabilities as an order, but from the distress of the farmers.' Mommsen, i. 279.)   [2] patres.

[3] quod (which is preferred to quia in giving the reason alleged *by others*); foll. by subj. of reported speech, quod non toleráret ...: Introd. p. 10.   [4] revoco.

[5] apud *eam* (=plebem).

[6] Say, *thus* (sic).

[7] Say, *the human limbs* (artus).

[8] Expr. pres. part. by cum and *subj.* of cerno.   [9] otiosus.

[10] Say, *parted from it* (dissideo).

[11] quo cum.

[12] deficio.   [13] *plur*.

[14] *to become reconciled with*, cum ... in gratiam redire.   [15] sic.

[16] valeo.   [17] motus.

9. WAR WITH THE GAULS.

When the Senonian Gauls [1] were besieging Clusium, a town of Etruria, three ambassadors were sent from Rome to [2] warn the Gauls to [3] desist from the siege. One of these, contrary to the law [4] of nations, went-forth [p] to battle, and [5] slew a chief of the Senones. Exasperated at this,[6] the Gauls, after [7] having in vain demanded the surrender of the ambassadors, made-for [8] Rome, and overthrew [9] the Roman army at the river Allia. They entered the city (as) [10] conquerors, where at first they reverenced as [10] gods the most noble of the old men, who-were-sitting [p] in their curule chairs, and clothed with their insignia of magistrates ; [11] afterwards, when [12] they perceived them to be (but) men, they put them to death. The rest [13] of the youth fled with Manlius into the Capitol, where they-were-besieged [p] (but) liberated by the valour of Camillus, who, being appointed dictator in-his-absence,[14] collected the citizens that-still-remained,[15] (and) overpowered the Gauls by-an-unexpected-(attack).[16]

---

[1] Galli Senŏnes.
[2] qui with *subj.*
[3] ut.   [4] jus gentium.
[5] Note that the use of a participle in the former clause renders the conj. 'and' superfluous.
[6] *rel.*
[7] cum with *pluperf. subj.*
[8] contendo.
[9] profligo.
[10] 'as conquerors ... as gods': the first 'as' must not be expressed, but the second is indispensable; see Ex. 7, Note 4.
[11] The order of the clauses is:

'where the noblest of the old men, sitting in chairs of state (sellae curules) and clothed with the insignia of magistrates, at first they reverenced as gods.'
[12] ut with *perf. indic.* (The perf. is also used after ubi, simul atque, postquam.)
[13] cetera or reliqua juventus :— keep the predicate singular throughout, the subject being juventus, *sing.*   [14] absens.
[15] reliquus: *abl. abs.*
[16] Say, (*he*) *unforeseen* overpowered the Gauls.

10. PISISTRATUS.

Pisistratus obtained[1] absolute-power by stratagem. For, on-one-occasion,[2] he voluntarily[3] submitted to be scourged at home, and, with his body (thus) mangled, went-forth[4] into-the-place-of-public-resort,[5] where he called[P] an assembly, and showed[4] his wounds to the people, complaining of[6] the cruelty of the aristocracy,[7] from whom he pretended that he had suffered this treatment.[8] Tears were[4] added to words,[9] and the credulous multitude was inflamed[4] by his invidious harangue, asserting,[10] as he did, that (it was) from-his-love to the populace that he was hated[11] by the Senate. By these artifices he obtained[12] the aid of a body-guard[13] for the custody of his person, by-whose-assistance[14] he seized-upon[P] the tyranny and reigned for thirty-seven years.

---

[1] occupo.   [2] aliquando.
[3] Say, *visited* (affectus) *with voluntary stripes at home.*
[4] *hist. pres.*   [5] in publicum.
[6] queror is *intrans.*, and must be foll. by de.   [7] principes.

[8] Say, *had suffered these* (*things*).
[9] voces.
[10] Say, *for he asserts* (affirmo).
[11] invisus, with *dat.*
[12] accipio.   [13] satellites.
[14] per quos.

11. METELLUS SCIPIO.

Q. Metellus Scipio, after[1] having unsuccessfully supported[p] in Africa the cause[2] of Cn. Pompey, his son-in-law, made-for Spain with his fleet. But when he had perceived that the ship, in which he was sailing,[3] had been captured by the enemy, he stabbed himself in the side.[4] And thereupon falling-prostrate[5] in the stern, to the enquiries[6] of Caesar's soldiers where[7] the general was, he replied, "The general is well;"[8] and would[9] only say just so much as was sufficient to[10] testify to the fortitude of his mind.

---

[1] Order: 'the cause of Cn. P., his son-in-law, unsuccessfully in Spain having been supported (defendo).'

[2] partes.   [3] vehor.

[4] Say, *stabbed* (percussit) *his side with a sword.*

[5] prostratus.

[6] Say, *to Caesar's soldiers en-* quiring (quaero).

[7] ubinam (more emphatic than simple ubi).

[8] *to be well*, bene se habere.

[9] tantumque eloqui voluit . . . ; and express *as* by the correl. of tantum (St. L. G. § 84).

[10] ad, with gerundive.

12. The Athenian Love of Liberty.

The Athenians were[1] utterly[2] unable to withstand the attack of the Persians. (Accordingly,) they resolved to abandon[p] the city, and—placing[p] their wives and children for safety[3] at Troezen—to take-to[4] their ships, and defend the independence[5] of Greece with their fleet; [and] they stoned-to-death[6] one Cyrsilus, (for) advising[p] (them) to[7] remain in the city and await (the arrival of) Xerxes.

---

[1] Say, *when* the Athenians, &c.; and form the entire paragraph into a single period.   [2] nullo modo.
[3] *to place for safety*, depono : use *perf. part. pass.*

[4] conscendo—ut and *subj.*
[5] Say, *freedom.*
[6] Say, *overwhelmed with stones* (which must come at the end of the period).   [7] ut.

---

13. Themistocles.

A certain learned man came to Themistocles and promised to teach[1] him the art of memory. Upon[2] his asking what[3] that art could effect, the teacher[4] replied, (that it would make him) remember[5] everything. And Themistocles answered, that[6] he would be doing him a greater kindness, if he taught[7] him to forget what he wished[8] (to forget) than if (he taught him) to remember.

---

[1] 'promised to teach'=*promised that he would teach* (trado, *to impart*), *fut. inf.*
[2] cum.
[3] quidnam, see Ex. 11, Note 7 : and remember that the question introduced by quidnam is *indirect.*
[4] doctor *ille.*

[5] ut with *subj.* Note, the *pluperf. subj.* of memini corresponds to the *imperf.* of ordinary verbs.
[6] Say, *that he would do (a thing) more pleasing to him.*
[7] *pluperf. subj.* of doceo; which come must at the end of the sentence.
[8] *imperf. subj.*, Introd. p. 10.

14. SOPHOCLES ACCUSED BY HIS SONS.

Sophocles composed[1] tragedies up-to[2] extreme old age. (And) when on account of this[3] pursuit he was thought[4] to neglect his private affairs,[5] he was summoned to trial by his sons, in order that the judges might remove him, on the ground of imbecility,[6] from (the management of) his property.[5] Then the old man is said to have read[7] to his judges the[8] play which he had in his hands, and which he had written last[9]— the Oedipus Colonēus,—and to have asked whether that poem seemed[10] to them (to be the work) of an imbecile. On reading this[11] he was discharged[12] by the verdict[13] of his judges.

---

[1] facio.   [2] ad.

[3] *rel.*: remember that the relative pron. is itself a connective, so that the conj. *and* must not be used. Also the rel. must come at the beginning of its clause.

[4] Say, *seemed*.   [5] res familiaris.

[6] Say, *as if being-imbecile* (desipiens).

[7] recito (to read *aloud*).

[8] When a noun is defined by a rel. clause, '*the*' is usually to be expressed by is, ea, id.

[9] proxime.

[10] What mood? see p. 10.

[11] *rel.* : *abl. abs.*

[12] libero.

[13] sententiis.

15. The Crime of Parricide.

Solon, when [1] he was asked, why he had appointed no punishment [2] for [3] a man who had killed [4] his parent, replied, that he did not think any one was likely to do that. [5] But the Romans, perceiving [6] that there was nothing so sacred which daring-wickedness [7] would not at-some-time-or-other [8] outrage, devised an extraordinary punishment for [9] parricides. They determined [10] that they should be sewn-up [11] alive in a sack and thrown [11] into the river.

---

[1] Expr. either by *perf. part.* or by cum with *imperf. subj.*

[2] supplicium (only used of severe punishment, such as scourging, torture, or death).   [3] in eum.

[4] Observe that though this form in English does not differ from the *indic.*, yet it conveys a pure supposition. It must therefore be in the *subj.*

[5] Say, *that he had thought that no one would do it.*

[6] cum with *imperf. subj.*

[7] audacia.

[8] aliquando.

[9] See Note 3.

[10] voluerunt, foll. by *inf.*: the verb volo often expresses a resolution of the people.

[11] *sewn-up . . . thrown.* Either these verbs may both be put in the inf. mood, or the former may be represented by a participle (p. 6), and the latter only be in *inf.*

16. Masinissa.

Masinissa, king of the Numidians, at-the-age-of[1] ninety years, when he had commenced[2] a journey on-foot, did not get on horseback[3] at all. When (he had set out) on horseback,[4] he did not dismount from his horse. No rain,[5] no cold induced him to[6] go[7] with his head covered; he was-wont-to-discharge all the duties and functions of a king.[8] Accordingly exercise and[9] temperance can preserve even in old age some of (one's) early vigour.[10]

---

[1] natus.

[2] ingredior.

[3] to get on horseback, in equum ascendere; or without prep., equum conscendere.

[4] abl. without prep.

[5] Say, by no rain ... was he induced (adduco).   [6] ut.

[7] Say, be with covered (opertus) head.

[8] Either the gen. of rex or the adj. regius may be here used: comp. Ex. 1, Note 4.

[9] et is here to be preferred to -que; partly because the two things are quite distinct, and partly for euphony. The enclitic -que is less frequent with words which have the accent on the antepenultima.

[10] aliquid pristini roboris.

17. XERXES.

Xerxes, though-loaded[1] with all the prizes and gifts of fortune, (was) content neither[2] with (his) cavalry, nor (his) infantry,[3] nor with the multitude of (his) ships, nor with (his) incalculable amount of gold, (but) offered[4] a reward to the man[5] who should invent[6] a new pleasure. And (yet) with this[7] very (pleasure) he was not content; so true is it that[8] unbridled-desire[9] will never find a limit.

---

[1] refertus.
[2] *neither ... nor ... nor,* non ... non ... non: and let the adj. contentus come at the *end* of the clause.
[3] pedestres copiae.   [4] propono.
[5] is: compare Ex. 14, Note 8.

[6] *pluperf.,* because the invention precedes the reward.
[7] *rel.,* and compare Ex. 14, Note 3.
[8] neque enim unquam.
[9] libīdo.

18. LEONIDAS.

Leonidas, king of the Lacedaemonians, when the alternative[1] of a base flight or a glorious death was presented to him, opposed[2] himself and the[3] three hundred men whom he had led out from Sparta to the enemy at Thermopylae.[4] Then to the Lacedaemonians as-they-

---

[1] There is no exact word for *alternative:* expr. by aut ... aut: when *either* base flight *or* a glorious death had been set before (propono) him.

[2] oppono.
[3] See Ex. 14, Note 8.
[4] in Thermopylis (Thermopylae not being the name of a town but of a pass).

set-out [p] for-the-place,[5] whence they thought [6] that they should never return, he said, "Proceed with a good courage,[7] Lacedaemonians! to-day perchance we shall sup with-the-shades-below." [8]

---

[5] eo: the adverb is defined by the adverbial clause, unde . . .

[6] arbitror: and use *subj.*, because the sense is, to *such* a place

of peril *that* they never expected to return.

[7] animus.

[8] apud inferos.

19. THE LACEDAEMONIANS.

A certain Lacedaemonian, when a Persian foeman had boastfully [1] asserted in the conference, "You will not see [2] the sun by-reason-of [3] the multitude of our spears and arrows," said, "Then [4] we shall fight in the shade." With-a-like-spirit [5] the Spartan-woman, when she had sent her son to battle and heard that he was slain, said, "For-this-cause [6] I had borne [7] him, that he might be (one) who should not hesitate [8] to meet death [9] on behalf of his country."

---

[1] Say, *boasting.*

[2] Direct narration : *indic.*

[3] prae, because a negative precedes. So, *he could not speak for tears*, prae lacrimis: St. L. G. p. 294.

[4] igitur.

[6] idcirco.

[7] gigno.

[5] similiter.

[8] When dubito means to hesitate *to do* something, it is foll. by *inf.*

[9] mortem *or* morti occumbere.

---

20. Epaminondas.

When Epaminondas had conquered the Lacedaemonians at[1] Mantinēa, and at-the-same-time[2] perceived
that he was dying[3] of a severe wound, as-soon-as[4] he
opened-his-eyes[5] he asked whether his shield were
safe.[6] When his comrades[7] weeping answered that it
was safe, he enquired whether the enemy were routed;
and when he had heard that (question) also (answered)
according to his wish,[8] he ordered the spear, with which
he was transfixed, to be plucked out. Upon-this[9] a
torrent[10] of blood gushed-out,[11] and he expired in[12]
(the midst of) joy and victory.

---

[1] ad or apud, the battle being
fought *near*, not *at* the town.

[2] simul.

[3] exanimo: *pres. inf. pass.*

[4] ut primum; and for the tense,
see Ex. 9, Note 12.

[5] dispicio.

[6] salvus; and give emphasis to
this word by putting it first in the
clause; appending to it the enclitic interrogative -ne.

[7] *his comrades*, sui: and again
keep the word for *safe* prominent.

[8] ut cupiebat.   [9] ita.

[10] Say, *much* blood, and use *abl.
abs.*

[11] Perf. part. pass. of perfundo.

[12] Repeat *prep.* before victoria.

21. FABRICIUS.

When Pyrrhus, king of Epirus, had without provocation engaged in war[1] against the Roman people, a deserter from him came into the camp of Fabricius, the Roman general, and promised him that, if he would offer[2] him a reward, he would return to the camp of Pyrrhus as secretly as[3] he had come, and would kill[4] him by poison. Fabricius had him taken back[5] to Pyrrhus; and that act of his was applauded by the senate.

---

[1] bellum ultro (=*without being injured or attacked*) inferre, with *dat.* of indirect object.

[2] *pluperf.*, because the offer was to *precede* the act.

[3] ut clam venisset (subj. of oblique narration, p. 10), sic clam . . .

[4] neco, which is regularly used of putting to death in a cruel or wicked way.

[5] *to have* a thing done, is expr. by curo (*to take care, see to it*) with *ger. part.*

---

22. MANIUS CURIUS.

Manius Curius, after[1] having held[2] triumphs over[3] the Samnites, the Sabines, and Pyrrhus, spent the end of his days[4] in-a-country-life.[5] When, as he[6] was sitting at his hearth, the Samnites brought him a great quantity of gold, he refused to accept it;[7] for he said that he did not think[8] it a fine thing to possess gold, but to rule over those who possessed it.

---

[1] cum.

[2] *to hold a triumph (for victories gained) over* . . ., triumphare de . . .

[3] Repeat *prep.* before each *abl.*

[4] extremum tempus aetatis.

[5] *loc.* of rus.

[6] Say, *to the same (man) sitting*

by (ad) *his hearth, when the Samnites* . . .

[7] Say, *they were rejected* (repudio, 1) *by him.*

[8] Expr. by videor: *that not the having* (inf.) *gold seemed to him fine* . . .

E 2

23. Ennius and Scipio Nasica.

Scipio[1] Nasica (once) went[2] to (call on) the poet Ennius, and the maid-servant told him upon his asking at the door[3] for Ennius, that he was not at home. Nasica however perceived that she had said so by order of her master, and that he was within. A few days after,[4] Ennius[1] came to (call on) Nasica, and enquired for him at the door, (when) Nasica called-out[5] that he was not at home. Then Ennius says,[6] "What! do I not recognise your voice?" Upon-this[7] Nasica replied, "You are an impudent (fellow); when[8] I enquired for you, I believed your maid-servant (when she said) that you were not at home; you do not believe me (when I tell you so) myself."[9]

---

[1] Begin, cum Scipio . . . and similarly in l. 6, cum Ennius . . .

[2] venio, *plup. subj.* after cum.

[3] Say, *to him asking-for* (quaero) *Ennius from the door* (ostium).

[4] paucis post diebus, in which phr., post is *adv.*, '*later by a few days.*'

[5] exclamo, *hist. pres.*

[6] inquit, which must follow some word or words of the question asked.

[7] hic.

[8] cum with *imperf. subj.*

[9] Emphasize 'myself' by ending sentence with ipsi.

24. C. MARIUS.

C. Marius, when he was (yet) far from the hope of (obtaining) the consulship, and[1] did not seem likely ever to be a candidate for it,[2] charged[3] Q. Metellus, whose lieutenant he was, and by whom he had been sent to Rome, before[4] the Roman people with[5] prolonging the war. If they made him consul, (he said) that he would in a short time bring[6] Jugurtha, either dead or alive, into the power of the Roman people. And so he[7] was indeed appointed consul, but he deviated[8] from good faith and justice in bringing[9] into discredit through a false charge an excellent and most influential citizen, whose lieutenant he was, and by whom he had been sent.

---

[1] *and . . . not*, nec.

[2] *likely to be a candidate for* (*it*), *fut. part.* of peto.

[3] criminor.　　[4] apud.

[5] Say, *that he* (illum) *was prolonging the war*. The idea of 'saying' is implied in criminor; hence *acc.* and *inf.*

[6] redigo: the constr. is that of *oratio obliqua*.

[7] ille.　　[8] discedo.

[9] *to bring into discredit*, in invidiam adducere. Expr. '*in* bringing' by qui with *perf. subj.*; denoting the *reason why* he is considered to have acted dishonourably.

25. The Filial Affection of T. Manlius.

M. Pomponius, a tribune of the people, brought [1] an accusation against L. Manlius, after [2] he had been dictator, on-the-ground-that [3] he had added on a few days to [4] (the period of) his holding the dictatorship; he also charged him with having banished [5] his son, Titus, from (the society of) men, and ordered him to dwell in the country.[6] When the young man, his son, heard of this,[7] he went-with-all-speed [8] to Rome, and at the first dawn of day [9] appeared at [10] the house of Pomponius. When this was announced to Pomponius,[11] thinking [12] that he would in his anger [13] bring him some fresh evidence [14] against his father, he rose [15] from his couch, and bidding all witnesses withdraw,[16] he ordered the young man to be brought to him. But he had no sooner entered [17] than he drew [p] his sword, and swore that he would kill Pomponius [18] on the spot,[19] unless he pledged him his oath [20] that he would abandon the prosecution against his father.[21] Compelled by this intimidation,[22] Pomponius took the (required) oath.[23]

---

[1] Say, *named* (dixit) *a day for* (*the trial of*), with *dat.* of person.

[2] cum.

[3] quod; with *subj.*, because it is simply what is alleged by the accuser. The indic. would mean that he really had so acted.

[4] ad with *ger. part.* (gero).

[5] relēgo, 1.   [6] *loc.* of rus.

[7] Begin with *rel. pron.*: *which when the young man had heard.*

[8] accurro; *hist. pres.*

[9] (cum) prima luce.

[10] Say, *comes into.*

[11] Instead of repeating the name,

use *rel.*, cui cum . . .

[12] quod arbitrabatur.

[13] Say, (*being*) *angry.*

[14] *bring some fresh evidence:* say, bring *something.*   [15] surgo.

[16] remotisque arbitris.

[17] Say, *as soon as* (ut) *he entered,* *immediately* (confestim) . . . : and for the tense after ut, see Ex. 9, Note 12.

[18] illum.   [19] statim.

[20] jusjurandum do: *pluperf. subj.*

[21] Say, *that he would make his father free-of-the-charge* (missus).

[22] terror.   [23] Say, *swore.*

26. THEMISTOCLES AND ARISTIDES.

Themistocles, after being victorious [1] in the war
which was (carried on) with the Persians, announced [2]
in the assembly, that he had a plan (which would be)
advantageous to the state, but [3] that there was no need
it should be (publicly) known.　He demanded, that the
people should appoint [4] some one, to whom [5] he could
communicate it.　They appointed [6] Aristides.　To him
Themistocles [7] (pointed out) that the Lacedaemonian [8]
fleet, which was hauled-on-shore [9] at [10] Gythēum, could
be secretly set-on-fire ; that if this [11] were done, the
resources of the Lacedaemonians must necessarily be
crushed.[12]　When Aristides heard this,[13] he returned to
the assembly amid [14] great expectation, and said that
the plan which Themistocles proposed [15] was very
advantageous, but by-no-means an honourable one.
Therefore the Athenians decided [16] that as [17] it was not
honourable, it was not advantageous either,[18] and by
the advice of [19] Aristides rejected the whole matter,
without [20] even having heard it.

---

[1] Say, after the victory of that
war . . .　　[2] dico.
[3] sed id sciri (palam fieri) non
opus esse.　　[4] do.
[5] quocum.
[6] Use *pass.*
[7] huic ille (a verb of *saying*
being understood).
[8] Say, the fleet *of* the Lacedaemonians.
[9] subduco : *subj.*, being oblique
narration, Introd. p. 10.　　[10] ad.
[11] *rel.*, and *abl. abs.*
[12] frangi necesse esse.　　[13] *rel.*
[14] *abl.* only.

[15] affero.　　[16] censeo.
[17] quod ; to be foll. by *subj.*, because it is the decision of the
people that is given, not a statement of the writer.
[18] Say, *not even advantageous :*
separate ne . . . quidem by the word
which these particles emphasize.
[19] auctore Aristide.
[20] Say, *which they had not even
heard.*　Finish the sentence with
the principal verb, *they rejected,*
which should be immediately preceded by the adverbial clause,
auctore Aristide.

27. THE RING OF GYGES.

Gyges, a shepherd of the king,[1] when the earth had parted-asunder[2] after heavy storms of rain,[3] descended into the[4] chasm, and perceived[5] a brazen horse, in whose sides there were doors. On opening these,[6] he saw a body of unusual size with[7] a gold ring on its finger ; this[8] he drew-off[9] and put on his own. Then he betook himself to the assembly[9] of the shepherds. There, when he had turned round the bezel[10] of the ring to the palm of his hand, he became invisible,[11] while[12] he saw everything himself; when he turned[13] the ring (back) to its place, he[14] was once-more[15] visible.

---

[1] adj.   [2] discedo.
[3] magnis imbribus.
[4] Use ille, which emphasizes the noun.   [5] animadverto.
[6] rel. and abl. abs.   [7] Say, and.
[8] Say, which drawn off he himself put on (induo): Introd. p. 6.
[9] concilium.
[10] i.e. the hollow for the jewel, pala.
[11] Say, he was seen (what tense ?)

by no one : remember that the abl. of nemo is not in use.
[12] ipse autem.
[13] iuverto: pluperf. ind.
[14] idem : which is very often used when a second predicate is introduced referring to the same subject.
[15] rursus : and express was visible acc. to Note 11.

28. CYRUS THE YOUNGER.

When Lysander, the Lacedaemonian, had come to Cyrus the younger at [1] Sardis, and had brought him presents from the allies, (Cyrus) was [2] courteous and kind to him with-regard-to-the-other-matters, and (in particular) showed him a [3] piece of ground fenced in and carefully planted. Whilst [4] Lysander was admiring the tallness [5] of the trees, the straightness [6] of the rows, and the fragrance of the perfumes which were wafted from the flowers, he remarked, [7] that he admired the ingenuity no less than [8] the industry of the man by whom all those things had been laid out [9] and designed. [9] And Cyrus answered him, "Well now, [10] I made [11] all the measurements you speak of, they are my [12] rows, my [12] designing, many even of those trees have been planted [13] by my own hand." Then Lysander, beholding his purple-robe, [14] the elegance [15] of his person, and his decorations [16] (consisting of) much Persian gold and many jewels, said, "They rightly call you happy, Cyrus, since in you good fortune is combined with moral excellence." [17]

---

[1] Say, *to* Sardis, *acc.*

[2] Connect the two following clauses by et . . . et: Introd. p. 1.

[3] ager quidam. [4] cum.

[5] *plur.*:—the trees were of different heights.

[6] Say, *the straight rows.* [7] dico.

[8] Say, *not only the industry, but also,* &c.

[9] What mood? See Introd. p. 10.

[10] atqui.

[11] Say, *laid-out all* those *things* (*you speak of*). Which demonstrative adj. should be used?

[12] Give emphasis to 'my' by position.

[13] sero. [14] purpura.

[15] nitor.

[16] ornatus, ûs, foll. by *abl.* of description.

[17] Say, *since to your virtue fortune has been joined.*

29. M. ATILIUS REGULUS.

When M. Atilius Regulus, the consul, was taken
prisoner in Africa by [1] an ambush, under the command
of Xanthippus the Lacedaemonian, he was sent to the
senate, bound by an oath [2] to return himself to Carthage unless certain noble captives were restored to the
Carthaginians.   When [3] he arrived at Rome, he came
into the senate, (and) explained his instructions, (but)
refused [4] to express [5] his opinion (on the matter), maintaining, that as long as he was bound [6] by the oath sworn
to the enemy, [7] he was not a senator.   And even the
proposition [8] that the prisoners should be restored, he
asserted [9] to be inexpedient, for that (he said) they
were in-the-prime-of-life, [10] and were good leaders, (but)
that he was now worn out with age.   And when his [11]
influence prevailed, the captives were retained, (and) he
himself returned to Carthage, nor did his affection for
his country or his-friends [12] retain him (at Rome).
And yet at that very time he well knew [13] that he was
departing to a most unmerciful enemy, and to tortures

---

[1] *ex* insidiis.

[2] Say, *having sworn*, foll. by ut.
The adverbial clause ' unless . . . '
must precede the other.

[3] is cum.

[4] recuso, with *inf.*

[5] sententiam dico.

[6] teneo ; *subj.*

[7] Say, oath *of* the enemy: the

Latin genitive having a much wider
range of meaning than Eng. '*of.*'

[8] illud, defined by *acc.* and *inf.*
following.

[9] Say, *denied to be expedient*
(utilis).

[10] juvenes.

[11] *rel.*   [12] sui.

[13] neque vero tum ignorabat . . .

of refined cruelty;[14] but he considered that his oath must be kept. And so, the Carthaginians having cut-off[15] his eyelids, and bound[P16] him on a scaffold,[17] left him to perish for want of sleep.[18]

---

[14] exquisīta supplicia.
[15] reseco: *abl. abs.*
[16] illigo: and see Introd. p. 6.

[17] machīna.
[18] Say, *killed him with going-with-out-sleep* (vigilando).

---

30. THE EMPEROR TITUS.

The Emperor Titus, who was naturally[1] of-the-most-benevolent-disposition,[2] was styled the darling and delight[3] of the human race. It was a principle of his[4] not to send away without hope any one who came[5] to him. When those-of-his-household[6] cautioned[P] him against making more promises than he would be able to perform,[7] he replied, "No one ought[8] to go away in sorrow[9] from an interview[10] with his sovereign." Moreover[11] on-one-occasion remembering[12] at supper time[13] that he had done nothing for-any-one[14] the whole day,[15] he uttered that memorable exclamation, worthy of all praise,[16] "(My) friends, to-day I have lost[17] a day!"

---

[1] *by nature.*   [2] *superl. adj.*
[3] amor ac deliciae.
[4] ei hoc erat propositum, foll. by *conj.*: and since a *purpose* is expressed, use ne ... quem (*not* ut neminem).
[5] Say, *of those coming* (accedo).
[6] domestici: and say, 'warning, *as if* he were promising,' &c.
[7] praesto.   [8] oportet.   [9] tristis.

[10] sermo; with *gen.*: see Ex. 29, Note 7.   [11] atque etiam.
[12] Use that word for *remember* which has *perf. part.*
[13] super cenam.
[14] =*any single person*, quisquam.
[15] *abl.*
[16] Say, *and deservedly praised.*
[17] perdo (which implies blame on the part of the loser).

31. ALEXANDER AND APELLES.

Alexander having inspected [1] at Ephesus a portrait of himself [2] by [3] Apelles, the most renowned painter of the age, [4] bestowed less praise upon [5] the painting than it (really) deserved. When however his horse, upon being brought in, [6] neighed at the horse represented in the picture, [7] as if this also were a (real) horse, Apelles remarked, [8] "O king, this horse seems a better judge [9] of the art of painting than you (are)."

[1] contemplor.   [2] imago sua.
[3] Say, *which Apelles, the most . . . had painted:* and note that this clause, being strictly adjectival, and defining *which* picture, must come immediately after the noun to which it refers.
[4] illius temporis.
[5] Say, *praised it less.*
[6] introduco.
[7] Say, *the painted horse.*
[8] inquit : see Ex. 23, Note 6.
[9] peritior (comp. of perĩtus).

32. DIOGENES.

Diogenes, when-at-the-point-of-death, [1] gave orders for his body [2] to be cast forth without-burial. [3] "What!" (objected) his friends, [4] "to the birds and wild beasts?" "On no account," [5] he replied; "but you-must-put [6] a little-stick near me that [7] I may drive them away." "How will you be able (to do that)?" they (rejoined), "for you will not feel (them)." "What harm, [8] then, (said he,) will the mangling of wild beasts do to me, if I have no feeling?" [9]

[1] moribundus.
[2] Say, *ordered himself to be cast forth.*
[3] inhumatus.   [4] tum amici.
[5] minime.
[6] *fut. imper.*, because it is not to be done till after his death.
[7] Say, *with which* = ut eo.
[8] *to do harm,* obsum, with *dat.*
[9] Say, *feeling nothing.*

33. THE GREEK SOLDIER.

Among[1] the Greeks, and especially the Lacedaemonians, nothing was (considered) more disgraceful to a soldier than to return from[2] battle without his shield. On-the-other-hand[3] it was his greatest[4] glory to be carried back[5] to his native place slain, with his wounds received-in-front, and laid upon his shield. For-this-reason[6] a Spartan woman[7] is reported to have said to her son, as she handed[P] (him his) shield on his setting out[8] for the war, "(Return) either with this or on this;" that is, either bring-home (this) shield, or be brought home[9] yourself lying[10] on this shield.

---

[1] apud; which has a more general sense than inter.

[2] e (not a), because the soldier is supposed to have been *in* the battle.

[3] contra. [4] summus.

[5] End the sentence with the clause 'to be carried back (reporto) to his native-place': which is thus preceded by the three adjuncts (i) 'with wounds in front,' (ii) 'slain,' (iii) 'laid on (in) his shield.'

[6] quare or idcirco.

[7] mulier Lacaena.

[8] Say, *to him setting out for* (ad) *the war.*

[9] *fut. imper. pass.* of reporto : see Ex. 32, Note 6.

[10] jacens; or as before, impositus.

34. Julius Drusus.

The house[1] of Julius Drusus was-open on several sides[2] to be overlooked[3] by the neighbours. A carpenter offered[4] to remedy[5] this inconvenience, if five talents were given him, and to contrive[6] that no part of it should be exposed to be overlooked. Whereupon Drusus replied—" I will give you ten (talents), if you will make[7] my house such, that not only (my) neighbours, but all the citizens may be able to see my manner of living in it."[8]

---

[1] aedes, *plur.*; to be preceded by *gen.* of possessor.

[2] pluribus ex partibus.

[3] Say, *to overlooking* (prospectus) *of neighbours.*

[4] polliceor: and for constr., see Ex. 13, Note 1.

[5] Arrange: 'this inconvenience a carpenter, if five talents ... to remedy (corrigo) promised.'

[6] Say, *that he would contrive,* efficio: and for what follows, see Ex. 30, Note 4.

[7] reddo; *fut. perf.*: in this clause use domus instead of aedes.

[8] Say, *how I live in it.*

N.B.—The latter part of the above paragraph should be rendered first in the Direct and then in the Indirect form. See p. 14.

35. GRECIAN VALOUR.

The glory[1] of Cynaegīrus, an Athenian soldier, has been highly extolled in history.[2] For when in the battle, which was fought under the leadership of Miltiades on the plains of Marathon,[3] he had made great havoc (among the enemy)[4] and had driven them[5] fleeing to their ships, he (caught hold of) a vessel laden[6] (with soldiers), first of all with his right hand, then, when this was cut-off,[p][7] with his left hand; lastly, when he had lost[p] this as well, he kept-hold[8] (of it) with his teeth. So desperate[9] was his valour, that, unexhausted[10] by the slaughter of so many foes,[11] unsubdued[12] (too) by the loss of both his hands, at-last mutilated (as he was), and with all the ferocity of a wild beast,[13] he fought-on[14] with his teeth.

---

[1] Comp. Ex. 34, Note 1: and remember that the noun in apposition must follow the noun with which it agrees.

[2] Say, *has been celebrated with great praises.*

[3] Marathonius, a, um.

[4] innumerabiles caedes effecisset.

[5] Use noun hostes.

[6] onustus.

[7] amputo ; *abl. abs.*

[8] retineo (*to hold back*). It is the use of this verb which renders it unnecessary to express 'he caught hold of,' above. [9] tantus.

[10] non . . . fatigatus.

[11] Say, *by so many slaughters.*

[12] non . . . victus: and express verbal noun 'loss' by *perf. part.* (amitto). Compare Ex. 2, Note 1.

[13] veluti rabida fera.

[14] dimico.

36. Patience under Insult.

(Whilst) Pericles [1] (was) transacting [P] public business [2] in the forum, a worthless and impudent fellow [3] kept railing at and abusing [4] (him). When (Pericles) bore it [5] quite patiently, and [6] said not a word in reply, [7] he kept it up [8] the whole day (long). In the evening Pericles returned home with countenance and gait (alike) unruffled, [9] the varlet [10] still [10] following and heaping every kind of obloquy [11] upon him. As-he-was-about-to-enter [P] his house, it being [12] now dark, [13] he ordered one of his servants to light [P] a lamp, [14] (and then) attend the man, and take-him-(safely)-home. [15]

---

[1] Make 'Pericles' the object of the verb 'to rail at.'   [2] *plur.*

[3] homo improbus et petulans.

[4] Say, *was assailing* (consector) *with abuse* (*plur.*).   [5] *rel.*

[6] *and . . . not*, nec.

[7] *to say . . . in reply*, repono.

[8] persevēro; and end sentence with Subject 'ille.'

[9] placidus.

[10] nebulo, onis; and express 'still' by idem: comp. Ex. 27, Note 14.

[11] Say, *overwhelming him with all insults* (opprobria, *neut. pl.*).

[12] Expr. by cum and *subj.*

[13] nox.   [14] *abl. abs.*

[15] reduco.

37. THE PATRIOTISM OF CODRUS.

Codrus, king of the Athenians, when the territory of Attica,[1] (already) weakened by the vast army of the enemy, was (now) being devastated by fire and sword, had-recourse[2] to the oracle of the Delphian Apollo, and enquired,[3] through deputies, in what way so disastrous a war[4] might be (successfully) repelled.[5] The god replied that, if he fell by the hand of-the-enemy,[6] an end would in-that-case[7] be (put) to the war.[8] This was noised about, not only at Athens, but in the enemy's camp; and orders were accordingly issued,[9] that[10] no one was to injure[11] the person of Codrus. When this[12] became known to him, he laid aside the badges of royalty,[13] and, clad in the dress of a slave,[14] threw-himself-in-the-way-of[15] a body of the enemy as they were foraging;[p] and by striking[16] one of their number with a scythe, compelled (the man) to kill him. Thus by his death[17] the fall of Athens was averted.[18]

---

[1] Attica regio.
[2] confugio. [3] sciscitor, 1.
[4] illud tam grave bellum.
[5] discutio, 3. [6] adj.
[7] ita. [8] ei.
[9] eoque factum est ut ediceretur.
[10] 'that no one': see Ex. 30, Note 4. [11] vulnero.
[12] Say, which when (postquam; see Ex. 9, Note 12) he learnt.

[13] imperium.
[14] Say, having put on the dress of-a-slave (servīlis).
[15] objicio, with pron. refl.
[16] Say, forced (compello) one of them struck with a scythe to (in) his own slaughter. [17] interitus.
[18] Say, it was brought about (efficio) that Athens should not perish: use ne.

38. Foolish Pride.

Socrates brought Alcibiades, (who was) a pupil of
his, (and) prided-himself[p][1] upon his wealth and the
extent of his landed property,[2] to a place in which a
map of the world[3] was hung up, and asked him to
look-for Attica in it. When he had found this,[4] he bade
him also look for his own farms, and point them out.
Upon[5] his answering that they were not represented on
the map,[6] Socrates said, "Are you not ashamed of
priding-yourself[7] upon the possession of lands which
form[8] no (appreciable) part of the world?"

---

[1] superbio takes *abl.* without
prep.   [2] agrorum multitudo.
[3] Say, *a picture comprising a
plan of the earth*, tabula quaedam
descriptionem terrae complectens.

[4] *rel*,.
[5] cum.
[6] Say, *that they were nowhere
represented* (pictos) *there*.
[7] *inf.*   [8] Say, *are*.

39. THE FOOLISH PHYSICIAN.

Menecrates, a physician, was so [1] puffed up with pride, that he styled himself Jupiter. Accordingly, Philip, king of Macedon,[2] having [3] on-one-occasion pre-pared-[4] a most sumptuous banquet, and invited him amongst others,[5] ordered a table to be laid [6] for him apart (from the rest), and a censer to be placed [7] (upon it), and frankincense and (other) perfumes to be burnt (therein). Meanwhile the rest partook of the feast.[8] Now Menecrates was at first delighted [9] with the divine honours [10] (which were paid to him); but when hunger gradually crept over him, and he was proved [11] to be a man—and, moreover,[12] a vain and stupid one, he rose up and went away, complaining that he had been insulted.[13]

---

[1] adeo.
[2] Say, *of the Macedonians.*
[3] cum.   [4] instruo.
[5] Say, *also* (quoque).
[6] apparo.   [7] appono.

[8] et ceteri quidem epulabantur.
[9] gaudeo.   [10] *sing.*
[11] convinco.   [12] isque.
[13] Say, *treated with insult* (injuriâ afficere).

40. A Father's Consolation for the Death of his Son.

When Xenophon was performing a customary [1] sacrifice, he received the intelligence [2] that the elder of his two sons, named [3] Gryllus, had fallen in the battle at Mantinèa.   He did not, however, [4] consider this [5] a sufficient reason for discontinuing the worship of the gods (when) once begun, but deemed [6] it sufficient to lay aside his (sacrificial) crown.   He then enquired? [7] how [8] he had met-with-his-death, [9] (and) was told [10] that he had fallen [11] whilst [12] fighting with-the-utmost-bravery. [13] He thereupon replaced the crown upon-his-head, calling-the deities, to whom he was sacrificing, -to-witness, that the pleasure he felt [14] at the valour of his son exceeded the grief occasioned by his death.

---

[1] sollennis; which originally meant *annual;* hence, *periodical, regular.*

[2] Say, *learned* (cognosco).

[3] nomine.   [4] nec ideo.

[5] Say, *that the worship of the gods begun* (instituo) *should be discontinued* (omitto, *ger. part.*).

[6] habeo.   [7] percontor.

[8] quonam modo: the —nam adds emphasis to the question.

[9] occido.

[10] audio.

[11] intereo.

[12] Remember that a participle, not being a finite verb, cannot have a conjunction before it, such as dum or cum.

[13] Say, *most bravely.*

[14] Say, *that he received* (capio) *greater pleasure from the valour of his son than grief from his death.*

41. DAMON AND PHINTIAS (PYTHIAS).

Damon and Phintias had formed[1] so strong a friend-ship for each other, that they were ready to die the one[2] for the other. When one of them[3] (had been) condemned[P] to death by Dionysius the tyrant, (and) had been allowed[4] time in which to go[P] home (and) arrange[5] his affairs, the other did not hesitate to offer himself to the tyrant as a surety for his-friend's[6] return, on-the-understanding that[7] if his-friend[8] had not returned by the (appointed) day, he himself would have to die.[9] Accordingly all, and especially Dionysius, eagerly awaited the issue of this strange[10] affair. (As) the appointed[11] day at length drew[P] near, and he did not[12] return,[P] everybody[13] began-to-blame the other's rashness in becoming bondsman;[14] but he asserted[15] that he had no fears[16] for the good faith of his friend. And by the stated day he appeared.[17] The tyrant, admiring their faithfulness, begged that he might be admitted[18] (as) a third in their friendship, and released from punishment the man[19] whom he had determined to put to death.

---

[1] jungo : for each other, inter se.
[2] alter.   [3] rel.
[4] Say, had obtained by request (impetro).   [5] subj.   [6] ejus.
[7] ita ut.   [8] ille.
[9] ger. part. (impers.).   [10] novus.
[11] definitus : and note, dies is usually fem. when it denotes an appointed day.

[12] and . . . not, nec.
[13] unusquisque.
[14] Say, that rash bondsman.
[15] praedico, 1.
[16] Say, that he feared nothing con-cerning . . .
[17] supervenio ; and expr. pron.
[18] Use act. voice.
[19] eum : see Ex. 14, Note 8.

42. The Crafty Ass-driver.

Alexander, king of Macedon, having been warned by an oracle[1] to order[2] that whoever was the first to meet him as he came out of the (city)-gate should be put-to-death, commanded[3] an ass-driver, who by chance came[P] in his way[4] before anybody else,[5] to be hurried off to death. Upon his asking[6] (the king) why he sentenced an innocent man (like) himself to capital punishment, (Alexander) recounted[7] the order of the oracle[8] as an excuse[9] for what he was doing. Then said the ass-driver, "Since that is the case,[10] O king, the oracle designed[11] another (than myself) to (undergo) this death; for the ass, which I was driving before me, (was) the first-of-the-two[12] to meet you." Alexander, well pleased with the man's crafty speech,[13] and at being[14] himself recalled from the mistake (he was making), made-a-victim-of[15] the ass.

---

[1] sors = *response.*

[2] Say, *that he should order him who first met him having gone out* . . . For the Mood of the verb '*met*,' comp. Ex. 15, Note 4.

[3] impero: here to be foll. by *acc.* and *inf.*   [4] obviam fieri.

[5] ante omnes.

[6] *abl. abs.*, or *dat.* in dependence upon verb 'he recounted' (*to him asking*).

[7] refero.   [8] oraculum.

[9] Say, *to excuse* (ad with *ger. part.*) *his act.*

[10] si ita est.   [11] destĭno.

[12] prior: in sentences like this the verb *to be* must not be used, prior tibi occurrit (*not* prior erat qui . . .).   [13] dictum.

[14] Expr. by quod; which must be followed by *subj.* if the feeling of the agent is indicated; or by the *indic.* if the fact is simply recorded by the writer.   [15] immŏlo.

43. Filial Affection.

Cleobis and Bito, the sons of a certain Argive priestess, are justly praised for [1] their remarkable dutiful-affection towards [2] their mother. For (once) when it was required [3] that she should be conveyed in a chariot a good way [4] from the town to the temple, for the customary sacrifice, and the beasts [5] (which were to draw her) were-behind-the-time, [6] those young men at once [7] took-off [p] their coats, [8] besmeared their bodies with oil, and harnessed [9] themselves to the carriage. So the priestess having arrived [10] at the temple, with [11] her sons drawing the chariot, is said to have prayed of [12] the goddess to give them for their dutiful affection the greatest reward which could be given to a human-being [13] by a god. [14] The young men—(so runs the story)—afterwards partook-of-the-feast [p][15] with their mother, fell asleep, [16] and in the morning were found dead.

---

[1] ob.   [2] in with *acc.*
[3] cum jus esset, foll. by *acc.* and *inf.*
[4] satis longe.
[5] jumenta: the general term for *baggage or draught cattle.*
[6] moror.   [7] tunc.
[8] veste posita.
[9] Say, *came up* (accedo) *to the yoke.*

[10] advehor.
[11] Say, *when the chariot had been drawn* (duco) *by her sons.*
[12] ab.
[13] homo.
[14] This sentence is to be given in the oblique form, fertur or some such verb being understood.
[15] epulor.
[16] Say, *gave themselves to sleep.*

44. THE LIBERTINE AND THE PHILOSOPHER.

There lived [1] at Athens a young man (named) Polemo, who revelled [2] in profligacy and debauchery. On one occasion he [3] had risen up from a banquet, not after sunset, but after sunrise, and (as he was) returning home found the gate of Xenocrates, the philosopher, wide-open [4]; half-intoxicated [5] (as he was), besmeared [6] with unguents, with garlands round his head, [7] and with a (thin) transparent garment flung about him, [8] he entered the philosopher's [9] school, (which was) filled [10] with a crowd of learned men, and interrupted the discussion with his foul speech. [11] Thereupon, as was natural, [12] general [13] indignation was aroused, [p] (but) Xenocrates, without changing [p] countenance, abandoned [p] the subject on which he was arguing, (and) began to discourse about moderation and temperance, with such power and earnestness, [14] that Polemo, as if awaking [15] out of a deep [16] sleep, came-to-his-senses. [17] First, he tore [p 18] the wreath from his head (and) threw it from him; shortly afterwards he drew back his arm inside his cloak, and laid aside the wanton merriment of his coun-

---

[1] Say, *was.* [2] *part.* (diffluo).
[3] qui cum. [4] patens.
[5] vino gravis. [6] delibutus.
[7] Say, *with head crowned* (redimĭtus) *with chaplets* (serta, *n. pl.*).
[8] Say, *wrapped about* (amictus) *with . . .* [9] ejus.
[10] refertus. [11] os.
[12] ut par erat.

[13] Say, indignation *of all* (in the same way express *adj. universal*).
[14] gravitas.
[15] expergiscor.
[16] gravis.
[17] resipisco.
[18] Say, *he threw from him the wreath ·torn off* (detraho); see Introd. p. 6.

tenance[19]; finally, he (completely) divested-himself-of[20] all profligacy and depravity, so that he afterwards became[21] a noted philosopher, and succeeded his master in the conduct of the school.[22]

---

[19] os.
[20] exuo (to strip off).
[21] evado, which may stand either in imperf. or perf. subj.: the latter

has more the character of an independent historical statement, and is therefore quite in place here.
[22] ger. part. (rego).

---

45. A STRANGE DREAM.

Two Arcadian friends,[1] in the course of a journey they were taking together, came to Megara; one put up[2] with an innkeeper, the other at (the house of) a friend.[3] After-supper[p] they[4] retired to rest[5]; in the middle of the night the man first mentioned[6] appeared in a dream to the other, who was in his friend's house, entreating (him) to come to his assistance, as his[7] death[8] was being compassed[9] by the innkeeper. At first he[10] rose up frightened by the dream; presently, when he had collected himself, and had come to the conclusion

---

[1] Begin: when certain two Arcadians (who were) friends (familiares) were taking (facio) a journey together . . .
[2] deverto, foll. by ad.
[3] hospes rather than amicus, because belonging to a different city.
[4] qui cum: see Introd. p. 2.
[5] quiesco.

[6] Arrange thus: seemed in sleep (in somnis) to the one (ei) who was in his friend's house (in hospitio) that other one to entreat him to come to his aid (subvenio).
[7] Say, to him (the speaker): quod sibi . . .
[8] interitus.   [9] paro.
[10] Begin with pron. (is).

. that the vision was of no moment,[11] he lay-down-again. Then, as he slept,[P] his friend [12] again appeared, to beg him that, since he had failed to come to his succour [13] (while) alive, he would (at all events) not [14] allow his death to be unavenged; he [15] had been murdered [P] (he said) by the innkeeper, (and his body) thrown into a waggon and covered over with dung; [16] he entreated [15] him to be [17] at the (city) gate in the morning, before the waggon could pass out of the town. Alarmed [18] by this dream, his friend [19] in the morning was in-attendance [20] at the gate: he asked the carter what was in the waggon. The carter [21] fled in-dismay [P]; the corpse [22] was dragged-out [23]; the innkeeper, when the matter was brought to light,[P] [24] suffered punishment.

---

[11] Say, *and had concluded* (duco) *that that vision was to be held of no account* (pro nihilo habere).

[12] idem ille.

[13] Say, *had not succoured.* [14] ne.

[15] Observe that this is oblique narration: see Introd. p. 9.

[16] Say, *and dung cast-on* (*it*) *above* (supra). [17] adsum.

[18] commotus. [19] ille.

[20] praesto, *adv.*

[21] Instead of repeating the noun, use ille. [22] mortuus.

[23] eruo. [24] patefacio.

46. An Eager Scholar.

Antisthenes used-to-urge his pupils to pay earnest[1] attention to philosophy, but few conformed-to-his-advice.[2] This at length roused his displeasure,[3] and he sent them all away; among the[4] number was Diogenes also. He, however,[5] being fired[6] with intense[7] eagerness to learn, kept coming[8] to Antisthenes, and refused[9] to go away. Antisthenes at length threatened to strike him on the head[10] with the staff which he was wont to carry in his hand; and as he was not frightened even by these threats, he once (actually) did so.[11] Even then,[12] Diogenes did not go away; but with a resolute[13] mind exclaimed, "Strike (on), if so it pleases you; here is my head for you:[14] but[15] you will never find[16] a cudgel so hard as to drive[17] me away from your discussions." Antisthenes at length admitted a pupil so desirous of learning, and became greatly attached to him.[18]

---

[1] Say, *earnestly* (*sedulo*) *to pay attention to*, operam dare.

[2] obtempero.

[3] Say, *accordingly at length being indignant.*   [4] *rel.*

[5] qui cum . . .

[6] incensus.

[7] magnus: note that in Latin, general adjectives like magnus, tantus, are preferred to those more descriptive.

[8] ventito, *frequent.*

[9] nec vellet . . .

[10] Say, *strike his head.*

[11] Say, *and him, not frightened by even these threats, once he struck.*

[12] neque tamen.

[13] obstinatus (which is used both in good and in bad sense).

[14] Say, *I offer* (praebeo) *you* (*my*) *head.*   [15] neque vero.

[16] *fut. perf.*   [17] quo abigas.

[18] *to become attached to* = love (amo, diligo).

47. The Banker and the Knight.

Canius, a Roman knight, having betaken himself to Syracuse, for the purpose of avoiding,[1] not of doing business,[1] gave out[2] that he wished to purchase some pleasure-grounds[3] to-which[4] he might ask[5] his friends, and where he might amuse himself without anybody to interfere with him.[6] When this had got-about,[7] one Pythius, a banker, told him that[8] he had (some) gardens :—(they were) not, indeed, for sale, but Canius was welcome to use them as (if they were) his own : at the same time he invited the man to sup[9] with him at his gardens on[10] the following day. The other[11] promised (to come) : thereupon Pythius, who,[12] as a banker, was likely to have a good deal of influence with all classes of men, called some fishermen to him, and begged of them to fish the next day[13] in-front-of his gardens ; and (further) told them what he wished them to do. At the (appointed) time Canius comes to supper. A sumptuous[14] banquet was prepared ; before their eyes was a multitude of boats. (Every[15] fisherman) brought on his own account what he had taken ;

---

[1] otior ... negotior (observe the play of words, otior, neg-otior).

[2] dictito.   [3] hortuli.

[4] rel. adv.   [5] invito.

[6] Say, without interrupters (inter-pellator).

[7] percrebresco.

[8] Say, that for sale (venales), indeed, gardens he had not, but that Canius (dat.) was at liberty (licere) to use them as (ut) his own.

[9] ad cenam.

[10] Say, for (in) the following day.

[11] cum ille ...

[12] Say, who was (subj. St. L. G. § 476) ... possessed-of-influence (gratiosus) with all classes-of-men (ordines).   [13] postridie.

[14] Expr. by adv. (opipare).

[15] pro se quisque.

the fish were thrown down before the feet of Pythius.
Then says Canius, " Pray,[16] Pythius, what is (all) this ?
Such a quantity [17] of fish, such a lot [17] of boats ? "
" Oh ! [18] " said he, " that's nothing strange ; [18] all [19] the
fish in Syracuse are at-this-spot ; those-fellows (you ask
about) [20] cannot do-without this house [21]." Canius, fired
with the desire (to possess it), earnestly-begs [22] Pythius
to sell (it).   (Pythius) at first raises-objections.[23]
(Well) to make a long story short,[24] the man obtains
(his wish): eager (to possess), and rich (withal), he
buys it at Pythius's own price,[25] and settles the business.   The next day Canius invites his friends ; he
arrives early himself ; he sees not a single boat.   He
asks of his nearest neighbour whether there was
some [26] holiday among the fishermen, as he saw [27] none
of them [28] (about).   " None that I know of [29]," replied
the other ; " but no (fishermen) are accustomed to fish
here, so I wondered what had happened yesterday."
Canius waxed wroth.[30]   But what was-he-to-do ? [31]

---

[16] quaeso. [17] tantumne.
[18] quid mirum.
[19] Use partitive expr., *whatever*
(quidquid) *of fish.* [20] isti.
[21] villa (strictly, *farm-house* ;
hence, *any country house*).
[22] contendit a Pythio.
[23] gravor ; and for Subject Pythius, use *ille.*

[24] quid multa. Lit. *why should
I say many things ?*
[25] *for so much* (gen. of Value) *as*
P. *wished.*
[26] quaedam.
[27] *subj.* (oblique narration).
[28] eos nullos. [29] quod sciam.
[30] stomachor (*hist. inf.*).
[31] quid faceret ?

48. The Critical Cobbler.

Apelles, the eminent painter, used-to-exhibit the works (he had) finished[P] in his studio[1] (in view of)-passers-by;[2] and, concealing-himself just[3] behind a picture, used to listen to the censures which were passed[4] (on it), considering the public to be a severer critic than himself. The-tale-goes[5] that a shoemaker[6] found some fault with the shoes (of a picture). Apelles accordingly altered[7] (them). On the following day the same shoemaker passed by, and, elated[8] at the alteration[9] (in the shoes), began to-make-captious-remarks[10] about the leg. Thereupon the painter indignantly[P] looked forth (from his hiding-place), and gave-him-to-understand[11] that[12] a shoemaker must not criticize above the shoe.

---

[1] pergula (used of various kinds of *stalls, shops,* or *schools*).

[2] dat. of part.

[3] Say, *behind the picture itself.*

[4] Say, *what faults* (vitia) *were noted* (nŏto): *subj.,* being indirect question.

[5] ferunt.

[6] Say, *that some defect* (vitium) *was reprehended by a shoemaker in the shoes.*

[7] emendo (*to free from faults*).

[8] superbus.   [9] emendatio.

[10] cavillor.   [11] denuntio.

[12] *that . . . not,* ne; denuntio being a verb of 'commanding.'

49. THE BURIED TREASURE.

Nitocris, queen of Babylon,[1] ordered a tomb to be built[2] for herself in a lofty[3] and conspicuous position over the most frequented gate of the city, and this inscription to be placed upon it[4]—"If any[5] of the kings, who after me shall reign over the Babylonians, shall be in want of money, let-him-open[6] (my) tomb, and take as much as he pleases.[7] But let him not open it, except he be in (urgent) need,[8] for he will gain nothing by doing so."[9] This sepulchre remained untouched, until the kingdom passed into the possession of[10] Darius, the son of Hystaspes, who broke-open[p 11] the tomb, (and) found, not the money[12] which he had hoped for, but (merely) the corpse, with[13] these words engraved[14] (upon the coffin):—"Were you not[15] too fond of base gain, and possessed[16] by an insatiable thirst for money, you would not violate the sepulchres of the dead."

---

[1] Say, *of the Babylonians*, Babylonii, orum.

[2] exstruo (only to be used of a *lofty* structure).   [3] editus.

[4] Say, *and* [this inscription] *to be inscribed*.

[5] Say, *if to any-one of the kings who after me shall rule in Babylon* (apud Babylonios imperium obtinere) *there shall be* (fut. perf.) *scarcity of money*.

[6] See Ex. 32, Note 6.

[7] *fut. perf.* (libet).

[8] indigeo, *fut. perf.*

[9] Say, *it will do no* (nil) *good to have opened* (it).   [10] pervenire ad.

[11] resĕro, 1 (*to unbar*).

[12] *plur.*   [13] et.

[14] exaro (*engraved;* lit. *ploughed out*).   [15] nisi.

[16] Expr. by act. voice, making 'thirst (cupīdo) *for money*' the Subject: 'did not an insatiable thirst for money *possess you*.'

.50. REVERENCE FOR AGE.

It was a law among the Lacedaemonians that young men should not only reverence [1] and obey their parents, but that they should also show-respect-to [2] all aged men. Consequently they made way [3] for them (when they met them), rose from [4] their seats, and stood in respectful silence [5] till they (had) passed-by [6]. (On one occasion) [7] at Athens an old man came into the theatre to witness the games, (and) in a crowded assembly [8] room was nowhere made [9] for him by his fellow-citizens. When, however, he came to the Lacedaemonian [10] ambassadors, who were-present-at [11] the games, they all rose-up-simultaneously [12] and gave him a seat in the place of-greatest-honour [13] amongst themselves. Upon witnessing [14] this (act) the people [15] vociferously [16] showed-their-approval-of [17] the politeness [18] of their guests. Whereupon one of the Lacedaemonians is said [19] to have remarked—"The Athenians know what is right, but do-not-choose [20] to do (it)."

---

[1] 'reverence and obey': when two verbs governing different cases have the same object, that object must be repeated with the second verb in pron. form: reverence *their* parents (acc.) *and* obey *them* (dat.).
[2] colo.   [3] de via decedo.
[4] e (ex).
[5] Say, *quiet and behaving-respectfully* (verecundor, 1 *dep.*).
[6] Subj.
[7] Connect the two co-ordinate sentences by means of cum.

[8] magno consessu.
[9] Say, *given.*
[10] Say, *ambassadors of the Lacedaemonians.*
[11] intersum.
[12] con-surgo.
[13] honoratus (*superl.*).
[14] aspicio.
[15] populus; which invariably takes sing. verb.
[16] Say, *with very-great applause.*
[17] comprŏbo.   [18] verēcundia.
[19] ferunt.   [20] nolo.

51. BROTHERLY LOVE.

Cato, (when he was) quite a boy, to the inquiry[p] of certain (people) whom he loved most of all, answered, " My brother."[1]   Upon their asking him again,[2] whom he loved next best,[3] he replied, " My brother."   When the question was put to him[4] a-third-time,[5] he gave the same answer, till they ceased[6] to question (him).   That (remarkable) fondness and reverence for his brother increased[7] as he grew up; he never left[8] his side; he obeyed[9] him in everything; at the age of[10] twenty years he had never supped, never even appeared[11] in the forum, nor gone away from home,[12] without his brother Caepio.   The character[13] of each was irreproachable[14]; but Cato's (mode of) life was the stricter (of the two).   Consequently Caepio, when his-own[15] frugality and temperance were-being-made-the-subject-of-praise, acknowledged that he might seem a temperate[16] man, compared[17] with many of the Romans.

---

[1] Remember that a verb is here understood.

[2] Expr. 'again' by idem: *to the same (persons) asking.*

[3] secundum maxime.

[4] Say, *being asked.*

[5] tertium or tertio.

[6] Here either *indic.* or *subj.* may be used: the former simply states the fact that *they did cease;* the latter indicates an intention on the part of the person questioned to persist in his answer *till they ceased.*

See preced. Ex., donec praeterirent.

[7] Begin the sentence with this verb, to which an emphasis is thus given. (So far from *abating*, this feeling *increased* with age.)

[8] discedo.

[9] praebebat se obedientem.

[10] natus.   [11] Use progedior.

[12] peregre.   [13] mores.

[14] probus.   [15] ipsius.

[16] frugi (strictly *dat.* = *for profit, thrift*).

[17] Say, *if he were compared.*

"But," he-went-on-to-say,[18] "when I compare my life with (that) of Cato, I seem to myself to be no better than [19] a Sippius." Now [20] the-said [21] Sippius was a worthless fellow, addicted to riotous-living.[22]

---

[18] inquiebat.
[19] Say, *to differ nothing from*.

[20] autem.   [21] ille.
[22] luxuria.

---

52. When do Kings hear the Truth?

Antiochus, king of Syria, whilst out hunting,[1] had [2] in the ardour of the chase [3] wandered away from his friends and servants, and entered, unrecognised,[4] the cottage of (some) poor men. (Whilst) supping with them he introduced [5] a conversation about the king, that he might discover what was the opinion (entertained) about him by [6] his hosts. Whereupon [7] he was told [8] that the king was in other respects [9] good and praiseworthy, but that from-his-intimacy-with [10] bad friends, he neglected many things, and, owing to [11] his excessive fondness [12] for hunting, frequently paid-no-attention-to [13] matters that were (really) necessary.

---

[1] in venatione.
[2] Say, *when he had wandered* . . . *entered*.
[3] Say, *of pursuing a wild-beast*.
[4] ignotus. ...   [5] injicio.
[6] Say, *of his hosts*.
[7] Use igitur,

[8] audio.
[9] Say, *things*,
[10] *part*. (utor).
[11] quod.
[12] Expr. by *adj.*: *because he was excessively fond* . . .
[13] nihil curo.

Antiochus said nothing[14] at the time.[15] But when at sunrise the royal-attendants[16] came to the cottage and brought (him his) purple robe and[17] diadem, he remarked, with-a-glance-at[p] those badges of-royalty,[18] "Verily,[19] yesterday (was the) first (time) since I put on these decorations (that) I heard the truth spoken about myself."

---

[14] taceo.
[15] Emphasize the particle of time by quidem (Gk. γέ).
[16] satellites.
[17] cum.   [18] adj.

[19] Arrange: *verily (certe)*, *said he, from the time when* (ex quo) *I assumed (*sumo*) these ornaments, yesterday first I heard true remarks* (sermones) *about myself.*

---

53. THE MACEDONIAN YOUTH.

According-to the ancient custom[1] of Macedonia, the boys belonging-to-the-noblest-families[2] attended[3] Alexander when he offered sacrifice.[p] One of these[4] had snatched-up[p] a censer (and) stood before the king,[5] (when) a red-hot coal fell[6] upon his[7] arm. (Yet) although it burnt[8] him so (severely) that the smell of scorched flesh[9] reached the nostrils of-those-who-stood-around,[p] he nevertheless repressed the pain without-uttering-a-sound,[10] and held his arm motionless, so as

---

[1] *abl.* alone.
[2] Say, *the noblest* (nobilis) *boys.*
[3] praesto esse.   [4] *rel.*
[5] Use ipse instead of rex.

[6] delabor.   [7] *rel.*
[8] Expr. by *pass.*: *by which although he was being burnt.*
[9] corpus.   [10] Say, *in silence.*

G 2

not to interrupt Alexander [11] in his sacrifice by shaking the censer,[12] or disturb the mind of the king by uttering a groan.[12]   The king also, delighted with the (brave) endurance of the boy, desired to make [13] a surer trial of his fortitude, and was purposely longer in sacrificing.[14] But not even by so doing [15] did he (succeed in) making him flinch [16] from his purpose.

---

[11] Say, *interrupt* (impedio) . *the sacrifice of Alexander.*
[12] *abl. abs.*   [13] sumo.

[14] Say, *sacrificed for a longer time.* (diutius).   [15] hac re.
[16] *to make to flinch,* repello.

---

54. A Noble Contest between Father and Son.

There lived [1] at Murgentium, which is a town of Sicily, a man named Cambalus, in wealth and renown the foremost of his state.   This man having (once) gone [2] out to hunt, had narrowly escaped falling [3] into the hands of robbers, and began to hurry back on foot to the town.   (Just) then, as-chance-would-have-it,[4] his father Gorgus met him on horseback.[5]   (He) immediately alighted,[6] and begged his son to mount [7] his horse and forthwith flee-for-refuge to the city.   Thereupon the

---

[1] erat.
[2] Use *dep.* verb, so as to be able to employ *perf. part.*
[3] Say, *had almost fallen.*

[4] forte.
[5] equo vehens : vehor is here *dep.*
[6] desilio may be foll. by ex equo or by *abl.* alone.

son refused[7] to save his own life at the risk of his father's; nor would the father consent to escape danger by abandoning[p 8] his son to certain death. And so (it happened that) whilst they were entreating each other[9] with tears[10] (to escape), and were both striving with each other, the robbers meantime overtook[p] them and put them both to the sword.[11]

---

[7] Say, *was unwilling to prefer to his father's safety his own.*

[8] projicio: and end sentence with filio.

[9] alter ... alterum.

[10] flentes.

[11] *put to the sword,* confodio.

---

55. DESIRE OF LEARNING.

The Athenians had passed a decree that[1] any citizen of Megara who set foot in Athens should be put to death, so intense was the hatred of[2] the Athenians for their neighbours[3] the Megareans. Euclides, who was a citizen of Megara, had already before this decree (was passed) been accustomed to frequent[4] Athens and attend the instructions of Socrates. But after the Athenians (had) passed[5] that decree, he used to come[6]

---

[1] Say, *that (he) who was a citizen at Megara should be put to death, if he brought* (infero, *pluperf. subj.*) *foot to Athens.*

[2] tanto odio flagrabant.

[3] finitimi homines (*obj. gen.*).

[4] Say, *to be at Athens and to hear Socrates.*

[5] sancio: for tense, see Ex. 9, Note 12.

[6] Arrange: *at nightfall, before it grew dark* (advesperasco), *clad . . . and wrapped . . . with head covered* (velatus), *from Megara to Athens he used to come* (commeo, 1).

to Socrates, from Megara to Athens, at the approach of
night, before it grew dark, clad in a woman's long
tunic, and wrapped in a cloak of-divers-colours,[7] and
with a veil on his head, that he might participate in
the wisdom and discourse of Socrates; and towards
daybreak[8] he again walked-back[9] (the distance of)
twenty miles, in the same disguise.[10]

---

[7] versicolor.
[8] sub lucem.

[9] redeo.
[10] eadem veste tecta.

---

56. The Persian's Offering.

When the king[1] of the Persians was on a journey
within the boundaries of his kingdom, it was the
custom for gifts to be offered him by all the Persians.
(Of those) who were engaged[2] in agriculture[3] some
gave oxen or sheep, others corn or wine; whilst[4] the
poorer class[5] (brought) milk, cheese, dates, and other
fruits of trees which grew[6] on their[7] lands. All these[8]
offerings were made by them individually[9] to the king,
as he marched[p] or rode[p] past them, not under the
name of tribute but of a gift.

---

[1] Arrange: to the king . . . journeying . . . it was the custom for
gifts to be offered.
[2] occupatus: or expr. by operam
dare.
[3] Say, (in) cultivating land.
[4] vero; which however must not

stand first in its clause.
[5] pauperiores.
[6] subj.
[7] in cujusque agro.
[8] rel.: and say, all which (things)
were offered.
[9] a singulis.

Now [10] a certain Persian, whose name was Sinaetas, had fallen in with Artaxerxes, surnamed [11] Mnemon, at a distance from his cottage,[12] and had nothing to [13] offer the king; he was loth, however, that he should seem to pass unhonoured by him. And so he ran [14] as fast as he could to a river that flowed hard by,[15] and taking up [p][16] water in both [17] hands, offered it to the king, enhancing [18] his present as much as he could with auspicious expressions.[19] Artaxerxes was wonderfully pleased both with the gift and the (good) feeling and language [20] of the giver, and holding [21] it a no less kingly act to receive small presents with gratitude than to confer [22] large ones (himself), said that he willingly accepted that (present of) water, and was no less pleased with it than (he could have been) with the most costly gift. Subsequently he sent the man a considerable sum of money,[23] with a Persian dress and a golden goblet, in which he might drink the water drawn from the river.

---

[10] Begin cum . . .

[11] cui cognomen (cognominatus only in late authors). The constr. may be varied by writing in the preceding clause, Sinaetas nomine.

[12] tugurium.

[13] rel. clause with subj.

[14] cursu contendere.

[15] proxime praeterfluentem.

[16] haurio: for constr. see Introd.

p. 6.

[17] utraque manu.

[18] exorno.

[19] faustis bonisque verbis.

[20] oratio.

[21] neque minus regium existimans.

[22] confero or tribuo.

[23] non parva pecunia (summa pecuniae in this sense is late and unclassical).

57. THE KING AND HIS COURTIER.

King Cambyses,[1] who was excessively addicted to wine, was warned by Prexaspes, one of his favourites,[2] to drink more sparingly: drunkenness, he said,[3] was disgraceful in any[4] man, most disgraceful in a king, on whom the eyes of all were[5] bent. To this he replied,[6] "That you may know that I never forget myself, and that I am always in my right senses,[7] I will now give-(you)-a-proof that both my eyes and my hands are even after drinking[8] fit for duty."[9] He then drinks more plentifully than at-other-times,[10] (and) from larger cups: and being now quite intoxicated,[11] orders the son of the man-who-had-rebuked[12] him to step forth beyond the threshold, and to stand with his left hand raised[13] above his head. Then he bent[P] his bow and shot[14] the youth right through the heart, which he had declared should be his aim. Whereupon[15] he pointed out to the father the arrow fixed in the very heart (of his son), and asked him whether he had a sufficiently steady hand. The father declared[16] that Apollo could not have sent an arrow with a truer aim.[17] What think you, boys, of such[18] a king and such a father?

---

[1] Use *act.* instead of *pass.* : *Prex-aspes . . . warned* (*imperf.*) *Cambyses;* and begin with the name of the king.

[2] carissimi.

[3] *pres. part.*, foll. by *acc.* and *inf.*

[4] quivis.

[5] *subj.*, acc. to the rules of oratio obliqua: Introd. p. 10 (2).

[6] inquit: see Ex. 23, Note 6.

[7] compos mentis.

[8] Say, *after wine.*

[9] in officio.

[10] alias, *adv.*

[11] gravis et temulentus.

[12] objurgator.

[13] allevo.

[14] Say, *he pierces the heart itself of the youth; for he had said that he was aiming at* (peto) *that.*

[15] quo facto.

[16] at ille negavit . . .

[17] Say, *more surely.*

[18] hic.

58. Diligence conquers all Difficulties.

Demosthenes[1] is said to have possessed such earnestness and such perseverance[2] that in the first place[3] he overcame his natural infirmities[4] by (sheer) diligence and application; and though he had such an impediment in his speech[5] that he could not pronounce[6] the first letter of the very art[7] he was studying, he accomplished (so much) by-dint-of-practice,[8] that no one was considered to have articulated[9] more clearly.[10] Then, though his respiration was (naturally) confined,[11] he succeeded so completely in keeping his breath[12] in speaking, that in one[13] sustained - effort - of - delivery were (sometimes) embraced two raisings[14] and lowerings[14] of the voice. He was also accustomed to put pebbles in his mouth,[15] (and then) to declaim a number of[16] verses at the top of his voice without drawing breath,[17] and that not[18] standing in (one) place, but walking-about,[19] and (even) going[20] up a steep ascent. He is also[21] said to have built an underground cham-

---

[1] Say, in Demosthenes there is said to have been . . .

[2] labor.   [3] primum.

[4] impedimenta naturae.

[5] cumque ita balbus (= lisping) esset.   [6] dico.

[7] i.e. rhetoric: he could not pronounce the letter r.

[8] meditor.   [9] loquor.

[10] planius.   [11] angustior.

[12] tantum continenda anima . . . assecutus est.

[13] continuatio verborum.

[14] contentiones . . . remissiones; use distrib. numeral, because the sense is two of each.

[15] conjicio (conicio): abl. abs.

[16] adj.

[17] Say, in one breath.

[18] neque is,

[19] inambulo.

[20] ingredior; foll. by abl. of place.

[21] Expr. by idem: this is highly idiomatic, when a second predicate has the same subject as the previous one.

ber,[22] in which at times he shut-himself-up[p] for two or
three months together,[23] and bestowed (great) attention [24] upon his voice and gesture; and that too [25] with
the crown [26] of his head shaved so that he could not go
abroad.[27]

---

[22] cella.	[23] continuus.	[25] et quidem.	[26] media pars.
[24] operam dare.		[27] in publicum prodire.	

---

59. A GENEROUS RIVAL.

Aeschĭnes, the orator, when he had left[1] Athens and
betaken himself to Rhodes, is reported to have read, at
the request of its inhabitants,[2] that admirable speech
which he had made[3] against[4] Ctesiphon in-opposition-
to Demosthenes. After having read[p] it[5] through, he
was asked[6] on the following day to read (to them) also
the (famous) speech[7] which had been delivered[8] by
Demosthenes in-defence-of Ctesiphon. After reading
this[9] in a most sweet and powerful[10] voice, he remarked
to his admiring (audience), "(Ah!) how much greater
would have been your admiration[11] had you but heard
(the orator) himself!"

---

[1] cedo.	[7] illam ('of celebrity').
[2] Say, *being asked by the Rhodians.*	[8] edo. [9] rel.
[3] dico. [4] in with *acc.*	[10] maximus.
[5] *rel.,* and *abl. abs.*	[11] Say, *by how much more would*
[6] Say, *it was asked* (peto) *of him.*	*you admire, if . . .*

60. ALEXANDER'S KINDNESS.

Alexander the Great was exceedingly courteous and generous. (One day)[1] a[2] common soldier in the Macedonian[3] army was driving a mule laden with gold belonging-to-the-king.[4] The animal[5] being wearied out, he took up[6] the packages himself and carried them on his own shoulders. The king saw him staggering[7] under-the-load, and, seeing how the matter stood,[8] said to him, (just) as the fellow[9] was going to lay his burden down, "Don't[10] tire-yourself-out,[11] but bring[12] the rest[13] of your journey to an end, and carry this home[14] to your own tent."

---

[1] Begin, cum . . .

[2] Say, *a certain* . . .

[3] Say, *in the army of the Macedonians.* [4] adj.

[5] jumentum: see Ex. 43, Note 5.

[6] See Introd. p. 6 : *he was carrying the packages taken up on-to (his) shoulders.*

[7] oppressus.

[8] re intellecta.

[9] ille.

[10] *imperative* of nolo.

[11] pass. in reflex. sense.

[12] *to bring to an end,* absolvo.

[13] reliquus, *adj.*

[14] *carry home,* defero.

---

61. THE SHREW.

Xanthippe, the wife of Socrates, the philosopher, is said to have been exceedingly morose and quarrelsome.[1] Alcibiades, astonished at her outrageous - conduct,[2]

---

[1] jurgii cupida.

[2] intemperies.

asked Socrates what[3] possible reason there was why
he did not drive such an ill-tempered woman from his
house. "Because," said Socrates, "by[4] patiently putting up with such a creature, at home, I am forming-
a-habit[5] and training-myself[6] to[7] bear with-greater
ease the wanton and unjust-treatment[8] of-the-rest-of-
the-world[9] also out of doors."

---

[3] 'what *possible* reason': emphasize *interrog. pron.* by suffix
-nam: cf. Ex. 40, Note 8.

[4] Say, *while I suffer* (perpetior)
her such (*as she is*).

[5] insuesco (but the best authors
use *as*-suesco).

[6] *pass refl.* [7] quo.

[8] petulantia et injuria.

[9] ceteri.

62. EXTRAORDINARY KNOWLEDGE OF LANGUAGES.

Mithridates, the renowned king of Pontus and Bi-
thynia, who was overcome in war by Cn. Pompey, was-
well-acquainted-with[1] the languages of the five-and-
twenty nations which he had under his dominion[2]; he
never[3] conversed with the men belonging-to-these-
nations[4] through an interpreter, but spoke with each in
his own[5] tongue no less skilfully[6] than if he had been
(a native) of the same state.

---

[1] percallesco, which is found with
acc. in Cic. [2] dicio.

[3] Begin, neque ... unquam ...

[4] *gen.*

[5] Should *sua* be used here or
ipsius? (ipsius: suus would refer
back to the Subject.)

[6] scite.

· 63. The Master-slave.

As Diogenes was sailing to the island of Aegina, he was taken ᴾ (prisoner) by pirates, and brought¹ to Crete, and there sold.² When the crier (at the auction) asked ᴾ him in what he was skilled,³ he replied, "in ruling⁴ men;" and at the same time pointed ⁵ with his finger to a certain Corinthian named Xeniades, (who was) decked out in gorgeous attire, and said, "Sell⁶ me to this man; for he wants a master.⁷" Xeniades accordingly purchased him, took ᴾ him home with him, and appointed him preceptor ⁸ to his sons; and set him over his whole house. In this office he conducted himself in such a manner, that Xeniades often remarked, "A good genius has entered my house."

---

¹ deduco.

² venundo (=vendo: but the longer form is commonly used of the sale of captured slaves). The auxiliary verb need only be expressed once; namely, with the latter of the two verbs.

³ calleo (strictly=to be horny-handed; hence, to be well practised in work): note that an intrans. verb is often found with acc. of neut. pron. and like words, St. L. G. § 253.   ⁴ inf.

⁵ to point to, monstro.

⁶ vendo.   ⁷ dominus.

⁸ Say, gave him as preceptor.

64. Diogenes and his Cup.

Diogenes used-to-carry with him everywhere a wooden cup, in which to[1] draw water from spring or river and to[1] drink (from). But one day[2] seeing[3] a boy taking up water (to drink)[4] in (the hollow of) his hands, he threw[5] away his cup with the words,[6] "Be-gone, what need I of thee? I can do-without thee; for my hands shall in future perform[7] the same service for me."

---

[1] *rel. and subj.*
[2] quondam or aliquando.
[3] cum and *subj.*
[4] Say, *for himself.*
[5] *pres. part.*, which implies that the words were said while he was *in the act of throwing away* the cup: abjecto poculo would mean he *first* threw away the cup.
[6] Use inquit: see Ex. 23, Note 6.
[7] praesto, 1.

---

65. Who is Happy?

Upon Socrates being asked[1] whether[2] he did not consider king Archelaus, the son of Perdiccas, who was then held[3] (to be) the most fortunate man of his time, a happy man, "I do not know[4]," he replied, "for I

---

[1] Say, *when it had been asked* (quaero) *of* (ex) . . .
[2] Direct question: nonne putas? In the indirect form, the only change needed is in the verb:—from 2 *pers.* to 3 *pers.*, and from *indic.* to *subj.*
[3] Still *subj.*, if part of the question; if an explanation by the writer, of course *indic.*
[4] haud scio or nescio.

have never conversed with him." "Can you not[5] then say even[5] of the great king of the Persians, whether he is happy ?" "How[6] could I," he replied, "when I am ignorant how learned a man he is, (or) how good ?" "What! do you consider a happy life consists[7] in that?" "Yes; I fully believe[8] that the good are happy; the wicked miserable." "Is Archelaus, then, miserable ?" "Certainly, if he is an unjust man."

---

[5] ne ... quidem; the clause 'of the great king of the Persians' separating these particles.

[6] an ego possim.
[7] to consist in, sitam esse in ...
[8] ita prorsus existimo.

---

66. THE PAINTER AND THE KING.

Apelles was an especial favourite[1] with Alexander the Great, both on account of his skill and his genial-disposition.[2] Thus it was that[3] the king frequently-came to his studio,[4] and had (moreover) forbidden, by an edict, his likeness to be taken[5] by (any) other (painter). On-a-subsequent-occasion,[6] when (Alexander) was making some ignorant remarks[7] in his studio about the art of painting, and about colours, Apelles remarked[8] good-temperedly, "Be-silent, pray,

---

[1] Say, most pleasing to.
[2] cōmitas (from cōmis, courteous; nothing to do with cōmes).
[3] Say, wherefore.
[4] officīna (also pergula, Ex. 48).

[5] Say, had forbidden himself to be painted ...
[6] postea.
[7] imperita multa disserere.
[8] inquit: see Ex. 23, Note 6.

or [9] you will get laughed at by the boys who are rubbing the colours." So great was his influence with a king, (who) in-general [10] (was) of a hasty temper. [11]

---

[9] Say, *lest you should be laughed at.*

[10] alioqui (lit. *otherwise, at other times*). [11] iracundus.

---

67. The Integrity of Phocion.

Phocion, the Athenian, was surnamed [1] "the good" on account of the integrity of his life. For he was never-otherwise-than [2] poor, though he might have amassed great wealth [3] from [4] the many [5] distinctions conferred [6] upon him, and the highest offices of state, which were given him by the people. Upon [7] his refusing large presents of money [8] from king Philip, the ambassadors urged him to accept it, and warned him at-the-same-time that although he could easily do-without it himself, still he should make provision [9] for his children, who [10] would find it difficult in very poor circumstances [11] to keep up the great reputation inherited from their father. [12] To them he replied, "If

---

[1] cognomine 'Bonus' est appellatus.

[2] perpetuo.

[3] Say, *when he was able to be very rich.*

[4] propter.

[5] frequens.   [6] defero.

[7] Say, *when he refused . . . and the ambassadors warned him . . .*

[8] munera magna pecuniae.

[9] For mood and tense see Introd. p. 11.

[10] Say, *to whom it would be difficult.*

[11] in summa paupertate (paupertas does not mean *destitution,* which is egestas).

[12] Say, *so great paternal glory.*

they prove [13] like me, this little farm, which has brought me to this high-honour,[14] will support [15] them; but if [16] they are going-to-be unlike me, I do not choose their extravagance to be maintained [15] and increased at my expense."

[13] Expr. by esse: and as the latter half of the sentence is future, clearly this verb must be so too.

[14] dignitas.   [15] alo.

[16] sin, which introduces a negative or contrary alternative.

68. THE AREOPAGUS.

The Areopagus [1] was the most sacred and the strictest court-of-law [2] at Athens. In it [3] the judges, that they might not be moved (to compassion) by the pitiable aspect of the accused, held the trials [4] in the depth of night [5] and without lights [6]; and amidst profound silence [7] they gave their verdict by ballot, in such a manner that no one (judge) knew the verdict of the other.[8]

These Areopagites once condemned (to death) a boy who was-in-the-habit-of [9] putting [10] out the eyes of quails, judging, that such an act [11] was the mark of

[1] Begin with the Locative "at Athens" and end with the Subject.
[2] consilium.
[3] ibi.
[4] judicia exercere.
[5] ipsa nocte.

[6] Say, no lights being employed (admoveo).   [7] summo silentio.
[8] Say, so that the one was-ignorant-of the verdict of the other.
[9] Say, had been accustomed to . . .
[10] eruo.   [11] id.

PR. LAT.—V.   H

a most destructive temper, and one fraught with evil to many,[12] if it were-(suffered)-to-grow-to-maturity.[13] These [14] same men used to make the most searching enquiry (as to) how each Athenian employed himself,[15] or by what occupation [16] he gained his livelihood,[17] in order that men might live honestly, bearing-in-mind [18] that they must render an account of their (mode of) life.

---

[12] Say, *about to be for evil to many* (double dative, St. L. G. § 297).

[13] *plup. subj.*

[14] Say, *by the same (men) it was wont (imperf.) to be most carefully investigated* (inquiro).

[15] Say, *what each of the Athenians did* (ago).

[16] questus.

[17] Say, *he sustained life.*

[18] memŏres.

---

69. THE LIBERALITY OF CIMON.

Cimon, a renowned general of the Athenians, was (a man) of such-extraordinary [1] liberality, that though he had farms and gardens in several places, he never placed [2] a guard over them for the sake of preserving the produce,[3] in order that no one [4] might be debarred from [5] enjoying what he liked of his property.[6] Atten-

---

[1] tantus: see Ex. 46, Note 7.

[2] The *perf. subj.* is to be used here according to Ex. 44, Note 21; but the *imperf.* would be no less correct, implying a regular practice.

[3] fructus.

[4] Where a purpose is denoted, always *ne quis, ne unquam*, etc.; not *ut nemo*, etc.

[5] quominus.

[6] quibus quisque vellet.

dants-on-foot [7] always followed him with [8] money, so that, if any one needed his aid, he might have something to give him on-the-spot, lest by postponing (relief) he should seem to deny (it altogether). Often when he saw some poor man but scantily clothed,[9] he gave him his own cloak. Supper was daily prepared [10] for him on-such-a-scale,[11] that he might invite-to-his-house [12] all whom he saw in the forum disengaged,[13] which on no day did he omit to do. He was the means of enriching [14] many; a-good-many poor people, who died without leaving sufficient to bury them,[15] he buried at his own expense. When this was the tenor of his conduct,[16] it is no wonder, surely, that [17] his life was an untroubled one, and his death a source-of-grief [18] to all.

---

[7] pedissequi.

[8] cum nummis (the prep. is necessary, as in phr., esse *cum* telo, *to carry arms*).

[9] minus bene vestitus.

[10] Say, *cooked* (coquo).

[11] sic.

[12] devoco.

[13] invocatus (*not invited anywhere*).

[14] Say, *he enriched.*

[15] qui unde efferrentur non reliquissent. The Subj. reliquissent implies that the reason is here given why he so acted (St. L. G. § 476).

[16] Say, *when he thus conducted* (gero) *himself.*

[17] Say, *it is by no means to be wondered at if his life was untroubled,* etc.: and use Indic., because what follows is stated as a fact, and not as a supposition.

[18] acerbus.

70. BUCEPHALUS, THE HORSE OF ALEXANDER THE GREAT.

The horse of king Alexander was called " Bucephalus." He had been purchased for thirteen talents, and presented to king Philip, the father of Alexander. With-regard-to [1] this horse it was a noteworthy feature,[2] that when [3] he was caparisoned and armed for battle, he never allowed himself to be mounted by any one but the king. When riding it [4] in the Indian war, Alexander, while [5] performing (sundry) deeds of valour, had charged,[6] somewhat incautiously,[7] a column [8] of the enemy. Weapons were showered [9] from-all-sides against Alexander, (and) the horse received several severe wounds.[10] Still, in a dying state (as he was), and with life fast ebbing,[11] he carried back the king at his topmost speed [12] from the midst of the enemy; and when [13] he had brought him out-of-reach-of [14] the weapons, he fell-down [15] on-the-spot [16] and expired [17]. Thereupon Alexander, after gaining the victory [18] in that war, built a town in those parts,[19] and called it Bucephalos in honour [20] of his horse.

---

[1] in. [2] dignum memoria visum.

[3] quod ubi, foll. by *indic.*

[4] in eo insidens.

[5] Say, *and doing brave feats.*

[6] irruo.

[7] Say, *not sufficiently cautious.*

[8] cuneus (lit. *a wedge;* hence, *a column formed for breaking an enemy's line;* or, as here, *a deep body of troops*).

[9] conjicio (conicio).

[10] Say, *was pierced* (perfodio) *with deep wounds.*

[11] prope jam exsanguis.

[12] vivacissimo cursu (so in Gellius; but the earlier and more classical sense of vivax is *long-lived*).

[13] ubi (*as soon as*); and for tense, see Ex. 9, Note 12.

[14] extra.   [15] concīdo.

[16] illico.

[17] animam exspiro.

[18] victoriam parĕre; and for the case of bellum, see Ex. 29, Note 7.

[19] Say, *places.*

[20] ob honorem.

71. THE SIBYLLINE BOOKS.

An old woman, who was a perfect stranger,[1] once came to Tarquinius Superbus, the seventh and last king of Rome,[2] bringing with-her nine books, which she declared to be the oracles of-the-gods[3]: she said she was willing to sell them. Tarquinius enquired the price: the woman asked[4] an extravagant and enormous (one). The king laughed, thinking[5] the old woman was in her dotage. Then she[6] placed[7] a brazier with fire (in it) before-him,[8] and burnt-up[7] three books out of the nine, and (then) asked the king whether he were willing to buy the remaining six at the same price. Tarquinius laughed much more, and said that beyond a doubt the old woman was now out-of-her-senses.[9] The woman immediately burned (to ashes) three more[10] books on-the-very-spot,[11] and once-more[12] quietly asked[13] the king the very same thing[14] (namely), to purchase the remaining three at the same price. Tarquinius, struck by the strangeness of the affair, perceived that such firmness and assurance were not to-be-trifled-with,[15] and purchased the three remaining books at just the same price[16] that had been asked[17] for all (the

---

[1] Say, an *unknown old-woman.*

[2] Romanorum.

[3] *adj.*   [4] posco.

[5] Expr. by quasi: *as if she were in her dotage: to be in one's dotage,* aetate desipere.   [6] illa.

[7] For the first two predicates use *hist. pres.*

[8] coram, as *adv.*

[9] deliro.   [10] alius.

[11] ibidem.   [12] denuo.

[13] *hist. pres.*

[14] id ipsum.

[15] contemno; *ger. part. sing.*

[16] nihilo minore pretio.

[17] peto.

nine). The woman [18] then left the presence of Tarquinius, but report says was never seen afterwards. The three books were deposited [P] in a shrine, and were called the "Sibylline (Books)." Special [19] priests consulted them as they would [20] an oracle, whenever the Romans decided [21] that the gods should be consulted on-behalf-of-the-state. [22]

---

[18] Say, *but they say* (ferunt) *that that woman, having parted* (digredior) *from Tarquin, was never afterwards seen.*

[19] quidam.

[20] *resorted to them* (adeo) *as if to an oracle.*

[21] censeo.

[22] publice.

===

72. Unjust Judges.

King Cambyses ordered Sisamnes, [1] one of the Persian [2] judges, to be punished [3] with death, for having given an unjust sentence for a bribe. [4] He was first killed [5] and then flayed; and the bench on which he had sat was covered with his skin. Then he chose [6] this man's [7] son Otanes to sit as judge in-the-same-place, and warned him never [8] to forget his father's fault or (its) punishment. Subsequently Artaxerxes, king

---

[1] Begin with the name of the judge, which of course must be followed by the descriptive clause, 'one of the Persian judges.'

[2] Say, *of the Persians.*

[3] plector (only found in *imperf.* tenses = *to be beaten, made to smart*).

[4] Say, *because, having received money, he had judged unjustly.*

[5] Say, *and with the killed* (interimo) (*man's*) *drawn off* (detraho) *skin he covered the bench,* etc.

[6] volo.

[7] ejus.

[8] ne unquam : see Ex. 30, Note 4.

of the Persians, was still more severe against some corrupt[9] judges. For he ordered them to be flayed alive,[10] and the benches of the other judges to be covered with their skins,[11] that they might have ever before their eyes a lively illustration[12] of injustice which had not gone unpunished.[13]

---

[9] malus.
[10] Emphasize the word for ʻaliveʼ by its position, nam vivis . . . : and see Note 5.

[11] iis.
[12] recens exemplum.
[13] Say, *of justice not with impunity violated.*

---

73. EXTRAORDINARY DEATHS.

When Aeschylus, the Athenian, who is called "the Father of Tragedy," was staying[1] in Sicily, and was sitting there in (some) sunny spot, an eagle dropped[2] a tortoise upon his smooth[3] (bald) head which it took[4] for a stone. He was killed by the[5] blow. Euripides, who has also[6] a great name among tragic poets, was torn to pieces by dogs, as he returned[P] home from a supper. Philippides, a writer of comedies, when beyond[7] his expectation he-came-off-victorious[8] in a contest among poets,[9] and was excessively[10] delighted[11] at his victory,[12] died[13] suddenly from sheer joy.[14]

---

[1] versor.
[2] immitto, with *acc.* and *dat.*
[3] glaber, bra, brum.
[4] habeo.   [5] *rel.*
[6] et ipse.   [7] praeter spem.

[8] vinco.
[9] See Ex. 29, Note 7.
[10] impense.   [11] Say, *rejoiced.*
[12] *abl.* alone.   [13] exstinguor.
[14] eo ipso gaudio.

74. Pericles and the Eclipse.

Pericles (was) on-the-point-of-setting-out[p] for the war with the Athenian[1] fleet, (and) had already gone on board his trireme.   It-happened-that[2] at that very time there was an eclipse of the sun.[3]   When darkness was spread-over[4] the sky, and terror had come upon all, as (though) some great prodigy were presented[5] (to their view), Pericles, seeing the helmsman (of his ship) stupefied with fear,[6] threw his cloak[7] over his eyes; and (when) thus muffled,[8] asked him whether this was anything to-be-frightened-at,[9] or[10] portended some disaster (to him).   He replied, "No."[11] Then said Pericles, "What difference is there[12] between this and that, except that that which has shrouded the heaven in darkness is larger[13] than a cloak?"

---

[1] Say, *of* the Athenians.
[2] forte.
[3] Say, *the sun failed*, defecit sol.
[4] obduco, *refl. pass.*
[5] oblatus—*abl. abs.*
[6] trepidus et stupens.

[7] chlamys.
[8] tectus.
[9] horrendus: and use *part. gen.* after *neut. pron.*
[10] aut.
[11] nego.
[12] interesse.
[13] grandis.

75. THE FAITHFUL DOG.

King Pyrrhus, while on a journey, fell in with a dog, which was keeping-guard-over the body[1] of a man (who had been) slain. Upon being told[2] that it had been sitting[3] there for now three days without[4] food, and would not leave[5] the corpse, he ordered the man to be buried,[6] but the dog to be taken along with him, and every[7] care taken of it. A few days after[8] there was held a review of his soldiers. They passed[9] before the king's seat in single file. The dog was there. He[10] was at first quiet, and made not a sound,[11] (but) as soon as he saw the assassins of his master passing by, he rushed furiously[12] forward and barked at them, again and again turning towards Pyrrhus, in such a way, too, that in-the-opinion-of-the-king,[13] as well as of all who were present, they were rendered objects of strong suspicion.[14] They were, accordingly, apprehended;[P] and an inquiry being held,[15] and some slight (confirmatory) evidence[16] adduced[17] from-other-quarters,[18] they confessed[P] the murder (and) suffered punishment.[19]

---

[1] A *dead body* is strictly cadaver; but corpus may also be used, as here.

[2] audio.

[3] assideo: *pres. inf.*, which indicates that the dog was *sitting there still*.

[4] expers, with *gen.*

[5] *pres. inf.* (discedo).

[6] Note, effero could not be used here as in Ex. 69 (Note 15), where *a formal interment* is implied. Use humo or sepelio.

[7] Say, *to be diligently taken care of.*

[8] paucis post diebus: in such cases the abl. denotes the measure *by how much* (St. L. G. § 321), and post is *adv.*: ' later *by a few days.*'

[9] Say, *they march past* (hist. pres.) *one by one* (singuli), *the king sitting.*

[10] Begin, is cum antea . . .

[11] tacitus.

[12] *part.* of furo.   [13] dat.

[14] Say, *they were brought* (adduco) *into great suspicion.*

[15] instituo.   [16] *plur.*

[17] accedo.   [18] aliunde.

[19] Expr. by poenas dare or supplicio affici.

76. HANNIBAL AT EPHESUS.

When Hannibal, on his expulsion [p] from Carthage, had come (as) an exile to Ephesus, he was invited by his hosts, should it be agreeable to him,[1] to[2] hear Phormio the philosopher.   Upon his saying that he should like (to do so), Phormio is stated to have spoken for some hours upon the duty of a commander, and upon military affairs in-general.[3]   Thereupon[4] all the rest of his audience[5] were marvellously[6] pleased, and asked[7] Hannibal what[8] he himself thought[9] of the[10] philosopher.   Upon this the Carthaginian[11] is said to have answered frankly, that he had often seen many crazy old men, but a crazier[12] than Phormio[13] he had never[14] seen.

---

[1] si vellet.   [2] ut.
[3] de omni re militari.
[4] Begin, tum cum.
[5] Say, *the rest who heard him.*
[6] vehementer.
[7] quaero, which is followed by ex, ab, de.

[8] quidnam.   [9] judico.
[10] ille.
[11] Poenus.
[12] Say, (one) *who was more crazy* (delīro): what mood?
[13] *nom.*
[14] Say, *he had seen no man.*

77. DIOGENES AND ALEXANDER.

The Greeks had assembled at[1] the Isthmus, for the purpose of[2] declaring war against the Persians, and appointed Alexander, king of Macedonia, general in this war. All-who[3] were renowned either for (military) exploits, or for learning, flocked together to Alexander, to-pay-their-respects,[4] and congratulate[4] him. Diogenes alone was wanting; he[5] was living[6] at that time near Corinth, (but) did not trouble-himself-at-all[7] about Alexander. He, however,[8] waited for him for, some considerable time,[9] (and) at length, in order to make the man's acquaintance,[10] went[11] himself to see him with his attendants. He found him sunning himself in the open air.[12] Diogenes, on the approach[13] of such a crowd[14] of men, raised[15] himself up a little, and looked at Alexander. Alexander greeted[16] him courteously, and asked him, if there was anything he could do for him,[17] to mention it. But Diogenes (replied), "All[18] I ask of you is to step aside[19] a little out of the sun." Alexander was dumbfounded at the spirit of a man who-was-indifferent-to[P][20] everything. And when his attendants, as they went away,[P] were turning-him-into-ridicule,[21] he remarked, "By my troth,[22] were I not Alexander, I would choose[23] to be Diogenes."

---

[1] in with acc. after verb of motion.
[2] ut decernerent.
[3] quicunque: but begin sentence with confluebant. [4] *pres. part.*
[5] *rel.* [6] dēgo.
[7] nihil curans.
[8] qui cum.
[9] satis diu. [10] cognosco.
[11] Say, *set out himself to him with attendants* (comites).
[12] sub dio (collat. form of divo:

divus or Jupiter being used by metonymy for *the sky;* like Bacchus = wine).
[13] accedo. [14] caterva.
[15] allēvo. [16] *hist. pres.*
[17] Say, *if he wanted* (opus) *anything.*
[18] Say, *this one* (thing).
[19] recedo. [20] contemno.
[21] derideo. [22] ego vero.
[23] volo.

78. Hannibal in Syria.

When Hannibal on his expulsion from Carthage was staying with Antiochus, king of Syria, the king passed before him in review [1] the immense forces which he had raised [2] with-the-object-of-making [3] war against the Roman people. He displayed-to [4] him an army decorated with gold and silver ornaments; he also brought on [5] (the field) chariots armed with scythes, [6] and elephants with towers, and cavalry glittering with their bits, housings, collars, and breast-trappings. And then [7] the king, elated at the survey [8] of an army so great (in numbers) and so splendidly equipped, [9] looked-to [10] Hannibal and remarked, "Do you think this army can be matched [11] with that-of-the-Romans? and (do you think) all this [12] is enough for the Romans?" Thereupon Hannibal, making-merry-with [13] the cowardice and weakness of his soldiers (though so) expensively equipped, replied, "It is my belief [14] that all this is enough, quite [15] enough, for the Romans, however

---

[1] Say, *showed* (ostendo) *him in the plain.*

[2] comparo.

[3] *fut. part.*: here use bellum facere, with *dat.*, which has the authority of Cic. and Caes.: it denotes the act of *beginning a war* = bellum inferre; whereas bellum gerere denotes the *carrying of it on.*

[4] exhibeo.   [5] induco.

[6] falcatus (also cum falcibus may be used; corresponding with cum turribus = turribus instructos, following).

[7] ibi.   [8] contemplatio.

[9] tam ornatus.

[10] *hist. pres.*

[11] confero.

[12] *plur.*   [13] eludo.

[14] credo.   [15] plane.

greedy [16] they may be." Nothing, certainly,[17] could have been said more smart [18] or cutting: [19] the king had put-the-question [20] with-respect-to [21] the number of the army, whether it would prove [22] a match for that of the Romans; Hannibal's answer had reference [23] to the booty (the Romans would acquire).

---

[16] Say, *even-if they should be most greedy* (avarus).

[17] prorsus.   [18] *adv.*

[19] neque tam lepide neque tam acerbe.

[21] de.

[20] quaero.

[23] futurus. !

[23] Say, *Hannibal answered about the booty.*

---

79. PLUTARCH AND HIS SLAVE.

Plutarch ordered his slave, a worthless and insolent fellow, but learned and well-read in the books of the philosophers, for some offence to be stripped [1] of his tunic and to be flogged.[2] When the flogging commenced,[3] the man [4] objected [5] that he did not deserve to [6] be beaten, that he had done nothing wrong,[7] (committed) no crime.[7] At last he began to call out [8] whilst

---

[1] *to strip,* tunicam detrahere, with *dat.* Put the ind. object (servo) immediately after the Subject.

[2] loro caedere: note that as caedo takes *acc.* of person, whereas detraho takes the *dat.*, the object must be repeated in pron. form:

et *eum* loro caedi jussit: comp. Ex. 50, Note 1.

[3] Say, *when he had begun to be flogged:* the *pass.* of coepi must be used before a *pass. inf.*

[4] *pron.*   [5] obloquor.

[6] ut.   [7] *part. gen.*

[8] vociferor, 1.

the beating was going on,[9] that[10] Plutarch was not acting as[11] became a philosopher; that it was disgraceful to be angry; that he[12] had often discoursed on the evil of anger[13]; moreover he had written a very beautiful treatise[14] on that subject; that it was by no means consistent[15] with all that was written in that treatise, that[16] he was now so angrily[17] inflicting[18] such a severe whipping upon him. Thereupon Plutarch observed, in a cool and quiet manner,[19] " Well now,[20] I am beating you, (it is true); but do I seem to you to be angry? Do you perceive from my countenance, or from my voice, or from my (heightened) colour, or even from my words, that I am carried away[21] by anger. My eyes, I think, are not fierce, nor is my face distorted,[22] nor do I cry out savagely, nor am I saying what I should be ashamed of[23] or regret,[23] nor am I at all agitated. All these things, though you may not be aware of it,[24] are the customary[25] signs of anger." And at the same time turning to the man who was flogging, he said, " In the mean time, whilst this (fellow) and I are discussing (the matter), do you go on with your task[26]."

---

[9] inter vapulandum.

[10] The words of the slave are here given in *oratio obliqua:* see Introd. p. 10.

[11] ita . . . ut.

[12] i.e. *Plutarch*, not the slave.

[13] de malo irae.

[14] Say, *book*.

[15] convenio, with *dat.*

[16] quod.

[17] *adj.*

[18] *to inflict a severe whipping on anyone*, aliquem multis plagis mulcare: use *sup.* of *adj.*

[19] lente et leniter.

[20] Quid autem.   [21] corripio.

[22] turbidus.   [23] *ger. part.*

[24] si ignoras.

[25] Say, *are wont to be the signs of anger.*   [26] hoc tu age.

80. THE BULL OF PHALARIS.

Perillus, a clever artificer, having come to Agrigentum, in order to please Phalaris, the tyrant of this state, constructed in the most ingenious manner[1] a bull of[2] brass. In its[3] side he placed a door (so contrived) that when any-one[4] (was) shut in,[p] (and) put to the torture by lighting a fire under it,[5] his cries resembled the bellowing of a bull rather than the voice of a man.[6] He offered this bull to the tyrant, whom he knew to be delighted with any fresh expedient for human torture,[7] and asked for a reward for his invention. The tyrant, however,[8] ordered (Perillus) himself to be the first to be shut up in the bull, and burnt-to-death[9].

---

[1] Say, a most *ingeniously-contrived* (artificiosus) *bull*.
[2] ex.
[3] rel.
[4] quis—which has the force of an *indef. pron.* after si, nisi, ne, cum, etc.

[5] subjectis ignibus.
[6] Say, *he seemed to emit a bellowing, not the voice of a human-being.*
[7] Say, *with new torments of men.*
[8] at, which must of course begin the sentence. [9] comburo.

81. APELLES AND PTOLEMY.

Apelles[1] when he was the companion of Alexander had (constant) feuds with Ptolemy. When the latter[2] had become king of Egypt, after the death of Alexander, Apelles during a voyage was driven ashore[3] at Alexandria[4] by a violent storm.[5] Thereupon (some) rivals of his secretly instigated[6] (some one) to invite him in the king's name to supper. Apelles was surprised[7] at receiving an invitation[8] from his old enemy, but nevertheless came to the supper. Ptolemy is indignant. "What do you mean?" he says. "Who asked you here?" As Apelles could not tell the name of the man who had invited him, he seized[p] a coal from a brazier, and sketched his likeness on the wall[9] with such-skill[10] that the king, from the very commencement of the sketch,[11] recognised the face of the-man-who-had-played-the-trick.[12]

---

[1] *dat.* with sum.
[2] *rel.*　[3] expello.
[4] *acc.*　[5] vi tempestatis.
[6] suborno.　[7] *hist. pres.*
[8] Say, *that he was invited, acc.*

and *inf.*
[p] *wall of a house,* paries, ĕtis, *m.*
[10] ita.
[11] protinus inchoata imagine.
[12] fraudator.

82. The Obedient Servant.

P. Piso, the orator, to prevent[1] his being interrupted (when) engrossed[2] in study, had ordered[3] his servants not to say anything unless they-were-asked-a-question[p]. It happened[4] (one day) that he directed Clodius, who was holding office[5] at that time, to be invited to a banquet. The supper-hour was close at hand[6]. All the other guests were present. Clodius alone was waited for. Piso several times sent out the servant who was wont to invite the guests, to see[7] whether[8] he was not coming. When evening came,[9] and his arrival was (now) despaired of, Piso said to his servant, " Tell me whether by (any) chance you failed[10] to invite Clodius." "I did invite (him)," replied he. "Why then has he not come?" "Because he declined[11] to come." "Why then didn't you tell me so at once?" "Because you never asked me[12] about it."

---

[1] ne.

[2] intentus in studia.

[3] praecipio.

[4] accidit ut, or simply forte.

[5] magistratum gero.

[6] insto.　　[7] sup.

[8] The direct question is, nonne venit? *is he not coming?* hence, indirect form, nonne veniret, Introd p. 10.

[9] vespere jam facto.

[10] ' fail to invite '=*not to invite.*

[11] Say, *denied that he would come:* nego.

[12] Say, *because I was not asked about it by you.*

---

83. The Talking Raven.

After the victory of Actium,[1] amongst those-who-were congratulating[P] Augustus, there came-to-meet[2] him a certain man holding a raven, which he had taught[3] to say, 'Hail Caesar, Conqueror, Emperor.' Caesar, surprised at such politeness in a bird,[4] bought it for 20,000 sesterces.[5] Being greeted in like manner by a parrot, he ordered it to be purchased. He was amused-at[P][6] the same (performance) on-the-part-of[7] a magpie, and it also he bought. These instances induced a poor shoemaker to train a raven to[8] (make) a similar salutation. Often when wearied with his task, (refer-ring) to the bird which-did-not-give-the-required-answer,[9] he would say, "I have lost my time and my trouble."[10] At length, however, the raven learnt to speak the salutation. Then he brought the bird to Augustus. He,[11] however, upon hearing the raven's greeting, remarked, "I have plenty[12] of such saluters at home." Whereupon the raven added very oppor-tunely, "I have lost my time and my trouble." At this[13] Augustus laughed, and ordered the bird to be purchased at a (still) higher price than he had hitherto given for the others.[14]

---

[1] Actiacus: note that battle or victory *of* is never expressed by *gen.*, but either by *adj.* or *prep.*, victoria Actiaca or ad Actium.

[2] occurrit (*hastens to meet*).

[3] instituo, foll. by ut.

[4] Say, *wondering at the polite bird*, avis officiosa [*full of courteous-ness and compliments*].

[5] a *sesterce* = twopence (about): hence 1000 sesterces = £8 3s. 4d.

[6] miratus.

[7] in.

[8] ad.

[9] Say, *not answering*.

[10] Use prov. phr., oleum et ope-rane perdidi (oleum, *lamp-oil;* hence, *the time represented by it*).

[11] qui cum.

[12] satis.

[13] quo facto.

[14] quanti nullam etiamtum eme-rat.

84. The Reward of Hospitality.

Seleucus, king of Syria, having lost all his forces in the battle against the Galatians, threw away his diadem, and fled [1] on horseback with three or four attendants. After wandering for a long time over unfrequented places, when already despairing of (finding) shelter,[2] he at length came to a cottage, and, meeting [3] by chance with its owner, asked for bread and water. The man not only (supplied him with) these, but also offered with liberality [4] and kindness [4] whatever else the country afforded.[5]   Moreover [6] upon his recognizing the king's face,[7] he (could) not suppress [8] his delight, and did not further [9] the king in his wish to preserve his incognito, but when he had led him into the road, as he quitted (him),[P] said, "Farewell, king Seleucus." Thereupon the king stretched out [P] his hand and drew him towards him,[10] as if to kiss [11] him; (at the same time) he signified [12] to one of his attendants with a nod to cut [13] off the man's head with his sword.   Now if he had but kept silent, and restrained himself a little,[14] he would shortly afterwards, when the king was again in flourishing circumstances,[15] have received perhaps a greater reward for his silence, than for his hospitality.[16]

---

[1] profugio.   [2] deverticulum.
[3] incido: cum and *subj.*   [4] *adv.*
[5] Say, *whatever things were in the country*.   [6] cumque.
[7] facies (which however does not mean *the face only*, but *the entire figure*, of which the face is the most conspicuous part).   [8] *indic.*
[9] Say, *nor did he aid the disguise of the king, desiring to-escape-notice* (lateo).

[10] Say, *with outstretched hand drawing him to him.*
[11] *fut. part.*   [12] praecipio.
[13] *to cut off the head of,* obtrunco.
[14] aliquantulum.
[15] Make this clause participial and say, *he would have received from the king again flourishing.*
[16] hospitium (hospitalitas occurs once in Cic., but only as technical term in ethics).

I 2

85. ANAXIMENES.

Alexander the Great had employed Anaximĕnes of Lampsacus [1] as his master in oratory, a circumstance which [2] was afterwards the means of saving [3] Lampsacus. For Alexander had determined upon destroying [4] the city, in consequence of its having taken the side [5] of Darius against himself. When therefore he beheld [P][6] Anaximenes coming forth from the city, not having a doubt but that he was coming to intercede on behalf of his native place, he swore by the gods that he would not grant [7] the petition the other was going to prefer. Upon hearing this, [8] the crafty orator begged the king to destroy Lampsacus. Thus-it-was-that [9] by reason of his oath and the ingenious [10] petition of his (former) teacher, he pardoned [11] the offence of the men of Lampsacus.

---

[1] Lampsacēnus : note that the genitive is never used in this connexion : thus, Timon *of Athens*, Atheniensis.

[2] Not res quae, but quae res (or id quod).

[3] salus, *dat.* of Purpose or Result : St. L. G. § 297.   [4] diruo, *inf.*

[5] Say, *because it had stood on the side of* (a partibus) *Darius.*

[6] conspicor (*to catch sight of*).

[7] Say, *that he would not do what the other* (ille) *was about to sue for.* Remember that this is *oratio obliqua*, and for the mood, see Introd. p. 10.

[8] *rel.*   [9] ergo.

[10] callidus.

[11] Lampsacenis gratiam (or veniam) delicti fecit.

86. The Death of Archimedes.

On the taking [P] of Syracuse, which Archimēdes had long defended with his wonderful engines, Marcellus, the Roman general, gave-orders,[1] that no one should injure [2] (the person of) Archimedes. He,[3] however,—while [4] with his attention [5] and eyes fixed upon the ground he was drawing [6] figures in the dust,—was asked [7] by a Roman soldier, who with drawn sword had forced-his-way into the house for the sake of plundering, who he was. In [8] the too-engrossing [9] ardour of his study, the only answer he returned was, "Don't [10] disturb my circles." He was consequently put to death by the soldier, who did not know [P] who he was.

---

[1] edico.

[2] vim facere, with *dat.* of ind. object.

[3] at is.

[4] dum, with *pres. indic.* : dum regularly takes *hist. pres.*, St. L. G. § 393, *Obs.*

[5] animus.   [6] describo.

[7] Say, *to a Roman soldier, who had forced . . . and with drawn sword had asked . . . he answers nothing-except* (nisi) *this . . .*

[8] propter.   [9] nimius.

[10] noli, with *inf.*, a frequent mode of expressing a prohibition. St. L. G. § 420, *Obs.* 1.

87. ZEUXIS AND PARRHASIUS.

There lived,[1] once upon a time, two celebrated painters, one called Zeuxis, the other Parrhasius. On one occasion these men entered into a competition in their art.[2] Zeuxis had painted (some) grapes, and imitated the reality[3] of nature so (successfully), that birds flew to the picture. Then Parrhasius brought a picture, in which he had painted a linen cloth. Zeuxis deceived (by the likeness) thought it was a real cloth, (intended) to[4] conceal the picture. Accordingly when Parrhasius seemed to be making a somewhat long delay,[5] he begged[6] (him) to remove[p] the cloth, and show the picture. Thereupon, perceiving his mistake,[7] he yielded the pre-eminence[8] to Parrhasius; for he[9] (he said) had (only) deceived the birds, (but) Parrhasius (had deceived one who was) himself an artist.[10] On another subsequent occasion[11] Zeuxis painted a boy carrying grapes. When a bird flew towards them,[12] Zeuxis remarked, "(Ah,) I have painted the grapes better than (I have) the boy: for if I had worked out this part of the picture as perfectly as the other,[13] the bird should[14] have been afraid (to approach)."

---

[1] Say, *were.*   [2] *gen.*

[3] Say, *truth.*

[4] *rel.* and *subj.* : turn the verb to pass., *by which the picture might be concealed* (occulto).

[5] diutius moror.

[6] flagito; which implies *urgency* or *loss of patience* on the part of the person asking.

[7] *abl. abs.*   [8] palmam defero.

[9] oratio obliqua.

[10] artifex: i.e. *a skilled craftsman (of any kind).*

[11] postea rursus.

[12] *rel.,* which (with *prep.*) must lead off the sentence.

[13] Say, *if I had perfectly-finished* (consummo) *this part of the picture also.*

[14] debeo: note that here and in like cases, the sign of the past tense, which in English is attached to the dependent verb, must in Lat. be represented by the past tense of the modal verb: hence, timere debuisset (*not* timuisse deberet).

88. THE TWO PAINTERS.

Apelles and Protogenes were the most renowned painters of their age. Protogenes was living at Rhodes; Apelles sailed thither,[1] eager to inspect[2] the works of Protogenes, (who was) only known to him by fame— and went[3] straightway to his studio. Protogenes[4] was not at home, but an old woman was (there) keeping-guard-over a canvas[5] of spacious size, (which stood) upon an easel.[6] She answered that Protogenes was out,[7] and asked, who she should say had inquired for him.[8] "(Say) this man,"[9] replied Apelles, and, seizing a brush, he drew[10] an extremely fine coloured line[11] along the canvas.[5] When[12] Protogenes returned, the old woman acquainted him with what had passed. The painter at once observing[13] the fineness of the line, observed, "Certainly Apelles has been here, for no one else could have done so delicate[14] a (piece of) work." Then he himself drew a still more delicate line in a different colour within the other[15] (line), and, as

---

[1] quo cum ...

[2] cognosco, *ger.*   [3] peto.

[4] Say, *he himself was absent.*

[5] tabula; strictly, *board* or *panel.*

[6] machina picturae aptata.

[7] foris; which is *loc. pl.* of obsolete fora, *door* (=foris, is, *f.*): comp. Ex. 90, Note 16.

[8] Say, *by whom she should say that he* (ipsum) *had been inquired for* (quaero).

[9] Of course it must be, '*by this* (man).'

[10] duco; which is applicable to anything extended or prolonged.

[11] Say, *of the utmost fineness* (tenuitas): expr. *coloured* by ex colore.

[12] Say, *to P. having returned, the old woman pointed what had been done* (gero).

[13] contemplor.   [14] subtilis.

[15] in illa ipsa.

he went away,[p] told [16] (the old woman) that if the
stranger [17] returned,[18] she was to show it him, and to
add that this was the man he sought. Apelles returned,
and intersected [19] the lines with a third colour, (thus)
leaving no more [20] room for any still-finer line. Upon
this Protogenes, confessing himself beaten, went-
straight [21] to the harbour to look [22] for his guest.

---

[16] praecipio.
[17] Say simply '*he*,' ille : comp.
Introd. p. 8.

[18] *plup. subj.*
[20] amplius.
[22] *pres. part.*

[19] seco.
[21] contendo.

---

89. Demosthenes as an Advocate.

Demosthenes [1] was once defending a man on a
capital charge,[2] and seeing the judges paying but in-
different attention,[3] said, "Give me your attention for
a few moments,[4] (and) I-will-relate [p] a strange and
amusing [5] circumstance." At these [6] words they pricked
up their ears,[7] (and) he said:—"A certain young man
had hired an ass, to [8] use on-a-journey [p 9] from Athens
to Megara. Whilst on his way,[10] the noontide heat
became (very) oppressive, and there being no shelter to
keep off the burning-heat of the sun, he took-off [p 11]

---

[1] Demosthenes cum . . .
[2] in causa capitali.
[3] Say, *indifferently* (parum) *attentive.*
[4] paulisper.
[5] auditu jucundus *or* festivus.

[6] *rel.* foll. by cum.
[7] aures arrigere.
[8] *rel.* and *subj.*
[9] proficiscor.
[10] jam in itinere cum . . .
[11] depono.

the pack-saddle, (and) sitting under the ass, sheltered himself with its shade. The driver,[12] however, forbad him to do so, thrusting the man away from there, and exclaiming that the ass (only) had been let-out-on-hire,[13] and not the ass's shadow. The other maintained, on the contrary, that he had hired[14] the shadow of the ass as well. So sharp grew[15] the quarrel between them, that they even came to blows.[16] At last they go off[17] to law."—When Demosthenes had spoken[P] thus far,[18] seeing the judges listening attentively, he suddenly stepped down[19] from the platform. Upon being called back by the judges, and requested to go on and[20] narrate the rest of the story, he said, "What, do you like[21] hearing about the shadow of an ass, (and yet) feel it a burden[22] to listen to the cause of a man who stands in peril of[23] his life?"

---

[12] Say, *that however the driver* (agàso) *was forbidding.*

[13] loco, *to let out, to put out on contract ;* the correlative to which is conduco, *to hire, to undertake a contract.*   [14] *pass.*

[15] adeo exarsit.   [16] manus.

[17] in jus ambulant.

[18] haec.   [19] descendo.

[20] Say, 'go on *to* relate.'

[21] libet.   [22] gravor.

[23] de.

90. THE GIANT ROBBER.

Hercules[1] once came into Italy from Spain, where he had killed[2] king Geryon and carried off his oxen, (which were) of remarkable beauty. Driving these oxen before[3] him, he swam across the river Tiber, and lay down on a grassy spot by its banks,[4] in order to refresh his cattle with rest and good[5] pasture, being himself, too, (somewhat) wearied with his journey. There, he was[6] overtaken with sleep, and a shepherd who-dwelt-near[7] that spot, named Cacus, presuming on[8] his strength, and captivated by the beauty of the oxen, determined to carry them off as his prey.[9] He was well aware, however, that, if he drove the herd into his cave, their very footmarks would (quickly) bring their owner in his search[9] to the spot. So he drew the oxen into the cave backwards[10] by their tails. Hercules at the dawn of day[11] roused-himself[9] from sleep, and, casting his eyes over[12] his herd, noticed that some of them were missing,[13] and (at once) proceeds to the cave hard by[14] if haply their footsteps led in-that-direction.[15] When however he saw all the footprints

---

[1] Arrange: 'Hercules once from Spain, where . . ., came into Italy.'

[2] Say, *where he carried off the oxen of king Geryon slain* (inter-imo).

[3] prae.

[4] prope eum.

[5] laetus (*abundant and good*).

[6] Say, *when sleep* (sopor) *had overtaken him.*

[7] accola.

[8] ferox with *abl.*

[9] Say, *to carry off* (averto) *that booty.*

[10] Say, *turned away*, i.e. *from the cave.*

[11] prima luce *or* ad primam auroram.

[12] oculis perlustro.

[13] Say, *that a part was absent.*

[14] proximus.

[15] eo.

turned outwards,[16] and leading in no other direction, he (was utterly) confounded and perplexed,[17] (and) began forthwith to drive his herd from the ill-omened[18] spot. Just then[19] some cows lowed, (as they were) driven away, out of regret[20] for their (companions) whom they were leaving behind,[p] and the lowing[21] being returned from the cattle shut up within the cave, at once brought Hercules (to the spot). Cacus[22] thereupon endeavoured by force to prevent his going[23] to the cave, (but) fell dead[24] with a blow[p] from the club of Hercules.[25]

---

[16] foras (strictly acc. plur. = to the doors: Ex. 88, Note 7).
[17] incertus animi.
[18] infestus.
[19] inde (=ex eo loco) cum . . .
[20] Say, moved by regret.
[21] Say, the voice of the imprisoned

(inclusus) cows being returned (reddo) from the cave, caused-to-turn (converto) Hercules.
[22] quem cum . . .
[23] vado.   [24] morte occumbere.
[25] Say, struck by the club of Hercules.

---

91. Sanctity of an Oath among the Romans.

Among the Romans an oath was most conscientiously[1] observed. After the battle of Cannae, Hannibal, the general of the Carthaginians,[2] sent to Rome ten (men) chosen from the Roman captives, and stipulated with them that, if it seemed (good) to the Roman people, an exchange of prisoners should be made. Before setting

---

[1] sanctissime: or, doubling adverbs, sancte inviolateque.

[2] Poeni is more usual than Carthaginienses.

out, he made[3] them take an oath to return to the Carthaginian[4] camp, in case the Romans would not exchange prisoners. The ten captives came to Rome and laid[5] before the senate the instructions of the Carthaginian commander. The senate refused[6] an exchange. The parents, kinsmen, and relatives[7] of the prisoners embraced[p] them, and entreated them not to return to the enemy. Then eight of them made answer that they were bound by their oath, and set out forthwith to Hannibal. The two remaining (prisoners) stayed at Rome, and declared that they were released from their oath, because, after they had gone out of the enemy's camp, they had returned[8] on the same day, as though they had forgotten something, and had thus complied with[9] the oath by which they had promised to return. This fraudulent cunning of theirs was considered so disgraceful, that they were universally[10] contemned and reviled,[11] and the censors subsequently punished[12] them with every-kind-of[13] (civil) penalty and disgrace because they had not acted in accordance with their oath.[14]

---

[3] adigo, *to drive* or *force to,* which takes two *acc.*; one, of the person, dependent on the verbal element (ago), and the other (jusjurandum) dependent on the prep. (ad).   [4] Punicus.

[5] in senatu exponunt (*hist. pres.*).

[6] Expr. by placeo with negative.

[7] affines; *connections by marriage.*

[8] *they had returned* (regredior): what mood? Introd. p. 10.

[9] satisfacio.   [10] vulgo.

[11] discerpo : in what tense of the subj. should this and the connected verbs stand? See Ex. 44, Note 20 ; St. L. G. § 424, end.

[12] afficio, with *acc.* and *abl.* This clause also is dependent upon the conj. ' that.'

[13] *every kind of, pl.* of omnis.

[14] Say, *had not done what they had sworn to do.*

92. ANDROCLUS AND THE LION.

Once at Rome a grand combat of beasts[1] was being
given to the people. Many wild beasts were there,
remarkable[2] either for their unusual figure or their
ferocity. But beyond everything else the immense-size
of the lions attracted (general) admiration,[3] and of one
above all the rest. That lion turned the attention and
eyes of all upon himself by his vast size,[4] his terrible
roaring, and his waving mane. The slave of a man of
consular rank was brought in among a number of
others (who were) condemned[p 5] to do battle with the
beasts. The name of that slave was Androclus. As
soon as the lion saw him in the distance, he suddenly
stood (still), as if in wonder[p]; then he gradually and
quietly approached him. Presently, as though he recognised the man, he wagged[6] his tail fondly, just like dogs
when they fawn[7] (upon you), went close up to him,[8]
and gently licked[9] with his tongue the legs and hands
of the man, (who was) already half dead[10] with fright.

During these caresses of a beast (naturally) so savage,
Androclus recovered the senses[11] (he had well-nigh)
lost, and by degrees brought[12] his eyes to look[13] at the

---

[1] venationis amplissimae pugna
(where venatio is collective, denoting a *number of wild-beasts obtained by hunting*).

[2] Say, *of either unusual form or
ferocity.*

[3] Say, *was for admiration* (Dat.
of Purpose or Result).

[4] corporis vastitas.

[5] ad pugnam bestiarum datus
(damnatus).

[6] *hist. pres.*: so in foll. predicates.

[7] more (ritu) adulantium canum.

[8] Say, *joined itself to the body of
the man.*   [9] lingua demulcere.

[10] prope exanimatus.

[11] animus.

[12] refero.   [13] *ger. part.*

lion. Then, as if the recognition were mutual,[14] the man and the lion stood joyfully greeting each other.[15] Tremendous [16] shouts arose [17] on the part of the people [18] at so wonderful an occurrence. Androclus was (immediately) sent for by the Emperor,[19] and asked why that fiercest of lions had spared him alone. Then Androclus recounts a marvellous story.

"When my master," said he, "was proconsul of the province of Africa,[20] I was compelled by undeserved [21] and daily-(inflicted) stripes to (take) flight, and that my hiding-place might be safer from (the pursuit of) my master, who-had-the-command [22] of that country, I retired into the solitudes of the plains and sandy-deserts;[23] and in case food failed me, I intended [24] to seek for death in some way or other.[25] Then during the scorching heat of the mid-day sun,[26] having lighted upon an out-of-the-way [27] cave, well-adapted-for-concealment,[28] I hid myself there. Not long after, this lion came to the same cave with one foot lamed and covered-with-blood; uttering groans and growlings,[29] showing [30] the pain and torture (caused him) by his wound.[31]   •

"At the first sight of the lion as he approached ? I was frightened; but afterwards when the lion entered

---

[14] Say, *a mutual recognition being made.*

[15] Say, *joyful and congratulating* (gratulabundi).

[16] maximus: see Ex. 46, Note 7.

[17] excito; *pass. refl.*

[18] *gen.*

[19] Caesar.

[20] Say, *held the province of Africa* with *proconsular authority* (imperium).

[21] iniquus.

[22] praeses, idis.   [23] arenae.

[24] consilium fuit.

[25] aliquo pacto.

[26] sole medio flagrante.

[27] remotus.   [28] latebrosus.

[29] murmura.   [30] significo.

[31] *gen.*

his lair,[32] and saw me trying-to-hide-myself[33] in the distance, he came up to me (with) mild and gentle (mien),[34] lifted up his foot to show me,[35] and seemed to hold it out as if for the purpose of craving my help. I then plucked out an immense splinter[36] (which was) fixed[37] in the sole[38] of his foot, squeezed out the matter, drained it very carefully[39] to-the-core,[40] for I was not much afraid now,[41] and wiped away the blood. Relieved by my help and treatment, he placed[P] his foot in my hands, lay down, and went to sleep.[42]

"From that day the lion and I lived for three whole years in the same cave and on the same food. For he used to bring[43] to the cave for me the richer portions of the beasts he hunted (down); and I, having no means of making a fire,[44] roasted[P] them in the mid-day sun, (and) ate them. But when I grew tired of this savage[45] life, the lion one day having gone forth to hunt, I left the cave; and after having travelled for about three days,[46] I was seen and captured by (some) soldiers, and brought from Africa to Rome to my master. He immediately had me condemned[47] on a capital charge and consigned to the beasts.[48] I conclude[49] that this

---

[32] habitaculum illud suum.

[33] delitesco (de, lateo).

[34] mitis et mansuetus.

[35] Say, *seemed to show and hold out to me his uplifted foot.*

[36] stirpes.   [37] haerens.

[38] vestigium.   [39] accuratius.

[40] penitus (=*from within;* hence, *to the heart* or *core; thoroughly*).

[41] sine magna jam formidine.

[42] quiesco.

[43] suggero: and say, *what beasts*

he was hunting, he used to bring to me the richer portions (opimiora membra).

[44] ignis copia.   [45] ferinus.

[46] viam ferme tridui permensus.

[47] *to have a thing done,* curare, with *ger. part.: to condemn on a capital charge,* rei capitalis or capitis damnare.

[48] Say, *given to the beasts* (ad bestias dandum: Gell.).

[49] intelligo.

lion, after my departure,[50] was also captured, and now shows his gratitude for the benefit and treatment[51] (he received from me)."   ·

Such was the story of[52] Androclus.   Thereupon by universal request[P] he was set free and discharged from punishment, and by the votes of the people the lion was presented to him.   Afterwards Androclus, with[53] the lion fastened to him by a slender thong, used to go round all the stalls throughout the whole city.[54]   Androclus was presented with money[55]; the lion was sprinkled with flowers.   Almost[56] all who met them used to say, "This is the lion (that was) the host of the man; this is the man who (was) doctor to the lion."

---

[50] *abl. abs.*
[51] medicina.   [52] haec dixit.
[53] Say, *and.*

[54] *abl.* alone.   [55] aes.
[56] fere, which is less definite than paene.

VOCABULARY.

A

abandon, (leave off) ōmitto, mīsi, ssum, 3 ; (forsake) rĕlinquo, līqui, lictum, 3.
able, be, possum, *irr.*
abode, dŏmĭcĭlium, ĭ, *n.* ; sēdes, is, *f.*
about = concerning, dē, with *abl.* Of numbers, fĕrē, circĭter.
above, (in comparisons) praeter, with *acc.*
absence, expr. by absens, ntis.
absolute power, dŏmĭnātĭo, ōnis, *f.*
abuse, convĭcium, ĭ, *n.*, oft. *plur.*
accept, accĭpĭo, cēpi, ceptum, 3.
accomplish, perfĭcĭo, confīcĭo, fēci, fectum, 3.
according to, ex (e), with *abl.*
accordingly, ĭtăque, ĭgĭtur.
account, rătĭo, ōnis, *f.* On — of, propter, ob, with *acc.* On no —, mĭnĭmē.
accuse, crīmĭnor, 1 *dep.* ; accūso, 1.
accused person, reus, ĭ, *m.* ; rea, ae, *f.*
accustomed, be, sŏleo, sŏlĭtus sum, 2. To become —, to accustom oneself, consuesco, insuesco, suēvi, tum, 3.
acknowledge, v. confess.
act, factum, ĭ, *n.*
Actium, Actium, ĭ, *n.* ; of —, Actĭăcus, a, um.
add, addo, addĭdi, tum, 3 ; adjĭcĭo, jēci, jectum, 3.
addicted, dēdĭtus, a, um.
address, allŏquor, cūtus, 3.
admirable, ēgrĕgĭus, a, um.
admiration, admĭrātĭo, ōnis, *f.*
admire, mĭror, admīror, 1.
admit, admitto, mīsi, ssum, 3.

advance, prōgrĕdĭor, ssus, 3.
advantage, commŏdum, ĭ, *n.* ; ūtĭlĭtas, tātis, *f.*
advantageous, ūtĭlis, (very) pĕrūtĭlis ; sălūtāris, e.
advice, consĭlium, ĭ, *n.* By my —, me auctore.
advise, suădeo, si, sum, 3 ; with *dat.*
Aegina, Aegĭna, ae, *f.*
Aeschines, Aeschĭnes, is, *m.*
Aeschylus, Aeschȳlus, ĭ, *m.*
affair, res, rĕi, *f.*
affection, cārĭtas, ātis, *f.* ; dutiful —, pĭĕtas, ātis, *f.*
Africa, Afrĭca, ae, *f.*
after, post, with *acc.*
afterwards, post, posteā, deindĕ.
again, rursus, ĭtĕrum. — and —, ĭdentĭdem.
against, adversus, contrā, in ; with *acc.*
age, aetas, tātis, *f.* ; (old —) sĕnectūs, tūtis, *f.* ; in gen. sense, tempus, ŏris, *n.*
aged, v. old.
agitated, to be, trĕpĭdo, 1.
Agrigentum, Agrigentum, ĭ, *n.*
Agrippa, Agrippa, ae, *m.*
aid, auxĭlium, ĭ, *n.* ; (ops), ŏpis, *f.*
— (*v.*), adjŭvo, jŭvo, jūvi, tum, 1, with *acc.*
aim at, pĕto, īvi, ĭtum, 3.
Alcibiades, Alcĭbĭădes, is, *m.*
Alexander, Ălexander, dri, *m.*
alight, dēsĭlĭo, uī, sultum, 4.
alive, vīvus, a, um.
all, omnis, e ; (together) cunctus, a, um. At —, omnĭno ; all but, v. almost.
Allia, Allia, ae, *f.*
allow, pătĭor, ssus, 3.
ally, sŏcius, ĭ, *m.*
almost, paenĕ.
alone, sōlus, a, um.

along, per, with *acc.* ; — with, (ūnā) cum.
already, jam.
also, ĕtiam, quŏquĕ.
altar, āra, ae, *f.*
alter, (for the better) ēmendo, 1.
alteration, ēmendātĭo, ōnis, *f.*
although, cum, etsi, quanquam, quamvis.
always, semper.
ambassador, lēgātus, ĭ, *m.*
ambush, insĭdiae, arum, *f.*
amid, inter, with *acc.*
among, inter, ăpud (in more general sense) ; with *acc.*
amount, (often) pondus, ĕris, *n.*
amuse, oblecto, 1.
amusing (*adj.*), festīvus, a, um.
Anaximenes, Ănaxĭmĕnes, ĭs, *m.*
ancient, vĕtus, ĕris ; vĕtustus (bearing the outward signs of antiquity); antiquus, a, um.
and, et, atque.
Androclus, Androclus, ĭ, *m.*
anger, ira, ae, *f.* ; in —, īrātus, a, um.
angry, to be, īrascor, īrātus, 3.
announce, nuntio, (publicly) prōnuntio, 1.
another, ălius, a, ud ; alter, ēra, ērum (a second one).
answer, respondeo, di, sum, 2.
Antiochus, Antĭŏchus, ĭ, *m.*
Antisthenes, Antisthĕnes, ĭs, *m.*
any, ullus, a, um ; — one, quisquam (any single person), quis (after si, ne, neu) ; quīvis, quīlibet (anyone you like ' anybody and everybody ').
apart, seorsum, *adv.*
Apelles, Ăpelles, is, *m.*
Apollo, Apollo, ĭnis, *m.*

APPEAR

appear, appāreo, 2; = seem, vĭdeor, vīsus sum, 2.

applaud, v. praise.

applause, plausus, ūs, *m.*

application, industria, ae, *f.*

apply, admŏveo, mōvi, mōtum, 2.

appoint, constĭtuo, ĭ, ūtum, 3: also, fācio (to make).

appointed (day), dictus, dēfinītus, a, um.

apprehend, comprĕhendo, di, sum, 3.

approach (v.), apprŏpinquo, 1; accēdo, ssi, ssum, 3; advĕnio, vēni, ventum, 4.

—— (subs.), adventus, ūs, *m.*; at the — of night, sub noctem.

Arcadian, Arcas, ădis, *m.*

Archelaus, Archĕlāus, i, *m.*

Archimedes, Archīmēdes, is, *m.*

ardour, stŭdium, ĭ, *n.*; ardor, ōris, *m.*

Areopagite, Ărĕŏpăgītes, ae, *m.*

Areopagus, Ărĕŏpăgus, i, *m.*

Argive, Argīvus, a, um.

argue, dispūto, 1.

arise, v. rise.

Aristides, Aristīdes, is, *m.*

aristocracy, princĭpes, um, *m.*

ark, arca, ae, *f.*

arm (subs.), bracchium, i, *n.*

arm (v.), armo, 1.

armour-bearer, armĭger, ĕri, *m.*

arms, arma, orum, *n. pl.*

army, exercĭtus, ūs, *m.*; (on march) agmen, ĭnis, *n.*

arouse, suscĭto, excĭto, 1.

arrange, ordĭno, 1.

arrival, adventus, ūs, *m.*

arrive, pervĕnio (vĕnio), vēni, ventum, 4; sŭpervĕnio (to come up at a critical time).

arrow, săgitta, ae, *f.*

art, ars, artis, *f.*

Artaxerxes, Artaxerxes, is, *m.*

artifice, ars, artis, *f.*; artĭficium, i, *n.*

artificer, artĭfex, ĭcis, *m.*

as, ut, quemadmŏdum; quam (in comparisons); — if, — though, quăsi, tanquam, vĕlut; — far —, usque ad; — well, v. also.

as soon as, ut, simul ac

ATTENDANT

(atque), postquam, with *perf. ind.*

ascent, ascensus, ūs, *m.*

ashamed, to be, pŭdet, uit, 2 *impers.*; with *acc.* of Eng. subject : *ger. part.* pŭdendus, a, um.

Asia, Ăsia, ae, *f.*

ask, rŏgo, 1; quaero, quaesīvi, ītum, 3; foll. by ex (e), de, ab (a). See also invite.

asleep, to fall, obdormio (-īsco), 4.

aspect, aspectus, ūs, *m.*

ass, ăsĭnus, i, *m.*

ass-driver, ăsĭnārius, i, *m.*

assail, aggrĕdior, gressus, 3.

assassin, (slayer) interfector, percussor, ōris, *m.*; (practised —, cutthroat) sĭcārius, i, *m.*

assault, impĕtus, ūs, *m.*

assemble, convĕnio, veni, ventum, 4.

assembly, contio, ōnis, *f.* (public); consessus, ūs (any assemblage of persons); concĭlium, i, *n.*

assert, v. say. Also affirmo, 1 (to assert positively).

assist, subvĕnio, vēni, ventum, 4, with *dat.* (to come to anyone's help); adjŭvo, juvo, v. aid.

assistance, auxĭlium, i, *n.*

assurance, confidentia, ae, *f.*

astonished at, to be, v. to wonder.

at, ăpud, ad (near) : loc. of names of towns and certain other words.

Athenians, Ăthēnienses, ium, *m.*

Athens, Ăthēnae, arum, *f.*

atrium, ātrium, i, *n.* (the hall of a Roman house).

attack (v.), oppugno, 1; aggrĕdior, gressus, 3; pĕto, īvi, ītum, 3.

—— (subs.), impĕtus, ūs, *m.*

attempt, make an —, cōnor, 1; tento, 1.

attend, (to accompany) cŏmĭtor, 1; (to listen to) audio, 4.

attendance, in, praesto, *adv.*, usu. with esse.

attendant, cōmes, ĭtis, *c.*; sătelles, ĭtis, *m.*; pedisĕquus, i, *m.* (used of servants following a great personage); servus, i, *m.*

BEAST

attention, (often) ănĭmus, i, *m.*

attention, to pay, cūro, 1 (to take care of); operam do, dĕdi, dătum, 1 (to devote care and effort to); aures praebeo, 2 (to listen attentively); two latter phr. foll. by *dat.*

attentive, attentus, a, um.

attentively, attentē, dilĭgenter.

Attica, Attĭca, ae, *f.*

attire, cultus, ūs, *m.*

aught, quid, quicquam : v. any.

Augustus, Augustus, i, *m.*

auspicious, faustus, a, um.

await, exspecto, 1.

aware of, to be, intellĭgo, lexi, ctum, 3.

away from home, fŏris, fŏrās (the former after a verb of rest; the latter after a verb of motion); pĕregrĕ (after verb of motion).

B

babe, infans, ntis, *c.*; pŭĕrŭlus, i, *m.*

Babylonian, Băbÿlōnius, a, um.

back, tergum, i, *n.*

backwards, expr. by āversus, a, um (turned away from).

bad, mălus, imprŏbus, a, um.

badges, insignia, ium, *n. pl.* (Strictly, *plur. neut.* of *adj.* insignis.)

ballot, tăbella, ae, *f.*

band, glŏbus, i, *m.* (compact body); mănus, ūs, *f.*

banish, expello, pŭli, pulsum, 3; in modified sense, rĕlēgo, 1.

bank, rīpa, ae, *f.* (of a stream).

banker, argentārius, i, *m.*

banquet, convīvium, i, *n.*

bar, prŏhĭbeo, 2; interclūdo, si, sum, 3.

bargain, nĕgōtium, i, *n.*

bark at, allātro, 1.

base, turpis, e.

battle, pugna, ae, *f.*; proelium, i, *n.*; — field, ăcies, ēi, *f.* esse.

be present, adsum, fui, esse.

bear, fĕro, 3 *irr.*; (a child) gigno, gĕnui, ĭtum, 3.

beast, bestia, ae, *f.*; wild —,

fĕra, ae, f. (strictly adj., with bestia understood) ; jūmentum, i, n. (— of burden, or draught).

beat, pulso, verbĕro, 1 ; to be beaten, vāpŭlo, 1. See also conquer.

beautiful, pulcher, chra, chrum.

beauty, pulchrĭtūdo, inis, f. ; spĕcies, ĕi, f.

because, quĭā, quod, proptĕreā quod.

—— of (prep.), propter, ob, with acc.

become, fīo, factus, irr. ; ēvādo, si, sum, 3.

——, to be becoming or fit, dĕcet, uit, 2 impers., with acc.

bed, cūbile, is, n. ; lectus, i, m.

before (prep.), ante, with acc. ; cōram, ăpud (in presence of), with abl.

—— (conj.), priusquam, antĕquam.

beg, ōro, 1 ; (urge) hortor, 1 ; pĕto, ivi, ĭtum, 3, foll. by ab ; exōro, 1 ; contendo, di, tum, 3 (to beg earnestly).

begin, incĭpio, cēpi, ceptum, 3 ; coepi, coeptus, def.

beginning, inĭtium, princĭpium, i, n.

begone, ăpăgĕ!

behalf of, on, pro, with abl.

behind (prep.), post, pōnĕ, with acc. As adv., a tergo, post tergum, pōnĕ.

behold, intueor, 2 dep.

believe, crēdo, dĭdi, dĭtum, 3, with dat. See also think.

bellowing, mūgītus, ūs, m.

belly, venter, tris, m.

below, infrā, with acc.

bench, subsellium, i, n. ; trĭbūnal, ālis, n.

bend (a bow), intendo, di, tum, 3.

benefit (conferred), bĕnĕfĭcium, i, n.

benevolent, bĕnĕvŏlus, a, um ; comp. -volentior ; sup. -volentissimus.

besides, expr. by ălius, a, ud ; praetĕreā.

besiege, obsĭdeo, sēdi, sessum, 2.

besmear, pĕrungo (-guo), xi, ctum, 3 : also, in p.p. dēlĭbūtus.

bestow, v. give.

betake (oneself), confĕro, tŭli, collātum, 3 irr. ; rĕcĭpio, cēpi, ceptum, 3 ; with pron. refl.

betray, prōdo, dĭdi, dĭtum, 3.

better (adv.), mĕlius.

between, inter, with acc.

beware, vĭdē! căvē!

beyond, ultrā, with acc. ; — all else, praeter omnia alia.

bezel (of ring), pāla, ae, f.

bid, jŭbeo, ssi, ssum, 2.

bind, vincio, nxi, nctum, 4 ; allĭgo, 1 (to fasten to something) ; ădĭgo, ēgi, actum, 3 (by oath, see Ex. 91).

bird, ăvis, is, f. ; vŏlucris, is, f.

bit, frēnum, i, n. ; pl. -i and -a, m. and n.

Bito, Bito, ōnis, m.

blame, culpo, vĭtŭpĕro, 1.

blandishment, blandīmentum, i, m.

blood, sanguis, ĭnis, m. ; cruor, ōris, m. (blood that has been shed). Covered with —, cruentus, cruentātus, a, um.

blow (subs.), ictus, ūs, m. (To come) to blows, ad manus venio, 4.

board, v. embark.

boast, glōrior, 1.

boat, cymba (cumba), ae, f.

body, corpus, ŏris, n. : — of troops, glŏbus, i, m.

body-guard, pl. of sătelles, ĭtis, m.

bold, audax, ācis.

boldness, audācia, ae, f.

bondsman, sponsor, ōris, m. ; vas, vădis, m.

book, lĭber, bri, m.

booty, praeda, ae, f.

bordering, finĭtimus, a, um.

born, to be, nascor, nātus, 3.

both, ambo, ae, o ; ūterque, utrăque, utrumque.

boundary, finis, is, m.

bountifully, mūnĭfĭcē.

bow, arcus, ūs, m.

bowl, pătĕra, ae, f.

boy, puer, ĕri, m. Of a —, boy's, puerĭlis, e.

brass (bronze), aes, aeris, m.

brave, fortis, e.

bravery, fortĭtūdo, ĭnis, f.

brazen, aeneus, a, um.

brazier (for coals), fŏcŭlus, i, m.

bread, pānis, is, m.

break, frango, frēgi, fractum, 3.

—— asunder, interrumpo, rūpi, ptum, 3.

—— open, rĕsĕro, 1.

breast-trappings, phălĕrae, arum, f.

breath, spīrĭtus, ūs, m. ; ănima, ae, f.

breathe, spīro, 1.

bribe, corrumpo, rūpi, ptum, 3, with or without pecuniā.

bridge, pons, ntis, m.

bring, affĕro, attŭli, allātum, 3 irr. ; of a person, dūco, perdūco, xi, ctum, 3.

—— against (of a charge), objĭcio, jēci, jectum, 3, with acc. and dat.

—— in, intrŏdūco, 3.

—— on, indūco, 3.

—— out or forth, effĕro, extŭli, ēlātum, 3 irr. ; of a person, prōdūco, 3.

brother, frāter, tris, m.

brush, pēnĭcillum, i, n.

brutality, atrōcĭtas, ātis, f.

Bucephalus, Būcĕphălus, i, m. ; Būcĕphălos, i, f. (name of town).

build, aedĭfĭco, 1 ; condo, dĭdi, dĭtum, 3.

bull, taurus, i, m.

burden, ŏnus, ĕris, n.

burn, ūro, ssi, stum ; (burn up) exūro, dēūro, combūro, 3 ; (set fire to) incendo, di, sum, 3.

bury, effĕro, extŭli, ēlātum, 3 irr. ; hūmo, 1.

business, nĕgōtium, i, n. Do — nĕgōtior, 1 ; opp. to ōtior, 1, to be unemployed.

but, at, sed, cētĕrum : but that, quin.

buy, ĕmo, ēmi, emptum, 3 ; mercor, 1.

by, of time, ad ; by means of, per, with acc.

C

Cacus, Cācus, i, m.

Caepio, Caepio, ōnis, m.

Caesar, Caesar, ăris, m.

Caius, Cāius, i, m. (C.)

call (= name), dīco, xi, ctum, 3 ; nōmĭno, appello, 1 ; (=summon), vŏco, advŏco, 1.

—— back, rĕvŏco, 1.

—— on (=invoke), invŏco,

K 2

1; (=visit) vĕnio, vēni, ntum, 4, with *prep.*
call upon (= appeal to), appello, 1.
—— **to witness**, testor, 1.
Cambalus, Cambălus, i, *m.*
Cambyses, Cambȳses, is, *m.*
Camillus, Cămillus, i, *m.*
camp, castra, orum, *n. pl.*
Campanian, Campānus, i, *m.*
can, possum, *irr.*
candidate for, to be, pĕto, ivi, itum, 3.
Canius, Canius, i, *m.*
Cannae, Cannae, arum, *f.* Of —, Cannensis, e.
capacious, căpax, ācis.
caparisoned, ornātus, a, um.
capital, căpĭtālis, e.
Capitol, Căpĭtōlium, i, *n.*
captivated, captus, a, um.
captive, captivus, i, *m.* To take —, căpio, 3.
capture, v. take.
care of, take, cūro, 1 *v. a* and *n.*
carefully, dīlĭgenter, accū-rātē.
caress, blandīmentum, i, *n.*
carpenter, făber lignārius.
carry, porto, 1; fĕro, dē-fĕro (carry home), tŭli, lātum, 3 *irr.*; gesto, 1 (carry habitually).
—— **away**, aufĕro, 3 *irr.*
—— **back**, rĕfĕro, 3 *irr.*; rēporto, 1.
—— **before, in front**, praefĕro, 3 *irr.*
—— **off**, (of things) aufĕro, abstŭli, ablātum, 3; (of persons also) răpio, ui, ptum, 3; (of cattle) āverto, ti, sum, 3.
—— **on** (war), gĕro, ssi, stum, 3.
—— **out**, effĕro, extŭli, ēlātum, 3 *irr.*
carter, būbulcus, i, *m.*
Carthage, Carthāgo, inis, *f.*
Carthaginian, Carthāginiensis, e; Poenus, i, *m.* (only as subst.); Pūnĭcus, a, um.
case, in, v. if.
cast, jăcio, jēci, jactum, 3.
—— **forth**, prōjĭcio, jēci, ctum, 3.
—— **on, upon**, injĭcio, 3.
catch, căpio, cēpi, captum, 3; — sight of, conspĭcio, exi, ctum, 3; conspĭcor, 1.
Cato, Căto, ōnis, *m.*

cattle, pĕcus, ŏris, *n.* (used both sing. collect. and pl.); bŏves, bŏvum & bŏum, *c.*
cause, causa, ae, *f.* For this —, idcirco.
caution, admŏneo, 2.
cautious, cautus, a, um.
cavalry, ĕquĭtātus, ūs, *m.*
cave, spēluncca, ae, *f.*; spē-cus, ūs, *m.*
cease, dēsisto, stĭti, stĭtum, 3.
celebrate, cĕlebro, 1.
celebrated, clārus, prae-clārus.
censer, ăcerra, ae, *f.*; tŭrĭbŭlum, i, *n.*
censor, censor, ōris, *m.*
certain (=sure), certus, a, um.
certain, a, quidam, quaedam, etc.
certainly, certē, plānē, prorsus.
chair, sella, ae, *f.*
challenge, prōvŏco, 1.
chance, by, fortē, căsū.
change, mūto, 1.
channel, alveus, i, *m.*
charge (*v.*), (in battle) irruo, i, ŭtum, 3, with *prep.*; =accuse, crimĭnor, 1.
charge (*subs.*), crimen, inis, *n.*
chariot, currus, ūs, *m.*
chasm, hiātus, ūs, *m.*
cheerfully, lĭbenter.
cheese, cāseus, i, *m.*
chief, princeps, ĭpis, *c.*
children, lĭbēri, orum, *m.*
choose, (foll. by *inf.*) vŏlo, *irr.*; not to —, nŏlo, *irr.*; = to select, ēlĭgo, dēlĭgo, ēgi, ectum, 3.
Cimon, Cimon, ōnis, *m.*
Cineas, Cineas, ae, *m.*
circle, circŭlus, i, *m.*
circumstance, res, rĕi, *f.* The very —, id ipsum.
citizen, civis, is, *c.*
city, urbs, bis, *f.*
clad, vestitus, indūtus, a, um.
clan, gens, ntis, *f.*
class, ordo, inis, *m.*
clever, ingĕniōsus, a, um.
cloak, pallium, i, *n.*; ămĭcŭlum, i, *n.*; chlămys, ȳdis, *f.*
clothe, induo, i, ŭtum, 3; vestio, 4.
clothes, clothing, vestitus, ūs, *m.*; vestis, is, *f.*
Clodius, Clōdius, i, *m.*

club, clāva, ae, *f.*
Clusium, Clūsium, i, *n.*
Cneius, Cnēius, i, *m.*
coal, carbo, ōnis, *m.*
coat, v. dress.
Cocles, Cocles, itis, *m.*
Codrus, Codrus, i, *m.*
cold, frigus, ŏris, *n.*
collar, mŏnile, is, *n.*
collect, colligo, lēgi, lectum, 3.
colour, cŏlor, ōris, *m.* Of different —s, versĭcŏlōris, e.
column, cŏlumna, ae, *f.*
combat, certāmen, inis, *n.*; pugna, ae, *f.*
combine, v. join.
come, vĕnio, vēni, ventum, 4; (regularly) commeo, 1; (frequently) ventĭto, 1.
—— **in the way of**, obviam flo, v. meet.
—— **out, forth**, prōdeo, ii, itum; 4 *irr.*; prōcēdo, ssi, ssum, 3.
—— **to**, pervĕnio, 4; accēdo, ssi, ssum, 3.
—— **to assistance of**, subvĕnio, 4, with *dat.*
—— **up with**, assēquor, cūtus, 3.
—— **upon**, incēdo, ssi, ssum, 3; also, incesso, ivi, 3; both with *acc.*
comedy, cōmoedia, ae, *f.*
command, impĕrium, i, *n.* Chief —, summa imperii. Under the — of, duce —, *abl. absol.*
commander, dux, dŭcis, *c.*; impĕrātor, ōris, *m.*
common soldier, grĕgārius miles.
commonwealth, respublica, rēipublicae, *f.*
communicate, commūnĭco, 1.
companion, (on a journey) cōmes, itis, *c.*; sŏcius, i, *m.*
company of dancers, chŏrus, i, *m.*
compare, compăro, 1.
compass (arrange, plan), păro, compăro, 1.
compel, cōgo, cŏēgi, cŏactum, 3.
competition, certāmen, inis, *n.*
complain, quĕror, stus, 3.
complete, absolvo, vi, lūtum, 3.
comply with, sătisfăcio, fēci, factum, 3, with *dat.*

COMRADE

comrade, sŏcius, i, *m.*; in plur., his —s, sui (pl. of suus).
conceal, occulto, 1: — oneself, lăteo, 2.
concerning, de, with *abl.*
concord, concordia, ae, *f.*
condemn, damno, condemno, 1.
conduct, = manage, rĕgo, xi, ctum, 3.
—— **oneself,** gĕro, ssi, stum, 3, with *pron. refl.*
confer, confĕro, dĕfĕro, tŭli, lătum, 3 *irr.*
conference, collŏquium, i, *n.*
confess, făteor, fassus, 2; confiteor, fessus, 2.
conform to, obtempĕro, 1, with *dat.*
confound, confundo, fūdi, sum, 3.
congratulate, grătŭlor, 1, with *dat.*
conquer, vinco, vici, victum, 3; sŭpĕro, 1.
conqueror, victor, ōris, *m.*
conscious, conscius, a, um.
consent, vŏlo, 3 *irr.*
consequence of, in, *v.* because of.
consequently, ită, ităque.
consider, *v.* think.
consist, expr. by sĭtus, a, um, foll. by in and *abl.*
consistent, be, convĕnio, vĕni, ventum, 4, with *dat.*
conspicuous, conspicuus, conspiciendus, a, um.
conspire, conjūro, 1.
construct, fabricor, 1.
consul, consul, ŭlis, *m.*
consular, of — rank, consŭlāris, e.
consulship, consŭlātus, ūs, *m.*
consult, consŭlo, ui, ltum, 3: of the Sibylline books, adeo, ii, ltum, 4 *irr.*
consume, consūmo, absūmo, mpsi, mptum, 3; exūro, 3 (burn up).
contain, căpio, cēpi, captum, 3.
contemn, contemno, psi, ptum, 3.
content, contentus, a, um.
contest, certāmen, ĭnis, *n.*
contrary, on the, contrā, *adv.*
—— **to,** contrā, with *acc.*

CRUELTY

contrive, efficio, fēci, fectum, 3.
conversation, sermo, ōnis, *m.*
converse, collŏquor, cūtus, 3.
convey, vĕho, xi, ctum, 3.
Corinth, Cŏrinthus, i, *f.*
Corinthian, Cŏrinthius, a, um.
Corioli, Cŏriŏli, orum, *m.*
corn, frūmentum, i, *n.*
corpse, cădāver, ĕris, *n.*
corrupt (*v.*), corrumpo, rūpi, ptum, 3.
—— (*adj.*), mălus, a, um.
costly, prĕtiōsus, a, um.
cottage, căsa, ae, *f.*; tŭgŭrium, i, *n.* (hut).
couch, lectus, i, *m.*
countenance, vultus, ūs, *m.*; ōs, ōris, *n.*
country, rūs, rūris, *n.* (opp. to town); rĕgio, ōnis, *f.* (tract of land).
courage, virtūs, ūtis, *f.*; ănimus (esp. with bonus); fortitūdo, ĭnis, *f.*
court (of law), jūdicium, consilium, i, *n.*
courteous, cōmis, e.
courteously, cōmiter.
courtesy, cōmitas, ātis, *f.*
cover, tĕgo, contĕgo, obtĕgo, xi, ctum, 3.
covered, ŏpertus, a, um (closed up); perfūsus, a, um (bathed with).
cow, bōs, bŏvis, *f.*
cowardice, ignāvia, ae, *f.*
crafty, callĭdus, a, um.
crave, *v.* beg.
crazy, dēlīrus, a, um: to be —, dēlīro, 1.
credulous, crēdŭlus, a, um.
creep over, obrēpo, psi, ptum, 3, with *dat.*
Cremera, Crĕmēra, ae, *f.*
Crete, Crēta, ae, *f.*
crier, praeco, ōnis, *m.*
crime, scĕlus, ĕris, *n.*
critic, criticize, *v.* judge.
cross, trajicio, jēci, jectum, 3; transeo, 4 *irr.*
crowd, turba, (troop) căterva, ae, *f.*
crowded, frĕquens, ntis.
crown, (wreath) cŏrōna, ae, *f.*; (royal) diădēma, ătis, *n.*
cruel, crūdēlis, e.
cruelly, crūdēliter.
cruelty, crūdēlitas, ātis, *f.*

DEBAUCHERY

crush, *v.* break.
cry out, clāmo, exclāmo, vōcĭfĕror, 1.
Ctesiphon, Ctēsiphou, ntis, *m.*
cudgel, fustis, is, *m.*
cunning (*adj.*), callĭdus, a, um.
—— (*subs.*), callĭditas, ātis, *f.*
cup, pōcŭlum, i, *n.*; scȳphus, i, *m.*
Curius, Cūrius, i, *m.*
current, flūmen, ĭnis, *n.*
curse, dēprĕcātio, imprĕcātio, ōnis, *f.*
curule, cūrūlis, e.
custody, custōdia, ae, *f.*
custom, mos, mōris, *m.*
customary, sollennis, e.
cut down=kill, occīdo, di, sum, 3; obtrunco, 1.
—— **off,** abscīdo, praecīdo, di, sum, 3; ampŭto, 1; = to destroy, intĕrĭmo, ēmi, emptum, 3.
cymbal, tympănum, i, *n.*
Cyrus, Cȳrus, i, *m.*

D

daily (*adv.*), cottīdiē (less correctly, quot-).
—— (*adj.*), cottīdiānus (quot-), a, um.
Damon, Dāmon, ōnis, *m.*
danger, pĕrīcŭlum, i, *n.* To incur or stand in —, pĕrĭclĭtor, 1.
dare, audeo, ausus, 2.
daring (*adj.*), audax, ācis: — wickedness, audācia, ae, *f.*
dark, it grows, advesperascit, 3 *impers.*
darkness, tĕnebrae, arum, *f.*; cālīgo, ĭnis, *f.* (like a mist).
darling, ămor, ōris, *m.*; dēlĭciae, arum, *f.*
date (fruit), dactylus, i, *m.*
daughter, filia, ae, *f.*
dawn, (prima) lux, lūcis, *f.*
day, dies, ēi, *c.*; plur. *m.* Two —s, three —s, bĭduum, triduum, i, *n.*
dead, mortuus, a, um.
death, mors, rtis, *f.*; nex, nĕcis, *f.* (murder). At point of —, mŏrĭbundus, a, um.
debar, impĕdio, 1.
debaucher , nēquitia, lux-

ūria, ae, *f.*; stuprum, i, *n.* (oft. plur.).

deceive, dēcĭpĭo, cēpi, pĭum, 3; fallo, fĕfelli, falsum, 3.

deck out, exorno, 1.

declaim, prōnuntio, 1.

declare, v. say. To — war, bellum indico, with *dat.* ; also bellum decerno (by public resolution).

decorate, orno, 1.

decoration, ornāmentum, i, *n.*

decree (*v.*), dēcerno, crēvi, tum, 3.

—— (*subs.*), dēcrētum, i, *n.*

deed, factum, i, *n.* ; fācĭnus, ŏris, *n.* (— of valour).

deem, v. think.

deep, altus, prŏfundus, a, um. Of sleep, grăvis, e.

defeat (*v.*), fŭgo, 1 ; vinco, vĭci, ctum, 3.

—— (*subs.*), clādes, is, *f.* (great —) ; incommŏdum, i, *n.*

defence of, in, prō, with *abl.*

defend, dēfendo, di, sum, 3 ; tūtor, 1 *dep.*

degrees, by, paulātim (paull-), sensim.

deity, nūmen, Inis, *n.*

delay, mŏror, 1.

delight (*v.*), dēlecto, 1: to be —ed, gaudeo, gāvĭsus, 2.

—— (*subs.*), dēlĭcĭae, arum, *f.* See also joy.

deliver, trădo, dĭdi, dĭtum, 3

Delphi, Delphi, orum, *m.*
Delphian, Delphĭcus, a, um.

deluge, dĭlŭvium, i, *n.*

demand, postŭlo, 1 ; posco, pŏposci, 3 ; flāgĭto, 1 (with urgency and impatience).

Demosthenes, Dēmosthĕnes, is, *m.*

deny, nēgo, 1.

depart, discēdo, ssi, ssum, 3 ; = to set out, prŏfĭciscor, fectus, 3.

deposit, condo, dĭdi, dĭtum, 3 ; dēpōno, pŏsui, ĭtum, 3.

depravity, turpĭtūdo, ĭnis, *f.*

deputation, lēgātĭo, ōnis, *f.*

deputy, lēgātus, i, *m.*

descend, descendo, di, sum, 3.

desert (*v.*), v. abandon.

—— (*subs.*), desertus locus ; (sandy) ārēnae, ārum, *f.* (bar-).

deserter, perfŭga, ae, *m.*

deserve, mĕreo & mĕreor, *dep.* 2.

deservedly, mērĭtō.

design (*v.*) = plan, descrĭbo, psi, ptum, 3.

—— (*subs.*) = purpose, consĭlĭum, i, *n.*

designing = planning, descriptĭo, ōnis, *f.*

desire (*v.*), cŭpio, ĭvi, ĭtum, 3 ; vŏlo, 3 *irr.*

—— (*subs.*), cŭpĭdĭtas, ātis, *f.* ; cŭpīdo, ĭnis, *f.* Unbridled —, lĭbīdo, ĭnis, *f.*

desirous, cŭpĭdus, a, um.

desist, dēsisto, stĭti, stĭtum, 3.

despair of, despēro, 1.

destine, destĭno, 1.

destroy, intĕrimo, pĕrimo, ēmi, emptum, 3 ; dĭruo, i, ŭtum, 3 (to demolish).

destruction, exĭtĭum, i, *n.*; pernĭcĭes, ēi, *f.*

destructive, pĕrnĭcĭōsus, a, um.

determine, stătuo, constĭtuo, i, ūtum, 3.

devastate, vasto, 1.

deviate from, discēdo, ssi, ssum, 3.

devise, excōgĭto, 1.

diadem, dĭădēma, ătis, *n.*

dictator, dictātor, ōris, *m.*

dictatorship, dictātūra, ae, *f.*

die, mŏrior, mortuus, 3 ; exstinguor, nctus, 3.

differ, differo, 3 *irr.*

difference, expr. by intersum, *irr.*

different, dīversus, a, um ; (sometimes) ălius, a, ud.

diligence, dīlĭgentĭa, ae, *f.*
Diogenes, Dĭŏgĕnes, is, *m.*
Dionysius, Dĭŏnȳsĭus, i, *m.*

dip, tingo (guo), nxi, nctum, 3.

direct (*v.*), v. order.

direction, (often) pars, rtis, *f.*

disaster, clādes, is, *f.*

disastrous, grăvis, e.

disburden, exŏnĕro, 1.

discharge, (perform) exsĕquor, cŭtus, 3 ; (set free) lībĕro, 1.

discord, discordia, ae, *f.*

discourse (*subs.*), sermo, ōnis, *m.*

—— (*v.*), dissĕro (ēdissēro), ui, rtum, 3. See also speak.

discover, invĕnio, vēni, ventum, 4 ; rĕpĕrio, reppĕri, rĕpertum, 4.

discuss, dispŭto, 1.

discussion, dispŭtātĭo, ōnis, *f.*

disease, morbus, i, *m.*

disgrace, ignōmĭnĭa, ae, *f.*

disgraceful, turpis, e.

disguise, dissĭmŭlātĭo, ōnis, *f.*

dismay, in, perterrĭtus, a, um.

dismount, descendo, di, sum, 3. See also alight.

disregard, neglĭgo, exi, ectum, 3.

distance, in the, longē, prŏcul.

distinction, v. honour.

distinguished, praestans, ntis ; insignis, e (not compared).

distribute, distrĭbuo, i, ūtum, 3.

disturb, turbo, 1.

divide, dīvĭdo, vĭsi, sum, 3.

divine, dīvīnus, a, um.

do, făcio, perfĭcio, 3; (something wrong) admitto, mīsi, ssum, 3.

—— **without**, căreo, 2, with *abl.*

doctor, v. physician.

dog, cănis, is, *c.*

dominion, impĕrium, i, *n.*; dĭcĭo, ōnis, *f.*

door, ostĭum, i, *n.*; fŏris, is, *f.* Out of —s, fŏris, forās : v. away.

dotage, to be in, dēsĭpio, 3.

doubt, expr. by dŭbius, dŭbĭto : without —, beyond a —, sine dubio ; I have no —, non dubito.

downfall, ruīna, ae, *f.*

drag, trăho, xi, ctum, 3.

drain, haurio, si, stum ; (to dry) sicco, 1.

draw, trăho, xi, ctum, 3 ; (in a carriage) vĕho, advĕho, xi, ctum, 3 ; (— a line) dūco, xi, ctum, 3 ; (sword) destringo, nxi, strictum, 3 ; (water) haurio, si, stum, 4.

—— **back**, rēdūco, 3.

—— **near**, insto, stĭti, stătum, 1 ; apprŏpinquo, 1.

draw off, dētrăho, xi, ctum, 3.

dream, somnium, i, *n.*

dress (*v.*), v. clothe.

—— (*subs.*), vestītus, ūs, *m.* ; vestis, is, *f.*

drink, bĭbo, i, ĭtum, 3.

drive, ăgo, ēgi, actum, 3.

—— **away, out,** ăbĭgo, exĭgo, ēgi, actum, 3.

—— **together,** compello, pŭli, pulsum, 3.

driver, ăgăso, ōnis, *m.*

drop, gutta, ae, *f.*

drunkenness, ēbrīētas, ātis, *f.*

dry, siccus, (parched) ārĭdus, a, um.

dumbfounded, be, obstŭpesco, stŭpui, 3.

dung, stercus, ŏris, *n.*

during, inter, with *acc.*

dust, pulvis, ĕris, *m.*

dutiful affection, pĭĕtas, ātis, *f.*

duty, offĭcium, i, *n.* In plur., mŭnĕra, um, *n.*

dwell, commŏror, 1 ; hăbĭto, 1.

dying, in a — state, mŏrĭbundus, a, um.

E

each, (of two) ūterque, v. both ; (of any number) quisque, ūnusquisque, both parts declined.

—— **other,** expr. by inter se.

eager, ăvĭdus, a, um.

eagerly, cŭpĭdē.

eagerness, cŭpĭdĭtas, ātis, *f.* ; cŭpĭdo, ĭnis, *f.*

eagle, ăquĭla, ae, *f.*

ear, auris, is, *f.*

early (*adv.*), (in the morning) mănē ; (in general) mātūrē.

earnestness, grăvĭtas, ātis, *f.* ; (zeal) stŭdium, i, *n.*

earth, terra, ae, *f.*

ease, ōtium, i, *n.* ; quies, ētis, *f.*

easily, with ease, făcĭlē.

easy, făcĭlis, e.

eat, ĕdo, ēdi, ēsum, 3.

eclipse, dēfectio, ōnis, *f.* ; or expr. by verb dēfĭcio, 3.

edict, ēdictum, i, *n.*

effect, effĭcio, fēci, ctum, 3.

Egypt, Aegyptus, i, *f.*

Egyptian, Aegyptus, a, um.

either . . . or, aut . . . aut.

elated, ēlātus, a, um.

elder (*adj.*), mājor.

elephant, ĕlĕphantus, i, *m.*

else, v. besides.

embark, conscendo, di, sum, 3, with navem (naves).

embrace, amplector, xus, 3 ; (to comprise) contineo, ui, tentum, 2.

eminent, ēgrĕgius, a, um.

emit, ēmitto, mĭsi, ssum, 3.

emperor, impĕrātor, ōris, *m.* Also, Caesar, ăris, *m.*

empire, impĕrium, i, *n.*

employ, v. use.

encounter, impĕtus, concursus, ūs, *m.*

end, i inis, is, *m.*

endeavour, cōnor, 1.

endurance, pătientia, ae, *f.*

endure, tŏlĕro, 1.

enemy, hostis, is, *c.* ; (personal) inĭmīcus, i, *m.*

——, **of the,** hostĭlis, e.

engaged, intentus, occŭpātus, a, um.

engine, māchĭna, ae, *f.*

engrave, exăro, 1.

enjoy, fruor, ĭtus, 3, with *abl.*

Ennius, Ennius, i, *m.*

enormous, immensus, a, um.

enough, sătis.

enquire, percontor, 1 ; quaero, sīvi, sītum, 3 : v. ask.

enquiry, quaestio, ōnis, *f.*

enrich, lŏcŭplēto, 1.

enter, ingrĕdior, ssus, 3 ; intro, 1.

—— **upon** or **into,** (fig.) ĭneo, 4 *irr.*

entertain, rĕcĭpio, cēpi, ptum, 3.

entreat, ōro, prĕcor, 1.

entreaty, (prex), prĕcis, em, e, *f.*

Epaminondas, Ēpămĭnondas, ae, *m.*

Ephesus, Ēphĕsus, i, *f.*

Epirus, Ēpīrus, i, *f.*

equal, pār, păris.

equip, compăro, exorno (orno), 1.

escape, fŭgio, effŭgio, fūgi, fŭgĭtum, 3.

especially, praesertim, imprīmis.

espy, conspĭcio, spexi, ctum, 3.

Etruscans, Etrusci, orum, *m.*

Euclides, Euclīdes, is, *m.*

Euphrates, Euphrātes, is, *m.*

Euripides, Eurĭpĭdes, is, *m.*

even, ĕtiam ; not —, ne . . . quĭdem.

evening, vesper, ĕris and ĕri, *m.*

ever, unquam : see also always.

every, omnis, e : — body, omnes ; — thing, omnia.

—— **where,** ŭbĭque.

evidence, indĭcium, i, *n.*

evil, mălum, i, *n.*

examine, of accounts, exĭgo, ēgi, actum, 3.

exasperate, exăcerbo, 1.

exceedingly, admŏdum.

excellence, (moral) virtūs, ūtis, *f.*

excellent, optĭmus, ēgrĕgius, a, um.

except (*conj.*), nĭsi ; (*prep.*) praeter, with *acc.*

excessive, nĭmius, a, um.

excessively, nĭmis.

exchange (*v.*), permūto, 1.

—— (*subs.*), permūtātio, ōnis, *f.*

exclamation, vox, vōcis, *f.*

exclaim, clāmo, exclāmo, 1.

excuse, excūso, 1.

exercise, exercĭtātio, ōnis, *f.*

exhibit, prōpōno, pŏsui, ĭtum, 3. See also show.

exile, exsul, ŭlis, *m.*

expectation, exspectātio, ōnis, *f.*

expedient, v. advantageous.

expel, ējĭcio (ēĭcio), jēci, ctum, 3 ; expello, pŭli, pulsum, 3.

expense, impensa, ae, *f.* (usu. *pl.*) ; sumptus, ūs, *m.*

expensive, prĕtiōsus, a, um.

expensively, prĕtiŏsē.

expire, (animam) exspīro, 1. See also die.

explain, expōno, pŏsui, ĭtum, 3.

exploit, făcĭnus, ŏris, *n.* ; in *pl.*, res gestae.

expose, expōno, pŏsui, ĭtum, 3 ; objecto, 1.

expression, (of counte-

nance) vultus, ûs, m. ; (words uttered) vox, vōcis, f. ; verbum, i, n. ; ōrătio, ōnis, f.
extent, magnitūdo, inis, f.
extraordinary, singūlāris, e.
extravagance, luxŭria, ae, f.
extravagant, nimius, a, um.
extreme, summus, a, um.
eye, ŏcŭlus, i, m.
eyelid, palpebra, ae, f.

F

Fabius, Făbius, i, m.
fable, făbŭla, ae, f.
Fabricius, Fabricius, i, m.
face, vultus, ûs, m. ; ōs, ōris, n. ; făcies, ēi, f.
fail, dēsum, fui, irr. ; dēficio, fēci, ctum, 3.
fainting, exsanguis, e.
faith, fĭdes, ĕi, f.
faithfulness, v. faith.
Falerii, Fălĕrii, orum, m.
fall, cădo, cĕcĭdi, căsum, 3 ; lābor, psus, 3 ; (prostrate) prosternor, strātus, 3 ; (to perish) occĭdi, di, casum, 3. See also perish.
—— **dead**, occumbo, cŭbui, ĭtum, 3.
—— **down**, concĭdo (collapse) ; dēcĭdo, di, 3.
—— **in with**, incĭdo, di, 3. See also meet.
—— **out with**, dissĭdeo, sēdi, ssum, 2.
—— **upon**, (one's sword) incumbo, cŭbui, ĭtum, 3.
false, falsus, a, um.
fame, făma, ae, f.
family, fămĭlia, ae, f.
famine, fămes, is, f.
fancy, crēdo, dĭdi, dĭtum, 3.
far, longē ; prŏcul (within view). As —— as, usque ad.
farewell, vălē, vălētē!
farm, fundus, i, m. ; praedium, i, n. Little —— ăgellus, i, m.
farther side of, on the, ultrā, with acc.
fasten, rĕvincio, nxi, nctum, 4.
father, păter, tris, m. ; părens, ntis, c. Of a ——, păternus, patrius, a, um.
fault, culpa, ae, f. ; (blemish) vĭtium, i, n.

fawn, ădŭlor, 1.
fear (v.), mĕtŭo, i, 3 ; tĭmeo, ui, 2.
—— (subs.), mĕtus, ûs, m. ; tĭmor, ōris, m.
feast, ĕpŭlor, 1.
feat, făcĭnus, ōris, n.
feel, sentio, si, sum, 4.
feeling, sensus, ûs, m. Often, ănĭmus, i, m.
fellow, hŏmo, ĭnis, m. ; often not expr., esp. in pl.
fellow-citizen, cĭvis, is, c.
feminine, mŭlĭebris, e ; fēmĭneus, a, um.
fence in, consaepio, psi, ptum, 4.
ferocity, fĕrĭtas, ātis, f. ; saevĭtia, ae, f.
fetter, compes, pĕdis, f. ; vincŭlum, i, n.
feud, sĭmultas, ātis, f.
few, pauci, ae, a.
fierce, trux, ŭcis (of aspect); atrox, ōcis.
fight (v.), pugno, 1 ; dīmĭco, 1 (of pitched battles). To —— a battle, pugnam committere.
—— (subs.), pugna, ae, f.
figure, forma, ae, f.
file, in single, singŭli, ae, a.
fill, impleo, ēvi, ētum, 2.
finally, dēnĭquē, postrēmo.
find, invĕnio, vēni, ventum ; rĕpĕrio, reppĕri, rĕpertum, 4.
—— **fault with**, reprĕhendo, di, sum, 3 ; vĭtŭpĕro, 1.
—— **out**, compĕrio, i, rtum, 4.
fine=thin, tĕnuis, subtĭlis, e : =grand, praeclārus, a, um.
finger, dĭgĭtus, i, m.
finish, perfĭcio, confĭcio, fēci, ctum, 3.
fire, ignis, is, m.
fired, incensus, a, um.
firmness, constantia, ae, f.
first, prīmus, a, um. At ——, prīmum, primo.
fish (subs.), piscis, is, m.
—— (v.), piscor, 1.
fisherman, piscātor, ōris, m.
fit, aptus, a, um.
fix, fīgo, xi, xum, 3. Steadily fixed, dēfīxus, a, um.
flame, flamma, ae, f.
flay, pellem dētrăho, 3, with dat. of person.
flee, fŭgio, fūgi, fŭgĭtum, 3; —— for refuge, confŭgio, 3.

fleet, classis, is, f.
flesh, căro, carnis, f.
flight, fŭga, ae, f.
flock, pĕcus, ōris, n. ; grex, grĕgis, m.
—— **together**, confluo, xi, xum, 3.
flog, verbĕro, 1 ; caedo, cĕcĭdi, caesum, 3.
flourish, flōreo, 2.
flow, fluo, xi, xum, 3.
flower, flos, ōris, m.
fly, vŏlo, 1 : see also flee.
—— **to**, advŏlo, 1.
foe, foeman, v. enemy.
follow, sĕquor, prōsĕquor, cutus, 3. As —— s, sic.
following, (of time) postĕrus, a, um.
fond, stŭdĭōsus, a, um.
fondly, (caressingly) blandē.
fondness, cārĭtas, ātis, f. ; bĕnĕvŏlentia, ae, f.
food, cĭbus, i, m. ; victus, ûs, m. ; (of animals) pābŭlum, i, n.
fool, stultus, i, m.
foot, pes, pĕdis, m.
foot-print or -mark, vestĭgium, i, n.
foot-soldier, pĕdes, ĭtis, m.
for, (of motion towards ; also of dates) in, with acc. ; (of purpose) ad with acc.
forage, pābŭlor, 1.
forbid, vĕto, ui, ĭtum, 1.
force (a way in), irrumpo, rūpi, ruptum, 3.
forces, cōpiae, arum, f.
ford (v.), vădo (abl. of vadum, a shallow place) or pedibus transeo.
foremost, princeps, ĭpis.
forget, oblīviscor, lĭtus, 3, with gen.
forgiveness, vĕnia, ae, f.
form, forma, ae, f.
—— (a plan) ĭneo, 4 irr. ; (friendship) jungo, nxi, junctum, 3.
forthwith, prōtĭnus, stătim.
fortitude, constantia, ae, f.
fortunate, fortūnātus, a, um ; fēlix, īcis.
fortune, fortūna, ae, f.
forum, fōrum, i, n.
foul, impūrus, a, um.
fragrance, suāvĭtas, ātis, f.
fragrant, suāvis, e.
frankincense, tûs, tûris, n.
frankly, lĭbĕrē.

FRAUDULENT

fraudulent, fraudŭlentus, a, um.

free, līber, ĕra, ĕrum: to set —, lībĕro, 1.

free-will, vŏluntas, ātis, f.

frequent, frĕquens, ntis.

frequented, cĕlĕber, bris, bre.

frequently, v. often.

fresh, rĕcens, ntis.

friend, ămīcus, i, m.; (from another city) hospes, ĭtis, c.

friendship, ămīcĭtĭa, ae, f.

frighten, terreo, perterreo, 2.

front, in, adversus, a, um. In — of, pro, with abl.; ante, with acc.

frugality, frūgālĭtas, ātis, f.

fruit, fructus, ūs, f.; frūges, um, f.

full, plēnus, a, um.

function, mūnus, ĕris, n.

furious, fūrens, ntis.

further (v.), v. aid.

—— (adv.), (besides) praetĕrĕā, amplius.

future, in or **for,** in postĕrum.

G

gain (v.), acquīro, quīsīvi, ītum, 3: — victories over, v. conquer.

—— (subs.), lucrum, i, n.

gait, gressus, ūs, m.

Galatians, Gălătae, arum, m.

game, (play) lūdus, i, m.

garland, sertum, i, n.

garment, vestis, is, f.

gate, (of city) porta, ae, f.; (of house) jānua, ae, f.

Gauls, Galli, orum, m.

general, v. commander.

generous, lībĕrālis, e.

generously, bĕnignē.

genius, (a spirit) gĕnius, i, m.

gentle, mansuētus, a, um.

gently, lēnĭter.

Geryon, Gēryon, ŏnis, m.

gesture, gestus, ūs, m.

get abroad, percrēbresco, crēbui, 3.

—— **the better of,** v. overcome.

gift, dōnum, i, n.; mūnus, ĕris, n.

GROW UP

give, do, 1 irr.; trĭbuo, i, ūtum, 3.

glance at, v. look at.

glitter, fulgeo, si, sum, 2.

glorious, glōriōsus, a, um.

glory, glōria, ae, f.; laus, dis, f.

go, eo, 4 irr. See also, set out.

—— **away,** ăbeo, 4 irr.; discēdo, ssi, ssum, 3.

—— **forth,** prōgrĕdior, ssus, 3; prōdeo, 4 irr.

—— **on,** pergo, perrexi, ctum, 3.

—— **on board,** v. embark.

—— **out,** exeo, 4 irr.; ēgrĕdior, 3.

goblet, v. cup.

god, deus, i, m. Of the —s, dīvīnus, a, um.

goddess, dea, dīva, ae, f.

gold, aurum, i, n.

golden, aureus, a, um.

good, bŏnus, a, um. To do —, prōsum, irr.

—— **will,** bĕnĕvŏlentia, ae, f.

—— **temperedly,** cōmĭter.

gorgeous, magnĭfĭcus, a, um.

govern, praesum, irr., with dat. See also rule.

government, impĕrium, i, n.

gradually, paulātim (paulla-), sensim.

grapes, cluster of, ūva, ae, f.

grassy, herbĭdus, a, um.

gratify, v. please.

gratifying, grātus, a, um.

gratitude, grātus animus. To show —, gratiam refero.

great, magnus, a, um. -est, (of qualities) summus, a, um.

greatly, magnŏpĕrē.

Greece, Graecia, ae, f.

Greek, Graecus, a, um.

greet, sălūto, 1.

greeting (subs.), sălūtātio, ōnis, f.

grief, dŏlor, ōris, m.

groan, gĕmĭtus, ūs, m.; murmur, ŭris, n.

ground, hŭmus, i, f.; terra, ae, f.

groundless, vānus, a, um.

grow, cresco, crēvi, tum, 3; nascor, nātus, 3.

—— **up,** ădŏlesco, ēvi, adultum, 3.

HESITATE

guard (subs.), custos, ōdis, c.

—— (v.), custōdio, 4.

guest, hospes, ĭtis, m.; (at a banquet) conviva, ae, m.

gush out, pass. of perfundo, fūdi, sum, 3.

Gyges, Gyges, is, m.

Gytheum, Gythēum, i, n.

H

hail, ăvē!

hair, căpillus, i, n.; lock of —, crinis, is, m.

hand, mănus, ūs, f.

—— **over,** trādo, ĭdi, ĭtum, 3.

hang up, suspendo, di, sum, 3.

Hannibal, Hannĭbal, ălis, m.

haply, fortĕ.

happen, ēvĕnio, vēni, ntum, 4; fīo, factus, fĭeri.

happy, beātus, a, um.

harangue, ōrātio, ōnis, f.

harbour, portus, ūs, m.

hard, dūrus, a, um.

hard by, v. near.

harm (v.), nŏceo, 2, with dat.

—— (subs.), mălum, i, n.

hastily, prŏpĕrē.

hasty, (of temper) īrācundus, a, um.

hate, ōdi, ōsus, def.

hateful, invīsus, a, um.

hatred, ŏdium, i, n.

haul up, ashore, subdūco, xi, ctum, 3.

have, hăbeo, 2; or sum, with dat.

havoc, caedes, is, f.

head, căput, ĭtis, n.

hear, audio, 4.

heart, cŏr, rdis, n.

hearth, fŏcus, i, m.

heat, călor, ōris, m.; (scorching) aestus, ūs, m.

heaven, caelum, i, n.

heavy, grăvis, e.

Hebrew, Hebraeus, i, m.

helmsman, gŭbernātor, ōris, m.

help, auxĭlium, i, n. See aid.

hence, hinc.

herd, armentum, i, n.; grex, grĕgis, m.

here, hīc; to be —, adsum, irr.

hesitate, dŭbĭto, 1.

hide, abdo, condo, dĭdi, dĭtum, 3.　To try to — oneself, dēlĭtesco, lĭtui, 3.

hiding - place, lătebrae, arum, *f.*　Full of —s, lătebrōsus, a, um.

high, altus, a, um; —est, summus, a, um.

high-priest, use săcerdos, ōtis, *c.*

highly, magnŏpĕrĕ.

hinder, impĕdio, 4.

hire (*v.*), condūco, xi, ctum, 3.

—— (*subs.*), to let out on —, lŏco, 1.

hither, hūc.

hitherto, adhūc.

hold, tĕneo, ui, tentum, 2; (of office) gĕro, ssi, stum, 3; (to esteem) hăbeo, 2; (an enquiry) instĭtuo, i, ūtum, 3; exerceo, 2; (a review) hăbeo, 2.

—— out, porrĭgo, exi, ectum, 3.

holidays, fērlae, arum, *f.*

home, dŏmus, ūs, *f.*

honestly, hŏnestĕ.

honey, mel, mellis, *n.*: — comb, făvus, i, *m.*

honour, honor, ōris, *m.*; (high —) dignĭtas, ātis, *f.*

honourable, hŏnestus, a, um.

hope, spes, ĕi, *f.*

—— for, spēro, 1.

Horatius, Hŏrātius, i, *m.*

horse, ĕquus, i, *m.*　On — back, equo; to get on —, equum conscendo, in equum ascendo.

hospitality, hospĭtium, i, n.

host, ācies, ĕi, *f.* (in battle); agmen, ĭnis, *n.* (on march); multĭtūdo, ĭnis, *f.*

—— = entertainer, hospes, ĭtis, *m.*

hot, călĭdus, a, um; (red —) ardens, ntis.

hour, hōra, ae, *f.*

house, aedes, ium, *f.*; dŏmus, ūs, *f.*

housings, ĕphippia, orum, *n.*

how, quŏmŏdŏ, quemadmōdum, ut; (of degree, before *adj.* or *adv.*) quam.

however, tămen, autem.

human, hūmānus, a, um: — being, hŏmo, ĭnis, *c.*

hunger, fămes, is, *f.*

hunt, vēnor, 1.

hurry, prŏpĕro, 1.

hurry off (*trans.*), abrĭpio, rĭpui, reptum, 3.

husband, mărĭtus, i, *m.*; conjux, ūgis, *c.*

Hystaspes, Hystaspes, is, *m.*

I

idle, ōtiōsus, a, um.

if, si; — not, nĭsi, ni.

ignorant, ignārus, nescius, a, um.　To be — of, ignōro, 1; nescio, 4.

ill, mălĕ.

—— omened, infestus, a, um.

—— tempered, ăcerbus, mōrōsus, a, um.

imbecile, dēsĭpiens, ntis.

imitate, ĭmĭtor, 1.

immature, impūbes and -is; *gen.* -ĕris and -is.

immediately, stătim, prōtĭnus.

immense, ingens, ntis; — size, immānĭtas, ātis, *f.*

impose, impōno, pŏsui, ĭtum, 3, with *acc.* and *dat.*

impudent, impŭdens, ntis; imprŏbus, a, um.

impunity, with, impūnĕ.

in, in, with *abl.*

incalculable, infinĭtus, a, um.

inconvenience, incommŏdum, i, *n.*

increase, (*trans.*) augeo, xi, ctum, 2; (*intrans.*) cresco, crēvi, tum, 3.

indeed, quidem; (emphatic) vēro, enĭmvēro.

independence, v. liberty.

independent, v. free.

Indian (*adj.*), Indĭcus, a, um.

indignant, be, indignor, 1.

indignation, indignātio, ōnis, *f.*

individually, expr. by quisque, singŭli.

induce, flecto, xi, xum, 3; permŏveo, mōvi, tum, 2; addūco, xi, ctum, 3.

industry, dĭlĭgentia, industria, ae, *f.*

inexpedient, ĭnūtĭlis, e.

infantry, pĕdĭtātus, ūs, *m.*; pĕdestres cōpiae.

inflame, incendo, di, sum.

inflict, expr. by afficio, fēci, ctum, 3, with *acc.* of person and *abl.* of punishment; mulco, 1 (to belabour).

influence, auctōrĭtas, ātis, *f.*

influential, grăvis, e; grātiōsus, a, um.

ingenuity, sollertia, ae, *f.*

inhabit, incŏlo, ui, cultum, 3.

inhabitant, incŏla, ae, *c.*; — of the neighbourhood, accŏla, ae, *c.*

injure, nŏceo, 2; vim făcio, 3; with *dat.*; see also wound.

injury, dētrīmentum, i, *n.*

inmost, intĭmus, a, um.

innkeeper, caupo, ōnis, *m.*

innocent, insons, ntis.

inquire, v. en-.

inscribe, inscrībo, psi, ptum, 3.

inside, intrā, *prep.* with *acc.*; intus, *adv.*

insignia, v. badges.

insolent, contŭmax, ācis.

instance, exemplum, i, *n.*

instead of, pro, with *abl.*

instigate, sŭborno, 1.

instruction = command, mandātum, i, *n.*

insult, injūria, ae, *f.*

integrity, integrĭtas, ātis, *f.*

intend, vŏlo, 3 *irr.*

intense, v. great.

intention, consĭlium, i, *n.*

intercede, dēprĕcor, 1.

interpreter, interpres, ātis, *c.*

interrupt, interpello, 1.

intimidation, terror, ōris, *m.*

into, in, with *acc.*

invent, v. find.

invention, inventio, ōnis, *f.*

invidious, invĭdiōsus, a, um.

invite, invĭto, 1; (to one's house) dēvŏco, 1.

involve, implĭco, 1.

iron, ferrum, i, *n.*

island, insŭla, ae, *f.*

Israelites, Israēlītae, a-rum, *m.*

issue (*v.*), ēgrĕdior, ssus, 3.

—— (*subs.*), exĭtus, ūs, *m.*

isthmus, isthmus, i, *m.*

Italy, Ītălia, ae, *f.*

J

Janiculum, Jănĭcŭlum, i, *n.*

jewel, gemma, ae, *f.*

join, jungo, conjungo, nxi, nctum, 3 : — battle, committo, misi, ssum, 3.

Jordan, Jordānes, is, *m.*

journey (*subs.*), iter, itǐnĕris, *n.*

———— (*v.*), iter facio, 3.

joy, laetǐtia, ae, *f.* ; gaudium, i, *n.*

joyfully, use laetus, a, um.

judge (*subs.*), jūdex, ǐcis, *c.*

———— (*v.*), jūdǐco, 1.

Jugurtha, Jūgurtha, ae, *m.*

Julius, Jūlius, i, *m.*

juncture, v. time.

Jupiter, Jūpǐter (Jupp.), Jōvis, *m.*

just (*adj.*), justus, a, um.

———— (*adv.*), mŏdŏ (only) ; just now) : — as, cum jam.

justice, justǐtia, ae, *f.*

justly, jūre, *abl.* of jus.

K

keep (oath) conservo, 1 ; (breath) contǐneo, ui, tentum, 2. To — coming, expr. by *frequent. v.* ventǐto, 1.

———— **guard over,** custōdio, 1.

———— **hold of,** rětǐneo, ui, tentum, 2.

———— **silence,** tăceo, 2.

———— **off,** v. ward off.

———— **up,** (maintain) tueor, 2.

kill, interfǐcio, fēci, ctum, 3 (most gen. term) ; nĕco, 1 (murder) ; intĕrǐmo, ēmi, emptum, 3 (destroy).

kind, bĕnignus, a, um ; hūmānus, a, um.

kindly, bĕnignē.

kindness, cōmǐtas, ātis, *f.* : with —, cōmǐter.

————, **act of,** bĕnefǐcium, i, *n.*

king, rex, rēgis, *m.* : —'s, rēgius, a, um.

kingdom, regnum, i, *n.*

kingly, rēgius, a, um.

kinsman, cognātus, i, *m.* ; affĭnis, is, *c.* (by marriage).

kiss, osculo, 1.

knight, ĕques, ǐtis, *m.*

know, scio, 4 ; (to get to —) cognosco, nōvi, nǐtum, 3.

known, cognǐtus, a, um.

L

labour, lăbor, ōris, *m.* ; ŏpĕra, ae, *f.* (effort, attention).

Lacedaemonian, Lăcedaemŏnius, a, um.

lacking, v. wanting.

laden, ŏnustus, a, um.

Laevinus, Laevīnus, i, *m.*

lake, lăcus, ūs, *m.*

lamed, dēbǐlis, e.

lamp, lūcerna, ae, *f.*

Lampsacus, Lampsăcum, i, *n.* or -us, i, *f.* Of —, Lampsăcēnus, a, um.

land, terra, ae, *f.* ; (for cultivation) ăger, gri, *m.*

language, lingua, ae, *f.*

large, grandis, e ; magnus, a, um.

last (*subs.*), crĕpǐda, ae, *f.*

———— (*adj.*), ultǐmus, a, um. At —, ad postrēmum, postrēmo, dēnǐque, tandem.

lastly, postrēmo.

latter, the, hic or ille.

laugh at, rǐdeo, si, sum, 2.

———— **scornfully,** dērǐdeo, 2.

law, lex, lēgis, *f.* (*a law*) ; jūs, jūris, *n.* (body of law, equity) : — court, jūdǐcium, consǐlium.

lay aside or **down,** dēpōno, pŏsui, ǐtum, 3.

———— **on** or **upon,** impōno, 3.

———— **out** = plan, dīmētior, mensus, 4.

———— **waste,** pŏpǔlo (pŏpǔlor), vasto, 1.

lead, dūco, xi, ctum, 3 ; (of a road) fĕro, 3 *irr.* ; (escort) dēdūco, 3.

———— **across,** trādūco, 3.

———— **out,** ēdūco, 3.

leader, dux, dǔcis, *c.*

leap down, dēsǐlio, ui, sultum, 4.

learn, disco, dĭdǐci, 3 ; (by heart) ēdisco, 3 ; (to become aware of) cognosco, nōvi, nǐtum, 3.

learned, doctus, ērǔdǐtus, a, um.

learning, doctrīna, ae, *f.*

least, at, saltem.

leave, rělinquo, līqui, ctum, 3 : v. abandon, depart.

left (*adj.*), laevus, a, um ; sǐnister, tra, trum.

leg, crūs, ūris, *n.*

length, at, tandem, dēnǐ-

quĕ ; (sometime or other) ălǐquando.

Leonidas, Leōnǐdas, ae, *m.*

less (*adv.*), minus.

lest, nē.

let go, dīmitto, misi, ssum, 3.

letter, (of alphabet) lǐttĕra, ae, *f.* ; (an epistle) lǐtterae, arum, *f.*

liberal, lībĕrālis, e.

liberate, lībĕro, 1.

liberty, lībertas, ātis, *f.*

lie, jăceo, ui, 2.

———— **down,** dēcumbo, prōcumbo, cǔbui, ǐtum, 3 ; (— again) rĕcumbo, 3.

lieutenant, lēgātus, i, *m.*

life, vīta, ae, *f.*

lift up, tollo, sustǔli, sublātum, 3.

light (*subs.*), lux, lūcis, *f.* To bring to —, pătĕfăcio, 3.

———— (*adj.*), lĕvis, e.

———— (*v.*), (kindle) accendo, di, sum, 3.

———— **upon** (= meet with), nanciscor, nactus, 3.

like, sǐmǐlis, e. In — manner, sǐmǐlǐter.

likeness, imāgo, ǐnis, *f.*

limit, fīnis, is, *m.*

line, līnea, ae, *f.*

linen cloth, linteum, i, *n.* (strictly *neut.* of *adj.* linteus).

lion, leo, ōnis, *m.*

listen, ausculto, 1 ; (— to) audio, 4.

little, a, paulūlum.

live, vīvo, xi, ctum, 3 ; (a certain kind of life) dēgo, 3.

load, ŏnus, ĕris, *n.*

loaded, v. loaded.

look, (of hair) crīnis, is, *m.*

lofty, ēdǐtus, celsus, a, um.

long (*adj.*), longus, a, um.

———— (*adv.*), diu. As — as, quamdiu.

look at or **to,** aspǐcio, exi, ectum, 3 ; contueor, ǐtus, 2.

———— **for,** v. search.

———— **forth,** prospǐcio, exi, ctum, 3.

lord, dōmǐnus, i, *m.*

lose, āmitto, misi, ssum, 3 ; (by one's own fault) perdo, dǐdi, tum, 3.

loth, be, nōlo, 3 *irr.*

loud, (of the voice) magnus, a, um.

love (*v.*), ămo, 1 ; dīlǐgo, exi, ctum, 3 (esteem).

———— (*subs.*), ămor, ōris, *m.*

LOW

low, mūgio, 4.
lower, infĕrior, us.
lowering, (of the voice) rĕmissio, ōnis, f.
lowing, mūgītus, ūs, m. ; also vox (boum).
Lucius, Lūcius, i, m. (L.).
Lysander, Lўsander, dri, m.

M

Macedon, Măcĕdŏnia, ae, f.
Macedonian, subst., Măcĕdo, ōnis, m. ; adj. Măcĕdŏnicus, a, um.
magistrate, măgistrātus, ūs, m.
magpie, pīca, ae, f.
maiden, virgo, ĭnis, f.
maid-servant, ancilla, ae, f.
maintain, (preserve) servo, 1 ; (feed, nurture) ălo, uĭ, ĭtum, 3 ; (in argument) contendo, dī, tum, 3.
make, făcio, fēci, factum, 3 ; (oneself) fio, factus, fĭĕri ; (to render) reddo, dĭdi, tum, 3. — for, pĕto, īvi, ĭtum, 3.
man, hŏmo, ĭnis, c. ; vir, vĭri, m.
mane, cōmae, arum, f.
mangle, lăcĕro, lănio, 1.
mangling, (by beasts) lănĭātus, ūs, m.
Manius, Mānius, i, m. (M').
manliness, virtūs, ūtis, f.
Manlius, Manlius, i, m.
manner, mos, mōris, m.
Mantinea, Mantĭnēa, ae, f.
mantle, pallium, i, n. ; (of women, and in tragedy) palla, ae, f.
many, multus, a, um. A good —, complūres, a.
march, ĭter, ĭtĭnĕris, n. — past, praetĕreo, 4 irr.
Marcius, Marcius, i, m.
Marcus, Marcus, i, m. (M.)
mark, signum, i, n. (oft. gen. of subst. only).
marriage, nuptiae, arum, f.
marvellous, mirĭfĭcus, a, um.
marvellously, (often) vĕhĕmenter.
Masinissa, Măsĭnissa, ae, m.
master, (teacher) măgister,

MITHRIDATES

tri, m. ; (owner) dŏmĭnus, i, m.
match (for), pār, păris. — with, confăro, tŭli, collātum, 3.
matter, res, rĕi, f. ; (from a sore) sănies, ēi, f.
maturity, grow to, v. grow up.
mean, vŏlo, 3 irr.
means, by no, mĭnĭmē.
meanwhile, meantime, intĕrim, intĕreā.
meet, occurro, i, rsum, 3 ; obviam fīo, irr. ; both with dat. : (to assemble) convĕnio, vēni, ventum, 4. To — death, oppĕto, īvi, ĭtum, 3 ; occumbo, cŭbui, ĭtum, 3 (morti, -em, -e).
Megara, Mĕgăra, ae, f., and -a, orum, n.
Megarean, Mĕgārensis, e.
member, membrum, i, n.
memorable, mĕmŏrābĭlis, e.
memory, mĕmŏria, ae, f.
Menecrates, Mĕnecrātes, is, m.
Menenius, Mĕnēnĭus, i, m.
mention, commĕmŏro, 1 ; dico, xi, ctum, 3.
merchant, mercātor, ōris, m.
mercy, mĭsĕrĭcordia, ae, f.
merely, mŏdŏ, sōlum.
merriment, hĭlărĭtas, ātis, f.
messenger, nuntius, i, m.
Metellus, Mĕtellus, i, m.
midday, mĕrīdies, ēi, m. ; adj., mĕrīdiānus, a, um.
middle, mĕdius, a, um.
midst of, in the, inter, with acc. Or expr. by mĕdius.
mighty, magnus, a, um.
mild, mītis, e.
mile, mille passus or -uum.
milestone, millĭārium, i, n.
military, mĭlĭtāris, e : — service, mĭlĭtia, ae, f.
milk, lac, lactis, n.
Miltiades, Miltĭādes, is, m.
mind, ănĭmus, i, m. ; mens, ntis, f.
mindful, mĕmor, ōris.
Minerva, Mĭnerva, ae, f.
miserable, miser, ĕra, ĕrum.
missing, be, absum, irr.
mistake, error, ōris, m.
Mithridates, Mithrĭdātes, is, m.

NEED

Mnemon, Mnēmon, ŏnis, m.
moderation, mŏdestia, ae, f.
money, pĕcūnia, ae, f. ; nummi, orum, m.
month, mensis, is, m.
morals, mōres, um, m.
more (adv.), măgis ; (besides) amplius.
moreover, quīnĕtiam.
morning, in the, mānē.
morose, mōrōsus, a, um.
mortal, mortālis, e : — man, hŏmo, ĭnis, c.
mother, māter, tris, f.
motionless, immōtus, a, um ; immōbĭlis, e.
mount, conscendo, di, sum, 3.
mountain, mount, mons, ntis, m.
move, mŏveo, commŏveo, ōvi, ōtum, 2.
much, multus, a, um. — how, quantus, a, um. — so, tantus, a, um. For so much as, tanti . . . quanti.
Mucius, Mūcius, i, m.
mule, mūlus, i, m.
multitude, multĭtūdo, ĭnis, f.
murder (v.), v. kill. — (subs.), hŏmĭcĭdium, i, n.
mutilated, truncus, a, um.
mutual, mūtuus, a, um.

N

name, nōmen, ĭnis, n.
narrate, narro, ēnarro, 1.
nation, gens, ntis, f.
native city or country, patria, ae, f.
naturally, nătūrā.
nature, nătūra, ae, f.
near (prep.), prŏpe, ăpud, with acc. — (adj.), prŏpinquus ; -est, proxĭmus, a, um.
nearly, paenē ; fermē (about).
necessarily, nĕcessē.
necessary, nĕcessārius, a, um.
need, indĭgeo, ui, 2, with gen. or abl. ; expr. by opus est, with abl.

NEGLECT

neglect, neglĭgo, exĭ, ectum, 3.

neigh at, ădhinnĭo, 4, with dat.

neighbouring, vīcīnus, fīnĭtĭmus, prŏpinquus, a, um. Also used subst. = neighbour.

neither, nĕque, nec.

never, nunquam.

nevertheless, tămen.

new, nŏvus, a, um.

next, proxĭmus, s, um. On the — day, postrīdĭē.

night, nox, noctis, f. By —, noctu. At — fall, sub noctem.

nineteenth, undēvīcēsĭmus, a, um.

Nitocris, Nĭtŏcris, ĭdis, f.

no, none, nullus, a, um.

no one, nobody, nēmo, ĭnis, c. (not in gen. or abl.).

noble, nōbĭlis, e.

nod, nūtus, ūs, m.

noised abroad, be, percrēbresco, crēbui, 3.

noontide, v. midday.

nostril, nāris, is, f.

not, non, haud.

noted, insignis, e.

nothing, nĭhil, indecl. n.

notice, sentio, si, sum, 4.

now, nunc, jam. As quasiconj., autem.

nowhere, nusquam.

number, nŭmĕrus, ĭ, m.: large —, v. multitude. A — of, multi, complūres: v. many.

Numidian, Nŭmĭda, ae, m.

nurse, nurture, nūtrĭo, 4.

O

oath, jusjūrandum, jurisjurandi, n.

obey, ŏbēdĭo, 4; păreo, 2; with dat.

object, grăvor, 1; (in words) oblŏquor, cūtus, 3.

obloquy, opprobrium, ĭ, n.

obnoxious, invīsus, a, um.

obscure, obscūrus, a, um.

observe, (notice) ănimadverto, ti, sum, 3; (attend to, keep) cŏlo, ui, cultum, 3; servo, 1: see also say.

obtain, ădĭpiscor, ădeptus, 3; (a wish) impĕtro, 1.

occasion, on one, v. once.

occupation, (calling) quaestus, ūs, m.

ORDER

occupied, occŭpātus, a, um.

occurrence, cāsus, ūs, m.; res, rēi, f.

Oedipus, Oedipus, ŏdis and i, m.

of, (concerning) de, with abl.

offence, dēlictum, ĭ, n.

offer, prŏpōno, pŏsui, ĭtum, 3; offĕro, obtŭli, lātum, 3 irr.; do, 1 irr.

—— sacrifice, sacrĭfĭco, 1.

offering, mŭnus, ĕris, n.

office, mŭnus, ĕris, n.; (of state) pŏtestas, ātis, f.

often, saepĕ, frĕquenter.

oil, ŏleum, ĭ, n.

old, (to denote how old) nātus, a; (of things) vĕtus, ĕris.

—— age, sĕnectūs, ūtis, f.

—— man, sĕnex, is, m.

—— woman, ănus, ūs, f.

omit, praetermitto, mĭsi, ssum, 3.

on, in, with acc. or abl.

once, (one time only) sĕmel; (— on a time, on one occasion) ălĭquando, quondam. — more, rursus, dēnuo. At —, v. immediately.

one, ūnus, a, um; (a certain) quĭdam, quaedam, etc. One . . . another, ălius . . . ălius; the —, the other, alter . . . alter.

only, mŏdŏ, sōlum, tantummŏdŏ. Not —, but also, non solum (modo) . . . sed (verum) etiam.

open (adj.), ăpertus, a, um; wide —, pătens, ntis. To be —, păteo, ui, 2.

—— (v.), ăpĕrio, ui, rtum, 4.

openly, ăpertĕ, pălam.

opinion, ŏpīnio, ōnis, f. To be of —, arbitror, 1.

opportunely, appŏsĭtē.

opportunity, occāsio, ōnis, f.; tempus, ŏris, n.

oppose, oppōno, pŏsui, ĭtum, 3 (to array against); objĭcio, jēci, ctum, 3.

opposition to, in, contrā, with acc.

oppress, vexo, 1.

oppression, injūria, ae, f.

oppressive, become, ingrăvesco, 3.

oracle, ōrācŭlum, ĭ, n.; sors (the response of an —).

orator, ōrātor, ōris, m.

oratory, ēlŏquentia, ae, f.

order (v.), jŭbeo, ssi, ssum,

PART

2, with acc.; praecĭpio, cēpi, ptum, 3, with dat.; (by proclamation) ēdīco, xi, ctum, 3, foll. by ut, ne and subj.

order (subs.), (jussus), ūs, m. (abl. only); mandātum, ĭ, n. In — that, ut; with neg., ne, quōmĭnus.

ornament, ornāmentum, ĭ, n.; dĕcus, ŏris, n.: see also badges.

Otanes, Otănes, is, m.

other, ălius, a, ud; the —, alter, ĕra, ĕrum; the —s, cētĕri, ae, a. In — respects, cētera; at — times, ălias; on the — hand, contrā.

ought, dēbeo, 2; ŏportet, ult, 2 impers., with acc. of Eng. subject.

out of reach of, extrā, with acc.

—— of doors, v. away.

outrage, vĭŏlo, 1.

outstretched, v. stretch.

over, sŭper, per, with acc.

overcome, sŭpĕro, 1. See also conquer.

overpower, opprĭmo, pressi, um, 3.

overtake, assĕquor, cūtus, 3; (in hostile sense; also of sleep) opprĭmo, pressi, ssum, 3.

overthrow, (in battle) prōflīgo, 1; dējĭcio (dēicio), jēci, ctum, 3.

overwhelm, obruo, ĭ, ŭtum, 3.

own, one's, suus, proprius, a, um.

owner, dŏmĭnus, ĭ, m.

ox, bŏs, bŏvis, c.

P

package, sarcĭna, ae, f.

pack-saddle, clītellae, ārum, f.

pain, dŏlor, ōris, m.

paint, pingo, nxi, pictum, 3.

painter, pictor, ōris, m.

painting, v. picture.

palm, (of hand) palma, ae, f.

pardon, ignosco, nōvi, nōtum, 3, with dat. Or expr. by vĕnia, grātia.

parent, părens, ntis, c.

Parrhasius, Parrhāsius, ĭ, m.

parricide, parrĭcīda, ae, m.

parrot, psittăcus, ĭ, m.

part, pars, rtis, f.

participate, partĭceps flo.

pass by, transeo, praetĕreo, 4 *irr.*

—— **out,** v. go out.

passage, translĭtus, ūs, *m.*

passion, in a, irătus, a, um.

pasture, pascuum, i, *n.*

patiently, pătienter.

pay, solvo, i, ŭtum, 3. To —— attention to, operam do, 1; —— one's respects to, sălŭto, 1.

peace, pax, pācis, *f.*

peaceful, tranquillus, a, um.

pebble, lăpis, ĭdis, *m.* ; (for voting) calcŭlus, i, *m.*

peep forth, prospĭcio, exi, ctum, 3.

penalty, damnum, i, *n.*

people, pŏpŭlus, i, *m.* ; plebs, plēbis, *f.* ; (=persons) hŏmĭnes, um, *m.*

perceive, intellĭgo, exi, ctum, 3.

Perdiccas, Perdiccas, ae, *m.*

perform, praesto, stĭti, stātum, 1 ; făcio, confĭcio, 3 ; (sacrifices) pērăgo, ēgi, actum, 3.

perfume, ŏdor, ōris, *m.*

perhaps, perchance, fortassē.

Pericles, Pĕrĭcles, is, *m.*

peril, v. danger.

perish, pĕreo, 4 *irr.* ; occumbo, cŭbui, ĭtum, 3.

perplexed, incertus, a, um.

perseverance, persĕvērantia, ae, *f.*

Persia, Persis, ĭdis, *f.*

Persian, Persa, ae, *m. Adj.* Persĭcus, a, um.

persistency, constantia, persĕvērantia, ae, *f.*

person, (body) corpus, ŏris, *n.* ; (man) hŏmo, ĭnis, *c.*

petition, expr. by pēto, īvi, ĭtum, 3.

Phalaris, Phălăris, ĭdis, *m.*

Philip, Philippus, i, *m.*

Philippides, Philippĭdes, is, *m.*

philosopher, phĭlŏsŏphus, i, *m.*

philosophy, phĭlŏsŏphia, săpientia, ae, *f.*

Phintias, Phintias, ae, *m.*

Phocion, Phōcion, ōnis, *m.*

Phormio, Phormio, ōnis, *m.*

physician, mĕdĭcus, i, *m.*

picture, pictūra, ae, *f.* ; tăbŭla, ae, *f.*

piece of land, ăger, gri, *m.*

pierce, transfĭgo, xi, xum, 3.

pirate, praedo, ōnis, *m.* ; pīrāta, ae, *m.*

Pisistratus, Pīsistrătus, i, *m.*

pitch, (camp) pōno, pŏsui, ĭtum, 3.

pitiable, mĭsĕrăbĭlis, e.

place (*subs.*), lŏcus, i, *m.* ; *pl.* -i and -a, *m. & n.* To take —, v. to happen.

—— (*v.*), pōno, pŏsui, ĭtum, 3 ; (for safety) dēpōno, 3.

—— **beneath,** subjĭcio, jēci, ctum, 3.

—— **before,** v. set over.

—— **on, over, upon,** impōno, appōno, 3.

plain, campus, i, *m.* Of the —, campester, tris, tre.

plan, consĭlium, i, *n.*

plant, (a tree, &c.) sēro, sēvi, sătum, 3 ; (ground) consēro, 3.

platform, suggestus, ūs, *m.*

play, (drama) făbŭla, ae, *f.*

please, (to give pleasure to) plăceo, 2, with *dat.* ; dēlecto, 1 ; (choose, will) lĭbet, 2 *impers.*, with *dat.* of Eng. subject. To be —d, gaudeo, gāvīsus, 2.

pleasing, grātus, jūcundus, a, um.

pleasure, vŏluptas, ātis, *f.*

plebeian order, plebs, ēbis, *f.*

plentifully, cōpiōsē.

pluck out, ēvello, i, vulsum, 3.

plunder (*v.*), praedor, 1.

plunge, mergo, submergo, si, sum, 3.

Plutarch, Plūtarchus, i, *m.*

poem, carmen, ĭnis, *n.*

poet, pŏēta, ae, *m.*

point out, indĭco, monstro, 1.

poison, vĕnēnum, i, *n.*

Polemo, Pŏlēmon, ōnis, *m.*

Pompey, Pompēius (trisyll.), i, *m.*

poor, pauper, ĕris, *m.*

populace, plebs, plēbis, *f.*

Porsena, Porsĕna, ae, *m.*

portend, portendo, di, tum, 3.

portrait, imāgo, ĭnis, *f.*

position, v. place.

possess, hăbeo, 2 ; (in fig.

sense, Ex. 7) tĕneo, ui, tentum, 2.

possession, possessio, ōnis, *f.*

—— **of, take,** occŭpo, 1.

postpone, differo, distŭli, dīlātum, 3 *irr.*

pour, fundo, fūdi, sum, 3.

poverty, paupertas, ātis, *f.* ; (destitution) ĕgestas, ātis, *f.*

power, pŏtestas, ātis, *f.* ; pŏtentia, ae, *f.* ; (energy, vigour) vis, *f.*

powerful, pŏtens, ntis.

practise, mĕdĭtor, 1 ; exerceo, 2.

praise (*subs.*), laus, dis, *f.*

—— (*v.*), laudo, 1.

praiseworthy, laude dignus, laudandus, a, um.

pray, prĕcor, 1. Colloq., pray ! quaeso, tandem.

preceptor, v. teacher.

prefer, (before *inf.*) mālo, *irr.* ; (before *subs.*) praefĕro, 3 *irr.* ; with *acc.* and *dat.*

prepare, păro, appăro, 1 ; (arrange) instruo, xi, ctum, 3 ; (to cook food) cŏquo, xi, ctum, 3.

present (*v.*), do, v. give ; dōno, 1 ; (to offer, set before one) prōpōno, pŏsui, ĭtum, 3.

—— (*subs.*), v. gift.

—— (*adj.*), to be —, adsum, intersum, *irr.*, with *dat.*

presently, mox, deindĕ.

preserve, servo, conservo, 1.

press on, insto, stĭti, stātum, 1.

pretend, simŭlo, 1.

prevail, (prove stronger) văleo, 2.

—— **upon,** commŏveo, mōvi, tum, 2 ; perpello, pŭli, pulsum, 3.

prevent, prŏhĭbeo, 2; obsto, stĭti, stātum, 1, with *dat.*

Prexaspes, Prexaspes, is, *m.*

price, prĕtium, i, *n.* At a high or low —, magni, parvi.

pride (*subs.*), sŭperbia, ae, *f.*

—— **oneself,** sŭperbio, 4.

priest, priestess, săcerdos, ōtis, *c.*

priesthood, săcerdōtium, i, *n.*

prison, carcer, ĕris, *m.*

prisoner, captĭvus, i, *m.*
prize, praemĭum, i, *n.*
proceed, pergo, perrexi, ctum, 3.·
proconsular, prōconsŭlāris, e.
prodigy, prōdĭgĭum, i, *n.*
profit, prōsum, *irr.,* with *dat.*
profligacy, luxŭria, nĕquĭtia, ae, *f.*
prohibition, interdictio, ōnis, *f.*
prolong, dūco, xi, ctum, 3.
promise (*v.*), pollĭceor, 2; prōmitto, mĭsi, ssum, 3.
———— (*subs.*), prōmissum, i, *n.*
pronounce, (utter) dico, xi, ctum, 3.
proof, give, prŏbo, 1.
propagate, prŏpăgo, 1.
property, res, *pl.*; res fămĭliāris; (landed) agri, ōrum, *m.*
propose, affĕro, attŭli, allātum, 3 *irr.*
Propylaea, Prŏpȳlaea, ōrum, *n.*
proscribe, proscrĭbo, psi, ptum, 3.
Protogenes, Prōtŏgĕnes, is, *m.*
prove, convinco, vici, ctum, 3.
province, prŏvincia, ae, *f.*
provision, make, prospĭcio, exi, ctum, 3, with *dat.*
provocation, without, ultro, *adv.*
prudence, prūdentia, ae, *f.*
Ptolemy, Ptŏlĕmaeus, i, *m.*
public (*adj.*), publĭcus, a, um; — place, publĭcum, after *prep.*
———— (*subs.*), (the common —) vulgus, i, *n.* and *m.*
publicly, often expr. by prefix: e.g. prōnuntio, 1 (to announce —).
puff up, inflo, 1.
pull down, (a house) dējĭcio (dēĭcio), jēci, ctum, 3.
——— **out,** rĕvello, i, vulsum, 3.
punish, poenā or supplĭcio afficio, 3 (to visit with punishment); to be —ed, plector, 3.
punishment, poena, ae, *f.*; (severe, capital) supplĭcium, i, *n.*
pupil, discĭpŭlus, i, *m.*

purchase, *v.* buy.
purple, — robe, purpŭra, ae, *f. Adj.* purpŭreus, a, um.
purpose, prŏpŏsĭtum, i, *n.* For the — of, grātiā, causā.
purposely, consultō.
pursue, insĕquor, (and overtake) persĕquor, cŭtus, 3.
pursuit, (favourite) stŭdium, i, *n.*
put, pōno, impōno, pŏsui, ĭtum, 3; also sometimes comps. of jăcio; as, injĭcio, conjĭcio (cōĭcio), jēci, ctum, 3.
——— **on,** induo, i, ŭtum, 3.
——— **to death,** *v.* kill.
——— **to the sword,** confōdio, fōdi, ssum, 3; obtrunco, 1.
——— **up at,** dēverto, ti, sum, 3.
Pyrrhus, Pyrrhus, i, *m.*

Q

quail, cŏturnix, icis, *f.*
quantity, pondus, ĕris, *n.*
quarrel, rixa, ae, *f.*
queen, rēgina, ae, *f.*
question, put a, *v.* ask.
questioning, percontātio, ōnis, *f.*
quiet, tranquillus, quiētus, a, um.
quietly, quiētē, tranquillē, plăcĭdē.
Quintus, Quintus, i, *m.* (Q.).
quit, *v.* depart.
quite, admŏdum.

R

race, gĕnus, ĕris, *n.*
rail at, insector, 1.
rain, imber, bris, *m.*
raise, tollo, sustŭli, sublātum, 3; allĕvo, 1.
raising, (of the voice) contentio, ōnis, *f.*
rank, (in army) ordo, ĭnis, *m.*
rash, tĕmĕrārius, a, um.
rashness, tĕmĕrĭtas, ātis, *f.*
rather, pŏtius, măgis: (— than any other) pŏtissimum.
raven, corvus, i, *m.*
reach, pervĕnio, vēni, ventum, 4.
read, lĕgo, lēgi, ctum, 3; (aloud) rĕcĭto, 1.
——— **through,** perlĕgo, 3.

ready, părātus, a, um.
real, vērus, a, um.
reality, vērĭtas, ātis, *f.*
rear, *v.* back.
reason (*subs.*), rătio, ōnis, *f.* By — of, *v.* account.
———— (*v.*), dissĕro, ui, rtum, 3.
recal, rĕvŏco, 1.
receive, accĭpio, cēpi, ptum, 3.
recognition, rĕcognĭtio, ōnis, *f.*
recognize, agnosco, uōvi, nĭtum, 3.
record, mĕmŏria, ae, *f.*
recount, *v.* relate.
recourse, have, convertor, sus, 3; confūgio, fūgi, fūgĭtum, 3.
recover, rĕcĭpio, cēpi, ptum, 3.
red-hot, ardens, ntis.
reflection, cōgĭtātio, ōnis, *f.*
refrain, abstĭneo, ui, tentum, 2.
refresh, rĕfĭcio, fēci, ctum, 3.
refuse, nĕgo, rĕcūso, 1. Expr. by non placet, with *dat.*
regret (*v.*), paenĭtet, 2 *impers.,* with *acc.*
———— (*subs.*), dēsĭdĕrium, i, *n.*
rehearse, rĕcĭto, 1.
reign, regno, 1.
reject, rĕpŭdio, 1.
relate, narro, (to the end) ēnarro, 1.
relation, *v.* kinsman.
release, lībĕro, 1.
relieve, lĕvo, exŏnĕro, 1.
reluctantly, *v.* unwillingly.
remain, măneo, si, sum, 2.
remark, *v.* say.
remarkable, insignis, e; ēgrĕgius, a, um.
remedy (*subs.*), rĕmĕdium, *n.*
———— (*v.*), (amend) corrĭgo, exi, ctum, 3.
remember, mĕmĭni, *def.*; rĕcordor, 1.
remote, rĕmōtus, a, um.
remove, rĕmŏveo, āmŏveo, 2 (*trans.*); migro, 1 (*intrans.*).
rend, scindo, conscindo, scĭdi, ssum, 3.
render, (account) reddo, dĭdi, dĭtum, 3; (thanks) grātias ago or habeo.

renew, rĕnŏvo, rĕdintegro, 1.

renown, glōria, ae, *f.*

renowned, clārus, inclĭtus, a, um. To be —, flōreo, 2.

repel, discŭtio, ssi, ssum, 3.

replace, rĕpōno, pōsui, ĭtum, 3.

reply, v. answer.

report, fĕro, 3 *irr.*; esp. ferunt, fertur, it is (currently) —ed.

reprehend, rĕprĕhendo, di, sum, 3.

repress, prĕmo, ssi, ssum, 3.

repudiate, v. reject.

reputation, v. glory, praise.

request (*v.*), pĕto, ivi, ĭtum, 3; rŏgo, 1. See also beg.

—— (*subs.*), expr. by pĕto, etc.

require, v. need.

rescue, ĕrĭpio, ui, reptum, 3; vindĭco, 1.

resolute, obstĭnātus, a, um.

resolve, stătuo, constĭtuo, i, ūtum, 3.

resources, ōpes, um, *f.*

respect, show, cōlo, ui, cultum, 3; rĕvĕreor, 2; (pay one's respects to) sălūto, 1.

respiration, spirĭtus, ūs, *m.*

rest (*subs.*), quies, ōtis, *f.*; = (remainder) rĕliquus, a, um; (of persons) cētĕri, rĕliqui, ae, a.

restore, (bring back) restĭtuo, i, ūtum, 3; (repay) reddo, didi, dĭtum, 3.

restrain, reprĭmo, pressi, um, 3.

retain, rĕtĭneo, ui, tentum, 2.

retire, concēdo, ssi, ssum, 3; (— to rest) quiesco, ēvi, ētum, 3.

return (*v.*), rĕdeo, 4 *irr.*; regrĕdior, ssus, 3; rĕvertor, sus, 3.

—— (*subs.*), rĕdĭtus, ūs, *m.*

reveal, indĭco, 1; ăpĕrio, ui, rtum, 4.

revel in, diffluo, xi, xum, 3.

reverence, vĕnĕror, 1; rĕvĕrcor, 2.

—— (*subs.*), rĕvĕrentia, ae, *f.*

review, lustrātio, ōnis, *f.*

revile, mălĕdico, xi, ctum, 3, with *dat.*

reward, praemium, i, *n.*

Rhodes, Rhŏdos, i, *f.*

Rhodian, Rhŏdius, a, um.

rich, dīves, itis; lōcuples, ētis; (of fare) ŏpĭmus, a, um.

ride on, insideo, sēdi, ssum, 2.

—— **past,** praetĕrĕquĭto, 1; praetervĕhor, ctus, 3.

right (*adj.*), rectus, a, um.

right-hand, dextĕra (tra), ae, *f.*

rightly, rĭtĕ, rectĕ, jūrĕ.

ring, annŭlus (ăn-), i, *m.*

rise, rise up, (from one's seat) surgo, surrexi, ctum, 3; (in honour of one) assurgo, 3, with *dat.*; (together) consurgo, 3. Of the sun, ōrior, ortus, ōrĭri, 3 and 4.

risk, v. danger.

rival, aemŭlus, i, *m.*

river, flŭvius, i, *m.*; flūmen, ĭnis, *n.*

road, via, ae, *f.*

roaring, frĕmĭtus, ūs, *m.*

roast, torreo, ui, stum, 2.

robber, lătro, ōnis, *m.*

rod, virga, ae, *f.*

Rome, Rōma, ae, *f.*; of —, Roman, Rōmānus, a, um.

room, (space) lōcus, i, *pl.* -i and -a, *m.* and *n.*

root, rādix, icis, *f.*

round (*prep.*), circum, with *acc.*

rouse, v. arouse.

rout, fŭgo, 1; fundo, fūdi, sum, 3.

row, ordo, ĭnis, *m.*

royal, rēgius, a, um.

royalty, impĕrium, i, *n.* Of —, v. royal.

rub, tĕro, trivi, tum, 3.

rule, impĕro, 1, with *dat.* See also govern.

rush forward, prōcurro, i, rsum, 3.

S

Sabines, Săbĭni, orum, *m.*

sack, culleus, i, *m.*

sacred, săcer, cra, crum; sanctus, a, um.

sacrifice (*v.*), immŏlo, 1 (*trans.*); sacrĭfĭco, 1 (*trans.* and *intrans.*).

—— (*subs.*), sacrĭfĭcium, i, *n.*

sad, tristis, e.

safe, salvus, a, um (not compared); tūtus, a, um; incŏlŭmis, e (unharmed).

safely, tūtō (in safety); or expr. by *adj.*, v. safe.

safety, sălūs, ūtis, *f.*

sail, nāvĭgo, 1; vĕhor, ctus, 3.

sake of, for the, grātiā, with *gen.*

sale, for, vēnālis, e.

salutation, sălūtātio, ōnis, *f.*

saluter, sălūtātor, ōris, *m.*

same, idem, eădem, idem.- At the — time, simul; in the — place, ibidem.

Samnites, Samnĭtes, ium, *m.*

sand, ărēna, ae, *f.* In *pl.*, = sandy deserts.

Sardis, Sardes, ium, *f.*

Sarpedon, Sarpēdon, ōnis, *m.*

satellite, (body-guard) sătelles, ĭtis, *m.*

savage, atrox, ōcis; (belonging to a wild-beast) fĕrinus, a, um.

savagely, immānĭter.

say, dico, xi, ctum, 3; (repeatedly) dictĭto, 1. To — nothing, tăceo, 2. Is said, (often) fertur: v. report.

Scaevola, Scaevŏla, ae, *m.*

scarcely, vix.

scarcity, inōpia, ae, *f.*

school, schŏla, ae, *f.*

Scipio, Scĭpio, ōnis, *m.*

scorch, ădūro, ssi, stum, 3; (to be very hot) flagro, 1.

scoundrel, scĕlestus hŏmo.

scythe, falx, cis, *f.* Armed with —s, falcātus, a, um.

sea, măre, is, *n.*

search for, quaero, quaesivi, situm, 3.

seat, sēdes, is, *f.*; (chair) sella, ae, *f.*

secede, sēcēdo, ssi, ssum, 3.

secret, arcānus, a, um.

secretary, scriba, ae, *f.*

secretly, clam, occultē.

seditious, sēdĭtiōsus, a, um.

see, vĭdeo, vidi, sum, 2; cerno, 3.

seek, quaero (v. search); pĕto, ivi, ĭtum, 3.

seem, vĭdeor, visus, 2.

seer, vătes, is, c.

seize, comprehendo, di, sum, 3; răpio, ui, ptum; arrĭpio, ui, eptum, 3; occŭpo, 1.

SELL

sell, vendo (venundo), dĭdi, dĭtum, 3.

senate, sĕnātus, ūs, m.

senator, sĕnātor, ōris, m.; pl. oft. patres.

send, mitto, misi, ssum, 3.

—— **away**, dimitto, 3.

—— **for**, arcesso, ivi, ītum, 3.

—— **out**, ēmitto, 3.

senses, mens, ntis, f.; esp. in phr. compos mentis, in one's —s.

sentence, addīco, xi, ctum, 3; foll. by dat. of penalty (to doom to).

sepulchre, sĕpulcrum, i, n.

servant, minister, tri, m.; servus, i, m.

service, ministĕrium, offĭcium, i, n. Military —, militia, ae, f.

sesterce, sestertius, i, m.

set, (foot) infĕro, 3 irr.

—— **free**, dimitto, misi, ssum, 3.

—— **on fire**, incendo, di, sum, 3.

—— **out**, prŏfĭciscor, fectus, 3.

—— **over**, praepōno, pŏsui, ĭtum, 3; with acc. and dat.

settle, (to dwell) consĭdo, sēdi, ssum, 3: — a business, confĭcio, fēci, ctum, 3.

several, plūres, complūres, a (a good many).

—————— **times**, ălĭquŏties.

severe, (harsh, strict) dūrus, sĕvērus, a, um; of a wound, grăvis, e.

sew up, insuo, i, ūtum, 3.

shade, shadow, umbra, ae, f.

shake, concŭtio, ssi, ssum, 3.

share, pars, rtis, f.

shave, abrādo, si, sum, 3.

sheep, ŏvis, is, f.

shelter (subs.), (from sun) umbrăculum, i, n.

—————— (v.), obtĕgo, xi, ctum, 3.

shepherd, pastor, ōris, m.

shield, (Greek) clĭpeus, i, m.; (Roman) scūtum, i, n.

ship, nāvis, is, f.

shoe, (sole, sandal) crĕpĭda, ae, f.

shoemaker, sūtor, ōris, m.

shortly, brĕvi, mox; paulo post.

shoulder, hŭmĕrus (um-), i, m.

SNATCH UP

shout, clāmor, ōris, m.

show, ostendo, di, tum, 3; monstro, 1.

shrine, sacrārium, i, n.

shroud, v. cover.

shut in, up, inclūdo, si, sum, 3.

Sibylline, Sĭbyllīnus, a, um.

Sicily, Sicĭlia, ae, f.

side, lătus, ĕris, n.; (in politics) partes, ium, f. On all —s, undīque.

siege, obsĭdio, ōnis, f.

sight, conspectus, ūs, m. To catch — of, conspĭcor, 1.

signal, signum, i, n.

silence, silentium, i, n.

silent, be, tăceo, 2.

silver (subs.), argentum, i, n.

—————— (adj.), argenteus, a, um.

similar, v. like.

Sinaetas, Sinaetas, ae, m.

since (adv.), ex quo.

—————— (conj.), quŏniam.

single, singŭlāris, e; ūnus, a, um: not a —, nullus, a, um.

Sisamnes, Sisamnes, is, m.

sister, sŏror, ōris, f.

sit, sĕdeo, sēdi, ssum, 2.

—— **down**, assĭdo, consĭdo, sēdi, ssum, 3.

site, sĭtus, ūs, m.

size, magnitūdo, ĭnis, f.

sketch, dēlineo, 1.

skilfully, scītē.

skill, sollertia, ae, f.

skilled, be, calleo, ui, 2.

skin, pellis, is, f.; (thin) cŭtis, is, f.

sky, caelum, i, n.

slaughter, caedes, is, f.

slave, servus, i, m.: of a —, servīlis, e. To be a —, servio, 4, with dat.

slay, v. kill.

sleep (subs.), somnus, i, m.; (deep) sŏpor, ōris, m. To go without —, vigĭlo, 1.

—————— (v.), dormio, 4.

slender, tĕnuis, e.

slenderness, tĕnuĭtas, ātis, f.

slight, lĕvis, e.

sling, funda, ae, f.

slow, tardus, a, um.

small, parvus, a, um.

smell, ŏdor, ōris, m.

snatch up, arrĭpio, ui, eptum, 3.

STALL

so, (with adj.) tam, ĭdeo. As conj., Ĭtā, Ĭtăquĕ.

—— **many**, tot, indecl.

—— **much**, tantum.

—— **great**, tantus, a, um.

Socrates, Sōcrătes, is, m.

sojourn, commŏror, 1.

soldier, miles, ĭtis, c.

solitude, sōlĭtūdo, ĭnis, f.

Solon, Sŏlōn, ōnis, m.

some, nonnullus, a, um; (— one, — thing), ălĭquis, qua, quid and quod; (of number) ălĭquot: — day or time, ălĭquando.

—————— **times**, ălĭquando, non-nunquam.

son, fīlius, i, m.

—— **in law**, gĕner, ĕri, m.

soon, mox, brĕvi. As — as, simul atque (ac), ut prīmum.

Sophocles, Sŏphocles, is, m.

sorrow, dŏlor, ōris, m.

sort, of what, quālis, e.

sovereign, princeps, ĭpis, m.

spacious, amplus, a, um.

Spain, Hispānia, ae, f.

spare, parco, pĕperci, parcĭtum and -sum, 3, with dat.

sparingly, parcē.

Sparta, Sparta, ae, f.

Spartan (subs.), Spartānus, i, m.

—————— (adj.), v. Lacedaemonian. A — woman, Lăcaena, ae, f.

speak, lŏquor, cūtus, 3.

spear, hasta, lancea, ae, f.

speech, (oration) ōrātio, ōnis, f.; (saying) dictum, i, n.

spend, (use quite up) consūmo, psi, ptum, 3; (time, life) āgo, ēgi, actum, 3.

spirit, ănĭmus, i, m.

spoil, (armour stripped off) spŏlia, ōrum, n.

sport, lūdĭbrium, i, n.

spot, v. place. On the —, illĭco, stătim. At this —, hic.

spread over, obdūco, xi, ctum, 3.

spring, fons, ntis, m.

spring from, nascor, nātus, 3.

sprinkle, spargo, si, sum, 3.

squeeze out, exprimo, essi, essum, 3.

staff, băcŭlus, i, m.; (a little —) băcillus, i, m.; (rod) virga, ae, f.

stall, tăberna, ae, f.

STAND	SYRIA	THEATRE

stand, sto, stĕti, stătum, 1.
—— **around**, circumsto, stĕti, stătum, 1.
—— **open**, păteo, ui, 2.
—— **still**, consisto, stiti, stitum, 3.
state (*subs.*), civitas, ătis, *f.*; respublica, reipublicae, *f.* On behalf of the —, publicē.
—— (*v.*), v. say.
stay, (dwell) commŏror, versor, 1.
steady, certus, a, um.
steep, arduus, a, um.
step forth, prōcēdo, ssi, ssum, 3.
stern, (of ship)puppis, is, *f.*
stick, v. staff.
still (*adj.*), v. motionless.
—— (*adv.*), ădhuc, ĕtiam-num.
—— (*conj.*), tămen. [3.
stipulate, păciscor, pactus,
stone, lăpis, ĭdis, *m.*; (large) saxum, i, *n.*
storm, tempestas, ătis, *f.*
story, făbŭla, ae, *f.*
straight, directus, a, um.
straightway, v. immediately.
strange, (novel) nŏvus, (wonderful) mirus, a, um.
strangeness, nŏvĭtas, ătis, *f.*
stranger, hospes, itis, *m.*
stratagem, fraus, dis, *f.*; dŏlus, i, *m.*
strength, vires, ium, *f.*
stretch out, porrĭgo, exi, ctum, 3.
strict, sĕvērus, a, um.
strike, fĕrio (percŭtio), percussi, ssum, 4 and 3; (by a missile) p. *part.* ictus, a, um.
strip off, exuo, i, ūtum, 3; (vestem) detrăho, 3, with *dat.*
stripes, verbĕra, um, *n.*
strive, certo, 1.
strong, vălĭdus, firmus, a, um.
struck(with astonishment), perculsus, a, um.
studio, officina, pergŭla, ae, *f.*
study (*subs.*), (pursuit) stŭdium, i, *n.*
—— (*v.*), stŭdeo, ui, 2, with *dat.*
stupid, stŏlĭdus, a, um.
style, v. call.
subdue, dŏmo, ui, ĭtum, 1; sŭbigo, ēgi, actum, 3; dēvinco, vici, ctum, 3.

subject, (matter) res, rĕi, *f.*
Sublician, sublicius, a, um (made of piles).
subsequently, v. afterwards.
succeed, succēdo, ssi, ssum, 3.
successor, successor, ōris, *m.*
succour, subvĕnio, vēni, ntum, 4, with *dat.*
such, tālis, e; (so large) tantus, a, um. In —a manner, ĭtā.
sudden, sŭbĭtus, a, um.
suddenly, sŭbĭtō, rĕpentē.
sue for, pĕto, ivi, ĭtum, 3.
suffer, pătior, ssus, 3. To —punishment, poenas do, 1.
sufficient, -ly, sătis. Not —, părum.
sum, (of money) pĕcūnia, ae, *f.*
summon, vŏco, 1.
sumptuous, lautus, a, um.
sun (*subs.*), sol, sōlis, *m.*: — rise, — set, sōlis ortus, occāsus, ūs, *m.*
—— **oneself**, apricor, 1.
sunny, apricus, a, um.
sup, cēno, 1.
supper, cēna, ae, *f.*
supply, cōpia, ae, *f.*
support, v. maintain.
supported, be, (rest on) innitor, subnitor, nisus and xus, 3.
suppress, contĭneo, ui, tentum, 2.
sure, certus, a, um.
surely, certē.
surety, vas, vădis, *m.*
surname, cognōmen, ĭnis, *n.*
surprised, be, miror, admiror, 1.
surrender, dēdĭtio, ōnis, *f.*
suspicion, suspicio, ōnis, *f.*
sustain, sustĭneo, ui, tentum, 2.
swear, jūro, 1: *p.p.* jūrātus, bound by oath.
sweet, suăvis, e; dulcis, e.
swift, cĕler, ĕris, e; vēlox, ōcis.
swiftness, vēlōcĭtas, cĕlĕrĭtas, ătis, *f.*
swim across, trāno, 1.
sword, glădius, i, *m.*
Syracuse, Syrăcūsae, ārum, *f.*
Syria, Syria, ae, *f.*

T

table, mensa, ae, *f.*
tail, cauda, ae, *f.*
take, căpio, cēpi, captum, 3. Of persons and animals, dūco, v. lead.
—— **away**, ădĭmo, ēmi, emptum; ēripio, ui, reptum, 3; both with *acc.* and *dat.*; aufĕro, abstŭli, ablātum, 3 *irr.*
—— **back**, (of persons) rēdūco, xi, ctum, 3.
—— **place**, v. happen.
—— **prisoner**, căpio, 3.
—— **to wife**, dūco, 3.
—— **up**, tollo, sustŭli, sublātum; sūmo, mpsi, mptum, 3: —a position, sto, consisto, v. stand.
talent, (money) tălentum, i, *n.*
tallness, prōcērĭtas, ătis, *f.*
Tarquinii, the, Tarquinii, ōrum, *m.*
task, lăbor, ōris, *f.*
taste, gusto, dēgusto, 1.
teach, dŏceo, ui, ctum, 2; see also train.
teacher, doctor, praeceptor, ōris, *m.*; măgister, tri, *m.*
tear (*subs.*), lacrĭma, ae, *f.*; flētus, ūs, *m.* (weeping).
tear out, ēruo, i, ūtum, 3.
—— **in pieces**, lăcĕro, dilănio, 1.
tell, v. say, order.
temper, (cast of mind) ingĕnium, i, *n.*; mens, ntis, *f.*
temperance, tempĕrantia, ae, *f.*
temperate, frūgi, *indecl.*
temple, templum, fānum, i, *n.*
tent, tentōrium, tăbernācŭlum, i, *n.*
tenth, dĕcĭmus, a, um.
terms, condicio, ōnis, *f.*
terrible, terrĭbĭlis, e.
terrify, terreo, ui, ĭtum, 2.
territories, fines, ium, *m.*
terror, terror, ōris, *m.*; mĕtus, ūs, *m.*
testify to, testor, 1.
than, quam.
that, ut, quo; — not, nē; but —, quin.
theatre, theātrum, i, *n.*

| THEMISTOCLES | TYRANT | USE |

Themistocles, Thĕmistŏcles, is, *m.*

then, tum, deindĕ.

there, Ibi ; from —, indĕ ; to be —, adsum, *irr.*

therefore, ergo, Ităquĕ, Igitur, Ideo (on that account).

thereupon, tum, deindĕ.

Thermopylae, Thermŏpўlae, ārum, *f.*

thing, res, rĕi, *f.* Or expr. by *neut.* of *adj.* or *pron.*

think, pŭto, existĭmo, arbitror, 1 ; reor, rătus, 2 : (to reflect, consider) cōgito, 1.

thirst, sitis, is, *f.* Fig., v. desire.

thong, lōrum, i, *n.*

thorn, spina, ae, *f.*

thoroughly, pĕnĭtus.

though, v. although. As —, quăsi.

threaten, mĭnor, 1 ; with *dat.* of person.

threats, mĭnae, ārum, *f.*

threshold, limen, Inis, *n.*

through, per, with *acc.*

throw away, down, abjĭcio, dējĭcio (dēĭcio), prōjĭcio, jēci, jectum, 3.

—— **in, into,** conjĭcio, 3.

—— **over,** objĭcio, 3.

thrust away, dēpello, pŭli, pulsum, 3.

Tiber, Tĭbĕris, is, im, *m.*

tidings, nuntius, i, *m.*

tie, v. bind.

time, tempus, ŏris, *n.* At that —, tum. At —s, v. sometimes.

tire, fătĭgo, (— out) dēfătĭgo, 1.

tired, fessus, a, um. To be —, taedet, uit and pertaesum est, 2 *impers.* ; with *acc.* of subject.

Titus, Titus, i, *m.* (T.)

to, ad, with *acc.* Before verb, oft., ut, qui, with *subj.*

to-day, hŏdiĕ.

together, ūnā ; co-, con-, in comp. ; (in succession) continuus, a, um.

tomb, sĕpulcrum, i, *n.*

tongue, lingua, ae, *f.*

too (also), et, quidem. See also excessively.

tooth, dens, ntis, *m.*

top of, summus, a, um, in agr. with subs.

torment (*subs.*), v. torture.

tortoise, testūdo, Inis, *f.*

torture (*v.*), torqueo, si, tum, 2.

torture (*subs.*), tormentum, supplicium, i, *n.* (usu. *pl.* in this sense) ; (acute suffering) crūciātus, ūs, *m.*

towards, ad ; (of feeling) ergā, with *acc.* In geog. sense, versus, with *acc.* ; put after its noun.

tower, turris, is, *f.*

town, oppidum, i, *n.*

tragedy, trăgoedia, ae, *f.*

tragic, trăgĭcus, a, um.

train, instĭtuo, i, ūtum, 3 ; exerceo, 2.

traitor, prōdĭtor, ōris, *m.*

transact, tractо, 1.

transfer, transfĕro, 3 *irr.*

transfix, v. pierce.

transparent, perlūcĭdus, a, um.

trappings, (of a horse) phălĕrae, ārum, *f.*

travel, permētior, mensus, 4, with viam.

treat, tracto, 1.

treatment, (in the way of cure) mĕdēla, ae, *f.*

treatise, lĭber, bri, *m.*

tree, arbor, ŏris, *f.*

trial, (legal) jūdĭcium, i, *n.* ; (experiment) expĕrimentum, i, *n.*

tribune, trĭbūnus, i, *m.*

tribute, trĭbūtum, i, *n.*

trireme, trĭrēmis, is, *f.*

triumph, hold a, triumpho, 1.

Troezen, Troezēn, ēnis, *f.*

troops, mīlites, cōpiae.

troth, by, vĕrō, sānĕ.

trouble (*subs.*), v. labour.

—— **oneself,** cūro, 1.

true, vērus, a, um.

truly, vērĕ.

truth, vērĭtas, ātis, *f.* Oft. = true things, vēra.

try, expĕrior, pertus, 4 ; tento, 1.

tunic, tŭnĭca, ae, *f.*

turn, verto, converto, inverto, ti, sum, 3.

—— **away,** āverto, 3.

—— **out,** (become) ēvĕnio, vēni, ventum, 4 ; ēvādo, si, sum, 3.

—— **round,** converto, 3.

tyranny, tўrannis, Idis, *f.*

tyrant, tўrannus, i, *m.*

U

unanimity, consensus, ūs, *m.* ; concordia, ae, *f.*

unavenged, inultus, a, um.

unburied, Inhŭmātus, a, um.

uncle, (mother's brother) ăvuncŭlus, i, *m.*

under, sub. with *acc.* and *abl.*

underground, subterrāneus, a, um.

undeserved, immĕrĭtus, Inĭquus, a, um.

unexpected, imprŏvīsus, a, um.

unforeseen, imprŏvīsus, a, um.

unfrequented, dēsertus, dēvius, a, um.

unguent, unguentum, i, *n.*

unharmed, incŏlŭmis, e.

unhonoured, Inhŏnōrātus, a, um.

unite, v. join.

universal, expr. by means of omnes.

unjust, injustus, a, um : — treatment, injūria, ae, *f.*

unjustly, injustĕ.

unknown, ignōtus, incognitus, a, um.

unless, nisi, ni.

unlike, dissimilis, e.

unmerciful, v. cruel.

unmindful, immĕmor, ōris.

unpopularity, invidia, ae, *f.*

unsuccessfully, infēlĭcĭter.

until, dōnec.

untouched, intactus, a, um.

untroubled, sēcūrus, a, um.

unusual, Inŭsĭtātus, a, um.

unwilling, to be, nōlo, 3.

unwillingly, expr. by invītus, a, um.

upon, in, sŭper, with *acc.* or *abl.* ; (concerning) de, with *abl.*

urge, hortor, 1.

use (*v.*), ūtor, with *abl.* See also accustomed.

148 VOCABULARY.

USE

use (*subs.*), ûsus, ûs, *m.*
usual, sŏlĭtus, a, um.
utmost, summus; a, um.
utter, ēdo, dĭdi, dĭtum, 3.

V

vain, vānus, a, um. In —, frustrā, nēquicquam.
valour, virtūs, ûtis, *f.*
vanquish, v. conquer, overcome.
vast, ingens, ntis.
Veientines, Vēientes, um, *m.*
Veii, Vēii, orum, *m.*
veil, with — on, vēlātus, a, um.
venture, v. dare.
verdict, sententia, ae, *f.*
verily, cērtē, ŏnimvēro.
verse, versus, ûs, *m.*
very (*adj.*), ipse, a, um.
vessel, v. ship.
victor, victorious, victor, ōris, *m.*; victrix, ĭcis, *f.* To be —, v. conquer.
victory, victōria, ae, *f.*
view, conspectus, ûs, *m.*
violate, do violence to, vĭŏlo, 1.
vision, visûm, i, *n.*
voice, vox, vōcis, *f.*
Volscians, Volsci, orum, *m.*
voluntarily, ultro.
voluntary, vŏluntārius, a, um.
vote, suffrāgium, i, *n.*
vow (*v.*), vŏveo, vōvi, tum, 2.
—— (*subs.*), vōtum, i, *n.*
voyage, nāvĭgātio, ōnis, *f.*

W

waft, (towards) afflo, 1.
wag, v. move.
wage, (war) gĕro, ssi, stum, 3.
waggon, plaustrum, i, *n.*
waggoner, būbulcus, i, *m.*
wait for, exspecto, 1; opperior, rtus, 4.

WHILE, WHILST

walk about, ĭnambŭlo, 1.
wall, (of a house) pāries, ĕtis, *m.*; of a town, mûrus, i, *m.*
wander, vāgor, 1; (away) āberro, 1.
want (*v.*), v. need.
—— (*subs.*), ĭnōpia, ae, *f.*
wanting, be, dēsum, *irr.*
wanton, effûsus, a, um (unrestrained).
war, bellum, i, *n.*
ward off, dēfendo, di, sum, 3.
warmth, v. heat.
warn, mŏneo, admŏneo, 2.
waste, lay, vasto, 1.
water, āqua, ae, *f.*
waving, fluctuans, ntis, *f.*
way, via, ae, *f.*; (manner) mŏdus, i, *m.*
weak, invălĭdus, a, um. To grow —, dēfĭcio, fēci, ctum, 3.
weaken, dēbĭlĭto, 1.
weakness, imbēcillĭtas, ātis, *f.*
wealth, dīvĭtiae, ārum, *f.*; ōpes, um, *f.*
wealthy, lōcuples, ĕtis.
weapon, tēlum, i, *n.*
wearied out, dēfessus, a, um.
weary, fessus, a, um. To be — of, taedet, uit and pertaesum est, 2, with *acc.* and *gen.*
weep, fleo, ēvi, ētum, 2.
welcome, excĭpio, cēpi, ptum, 3.
well, bĕnĕ.
—— omened, faustus, a, um.
—— read, versātus, a, um, foll. by in.
what sort of, quālis, e.
whatever, quidquid (quicquid).
when, cum, ŭt, ûbi.
whence, undĕ.
whenever, quŏties (-ens).
where, ûbi, ûbinam.
whereas, cum.
wherefore, prŏindĕ.
whereupon, quārē, tum; quo facto.
whether, in ind. questions, num or -nĕ.
while, whilst, dum, with *pres. ind.*

WORSHIP

whipping, (stripes) plāgae, ārum, *f.*
whoever, quicunque, etc.
whole, tōtus, a, um.
why, cûr, quārē.
wicked, imprŏbus, scēlestus, a, um.
wife, uxor, ōris, *f.*; conjux, ûgis, *c.* (spouse).
wild-beast, fēra, ae, *f.* Collect. vēnātio, ōnis, *f.* (—s taken in hunting).
will (*subs.*), vŏluntas, ātis, *f.*
willing, be, vŏlo, 3 *irr.*
willingly, lĭbenter.
wine, vīnum, i, *n.*
wipe away, dētergeo, si, sum, 2.
wise, săpiens, ntis.
wish, vŏlo, 3 *irr.*
with, cum, with *abl.*; (at a person's house) ăpud, with *acc.*
withdraw, (*trans.*) āmŏveo, rĕmŏveo, mōvi, tum, 2; (*intrans.*) rĕcēdo, ssi, ssum, 3.
within, intus.
without, sĭne, with *abl.* Also *adj.* expers, rtis (void of), with *gen.* or *abl.*
withstand, sustĭneo, ui, tentum, 2.
witness (*subs.*), testis, is, *c.* To call to —, testor, invŏco, 1.
—— (*v.*), (look at) specto, 1; aspĭcio, exi, ectum, 3.
wits, in possession of, mentis compos, ōtis.
woman, fēmĭna, ae: mūlier, ēris, *f.*: —'s, mŭliebris, e.
wonder at, miror, admīror, 1.
wonderful, mirus, a, um; mīrābĭlis, e; mīrĭfĭcus, a, um.
wonderfully, mīrē.
wont, v. accustomed.
wood, silva, ae, *f.*
wooden, ligneus, a, um.
word, verbum, i, *n.*; dictum, i, *n.*
work, ŏpus, ĕris, *n.*
world, orbis terrae or -arum.
worn out, confectus, a, um.
worship (*v.*), cŏlo, ui, cultum, 3.
—— (*subs.*), cultus, ûs, *m.*

WORTHLESS	YEAR	ZEUXIS

worthless, nĕquam, *indecl.*

worthy, dignus, a, um, with *abl.*

wound (*subs.*), vulnus, ĕris, *n.*

——— (*v.*), vulnĕro, 1.

wrap, (round) ămicio, ui, ctum, 4.

wreath, cŏrōna, ae, *f.*

write, scrĭbo, psi, ptum, 3.

writer, scriptor, ōris, *m.*

wrong, in moral sense, mălus, a, um.

X

Xanthippe, Xanthippē, ēs, *f.*

Xenophon, Xĕnŏphon, ontis, *m.*

Xerxes, Xerxes, is, *m.*

Y

year, annus, i, *m.* Two, three —s, biennium, triennium.

yesterday, hĕri.

yet, (still) adhūc; (however) tămen.

yield, (the palm) dēfĕro, 3 *irr.*

young, jŭvĕnis, is, *c.* ; —er, minor.

youth, jŭvĕnis, is, *c.* ; (the period of —) jŭvĕntūs, ūtis, *f.*

Z

Zeuxis, Zeuxis, is and ĭdis, *m.*

APPENDIX.

PASSAGES FROM ENGLISH AUTHORS
FOR RENDERING INTO LATIN.

1. BEFORE MARATHON.

Athens now alone remained to fulfil the object of the expedition, and Athens had to bear the brunt[1] of the danger by herself. There is no reason to suppose that Sparta evaded her obligations[2]; but the direct movement of the Persians across the Aegaean had probably taken all Greece somewhat by surprise[3]; and when the crisis came, a religious scruple caused[4] a delay which might have been fatal. The courier, Pheidippides, despatched from Athens as soon as Eretria had fallen, performed the journey of 150 miles, on foot, in forty-eight hours. He laid before[5] the Ephors an urgent request for aid, which was readily promised. But it wanted nearly a week to the full moon, and religious scruples would not permit a march during the interval. That this was no mere excuse[6] is proved by the rapid march of the 2000 Spartans, who, having started as soon as the moon had changed, reached the frontier of Athens on the third day. But on the day before, the fate of Greece had been decided,[7] and immortal glory gained by Athens.

(P. SMITH.)

---

[1] impetus.   [2] ab officio deficere.
[3] Expr. by improvisus.
[4] esse with *dat*.   [5] defero.

[6] hoc illos satis honeste nec per calumniam fecisse.
[7] Expr. by aleam jacere.

2. The Embassy of Fabius.

When the news of the fall of Saguntum reached Rome, ambassadors were immediately sent to Carthage: M. Fabius Buteo, who had been consul seven-and-twenty years before, C. Licinius Varus, and Q. Baebius Tamphilus. Their orders were simply[1] to demand that Hannibal and his principal officers[2] should be given up for their attack upon the allies of Rome in breach of the treaty, and, if this[3] were refused, to declare war. The Carthaginians tried to discuss the previous question,[4] whether the attack on Saguntum was a breach of the treaty; but to this the Romans would not listen. At length M. Fabius gathered up his toga, as if he was wrapping up something in it, and, holding it out thus folded together, he said, "Behold, here are peace and war; take which you choose!" The Carthaginian[5] suffete or judge answered, "Give whichever thou wilt." Hereupon Fabius shook out the folds of his toga,[6] saying, "Then here we give you war;" to which several members of the council shouted in answer, "With all our hearts[7] we welcome it." Thus the Roman ambassadors left Carthage, and returned straight[8] to Rome.   (Arnold.)

[1] His nil aliud mandatum nisi.   [4] illud potius disceptare. [8] gen. pl.
[2] duces.   [8] rel.   [6] sinu excusso.   [7] bono animo.

3. Artemisia.

Artemisia, the queen of Halicarnassus, whose good advice before the battle had been rejected by Xerxes, having fought her ship with distinguished gallantry,[1]

[1] cum nave sua rem fortissime gessisset.

was escaping from the rout, hotly pursued[2] by the Athenian Ameinias. The ship of another Carian prince lay full in her course; she charged it and sank it with its whole crew.[3] Ameinias, not knowing[4] that the ship before him was that of the obnoxious[5] woman who had dared to fight with men, and for whose capture the Athenians had offered a high reward, took[6] this act as a sign of desertion to the Greeks, and gave up the pursuit. Xerxes noticed the deed,[7] and his courtiers,[8] knowing Artemisia's vessel by her flag, exclaimed, "Seest thou, Master, how well Artemisia fights, and how she has just[9] sunk a ship of the enemy?" "Yes," replied the king, "my men have behaved like women; my women like men!"   (P. SMITH.)

[2] insto, insequor.
[3] una cum cunctis qui in ea vehebantur.
[4] subj.: St. L. G. 476.
[5] invisus.
[6] hoc factum interpretatus quasi (with *subj.*).   [7] *rel.*
[8] purpurati.
[9] nunc cum maxime, or simply modo.

4. HANNIBAL STIMULATES HIS SOLDIERS.

At length Hannibal received the news of the Roman embassy to Carthage, and the actual declaration[1] of war; his officers also had returned from Cisalpine Gaul. "The natural difficulties[2] of the passage of the Alps were great," they said, "but by no means insuperable; while the disposition of the Gauls was most friendly,[3] and they were eagerly expecting his arrival." Then Hannibal called his soldiers together, and told them openly that

[1] *part.*
[2] Alpes quidem trajectu difficiles esse.
[3] ipsos Gallos Poenis favere.

he was going to lead them into Italy. " The Romans," he said, " have demanded that I and my principal officers should be delivered up to them as malefactors. Soldiers, will you suffer such an indignity⁴? The Gauls are holding out their arms to us, inviting us to come to them, and to assist them in revenging their manifold injuries. And the country which we shall invade, so rich in corn and wine and oil, so full of flocks and herds, so covered with flourishing cities, will be the richest prize⁵ that could be offered by the gods to reward your valour." One common⁶ shout from the soldiers assured him of their readiness to follow him. He thanked them, fixed the day on which they were to be ready to march, and then dismissed them. (ARNOLD.)

---

⁴ tam indigna.   ⁵ quo nihil opulentius . . .

⁶ cunctorum.

---

5. JOANNA OF CASTILE.

The whole royal authority in Castile¹ ought of course to have devolved² upon Joanna. But the shock³ occasioned by a disaster so unexpected as the death of her husband, completed the disorder⁴ of her understanding, and her incapacity⁵ for government. During all the time of Philip's sickness,⁶ no entreaty could prevail upon her to leave him for a moment. When he expired, however, she did not shed one tear or utter a single groan. Her grief was silent and settled. She continued to watch⁷ the

---

¹ apud Castilienses.   ⁴ part.   ⁵ adj.
² pervenio.   ⁶ valetudo.
³ offensio (with gen. only).   ⁷ assideo.

body with the same tenderness and attention as if it had
been alive; and though at last she permitted it to be
buried, she soon removed it from the tomb to her own
apartment.[8]   There it was laid upon a bed of state, in a
splendid [9] dress; and having heard from some monk a
legendary tale [10] of a king who revived after he had been
dead fourteen years, she kept her eyes almost constantly
fixed on the body, waiting for the happy moment of its
return to life.   (ROBERTSON.)

---

[8] camera.   [9] magnificus.   [10] fabula commenticia.

---

6. MARDONIUS COUNSELS XERXES AFTER HIS DEFEAT AT SALAMIS.

Mardonius framed [1] his advice to suit the king's in-
clination and his own ambition.   "Grieve [2] not, Master,"
said he, " over thy loss.   Our hopes do not rest on a few
planks, but on our brave steeds and horsemen.   Not one
of these men will dare to land and meet our army.   The
shame of defeat affects only the Phœnicians and Egyptians, the Cyprians and Cilicians.   Thy own faithful
Persians are unbroken and undisgraced.[3]   Make them not
a laughing-stock to the Greeks."   He advised Xerxes to
advance upon Peloponnesus, either immediately or at his
leisure,[4] for it was completely in his power; or, if the
king were minded to return home, Mardonius asked to
be left behind with 300,000 chosen troops, and he would
bring Greece beneath his sway.   This advice was

---

[1] accommodo.

[2] Give the advice of Mardonius in the oblique form.

[3] dedecoris expertes.

[4] tempore suo.

seconded[5] by Artemisia, who represented[6] that the whole danger would fall upon Mardonius and his troops.   Nor did she[7] omit to flatter the king with the idea that he would now return in triumph,[8] since the chief purpose of his expedition was fulfilled by the destruction of Athens.   This advice was the more acceptable to Xerxes as it exactly reflected[9] his own thoughts.   (P. Smith.)

---

[5] suffrägor, 1 *dep.*, with *dat.*   [8] *part.*
[6] affirmo.   [7] eadem.   [9] congruo.

---

7. After Cannae.

Less than six thousand men of Hannibal's army had fallen : no greater price had he paid[1] for the total destruction[2] of more than eighty thousand of the enemy, for the capture[3] of their two camps, for the utter annihilation,[3] as it seemed, of all their means for offensive warfare.   It is no wonder that[4] the spirits of the Carthaginian officers were elated by this unequalled[5] victory. Maharbal, seeing what his cavalry had done, said to Hannibal, "Let me advance instantly with the horse, and do thou follow to support me; in four days from this time thou shalt sup in the Capitol."   There are moments when rashness is[6] wisdom; and it may be that this was one of them.   The statue of the goddess Victory in the Capitol[7] may well have trembled in every limb on that day, and have

---

[1] tanti (*or* tantuli) constitit.   Note 17.
[2] internecio.   [3] *part.*
[4] si with *indic.*   Comp. Ex. 69,   [5] singularis.   [6] partes sustinet.
      [7] Victoria illa Capitoliensis.

dropped her wings, as if for ever. But Hannibal came not; and if panic had for one moment unnerved the iron courage of the Roman aristocracy,[8] on the next their inborn spirit revived. (ARNOLD.)

---

[8] principes *or* optimates.

---

8. RETIREMENT OF CHARLES V.

Nor was he satisfied with these acts of mortification,[1] which, however severe, were not unexampled.[2] . . . He resolved to celebrate his own obsequies before his death.[3] He ordered his tomb to be erected in the chapel of the monastery. His domestics marched thither in funeral procession, with black tapers[4] in their hands. He himself followed in his shroud.[5] He was laid in his coffin with much solemnity. The service for the dead was chanted, and Charles joined in the prayers which were offered up for the rest of his soul, mingling his tears with those which his attendants shed, as if they had been celebrating a real funeral. The ceremony closed with sprinkling holy water[6] on the coffin in the usual form; and all the assistants retiring, the doors of the chapel were shut. Then Charles rose out of the coffin, and withdrew to his apartment, full[7] of those awful sentiments[8] which such a singular solemnity was calculated to inspire. But either the fatiguing length[9] of the

---

[1] his sui tormentis.
[2] parum novus.
[3] vivus.   [4] candēla.
[5] tunica funebri amictus.

[6] aqua lustralis.
[7] imbutus.
[8] sanctae sententiae.
[9] nimis productae precationes.

ceremony, or the impression which the image of death [10] left on his mind, affected him so much, that next day he was seized with a fever. His feeble frame could not long resist its violence, and he expired on the twenty-first of September. _____ (ROBERTSON.)

[10] mors repraesentata.

9. GLORY OF MILTIADES.

The glory of Marathon belongs [1] to Miltiades alone. Of all the generals, he only had experience [2] to discern those elements of Oriental weakness which were yet to be revealed, and the skill to suit his plan of battle to the enemy. He saw, not only that safety lay in victory, but that the very [3] isolation of Athens opened a boundless prospect [4] to her ambition. He implored Callimachus to earn for himself a name more glorious than that of Harmodius and Aristogeiton,[5] by at once saving his country from the fate prepared for her under Hippias, and raising her to become the first state in Greece. If they delayed to fight, the disturbance of men's minds [6] at Athens would soon end in submission; but if the battle were fought before unsoundness [7] revealed itself in the city, and while Heaven still granted them fair play,[8] they were well able to overcome the enemy. Callimachus gave his vote for battle [9]; and the four generals who had supported Miltiades in the debate, gave up to him their turn of command. (P. SMITH.)

[1] penes est.
[2] experimento facto.
[3] illud ipsum quod . . .
[4] spes.
[5] illā Harmodii et A. laude majorem sibi compararet.

[6] adeo omnium animos confusos esse.
[7] vitiosum illud.
[8] Use ex aequo.
[9] secundum dimicationem (proelii discrimen).

10. THE THAW, FEBRUARY 1784.

I congratulate you on the thaw[1]; I suppose it is an universal blessing, and probably felt all over Europe. I myself am the better for it,[2] who wanted nothing that might make the frost supportable[3]; what reason, therefore, have they to rejoice, who, being in want of all things, were exposed[4] to its utmost rigour[5]! The ice in my ink,[6] however, is not yet dissolved. It was long before the frost seized it,[7] but at last it prevailed. The 'Sofa'[8] has consequently received little or no addition since.[9] It consists at present of four books and a part of a fifth; when the sixth is finished, the work is accomplished[10]; but if I may judge by my present inability, that period is at a considerable distance.

It makes a capital figure[11] among the comforts we enjoyed during the long severity of the season, that the same *incognito*[12] to all except ourselves, made us his almoners this year likewise, as he did the last, and to the same amount. Some we have been enabled, I suppose, to save from perishing, and certainly many from the most pinching necessity.   (COWPER, *Letters.*)

---

[1] tempestatis (temporis) mitigatio.   [2] eo.
[3] ad frigora toleranda.
[4] obnoxius.
[5] inclementia.
[6] atramentum gelu concretum.

[7] Say, *it long resisted the cold.*
[8] 'Sofa' carmen.
[9] nihil auctius.   [10] absolvo.
[11] haud minimum.
[12] ille beneficiorum suorum dissimulator.

---

11. DEATH OF BAYARD.

He put himself at the head of the men at arms,[1] and, animating them by his presence and example to sustain

[1] graviter armati (gravis armaturae) equites.

the whole shock of the enemy's troops, he gained time
for the rest of his countrymen to make good their retreat.
But in this service he received a wound which he immediately perceived to be mortal, and being unable to
continue any longer on horseback, he ordered one of his
attendants to place him under a tree with his face
towards the enemy; then fixing his eyes on the guard[2]
of his sword, which he held up instead of a cross,[3]
he addressed his prayers to God, and in this posture,
which became his character both as a soldier and as a
Christian, he calmly awaited the approach of death.
Bourbon, who led the foremost of the enemy's troops,
found him in this situation, and expressed regret and
pity at the sight. "Pity not me," cried the high-spirited
Chevalier[4]: "I die[5] as a man of honour ought, in the
discharge of my duty. They, indeed, are cbjects of pity
who fight against their king, their country, and their
oath." He died, as his ancestors for several generations
had done, on the field of battle.   (ROBERTSON.)

[2] capulus, *handle*; of which the guard was part.   [3] sancta crux.

[4] Simply, inquit. See p. 8, par. 2.   [5] ita morior . . .

12. PYTHAGORAS.

The chief distinctive doctrine of Pythagoras[1] was that
of the transmigration[2] of souls from body to body both
of men and animals, which, as we have seen, was held by
the Egyptians from a remote period. This doctrine was
used to account for those strange phenomena[3] of con-

[1] Pythagorae nil magis pro-prium . . .

[2] Expr. by verb (migro).

[3] quae in mentibus hominum mi-rabiliter geruntur (fiunt).

sciousness which Plato represents Socrates also as referring to knowledge[4] acquired in a former state of
existence. Pythagoras found it useful too for acquiring[5]
religious ascendency over his disciples. He did not
disdain the arts by which intellectual reformers[6] have
often appealed to the imaginations of common men. He
declared that he himself had lived on earth in the person
of the Trojan hero Euphorbus, whom Menelaus had slain
and dedicated his shield in the temple of Hera near
Mycenae; and, in proof of the assertion, Pythagoras took
down the shield from the midst of all the other votive
offerings[7]. . . . He was reverenced by his disciples as
a superior being.[8] Their unquestioning faith in his
teaching has passed into the proverb, *Ipse dixit* —" *He
has said it.*" (P. SMITH.)

[4] cognitiones. [5] concilio, 1. [7] donaria.
[6] doctrinarum auctores atque [8] divino quodam afflatu praedi-
emendatores. tus; *or* deus.

13. PHOKION (1).

Phokion was a citizen of small means, son of a pestle-
maker.[1] Born about the year 402 B.C., he was about
twenty years older than Demosthenes. At what precise
time his political career commenced,[2] we do not know;
but he lived to the great age of 84, and was a conspicuous
man throughout the last half-century of his life. He
becomes known first as a military officer,[3] having served

[1] pistillorum faber; or perhaps, ferrarius, intestinarius, etc.)
pistillarius, though the word ap- [2] Expr. by ad rempublicam acce-
pears not to occur. (Cf. faber dere. [3] rebus bellicis.

under Chabrias,[4] to whom he was greatly attached,[5] at
the battle of Naxos in 376 B.C. He was a man of thorough
personal bravery, and considerable talents for command;
of hardy and enduring temperament, insensible to cold
or fatigue; strictly simple in his habits, and, above all,
superior to every kind of personal corruption.[6] His
abstinence[7] from plunder and peculation, when on naval
expeditions, formed an honourable contrast[8] with other
Athenian admirals, and procured[9] for him much esteem
on the part of his maritime allies. Hence probably his
surname of Phokion the Good.   (GROTE.)

[4] Chabria duce.
[5] cujus familiaritate plurimum
utebatur.
[6] adversus omnes cupiditatis ille-

cebras incorruptissimus.
[7] Simply, abstinentia.
[8] enituit.
[9] effecit ut . . .

14. PHOKION (2).

He was no orator[1]—from disdain rather than incom-
petence. Once when about to speak in public, he was
observed to be particularly absorbed in thought.[2] "You
seem meditative, Phokion," said a friend. "Ay, by
Zeus," was the reply,—"I am meditating whether I cannot
in some way abridge[3] the speech which I am just about to
address to the Athenians." He knew so well, however, on
what points[4] to strike, that his telling[5] brevity, strength-
ened by the weight of character and position, cut through[6]
the fine oratory of Demosthenes more effectively than any

[1] parum disertus.
[2] praeter solitum in cogitationi-
bus defixus.

[3] in brevius cogere.
[4] quos quasi articulos rerum.
[5] acris.   [6] discutio.

counter-oratory from men like Æschines. Demosthenes himself greatly feared Phokion as an opponent, and was heard to observe, on seeing him rise to speak, "Here comes the cleaver[7] of my harangues." Polycletus—himself an orator and friend of Demosthenes—drew a distinction highly complimentary[8] to Phokion, by saying, "That Demosthenes was the finest orator, but Phokion the most formidable in speech." (GROTE.)

---

[7] securis.   [8] non sine insigni hujus honore.

---

15. DOMESTIC LIFE OF THE EARLY GREEKS.

The life of the Greeks at home preserved a high degree of the patriarchal order[1] and simplicity. The father's authority was the real and supreme law; his blessing was sought like that of Jacob by his children; and the curse of Œdipus was the direst of the woes that befell his sons. The wife held her due[2] place of honour, though she was purchased from her parents with costly gifts, as was the custom also among the Hebrews. The seclusion of the women in their separate apartments was a later usage[3] borrowed from the Asiatic Greeks. They were equally in their own sphere, when directing their maidens in private at the spinning-wheel[4] and loom, or coming forth to exercise that hospitality which was a chief grace of the heroic age. The stranger guest was freely welcomed; and if he came as a suppliant, it was a sacred duty to receive him. Not till[5] he was refreshed with the bath

---

[1] pristina illa potestas paterna.
[2] honos suus.
[3] Say, *the custom was borrowed* (sumptus) *from the Asiatics* . . .

that . . .
[4] colo seu telae operam dare.
[5] demum after *part.*

and banquet, was any inquiry made about his name or object. The banquet was plentiful, but simple, and enlivened [6] by the strains of the bard, reciting the loves of the gods, or the martial deeds of heroes.

(P. SMITH.)

[6] non sine.

16. THE BATTLE OF PAVIA.

The rout became universal [1]; and resistance ceased in almost every part but where the king was in person, who fought now, not for fame or victory, but for safety. Though wounded in several places, and thrown from his horse, which was killed under him,[2] Francis defended himself on foot with an heroic courage. Many of his bravest officers, gathering round him, and endeavouring to save his life at the expense [3] of their own, fell at his feet. Among these was Bonnivet, the author of this great calamity, who alone died unlamented. The king, exhausted [4] with fatigue, and scarcely capable of further resistance, was left almost alone, exposed [5] to the fury of some Spanish soldiers, strangers to his rank and enraged at his obstinacy. . . . At length he surrendered his sword to Lannoy, who happened likewise to be near at hand; which he, kneeling [6] to kiss the king's hand, received with profound respect; and taking his own sword from his side, presented it to him, saying, that it did not become so great a monarch to remain disarmed in the presence of one of the Emperor's subjects.[7] (ROBERTSON.)

[1] Expr. by *hist. inf.*
[2] cum ipse equus confossus esset.
[3] *part* of projicio (proicio).
[4] defatigatus.
[5] obnoxius.
[6] genibus nixus. [7] cives.

M 2

17. A WARM SPRING, 1781.

The season is wonderfully improved[1] within this day or two; and if these cloudless skies are continued to us, or rather, if the cold winds do not set in[2] again, promises you a pleasant excursion,[3] as far, at least, as the weather can conduce to make it such. You seldom complain of too much sunshine; and if you are prepared for a heat somewhat like that of Africa, the south walk[4] in our long garden will suit you. Reflected from the gravel, and from the walls, and beating[5] upon your head at the same time, it may possibly make you wish[6] you could enjoy for an hour or two that immensity of shade afforded by the trees still growing in the land of your captivity. If you could spend a day now and then in those forests, and return with a wish to England, it would be no small addition[7] to the number of your best pleasures.

(COWPER, *Letters.*)

---

[1] commodior.	[2] ingravesco.	[6] desidero, after which ' to enjoy '
[5] iter.	[4] ambulatio.	need not be expressed.
[5] dejicio (deicio), with *pron. refl.*		[7] appendix.

---

18. CAUSES WHICH SAVED ROME AFTER TRASIMENUS AND CANNAE.

How[1] could it happen that a confederacy so formidable was only formed to be defeated[2]?—that the revolt of Capua was the term of Hannibal's progress?—that from

---

[1] Begin, operae pretium est quae-rere, to avoid the abruptness of the	English.
	[2] nonnisi ad perniciem suam.

this day forwards his great powers[3] were shown rather in repelling defeat than in commanding victory?—that, instead of besieging Rome, he was soon employed in protecting and relieving Capua?—and that his protection and his succours were alike unavailing? No single cause[4] will explain a result so extraordinary. Rome owed her deliverance principally to the strength of the aristocratical interest throughout Italy,—to her numerous colonies of the Latin name,—to the scanty numbers of Hannibal's Africans and Spaniards, and to his want of an efficient artillery.[5] The material[6] of a good artillery must surely have existed at Capua; but there seem to have been no officers[7] capable of directing it; and no great general's operations exhibit so striking a contrast of strength and weakness, as may be seen in Hannibal's battles and sieges. And when Cannae had taught the Romans[8] to avoid pitched battles in the open field,[9] the war became necessarily a series of sieges, where Hannibal's strongest arm,[10] his cavalry, could render little service, while his infantry was in quality not more than equal to the enemy, and his artillery was decidedly inferior.　　　　　　　　　　　　　　　(ARNOLD.)

---

[3] insignis illa bellica virtus.

[4] pluribus de causis . . .

[5] tormenta.

[6] Say, *these could be manufactured at Capua.*

[7] defuisse videntur qui . . .

[8] Cannensi clade docti.

[9] universae rei dimicationes.

[10] quo genere copiarum maxime pollebat.

19. BATTLE OF MARATHON.

So, when Miltiades had sacrificed,[1] and the omens were pronounced favourable, the whole Greek line crossed the mile of ground which divided them from the enemy at a run, and fell upon them while astonished at this novel charge. But the battle was not yet gained[2]; the front ranks joined in furious conflict, and the cloud[3] of arrows from the Persian rear darkened the heavens above them. The phalanx[4] of Greek spearmen on the wings, protected by their shields and armour, found no match in the light bucklers and scimetars[5] of the Asiatics: but in the centre, where spears were opposed to spears, and the Athenians were met by the Persian veterans, the force of numbers prevailed. How far the Greek centre gave way is one of the problems of the battle. Herodotus represents them as flying in full rout up[6] the valley of Marathon or Œnoë, pursued by the main body of the Persians. But the victorious wings fell[7] upon the flanks of the crowded column; the fugitives rallied in its front; the tide of battle turned; and the Persian host fled for refuge to their ships.   · (P. SMITH.)

---

[1] lito, 1. This implies favourable sacrifice, so that the following clause may be omitted.

[2] nondum parta victoria.

[3] multitudo.

[4] Begin, Graecis gravis armaturae . . .

[5] falcati enses.

[6] abl. only.

[7] conversis signis incurrunt.

20. The Northern Barbarians.[1]

The character of the people with whom the Romans had to contend was, in all respects, the reverse [2] of theirs. Those northern adventurers,[3] or Barbarians, as they are called, breathed nothing but war; their martial spirit was yet in its vigour [4]; they sought a milder climate and lands more fertile than their forests and mountains: the sword was their right; and they exercised it without remorse, as the right of nature. Barbarous they surely were; but they were superior to the people they invaded in virtue as well as in valour. Simple [5] and severe in their manners, they were unacquainted with the word luxury: anything was sufficient for their extreme frugality. Hardened by exercise and toil, their bodies seemed inaccessible to disease or pain. War was their element: they sported with danger and met death with expressions of joy. Though free and independent, they were firmly attached to their leaders, because they followed them from choice, not from constraint,[6] the most gallant being always dignified with the command. Nor were these their only virtues. They were remarkable for their generous hospitality; for their detestation of treachery and falsehood: they possessed many maxims of civil wisdom,[7] and wanted only the culture of reason to conduct them to the true principles of social life.   (Gibbon.)

---

[1] This passage may with advantage be rendered in the style of the Germania of Tacitus: brief and with few connectives.

[2] Expr. by tanta ... quanta potest esse distantia.

[3] praedones. Or use simply advenae.

[4] floreo.

[5] Say, *simple and severe manners*.

[6] (vi) coacti.

[7] civilis prudentiae multum.

21. Age of Homer.

While the works[1] of Homer have exercised an influence[2] which has been greater than that of any other poet, and which is rising apparently at the present time, nothing is known of his person. With respect to the date at which he lived, nothing is known.[3] Herodotus places him at four hundred years before himself, in the ninth century before Christ. This would bring him nearly to the epoch[4] of Lycurgus. But the state of society in Greece depicted[5] by him is far anterior not only to that legislator,[6] but to the historic period, which is commonly said to begin with the Olympiad of Corœbus, B.C. 776.[7] The date of 1183 B.C. is fixed by Eratosthenes for the fall of Troy; but it has long been known to be no more than conjectural.[8] In my opinion, that event is quite as likely to have been older as to have been more recent.   (W. E. Gladstone.)

---

[1] Not opera: say, *poems*.
[2] 'influence' is difficult to express. Here perhaps, vis ad hominum animos impellendos.
[3] nihil compertum habemus, or parum constat.

[4] Expr. by aequalis, *contemporary*.
[5] describo or expono.
[6] Say, *him*.
[7] Of course ordinal numerals.
[8] Expr. by conjectura niti.

---

22. Hannibal appeals to his Prisoners.

Hannibal addressed the prisoners by an interpreter; he told the soldiers who had surrendered to Maharbal, that their lives, if he pleased, were still forfeited,[1] for Maharbal had no authority to grant terms without his

---

[1] Expr. by morti obnoxius.

consent [2]: then he proceeded, with the vehemence often displayed by Napoleon in similar circumstances, to inveigh against [3] the Roman government and people, and concluded by giving all his Roman prisoners to the custody of the several divisions of his army. Then he turned to the Italian allies: they were not his enemies, he said; on the contrary, he had invaded Italy to aid them in casting off the yoke [4] of Rome; he should still deal with them as he had treated his Italian prisoners taken at the Trebia; they were free from that moment, and without ransom.[5] This being done, he halted for a short time to rest his army, and buried with great solemnity thirty of the most distinguished of those who had fallen on his own side in the battle. His whole loss [6] amounted only to 1500 men, of whom the greater part were Gauls.   (ARNOLD.)

[2] injussu suo.
[3] insector.
[4] Avoid the metaphor.

[5] nullo pretio.
[6] Say, *not more than* ... *were lost*.

23. BATTLE OF CHÆRONEIA.

In the field of battle [1] near Chæroneia, Philip himself commanded a chosen body of troops opposed to the Athenians; while his youthful son Alexander, aided by experienced officers, commanded [2] against the Thebans on the other wing. Respecting the course of the battle, we are scarcely permitted to know anything. It is said to have been so obstinately contested, that for some time the result was doubtful.[3] The Sacred Band of Thebes ex-

[1] Begin, *Postquam duae acies* ... *constiterunt.*
[2] curo.
[3] in incerto stare.

hausted all their strength[4] and energy in an unavailing
attempt to bear down the stronger phalanx and multiplied
pikes[5] opposed to them.   The youthful Alexander here
first displayed[6] his great military energy and ability.
After a long and murderous struggle, the Theban Sacred
Band were all overpowered, and perished in their ranks,
while the Theban phalanx was broken and pushed back.
Philip on his side was still engaged in undecided conflict
with the Athenians, whose first onset is said to have been
so impetuous, as to put to flight[7] some of the troops in
his army. . . . Philip became emulous on witnessing the
success of his son, and redoubled his efforts, so as to
break and disperse them.   The[8] whole Grecian army was
thus put to flight with severe loss.   (GROTE.)

---

[4] totis viribus conixi.   [7] in fugam conjicere (conicere).
[5] sarissae.   [6] specimen edere.   [8] Connect by quo facto.

---

24. TEMPEST DURING BATTLE BETWEEN GREEKS AND CARTHAGINIANS IN SICILY, B.C. 340.

A storm of the most violent character[1] began.   The[2]
hill-tops were shrouded in complete darkness; the wind
blew a hurricane[3]; rain and hail poured abundantly, with
all the awful accompaniments of thunder and lightning. To
the Greeks this storm was of little inconvenience, because
it came[4] in their backs.   But to the Carthaginians, pelting
as it did directly in their faces, it occasioned both great
suffering and soul-subduing[5] alarm.   The rain and hail

---

[1] atrox, sup.   ventus.   [4] ingruo, 3.
[2] Connect by cum.   [5] Omit. The preceding adj. is
[3] vehementissimus (se) erupit   sufficient.

beat, and the lightning flashed, in their faces, so that they could not see [6] to deal with hostile combatants : the noise of the wind, and of hail rattling against their armour, prevented the orders of their officers from being heard : the folds of their voluminous [7] military tunics were sur- charged with water, so as to embarrass their movements : the ground presently became so muddy that they could not keep their footing [8]; and when they once slipped, the weight of their equipment forbade all recovery. . . . At length when the four hundred front men of the Cartha- ginians had perished by a brave death in their places, the rest of the White-shields [9] turned their backs and sought safety in flight.   (GROTE.)

---

[6] Expr. by oculis capti, *disabled as to their eyes*, *blinded*.
[7] Put the adj. with the noun

'folds' (amplus).
[8] pedibus insistere.
[9] Leucaspides.

---

25. MARY, QUEEN OF SCOTS, LEAVING FRANCE.

It is said [1] that, after Mary was embarked, she kept her eyes fixed on the coast of France, and never turned them from that beloved object,[2] till darkness fell and inter- cepted [3] it from her view. She then ordered a couch to be spread for her in the open air,[4] and charged the pilot, that if in the morning the land were still in sight, he would awake her, and afford her one parting view of that country in which all her affections were centered.[5] The weather proved calm, so that the ship made little way in the night-time; and Mary had once more an opportunity [6]

---

[1] Use personal form, fertur Maria (not Mariam).   [2] Say, *land*.
[3] intercludo. For the Mood see

p. 36, Ex. 3, Note 9.
[4] sub divo.   [5] defixus.
[6] contigit.

of seeing the French coast. She sat upon her couch, and still looking towards the land, often[7] repeated these words :—" Farewell, France, farewell; I shall never see thee more." (ROBERTSON.)

[7] identidem.

26. DEATH OF BECKET.

When the king heard of this conduct, the anger which had been boiling within him, but which circumstances had obliged him to suppress, broke loose,[1] and he accused his courtiers of caring[2] nothing for him, since they suffered this audacious[3] priest to live. Four knights took him at his word,[4] hurried across to England, collected followers among his enemies, and, proceeding to Canterbury, demanded the immediate removal of his excommunication.[5] The monks in terror hurried the archbishop to the cathedral, and wished to shut the doors, believing him then in safe sanctuary, but he would not allow any sign of weakness.[6] The knights, at the head of an armed mob, still demanded the removal of the excommunication, were still refused, and killed him at the altar. The outcry[7] which rose throughout Europe told Henry that he had lost his cause. He at once declared himself innocent, refused food, took on him all the outward signs of penitence, and despatched a mission to exculpate[8] him at the court of the Pope. (BRIGHT.)

[1] Say, *no longer master* (potens) *of his anger long suppressed* (premo).
[2] Expr. by quasi. [3] temerarius.
[4] hac tanquam certa regis volun-tate accepta. [5] excommunicatio.
[6] animus infirmus, imbecillus.
[7] adversa acclamatio.
[8] purgo.

27. ROME AND FOREIGN RELIGIONS.

Rome,[1] the capital of a great monarchy, was incessantly
filled with subjects and strangers from every part of the
world, who all introduced and enjoyed the favourite
superstitions of their native country. Every city in the
empire was justified in maintaining the purity[2] of its
ancient ceremonies; and the Roman Senate, using the
common privilege, sometimes interposed to check this
inundation of foreign rites. The Egyptian superstition,[3]
of all the most contemptible and abject, was frequently
prohibited; the temples of Serapis[4] and Isis demolished,
and their worshippers banished from Rome and Italy.
But the zeal of fanaticism prevailed over the cold and
feeble efforts of policy.[5] The exiles returned, the pro-
selytes[6] multiplied, the temples were restored with in-
creasing splendour, and Isis and Serapis at length
assumed their place among the Roman deities. Nor was
this indulgence a departure[7] from the old maxims of
government. In the purest ages of the Commonwealth,
Cybele and Æsculapius had been invited by solemn
embassies; and it was customary to tempt the protectors
of besieged cities by the promise of more distinguished
honours than they possessed in their native country.
Rome gradually became the common temple of her
subjects; and the freedom of the city was bestowed on.
all the gods of mankind.   (GIBBON.)

----

[1] Begin with acc. Romam, con-
verting the predicative verb to the
active voice.   [2] Expr. by adj.

[3] dat.: the sentence ending with
interdictum est.

[4] Serăpis has gen. in is and Idis.

[5] Expr. by part., lente timide-
que consulentium conata.   Comp.
St. L. G. 638, Obs. 3.

[6] externarum religionum secta-
tores.

[7] Neque ita ... discessum est.

28. ALEXANDER KILLS KLEITUS.

Remarks[1] such as these provoked loud contradiction from many, and gave poignant offence to Alexander. But wrath and contradiction, both from him and from others, only made Kleitus more reckless[2] in the outpouring of his feelings, now discharged with delight after being so long pent up. He passed[3] from the old Macedonian soldiers to himself individually. Stretching forth his right hand towards Alexander, he exclaimed, "Recollect that you owe your life to me; this hand preserved you at the Granikus. Listen to the outspoken language of truth, or else abstain[4] from asking freemen to supper, and confine yourself to the society of barbaric slaves." All these reproaches stung[5] Alexander to the quick.[6] . . . At length wrath and intoxication together drove him into uncontrollable fury. He started from his couch, and felt for his dagger to spring at Kleitus; but the dagger had been put out of reach by one of the attendants. In a loud voice and with the Macedonian word[7] of command, he summoned the body-guards and ordered the trumpeter to sound an alarm.[8] But no one obeyed so grave an order, given in his condition of drunkenness. His principal officers, Ptolemy, Perdikkas and others, clung round him, held his arms and body, and besought him to abstain from violence ; others at the same time tried to silence Kleitus and hurry him out of the hall, which had now become a scene of tumult and consternation. But Kleitus was not in a humour to confess himself in the wrong by retiring; while Alexander, furious at the opposition now, for the first time,

---

[1] Dum Clitus haec taliaque opprobria ingerit.
[2] Clito audacia augetur.
[3] omissis.   [4] noli.

[5] mordeo.
[6] *adv.*
[7] signum.
[8] ad arma canere.

offered to his will, exclaimed that his officers held him in
chains,[9] as Bessus had held Darius, and left him nothing
but the name of a king. Though anxious to restrain his
movements, they doubtless did not dare to employ much
physical force; so that his great personal strength, and
continued efforts, presently set him free. He then
snatched a pike from one of the soldiers, rushed upon
Kleitus, and thrust him through on the spot, exclaiming,
" Go now to Philip and Parmenio." (GROTE.)

[9] vinctum se teneri a suis.

29. VILLAGE GOSSIP.

When I began, I expected no interruption. But if I
had expected interruptions without end, I should have been
less disappointed.[1] First came the barber[2]; who, after
having embellished the outside of my head, has left the
inside just as unfurnished as he found it. Then came
Olney bridge,—not into the house,[3] but into the conversation. The cause relating to it was tried on Tuesday[4] at
Buckingham. The judge directed the jury to find a
verdict favourable to Olney.[5] The jury consisted of one
knave and eleven fools. The [6] last-mentioned followed
the afore-mentioned, as sheep follow a bell-wether,[7] and
decided in direct opposition to the said judge. Then a
flaw[8] was discovered in the indictment. The indictment
was quashed,[9] and an order made for a new trial. The
new trial will be in the King's Bench, where said knave

[1] de spe dejici.
[2] ecce tonsor adest.
[3] non ille quidem in aedes.
[4] die Martis.
[5] secundum Olneienses.
[6] Begin, quorum dum hi . . .
[7] dux. [8] vitium in actione.
[9] rescindo.

and said fools will have nothing to do with it. So the men of Olney fling up their caps,[10] and assure themselves of a complete victory.   (COWPER, *Letters.*)

[10] in caelo sunt.

30. BEFORE METAURUS.

The red ensign was hoisted [1] as soon as the council broke up; and the [Roman] soldiers marched out and formed in order of battle. The enemy, whose camp, according to the system of ancient warfare, was only half a mile distant from that of the Romans, marched out and formed in line to meet them. But as Hasdrubal rode forward to reconnoitre the Roman army, their increased numbers [2] struck him; and other circumstances, it is said, having increased his suspicions, he led back his men into their camp, and sent out some horsemen to collect information. The Romans then returned to their camp; and Hasdrubal's horsemen rode round it at a distance to see if it were larger than usual, or in the hope of picking up [3] some stragglers. One thing alone, it is said, revealed the secret: the trumpet, which gave the signal for the several duties of the day, was heard to sound as usual once in the camp of the prætor, but twice in that of Livius. This, we are told, satisfied Hasdrubal that both the consuls were before him: unable to understand how Nero had escaped from [4] Hannibal, and dreading the worst,[5] he resolved to retire to a greater distance from the enemy; and having put out all his fires, he set his army in motion as soon as night fell, and retreated towards the Metaurus.   (ARNOLD.)

[1] vexillo proposito.   [3] excipio.   [4] fallo.
[2] multitudo auctior.   [5] metuens de summa rerum.

LONDON: PRINTED BY WILLIAM CLOWES AND SONS, LIMITED, STAMFORD STREET AND CHARING CROSS.

50ᴬ, ALBEMARLE STREET, LONDON, W.
January, 1902.

MR. MURRAY'S
LIST OF SCHOOL BOOKS.

NATIONAL EDUCATION. ESSAYS TOWARDS A CONSTRUCTIVE POLICY. Edited by LAURIE MAGNUS, M.A., Magdalen College, Oxford. 8vo. *7s. 6d. net.*

Chap. 1.—AIMS AND METHODS. By the EDITOR.

Chap. 2.—CHURCH SCHOOLS AND RELIGIOUS EDUCATION. By the Rev. BERNARD REYNOLDS, M.A., Prebendary of St. Paul's, Diocesan Inspector of Schools, London.

Chap. 3.—REGISTRATION AND TRAINING OF TEACHERS. By FRANCIS STORR, B.A., Editor of the "Journal of Education."

Chap. 4.—THE INSPECTION OF SECONDARY SCHOOLS. By Sir JOSHUA G. FITCH, LL.D., formerly H.M. Chief Inspector of Training Colleges.

Chap. 5.—SCIENCE IN EDUCATION—THE NEED OF PRACTICAL STUDIES. By Prof. H. E. ARMSTRONG, LL.D., Ph.D., F.R.S., Professor of Chemistry at the Central Technical College.

Chap. 6.—INDUSTRIAL NEEDS. By A. D. PROVAND, formerly M.P. for Glasgow.

Chap. 7.—COMMERCIAL EDUCATION :—

    (a) *Secondary.* By T. A. ORGAN, B.A.. L.C.C., formerly Chairman of the Technical Education Board.

    (b) *University.* By Prof. W. A. S. HEWINS, Director of the London School of Economics and Political Science.

Chap. 8.—AGRICULTURAL EDUCATION. By JOHN C. MEDD, M.A., Executive Member of the Agricultural Education Committee.

Chap. 9.—THE TEACHING OF MODERN LANGUAGES. By H. W. EVE, formerly Headmaster of University College School.

BIBLIOGRAPHICAL NOTE, &c.

"Professor ARMSTRONG writes vigorously on the need for 'drastic reform' in the schools in which our governing classes are educated, as the most important feature in the reorganization of a national educational programme."—*Times.*

"The contributors are all men of high standing in the educational or commercial world, so that what they have to say comes to us with the added weight of authority. . . . It is a work which deserves the most careful attention, for in it will be found one explanation of the failure of England to hold her own in a world of progress."—*Daily Mail.*

MR. MURRAY'S NEW SERIES

OF

SECONDARY EDUCATION TEXT-BOOKS.

Edited by LAURIE MAGNUS, M.A.,

MAGDALEN COLLEGE, OXFORD.

COMMERCIAL FRENCH. In Two Parts. By W. MANSFIELD POOLE, M.A., Magdalen College, Oxford; Secretary to the Modern Language Association, and Assistant-Master at Merchant Taylors' School, AND MICHEL BECKER, Professor at the Ecole Alsacienne, Paris; Author of "L'Allemand Commercial," and "Lectures Pratiques d'Allemand Moderne." With a Map in each Volume.

PART I.—Consisting of Simple Sentences and Passages in French, with occasional Business Letters, and containing in an Appendix a clear system of French Grammar, with special reference to the Verb. Crown 8vo. *2s. 6d.*

". . . a most careful piece of work . . . an excellent book . . . we warmly recommend to all who have to teach Commercial French."
—*Educational Times.*

". . . . is in every respect excellent, and we commend it to the best attention of all students of Commercial French."—*Birmingham Gazette.*

PART II.—Comprising an Advanced Commercial Reader. Crown 8vo. *2s. 6d.*   [*Just out.*

BRITAIN OVER THE SEA. A Reader for Schools. Compiled and edited by ELIZABETH LEE, Author of "A School History of English Literature," etc.; Editor of "Cowper's Task and Minor Poems," etc. With Four Maps of the British Empire at different periods. Crown 8vo. *2s. 6d.*

This School Reader is conceived on novel lines. The extracts are arranged in sections, comprising "The English Colonies up to 1900," "Australia," "India," "South Africa," etc.; and the selections range from the works of Sir Walter Raleigh to the speeches of Lord Beaconsfield. It contains a literary introduction, and the name of the author, who is a contributor to the *Dictionary of National Biography*, carries assurance that the editorial work is well done.

MR. P. A. BARNETT (H.M. Inspector of Training Colleges).—"I congratulate you on the production of a very excellent piece of work. I hope the schools will use it; but it is almost too good for them."

The Globe says:—". . . . a very happy thought, very successfully carried out. . . . We should like to see this book in use in every school in England."

Secondary Education Text-Books—continued.

COMMERCIAL KNOWLEDGE. A Manual of Business Methods and Transactions. By ALGERNON WARREN. Crown 8vo. 2s. 6d.

This text-book of *Handelswissenschaft* is designed for the use of students who intend to enter the higher branches of commercial life. It includes chapters on Supply and Demand; Free Trade and Protection; Partnership; Companies, Syndicates, and Trusts; Principal and Agent; Contracts; Banking; Transit; Insurance; Tariffs; Employers' Liability; Commercial Travellers; Consuls, etc.

" The book should be used in every senior class both of our board and private schools, and as an introduction to business life it should prove of great value."— *Statist.*

". . . . contains concise and accurate descriptions of all kinds of commercial routine, from the functions of the Board of Trade to a *facsimile* of a Bill of Lading and should be in the possession of everyone who intends to embrace a commercial career."— *The Scotsman.*

COMMERCIAL GERMAN. In Two Parts. By GUSTAV HEIN, University of Berlin, and Lecturer in German (Honours) to the University of Aberdeen, and MICHEL BECKER, Professor of Modern Languages in the Ecole Alsacienne, Paris.

PART I. with a Map will be published shortly.

This manual is uniform with the first part of *Commercial French* by Poole and Becker, and is specially adapted for the use of students in commercial classes and continuation schools.

FRENCH COMMERCIAL CORRESPONDENCE. By Professor CHARLES GLAUSER, and W. MANSFIELD POOLE, M.A., Magdalen College, Oxford ; Secretary to the Modern Language Association, and Assistant-Master at Merchant Taylors' School. Crown 8vo. [*In the Press.*

INTERMEDIATE FRENCH ACCIDENCE AND OUT-LINES OF SYNTAX, with Historical Notes. By G. H. CLARKE, M.A., of Hymers College, Hull, and L. R. TANQUEREY, B.ès.L. [*In the Press.*

THE SOIL. By A. D. HALL, M.A., Principal of the South Eastern Agricultural College.

This volume, by the Principal of the County Council College at Wye, is the first of a group of text-books intended for the use of students in Agriculture. Other volumes, which will be duly announced, will deal with " Plant Physiology," " Manures," etc. [*In active preparation.*

AN INTRODUCTION TO THE STUDY OF POETRY. By LAURIE MAGNUS.

Designed to instruct pupils in the middle and upper forms of schools with the elements of taste and judgment in poetry by the natural or direct method of literature-teaching. [*In active preparation.*

OTHER VOLUMES TO FOLLOW.

Mr. MURRAY'S

HOME AND SCHOOL LIBRARY

Edited by LAURIE MAGNUS, M.A.,

MAGDALEN COLLEGE, OXFORD.

———

This series of volumes is intended for the general reader as well as for school use. There are many subjects, formerly described as educational, on which the intelligent reader of to-day is required, or desires, to inform himself, for the purposes of his business or his recreation. To this end the various volumes have been entrusted to experts in the subjects with which they deal, and, it is hoped, that the series will ultimately be found o cover in convenient and readable volumes a wide field of human knowledge.

Several of the volumes contain appropriate illustrations, maps, diagrams, &c., and their prices will vary from a shilling to half-a-crown. The following are now ready:—

ALGEBRA. Part I. By E. M. LANGLEY, M.A., Senior Mathematical Master, Modern School, Bedford, and S. N. R. BRADLY, M.A., Mathematical Master, Modern School, Bedford. F'cap 8vo, 1s. 6d.

> This volume is specially adapted to the requirements of the First Stage of the Directory of the Board of Education, South Kensington. Answers, for teachers only, can be obtained separately.
> Professor JOHN PERRY, of the Royal College of Science, South Kensington, writes:—"I never do praise a book unless I believe it to be good. Your Algebra (regarded as a book for beginners) pleases me very much indeed. I cannot imagine an Algebra prepared for schools in general, and especially for use by teachers in general, which would come nearer to my notion of what an Algebra ought to be, than yours."

A FIRST COURSE OF PRACTICAL SCIENCE, with full directions for experiments and numerous Exercises. By J. H. LEONARD. B.Sc. Lond. With a Preface by Dr. GLADSTONE, F.R.S. F'cap 8vo. 1s. 6d.

> These Lessons are taught on the heuristic method, with a view to stimulating the learner's powers of observation and experiment.
>
> "The exercises described are suitable for quite young beginners, and they will serve the double purpose of applying the pupil's knowledge of arithmetic and developing a scientific frame of mind . . . The experiments are described concisely and are well arranged."—*Nature.*

FIRST MAKERS OF ENGLAND. Julius Cæsar, King Arthur, Alfred the Great. By Lady MAGNUS, Author of "Boys of the Bible," etc. With Illustrations. F'cap 8vo. 1s. 6d.

> This volume is based on the recommendations for history teaching made by Professor Withers at the invitation of the School Board for London.

Home and School Library—continued.

IN THE PRESS.

A SHORT HISTORY OF COINS AND CURRENCY.
By Lord AVEBURY, F.R.S., &c. With many Illustrations.

HEROES OF THE WEST, A BIOGRAPHICAL SKETCH OF
MODERN HISTORY, by the Rev. A. J. and Mrs. CARLYLE and
F. S. MARVIN, M.A. 2 vols.

TELEGRAPHS AND TELEPHONES. By Sir W. H.
PREECE, K.C.B., etc., sometime President of the Institute of
Civil Engineers.

ELECTRIC WIREMEN'S WORK. By W. C. CLINTON,
B.Sc. (Lond.), Demonstrator in the Pender Laboratory, University
College, London.

> The above two volumes are written with particular reference to the require-
> ments of the examinations of the City and Guilds of London Institute.

VILLAGE LECTURES ON POPULAR SCIENCE. By
the Rev. C. T. OVENDEN, D.D., Canon of St. Patrick's, Rector
of Enniskillen. With numerous Diagrams. Two Vols.

PLATO'S 'REPUBLIC.' By Prof. LEWIS CAMPBELL, Hon.
Fellow of Balliol College, Oxford.

IN ACTIVE PREPARATION.

OUTLINE OF THE HISTORY OF COMMERCE. By
C. S. FEARENSIDE, M.A., Cantab., Author of "*The Tutorial
History of England.*'

THE LIFE OF CHRIST. By the Rev. H. C. BEECHING,
M.A., Chaplain to Lincoln's Inn, Editor of *Lyra Sacra*, &c.

MUSIC. By A. KALISCH, B.A.

INTRODUCTION TO THE STUDY OF PHILOSOPHY.
By S. RAPPOPORT, Ph D.

THE CALCULUS FOR ARTISANS. By Prof. O. HENRICI,
F.R.S., etc.

TENNYSON'S 'ŒNONE.' By LAURIE MAGNUS, M.A.

MURRAY'S
HANDY CLASSICAL MAPS.

Edited by G. B. GRUNDY, M.A.,
BRASENOSE COLLEGE, OXFORD.

The Maps in Sir WILLIAM SMITH's Classical Atlas, engraved at a cost of several thousands of pounds, are regarded as amongst the best of the kind in existence, but hitherto they have only been published in a costly form, and are practically inaccessible to school-boys and many students.

Mr. G. B. GRUNDY, of Brasenose College, Oxford, whose name is a sufficient guarantee of the excellence and scholarly character of the work, has undertaken to edit the series, to bring it up to date in the light of modern research, and to make it suitable for school and college use.

The form of their issue is entirely novel, and will, we think, commend itself to teachers.

The maps will be published *separately*, mounted on cloth, with an index of names, and folded in a cover similar to those used for tourists and cycling maps, though somewhat larger.

By this means, instead of having to purchase at one time and bring into School or Lecture Room an expensive and bulky atlas, the student will be enabled to carry only the map required for the lecture or lesson in hand.

The old method of engraving and hatching the mountain ranges has been supplemented by colouring the contours with flat brown and green tints, which is now recognised as the best and most intelligible way of denoting the configuration of the land.

LIST OF MAPS IN THE SERIES:

GRAECIA	Northern Greece South and Peloponnesus	*Two sheets in one case, 3s. cloth ; 1s. 6d. net, paper.* [NOW READY.
GALLIA - - - - -		*One sheet, 2s. cloth ; 1s. net, paper.* [NOW READY.
BRITANNIA - - - -		*One sheet, 2s. cloth ; 1s. net, paper.* [NOW READY
HISPANIA - - - - -		*One sheet, 2s. cloth ; 1s. net, paper.* [NOW READY.
ITALIA	Northern Italy South and Sicily.	*Two sheets in one case, 3s. cloth ; 1s. 6d. net, paper.* [NOW READY.
GERMANIA, RHAETIA, ILLYRIA, MOESIA, etc.		*One sheet, 2s. cloth ; 1s. net, paper.* [NOW READY.
PALESTINE, SYRIA, and part of MESOPOTAMIA, and a Map showing St. Paul's Voyages		*Three Maps on one sheet, 2s. cloth ; 1s. net, paper.* [NOW READY.

Murray's Handy Classical Maps—continued.

ASIA MINOR and MARE AEGAEUM } *Two Maps on one sheet,* 2s. *cloth;* 1s. *net, paper.*

THE ROMAN EMPIRE (at different epochs) } *Two Maps on one sheet,* 2s. *cloth;* 1s. *net, paper.*

EGYPT and the EASTERN EMPIRES } *Two Maps on one sheet,* 2s. *cloth;* 1s. *net. paper.*

An Index is bound in each case.

"These maps of Mr. Murray's are far better than anything which has yet been attempted in the direction of teaching the physical features of ancient geography, and they deserve all attention from students and schoolmasters."—*Athenæum.*

". . . admirably executed maps . . . likely to be of high utility to students, Biblical and others . . . may be consulted with much advantage."
—*Notes and Queries*

". . . are admirable, and will prove of great assistance to students of ancient history. We have before warmly praised the colour-system of the maps and we need only say of this one (Graecia) that it will help those that use it to realize the relations and circumstances of the Ancient Greek States far better than any other map with which we are acquainted."—*Educational Times.*

"t is likely to take rank as the best map of Greece."—*Daily Chronicle.*

CHINA: HER HISTORY, DIPLOMACY AND COMMERCE, FROM THE EARLIEST TIMES TO THE PRESENT DAY. By E. H. PARKER, Professor of Chinese at the Owens College; Acting-Consul-General in Corea, Nov., 1886—Jan., 1887; Consul in Hainan, 1891-2, 1893-4; and in 1892-3, Adviser in Chinese Affairs to the Burma Government. With 19 Maps, &c. Large Crown 8vo. 8s. net.

"Mr. E. H. Parker brings to bear upon his subject an experience, an amount of personal insight, and a capacity for criticism so unusual, as to endow his pages with an intrinsic merit practically unequalled. . . . Mr. Parker has produced a book which will be of value both on account of its wealth of information and independent criticism, and for the additional light it sheds on Chinese topics treated of in other standard works."—*Pall Mall Gazette.*

"Mr. Parker may be congratulated upon his lucid exposition of the system of government. It conveys a more vivid impression of the ins and outs of Chinese administration than almost anything on the subject that has yet appeared in print. . . . The author's method is excellent."—*Standard.*

ELEMENTARY TEACHERS' CERTIFICATE, 1902.

STANLEY'S LIFE OF ARNOLD. With a Preface by Sir JOSHUA FITCH, LL.D., formerly H.M. Chief Inspector of Training Colleges. Large type, 800 pages, in 1 volume. With Photogravure Portrait and 16 half-tone Illustrations. Crown 8vo. 6s. [*Just out.*

"Stanley's Life of Arnold has been selected by the Board of Education as a subject of examination for intending teachers, so that this edition will be heartily welcomed."—*Educational Times.*

"The Board of Education have lately included the book in the curriculum for candidates for the teachers' certificate, apparently in the hope that the young men and women engaged in elementary schools be helped by its study to infuse into their labours something of the spirit which gives Arnold his unique position among teachers. A more excellent work for this section of the community does not exist in the language."—*The Standard.*

HALLAM'S CONSTITUTIONAL HISTORY OF ENG-LAND, Chapters I. to IX. Bound together in 1 Volume for the special use of candidates for the London University Examinations. Crown 8vo. 5s. [*Just out.*

AN HISTORICAL REVIEW OF THE DEVELOPMENT OF GREATER BRITAIN.

THE GROWTH OF THE EMPIRE. By A. W. JOSE. With many Coloured and other Maps and Diagrams. Cr. 8vo. 6s.

". . . . an eminently useful book . . . . as serviceable as it is readable. It is systematic in method and accurate in statement."—*The Globe.*
". . . . this excellent manual is written by an Australian Briton. . . . That the colonial history of Great Britain should be worthily told was a crying need, and we congratulate Australia upon producing the historian, and the historian upon the production of an admirable book."—*Daily Chronicle.*

NEW TESTAMENT TEACHINGS FOR SECONDARY SCHOOLS.

THE SUNRISE OF REVELATION. A Sequel to "The Dawn of Revelation." By Miss M. BRAMSTON, Author of "The Dawn of Revelation," "Judæa and her Rulers," etc. Crown 8vo. 5s. net.
[*Just out.*

"We do not think that any good Judge will get far in the book without discovering that it is one of rare merit and exceptionally well suited to the class to whom it is addressed. We do not know of any book likely to be more useful to the teachers of secondary schools in the preparation of their Scripture lessons than this. It is clear, accurate, and full of instruction and suggestiveness. Miss Bramston shows a competent knowledge of the present position of criticism as to the Gospels and Acts, but she wisely keeps her learning in the background, and it only betrays itself by an occassional sentence or epithet. It is a great deal to say of any book dealing with the Scripture history that it is scholarly without being dry, and reverent without any trace of 'preaching.' Yet Miss Bramston has succeeded in all this and more. We do not often praise a book so unreservedly, but we shall be surprised if she does not attract a circle of readers far larger than that to which she has addressed herself in the first instance."—*The Guardian.*

THE PUBLIC SCHOOL SPEAKER. Compiled by F. WARRE CORNISH, M.A., Vice-Provost of Eton College. Large 8vo. 7s. 6d.

This work, as its name implies, is a collection of pieces suitable for recitation at school "speeches." The Editor has made his selection in the widest manner and from various languages—Greek, Latin, English, German, French and Italian. He has included drama, general poetry, orations and other prose pieces, ancient and modern. The Editor is in hopes that no serious omissions can be found, unless it be those intentional ones from classics that are at everyone's command, which he has left out to make room for those more difficult of access.
It will be noticed that he has in many cases given an extract longer than is sufficient for a single recitation—he has done this advisedly with a view to affording greater scope for individual requirements and individual taste.
The publisher is of opinion that the Speaker will be found the most complete extant.
"The Vice-Provost of Eton College has very worthily performed a task which certainly needed to be done. . . . Mr. Cornish's volume is specially suited and designed for schools which have their regular speech days . . . in the upper forms of a public school, and in the library of all literary schools, it is precisely what we have needed for a long time past."—*Educational Times.*
"No such comprehensive work has hitherto been issued, and in our opinion 'The Public School Speaker' has leaped at a single bound into the very foremost rank, and has become the classic of its kind."—*The Bookseller.*

MURRAY'S STUDENT'S MANUALS.

A Series of Class-books for Advanced Scholars.

FORMING A CHAIN OF HISTORY FROM THE EARLIEST AGES DOWN TO MODERN TIMES.

English History and Literature.

" The great foundation for all useful knowledge we hold, without any doubt, to be the knowledge of the history and literature of our own country. On this ground Mr. Murray is especially strong. We are acquainted with many admirable books on these subjects, issued by various firms of high standing, some of which, such as Mr. Green's and Mr. Bright's, have universally recognised merits ; but for the utility and completeness of the course we give the first place to Mr. Murray's series."—*Literary Churchman.*

THE STUDENT'S HUME: A HISTORY OF ENGLAND, FROM THE EARLIEST TIMES TO THE REVOLUTION IN 1688. By DAVID HUME. Incorporating the Researches of recent Historians. Revised, corrected, and continued to the Treaty of Berlin in 1878, by J. S. BREWER, M.A. With Notes, Illustrations, and 7 Coloured Maps and Woodcuts. Crown 8vo. 7s. 6d.

** **Also in Three Parts.** 2s. 6d. each.

I. FROM B.C. 55 TO THE DEATH OF RICHARD III., A.D. 1485.

II. HENRY VII. TO THE REVOLUTION, 1688.

III. THE REVOLUTION TO THE TREATY OF BERLIN, 1878.

** *Questions on the "Student's Hume."* 12mo. 2s.

STUDENT'S CONSTITUTIONAL HISTORY OF ENG-LAND. FROM THE ACCESSION OF HENRY VII. TO THE DEATH OF GEORGE II. By HENRY HALLAM, LL.D. Crown 8vo. 7s. 6d.

STUDENT'S MANUAL OF THE ENGLISH LAN-GUAGE. By GEORGE P. MARSH. Crown 8vo. 7s. 6d.

STUDENT'S MANUAL OF ENGLISH LITERATURE. A History of English Literature of the chief English Writers, founded upon the Manual of THOMAS B. SHAW. A new Edition thoroughly revised. By A. HAMILTON THOMPSON, B.A., of St. John's Coll., Cambridge, and Univ. Extension Lecturer in English Literature. With Notes, etc. Crown 8vo. 7s. 6d.

STUDENT'S SPECIMENS OF ENGLISH LITERA-TURE. Selected from the BEST WRITERS, and arranged Chrono-logically. By T. B. SHAW, M.A. Crown 8vo. 5s.

Scripture and Church History.

STUDENT'S OLD TESTAMENT HISTORY. From the Creation of the World to the Return of the Jews from Captivity. With an Introduction to the Books of the Old Testament. By PHILIP SMITH, B.A. With 40 Maps and Woodcuts. Crown 8vo. 7s. 6d.

STUDENT'S NEW TESTAMENT HISTORY. With an Introduction, containing the Connection of the Old and New Testaments. By PHILIP SMITH, B.A. With 30 Maps and Woodcuts. Crown 8vo. 7s. 6d.

STUDENT'S MANUAL OF ECCLESIASTICAL HISTORY. A History of the Christian Church to the Reformation. By PHILIP SMITH, B.A. 2 Vols. Crown 8vo. 7s. 6d. each.
> PART I.—A.D. 30—1003. With Woodcuts.
> PART II.—A.D. 1003—1614. With Woodcuts.

STUDENT'S MANUAL OF ENGLISH CHURCH HISTORY. By G. G. PERRY, M.A., Canon of Lincoln. 3 Vols. 7s. 6d. each.
> *1st Period.* From the Planting of the Church in Britain to the Accession of Henry VIII. A.D. 596—1509.
> *2nd Period.* From the Accession of Henry VIII. to the Silencing of Convocation in the Eighteenth Century. A.D. 1509—1717.
> *3rd Period.* From the Accession of the House of Hanover to the Present Time. A.D. 1717—1884.

———

A POPULAR HISTORY OF THE CHURCH OF ENGLAND. From the Earliest Times to the Present Day. By the Rt. Rev. WILLIAM BOYD CARPENTER, The Lord Bishop of Ripon. Illustrated. Crown 8vo. 6s.
> "The title is, perhaps, hardly wide enough for the contents; one would almost call the book a history of Christianity in England. . . . He has the true judicial spirit, and is passionately eager to be entirely fair to every one. His history is impartial to the last degree. . . . His book should have a very wide circulation, and can do nothing but good wherever it is read."—*Morning Post.*

THE EVOLUTION OF THE ENGLISH BIBLE. Being an Historical Sketch of the Successive Versions from 1382—1885. By H. W. HOARE, late of Balliol College, Oxford, now an Assistant Secretary to the Board of Education, Whitehall. With Portraits and Specimen-pages from Old Bibles. Demy 8vo.
> "Mr. Hoare . . . has read well and widely . . . We cordially commend this book for what it professes to be—an amateur guide to amateur students and lovers of 'the greatest of English classics and the most venerable of national heirlooms.'"—*The Times.*

THE REFORMATION. A Religious and Historical Sketch. By the Rev. J. A. BABINGTON, M.A., Assistant Master at Tonbridge School, formerly Scholar of New College, Oxford. Demy 8vo. 12s. net.
> "This masterly essay . . . gives evidence on every page f wide reading and of a remarkable power of condensation. . . . It is a notable piece of work, one that deserves to be widely read."—*Daily Chronicle.*

Ancient History.

STUDENTS ANCIENT HISTORY OF THE EAST.
FROM THE EARLIEST TIMES TO THE CONQUESTS OF ALEXANDER
THE GREAT, including Egypt, Assyria, Babylonia Media, Persia,
Asia Minor, and Phœnicia. By PHILIP SMITH, B.A With 70
Woodcuts. Crown 8vo. 7s. 6d.

STUDENTS HISTORY OF GREECE. FROM THE
EARLIEST TIMES TO THE ROMAN CONQUEST. With Chapters on
the History of Literature and Art. By SIR WM. SMITH, D.C.L.
Thoroughly revised and in part rewritten by G. E. MARINDIN, M.A.
With many new Maps and Illustrations. Crown 8vo. 7s. 6d.

STUDENTS HISTORY OF ROME. FROM THE EARLIEST
TIMES TO THE ESTABLISHMENT OF THE EMPIRE. With Chapters
on the History of Literature and Art. By DEAN LIDDELL.
New and Revised Edition, incorporating the results of Modern
Research, by P. V. M. BENECKE, M.A., Fellow of Magdalen
College, Oxford. With Coloured and other Maps and numerous
Illustrations nearly all prepared specially for this Edition.
Crown 8vo. 7s. 6d.

STUDENTS HISTORY OF THE ROMAN EMPIRE.
FROM THE ESTABLISHMENT OF THE EMPIRE TO THE ACCESSION OF
COMMODUS, A.D. 180. With Coloured Maps and Numerous Illustra-
tions. By J. B. BURY, Fellow and Tutor of Trin. Coll., Dublin.
Crown 8vo. 7s. 6d.

STUDENTS GIBBON. A HISTORY OF THE DECLINE AND FALL
OF THE ROMAN EMPIRE. Abridged from the Original Work by
SIR WM. SMITH, D.C.L., LL.D. A New and Revised Edition
in Two Parts. Crown 8vo. 5s. each.
PART I.—FROM THE ACCESSION OF COMMODUS TO THE DEATH
OF JUSTINIAN. By A. H. J. GREENIDGE, M.A., Lecturer and
Late Fellow of Hertford College, Lecturer in Ancient History at
Brasenose College, Oxford.
PART II.—FROM A.D. 565 TO THE CAPTURE OF CONSTANTINOPLE
BY THE TURKS. By J. G. C. ANDERSON, M.A., late Fellow of
Lincoln College, Student and Tutor of Christ Church, Oxford.
With Maps and Illustrations.

HERODOTUS. THE TEXT OF CANON RAWLINSON'S TRANSLATION.
With the Notes abridged for the use of Students. By A. J.
GRANT, M.A., of King's College, Cambridge; Professor of History,
Yorkshire College, Leeds; Author of "Greece in the Age of
Pericles." With Map and Plans. 2 Vols. Crown 8vo. 12s.
"The delightful pages of the old Greek whose flavour has been so admirably
presented by Canon Rawlinson, will thus be made accessible to a far wider circle
than heretofore. There is no better introduction to Greek history and literature
than Herodotus, and the English reader gets him here under the best possible
conditions."—*Literary World.*

**THE STORY OF THE PERSIAN WARS AS TOLD
BY HERODOTUS.** In English. Selected, arranged and edited,
so as to form a History Reading Book for Schools. By the REV.
C. C. TANCOCK, Head Master of Tonbridge School. With
Illustrations, Map and Plans. Crown 8vo. 2s. 6d.

Europe.

STUDENT'S HISTORY OF MODERN EUROPE.
FROM THE CAPTURE OF CONSTANTINOPLE BY THE TURKS, 1453,
TO THE TREATY OF BERLIN, 1878. By RICHARD LODGE, M.A.,
Fellow and Tutor of Brasenose College, Oxford. 4th Edition,
thoroughly revised. Crown 8vo. 7s. 6d.

**STUDENT'S HISTORY OF EUROPE DURING THE
MIDDLE AGES.** By HENRY HALLAM, LL.D. Crown 8vo.
7s. 6d.

EUROPE IN THE MIDDLE AGES. By OLIVER J.
THATCHER, PH.D., and FERDINAND SCHWILL, PH.D.
Large Crown 8vo. 9s.

This work has been written by men who have had long experience in teaching,
to supply the want of a compendious History of Mediæval Europe, from the
middle of the Fourth to the close of the Fifteenth Century, which has been long
felt in the universities and schools. A distinguished Professor of Modern History
in one of our leading universities, to whom a copy has been sent, writes:

"The book covers ground on which it has always been hard to get a suitable
book for educational purposes, and, so far as I can judge—I have as yet only
examined the German History of the 10th Century—it is thoroughly sound and
clear."

A GENERAL HISTORY OF EUROPE, 850–1900.
By OLIVER J. THATCHER and FERDINAND SCHWILL,
Authors of "Europe in the Middle Ages." Revised and adapted to
the requirements of English Colleges and Schools, by ARTHUR
HASSALL, M.A., Christ Church, Oxford. With Bibliographies at the
end of each section. With Maps, Genealogical Tables. Crown 8vo.
9s. [*Just out.*

The Mediæval Period. The Empire, the Church, and the Invasion
of the Germans—The Franks—The Dismemberment of the Empire
—England and the Norsemen—Germany and France—Feudalism
—Growth of the Papacy—Monasticism — Mohammed and the
Crusades—Italy to 1494, etc.

The Modern Period. The Reformation and Counter Reforma-
tion—Spain under Charles I. and Philip II.—England under the
Tudors—The Revolt of the Netherlands—The Reformation in
France to the Edict of Nantes—The Thirty Years' War—England
in the XVII. Century—Ascendancy of France under Louis XIV.—
Rise of Prussia—The French Revolution—The Holy Alliance—
The Revolution of 1830 and 1848—France under Napoleon III.—
The Unification of Italy—and of Germany—Great Britain and
Russia.

". . . a model of condensation, omitting no essential facts. . . . The
volume is greatly enhanced by a wealth of maps and chronological and genealogical
tables. Among general histories this will take a leading place."—
Dundee Advertiser.

France.

STUDENT'S HISTORY OF FRANCE. FROM THE EARLIEST
TIMES TO THE FALL OF THE SECOND EMPIRE. By W. H. JERVIS,
M.A. A New Edition, thoroughly revised, and in great part re-
written, by ARTHUR HASSALL, M.A., Censor of Christ Church,
Oxford. With a Chapter on Ancient Gaul by F. HAVERFIELD,
M.A., Student of Christ Church, Oxford. Coloured Maps, and
many new Woodcuts. Crown 8vo. 7s. 6d.

Geography.

STUDENT'S MANUAL OF ANCIENT GEOGRAPHY.
By Canon BEVAN, M.A. 150 Woodcuts. Crown 8vo. 7s. 6d.

STUDENT'S GEOGRAPHY OF BRITISH INDIA.
Political and Physical. By GEORGE SMITH, LL.D. With
Maps. Crown 8vo. 7s. 6d.

Geology.

STUDENT'S ELEMENTS OF GEOLOGY. By Sir
CHARLES LYELL. Thoroughly revised by Prof. J. W. JUDD.
Crown 8vo. With 600 Woodcuts. 9s.

Law and Philosophy.

**STUDENT'S EDITION OF AUSTIN'S JURISPRU-
DENCE.** Compiled from the larger work. By ROBERT
CAMPBELL. Crown 8vo. 12s.

AN ANALYSIS OF AUSTIN'S JURISPRUDENCE.
By GORDON CAMPBELL. Crown 8vo. 6s.

Sir Wm. Smith's Smaller Manuals.

These Works have been drawn up for the Lower Forms, at the
request of several teachers, who require more elementary books
than the STUDENT'S HISTORICAL MANUALS.

**SMALLER SCRIPTURE HISTORY OF THE OLD
AND THE NEW TESTAMENT.** In Three Divisions:—I. Old
Testament History. II. Connection of Old and New Testaments.
III. New Testament History to A.D. 70. Edited by Sir WM. SMITH.
With Coloured Maps and 40 Illustrations. Small Crown 8vo. 3s. 6d.

" This book is intended to be used with, and not in place of, the Bible. The
result is most satisfactory,"—*The Standard.*

SMALLER ANCIENT HISTORY OF THE EAST.
From the Earliest Times to the Conquest of Alexander the
Great. By PHILIP SMITH, B.A. With 70 Woodcuts. Small
Crown 8vo. 3s. 6d.

Sir Wm. Smith's Smaller Manuals—continued.

SMALLER HISTORY OF GREECE. From the Earliest
Times to the Roman Conquest. By Sir WM. SMITH. With
Coloured Maps, Plans, and Illustrations. Thoroughly revised by
G. E. MARINDIN, M.A. Crown 8vo. 3s. 6d.

> "Most excellently suited to its purpose; distinguished above all things by its
> lucidity. Altogether the book is excellent."—*Guardian.*

SMALLER HISTORY OF ROME. From the Earliest
Times to the Establishment of the Empire. Thoroughly
revised by A. H. J. GREENIDGE, M.A., Fellow of Hertford College,
Oxford. With a Supplementary Chapter on the Empire to 117 A.D.,
by G. MIDDLETON, M.A., under the Direction of Prof. W. M.
RAMSAY, M.A., D.C.L. With Coloured Map, Plans, and Illustrations. Crown 8vo. 3s. 6d.

> The "Smaller History of Rome" has been written and arranged on the same
> plan, and with the same object, as the "Smaller History of Greece." Like that
> work it comprises separate chapters on the institutions and literature of the coun-
> tries with which it deals.

SMALLER CLASSICAL MYTHOLOGY. With Translations
from the Ancient Poets, and Questions on the Work. By H. R.
LOCKWOOD. With 90 Woodcuts. Small Crown 8vo. 3s. 6d.

> This work has been prepared by a lady for the use of schools, and young persons
> of both sexes. In common with many other teachers, she has long felt the want
> of a consecutive account of the heathen deities, which might safely be placed in
> the hands of the young, and yet contain all that is generally necessary to enable
> them to understand the classical allusions they may meet with in prose or poetry,
> and to appreciate the meanings of works of art.
> A carefully prepared set of QUESTIONS is appended, the answers to which will
> be found in the corresponding pages of the volume.

SMALLER MANUAL OF ANCIENT GEOGRAPHY.
By Canon BEVAN, M.A. With Woodcuts. Small Crown 8vo.
3s. 6d.

SMALLER HISTORY OF ENGLAND. From the Earliest
Times to the Year 1887. Revised and enlarged. By RICHARD
LODGE, M.A. With Coloured Maps and 68 Woodcuts. Crown 8vo.
3s. 6d.

SMALLER HISTORY OF ENGLISH LITERATURE.
Giving a Sketch of the Lives of our Chief Writers. By JAMES
ROWLEY. Small Crown 8vo. 3s. 6d.

> The important position which the study of English literature is now taking in
> education has led to the publication of this work, and of the accompanying volume
> of specimens. Both books have been undertaken at the request of many eminent
> teachers, and no pains have been spared to adapt them to the purpose for which
> they are designed—as elementary works to be used in schools.

SHORT SPECIMENS OF ENGLISH LITERATURE.
Selected from the Chief Authors and arranged chronologically. By
JAMES ROWLEY. With Notes. Small Crown 8vo. 3s. 6d.

> While the "Smaller History of English Literature" supplies a rapid but trust-
> worthy sketch of the lives of our chief writers, and of the successive influences
> which imparted to their writings their peculiar character, the present work supplies
> choice examples of the works themselves, accompanied by all the explanations
> required for their perfect explanation. The two works are thus especially designed
> to be used together.

Mrs. Markham's Histories.

"**Mrs. Markham's Histories are constructed on a plan which is novel and we think well chosen, and we are glad to find that they are deservedly popular, for they cannot be too strongly recommended.**"—**JOURNAL OF EDUCATION.**

HISTORY OF ENGLAND. FROM THE FIRST INVASION BY THE ROMANS TO 1878. With Conversations at the end of each Chapter. 100 Woodcuts. 3s. 6d.

HISTORY OF FRANCE. FROM THE CONQUEST OF GAUL BY JULIUS CÆSAR TO 1878. Conversations at the end of each Chapter. 70 Woodcuts. 3s. 6d.

HISTORY OF GERMANY. FROM ITS INVASION BY MARIUS TO 1880. 50 Woodcuts. 3s. 6d.

Little Arthur's Histories.

HISTORY OF ENGLAND. By LADY CALLCOTT. New and Revised Edition. Continued down to 1878. With 36 Woodcuts. 16mo. 1s. 6d.

"I never met with a history so well adapted to the capacities of children or their entertainment, so philosophical, and written with such simplicity."—Mrs. MARCETT.

HISTORY OF FRANCE. FROM THE EARLIEST TIMES TO THE FALL OF THE SECOND EMPIRE. With Map and Illustrations. 16mo. 2s. 6d.

"The jaded schoolboy, surfeited with tales and the 'over-pressure' arising from long attention to lives and adventures, will, towards the latter part of his holiday, turn with some relief to this book, and begin feasting afresh. Those who know what 'Little Arthur's England' did to popularise the subject among little folks, will know what to expect in this 'France.' The book is capitally illustrated, and very wisely the compiler does not reject the exciting and legendary parts of the subject."—*Schoolmaster.*

HISTORY OF GREECE. By A. S. WALPOLE, M.A. With Map, Plans and Illustrations. Fcap 8vo. 2s. 6d. [*Just out.*

PREPARATORY GEOGRAPHY for IRISH SCHOOLS. With numerous Coloured Maps, Relief Maps, Plans, and Views of well-known Places in Illustration of Geographical Terms. By JOHN COOKE, M.A., Lecturer in Geography, Church of Ireland Training College; and Examiner to the Board of Intermediate Education. Small Crown 8vo. 1s. 6d.

"Mr. Cooke's eminent services to the literature of education have seldom been better illustrated than in this Geography for Irish Schools. . . . Mr. Cooke claims that his Geography is suggestive rather than exhaustive. He might reasonably have gone a step further, and claimed the high merit of charm of attractiveness. With such a wealth of apt illustration drawn from our own country, no child could for a moment fail to comprehend what he sees and hears."—*The Irish Times.*

Sir Wm. Smith's Biblical Dictionaries.

DICTIONARY OF THE BIBLE: COMPRISING ITS ANTIQUITIES, BIOGRAPHY, GEOGRAPHY, AND NATURAL HISTORY. By Various Writers. With Illustrations. 3 vols. Enlarged and revised Edition. Medium 8vo. £4 4s.

. *Arrangements have now been made with the Booksellers, enabling them to offer Special Terms for the Complete Work.*

Intending purchasers should make application to their Bookseller, from whom all particulars may be obtained.

CONCISE DICTIONARY OF THE BIBLE. Condensed from the larger Work. For Families and Students. With Maps and 300 Illustrations. Medium 8vo. 21s.

A Dictionary of the Bible, in some form or another, is indispensable for every family. To students in the Universities, and in the Upper Forms at Schools, to private families, and to that numerous class of persons who desire to arrive at *results* simply, this CONCISE DICTIONARY will, it is believed, supply all that is necessary for the elucidation and explanation of the Bible.

SMALLER DICTIONARY OF THE BIBLE. Abridged from the larger Work. For Schools and Young Persons. With Maps and Illustrations. Crown 8vo. 7s. 6d.

"An invaluable service has been rendered to students in the condensation of Dr. Wm. Smith's Bible Dictionary. The work has been done as only a careful and intelligent scholar could do it, which preserves to us the essential scholarship and value of each article."—*British Quarterly Review.*

The two following Works are intended to furnish a complete account of the leading Personages, the Institutions, Art, Social Life, Writings, and Controversies of the Christian Church from the time of the Apostles to the Age of Charlemagne. They commence at the period at which the "Dictionary of the Bible" leaves off, and form a continuation of it.

DICTIONARY OF CHRISTIAN ANTIQUITIES. The History, Institutions, and Antiquities of the Christian Church. Edited by SIR WM. SMITH, D.C.L., and ARCHDEACON CHEETHAM, D.D. With Illustrations. 2 Vols. Medium 8vo. £3 13s. 6d.

"The work before us is unusually well done. A more acceptable present for a candidate for holy orders, or a more valuable book for any library, than the 'Dictionary of Christian Antiquities' could not easily be found."—*Saturday Review.*

DICTIONARY OF CHRISTIAN BIOGRAPHY, LITERATURE, SECTS, AND DOCTRINES. Edited by SIR WM. SMITH, D.C.L., and HENRY WACE, D.D. 4 Vols. Medium 8vo. £6 16s. 6d.

"The value of the work arises, in the first place, from the fact that the contributors to these volumes have diligently eschewed mere compilation. In these volumes we welcome the most important addition that has been made for a century to the historical library of the English theological student."—*Times.*

Classical and School Dictionaries.

"I am extremely glad of the opportunity of expressing to you the strong sense of obligation which I, in common with all teachers and lovers of classical literature, feel to you for your admirable Dictionaries."—Rev. Dr. HAWTREY, late Head Master of Eton College.

A Complete Cyclopædia of Classical Antiquity. By Various Writers. Edited by Sir WM. SMITH, D.C.L., LL.D.

A DICTIONARY OF GREEK AND ROMAN ANTI-QUITIES. INCLUDING THE LAWS, INSTITUTIONS, DOMESTIC USAGES, PAINTING, SCULPTURE, MUSIC, THE DRAMA, ETC. Edited by SIR WM. SMITH, LL.D., Hon. D.C.L., Oxford, Hon. Ph.D., Leipzig ; WILLIAM WAYTE, M.A., Late Fellow of King's College, Cambridge; G. E. MARINDIN, M.A., Late Fellow of King's College, Cambridge. Third Revised and Enlarged Edition. With 900 Illustrations. 2 Vols. Medium 8vo. 31s. 6d. each.

A CONCISE DICTIONARY OF GREEK AND ROMAN ANTIQUITIES. Based on Sir Wm. Smith's larger Dictionary, and Incorporating the Results of Modern Research. Edited by F. WARRE CORNISH, M.A., Vice-Provost of Eton College. With over 1,100 Illustrations taken from the best examples of Ancient Art. Medium 8vo. 21s.

A SMALLER DICTIONARY OF ANTIQUITIES. Abridged from Sir Wm. Smith's larger Dictionary. With 200 Woodcuts. Crown 8vo. 7s. 6d.

A DICTIONARY OF GREEK AND ROMAN BIO-GRAPHY AND MYTHOLOGY. By Various Writers. Edited by SIR WILLIAM SMITH, D.C.L., LL.D. Illustrated by 564 Engravings on Wood. In 3 Vols. Medium 8vo. 84s.

A CLASSICAL DICTIONARY OF MYTHOLOGY, BIOGRAPHY, AND GEOGRAPHY, compiled from Sir Wm. Smith's larger Dictionaries. In great part re-written by G. E. MARINDIN, M.A., late Fellow of King's College, Cambridge, some time Assistant Master at Eton College. With over 800 Woodcuts. New and thoroughly Revised Edition. 8vo. 18s.

A SMALLER CLASSICAL DICTIONARY, abridged from the above Work. With 200 Woodcuts. In great part re-written by G. E. MARINDIN, M.A., some time Assistant Master at Eton College. Crown 8vo. 7s. 6d.

A DICTIONARY OF GREEK AND ROMAN GEO-GRAPHY. Illustrated by 534 Engravings on Wood 2 Vols. Medium 8vo. 56s.

Sir Wm. Smith's Latin Dictionaries.

"I consider Dr. Wm. Smith's Dictionaries to have conferred a great and lasting service on the cause of classical learning in this country."—Dean LIDDELL.

"I have found Dr. Wm. Smith's Latin Dictionary a great convenience to me. I think that he has been very judicious in what he has omitted, as well as what he has inserted."—Dr. SCOTT.

A COMPLETE LATIN-ENGLISH DICTIONARY. BASED ON THE WORKS OF FORCELLINI AND FREUND. With Tables of the Roman Calendar, Measures, Weights, Money, and a DICTIONARY OF PROPER NAMES. By SIR WM. SMITH, D.C.L., and LL.D. Medium 8vo. 22nd Edition. 16s.

"This work aims at performing the same service for the Latin language as Liddell and Scott's Lexicon has done for the Greek. Great attention has been paid to Etymology, in which department especially this work is admitted to maintain a superiority over all existing Latin Dictionaries.

A SMALLER LATIN-ENGLISH DICTIONARY. WITH A SEPARATE DICTIONARY OF PROPER NAMES, TABLES OF ROMAN MONEYS, &c. Thoroughly revised and in great part re-written. Edited by SIR WM. SMITH and T. D. HALL, M.A. The Etymological portion by JOHN K. INGRAM, LL.D. Square 12mo. 7s. 6d.

This edition of Dr. Smith's 'Smaller Latin-English Dictionary' is to a great extent a new and original Work. Every article has been carefully revised.

A COPIOUS AND CRITICAL ENGLISH-LATIN DIC-TIONARY. Compiled from Original Sources. By SIR WM. SMITH, D.C.L., and T. D. HALL, M.A. Medium 8vo. 16s.

It has been the object of the Authors of this Work to produce a more complete and more perfect ENGLISH-LATIN DICTIONARY than yet exists, and every article has been the result of original and independent research.

Each meaning is illustrated by examples from the classical writers: and those phrases are as a general rule given in both English and Latin.

A SMALLER ENGLISH-LATIN DICTIONARY. Abridged from the above Work, by SIR WM. SMITH and T. D. HALL, M.A., for the use of Junior Classes. Square 12mo. 7s. 6d.

"An English-Latin Dictionary worthy of the scholarship of our age and country. It will take absolutely the first rank, and be the standard English-Latin Dictionary as long as either tongue endures. Even a general examination of the pages will serve to reveal the minute pains taken to ensure its fulness and philological value, and the 'work is to a large extent a dictionary of the English language, as well as an English-Latin Dictionary.'"—*English Churchman.*

A NEW GRADUS AD PARNASSUM.

AN ENGLISH-LATIN GRADUS, OR VERSE DIC-TIONARY, for Schools. By A. C. AINGER, Trinity Coll., Cambridge, Assistant-Master at Eton College, and the late H. G. WINTLE, M.A., Christ Church, Oxford. This Gradus is on a new plan, intended to simplify the Composition of Latin Verses by Classical Meanings, selected Epithets and Synonyms, etc. Crown 8vo. 9s.

Sir Wm. Smith's Educational Series.

Latin Course.

THE YOUNG BEGINNER'S COURSE.
2s. each.

I. **FIRST LATIN BOOK.**—Grammar, Easy Questions, Exercises and Vocabularies.

II. **SECOND LATIN BOOK.**—An easy Latin Reading Book with Analysis of Sentences.

III. **THIRD LATIN BOOK.**—Exercises on the Syntax, with Vocabularies.

IV. **FOURTH LATIN BOOK.**—A Latin Vocabulary for Beginners, arranged according to Subjects and Etymologies.

PRINCIPIA LATINA, Part I. First Latin Course, Grammar, Delectus, Exercises, and Vocabularies. 38th Edition. Thoroughly revised so as to meet the requirements of Modern Teachers and Scholars. Crown 8vo. 3s. 6d.

APPENDIX TO PRINCIPIA LATINA, Part I. Containing Additional Exercises, with Examination Papers. Crown 8vo. 2s. 6d.

PRINCIPIA LATINA, Part II. Reading Book. An Introduction to Ancient Mythology, Geography. Roman Antiquities, and History. With Notes and a Dictionary. Crown 8vo. 3s. 6d.

PRINCIPIA LATINA, Part III. Poetry. 1. Easy Hexameters, and Pentameters. 2. Eclogæ Ovidianæ. 3. Prosody and Metre. 4. First Latin Verse Book. Crown 8vo. 3s. 6d.

PRINCIPIA LATINA, Part IV. Prose Composition. Rules of Syntax, with Examples, Explanations of Synonyms, and Exercises on the Syntax. Crown 8vo. 3s. 6d.

PRINCIPIA LATINA, Part V. Short Tales and Anecdotes from Ancient History for Translation into Latin Prose. With an English-Latin Vocabulary. By Sir WM. SMITH, LL.D. Revised and considerably enlarged. By T. D. HALL, M.A. 3s. 6d.

THE STUDENT'S LATIN GRAMMAR. For the Use of Colleges and the Higher Forms in Schools. By Sir WM. SMITH, LL.D., and T. D. HALL. Crown 8vo. 6s.

SMALLER LATIN GRAMMAR. For the Middle and Lower Forms. Crown 8vo. 3s. 6d.

TRANSLATION AT SIGHT; or, Aids to Facility in the Translation of Latin. Passages of Graduated Difficulty, carefully selected from Latin Authors, with Explanations, Notes, &c. By Professor T. D. HALL, M.A. Crown 8vo. 2s.

A CHILD'S FIRST LATIN BOOK. Comprising Nouns, Pronouns, and Adjectives, with the Verbs. With ample and varied Practice of the easiest kind. Both old and new order of Cases given. By T. D. HALL, M.A. Enlarged Edition, including the Passive Verb. 16mo. 2s.

Sir Wm. Smith's Greek Course.

INITIA GRÆCA, Part I. A FIRST GREEK COURSE, containing Grammar, Delectus, Exercise Book, and Vocabularies. 25th Edition. Edited and carefully revised by FRANCIS BROOKS, M.A., Lecturer in Classics at University College, Bristol, and formerly Classical Scholar of Balliol College, Oxford. Crown 8vo. 3s. 6d.

The great object of this work, as of the "Principia Latina," is to make the study of the language as easy and simple as possible, by giving the grammatical forms only as they are wanted, and by enabling the pupil to translate from Greek into English and from English into Greek as soon has he has learnt the Greek characters and the First Declension. For the convenience of teachers the cases of the nouns, &c., are given according to the ordinary grammars as well as according to the arrangement of the Public Schools Latin Primer.

APPENDIX TO INITIA GRÆCA, Part I. Containing Additional Exercises, with Examination Papers and Easy Reading Lessons with the Sentences Analysed, serving as an Introduction to INITIA GRÆCA, Part II. Crown 8vo. 2s. 6d.

INITIA GRÆCA, Part. II. A READING BOOK. Containing short Tales, Anecdotes, Fables, Mythology, and Grecian History. With a Lexicon. Crown 8vo. 3s. 6d.

INITIA GRÆCA, Part III. PROSE COMPOSITION. Containing the Rules of Syntax, with copious Examples and Exercises. Crown 8vo. 3s. 6d.

THE STUDENT'S GREEK GRAMMAR. FOR THE HIGHER FORMS. By PROFESSOR CURTIUS. Edited by SIR WM. SMITH, D.C.L. Crown 8vo. 6s.

A SMALLER GREEK GRAMMAR. FOR THE MIDDLE AND LOWER FORMS. Abridged from the above Work. Crown 8vo. 3s. 6d.

A GREEK GRAMMAR FOR SCHOOLS. By JOHN THOMPSON, M.A., late Scholar of Christ's College, Cambridge; Senior Classical Master, High School, Dublin. Crown 8vo.
[*In preparation.*

One of the chief objects of this book is to bring within the reach of the younger generation of students and schoolboys some of the results of the linguistic discoveries of the present day. It is therefore written in accordance with the philological views of the *Grundriss der Vergleichenden Grammatik* of Professors Brugmann and Delbrück, of P. Giles' *Manual of Comparative Philology*, of G. Meyer's *Griechische Grammatik* and of other scholars. Use has also been made of the Third Edition, revised by Drs. Blass and Gerth, of Kühner's *Ausführliche Grammatik der Griechischen Sprache*, and of several school Greek Grammars in use in Germany.

The Grammar consists of two parts in one volume, Part I. containing the Accidence, and Part II. the Syntax. The forms and spelling in use in Attic Greek are given according to the latest authorities, and there are special notes on Homeric peculiarities. There are also tables of Greek verbs arranged on a new plan, including (a) a list of the chief types of verbs, (b) a list of common Attic verbs regular according to the types in (n), and (c) a list of the irregular verbs with the irregular forms printed in special type. This arrangement is intended to remove many misconceptions about Greek verbs. Brief notes on syntax, &c., are given with each verb stating the ordinary constructions and any special uses. There will also be Appendices on (1) Greek Weights, Measures, and Dates, (2) Accents, and (3) Sound Changes. Particular attention has been given to the type, so that the essential part of Greek Grammar may be made specially clear, and that the beginner may have no difficulty in distinguishing the more important sections.

AN ENTIRELY NEW AND CHEAPER EDITION.

GREEK TESTAMENT READER. For Use in Schools, comprising consecutive Extracts from the Synoptic Gospel and Passages from the Epistles of St. Paul. By Theophilus D. Hall, M.A. Crown 8vo. 2s. 6d.

Sir Wm. Smith's French Course.

FRENCH PRINCIPIA, Part I. A First French Course, containing Grammar, Delectus and Exercises, with Vocabularies and Materials for French Conversation. Crown 8vo. 3s. 6d.

This work has been compiled at the repeated request of numerous teachers who, finding the "Principia Latina" and "Initia Græca" *the easiest books for learning Latin and Greek,* are anxious to obtain equally elementary French books on the same plan. There is an obvious gain in studying a new language on the plan with which the learner is already familiar. The main object is to enable a beginner to acquire an accurate knowledge of the chief grammatical forms, to learn their usage by constructing simple sentences as soon as he commences the study of the language, and to accumulate gradually a stock of words useful in conversation as well as in reading.

⁎⁎⁎ Keys may be had by AUTHENTICATED TEACHERS *on application.*

APPENDIX TO FRENCH PRINCIPIA, Part I. Containing Additional Exercises and Examination Papers. Cr. 8vo. 2s. 6d.

FRENCH PRINCIPIA, Part II. A Reading Book. Containing Fables, Stories, and Anecdotes, Natural History, and Scenes from the History of France. With Grammatical Questions, Notes, and copious Etymological Dictionary. Crown 8vo. 4s. 6d.

FRENCH PRINCIPIA, Part III. Prose Composition. Containing a Systematic Course of Exercises on the Syntax, with the Principal Rules of Syntax. Crown 8vo. 4s. 6d.

THE STUDENT'S FRENCH GRAMMAR: Practical and Historical. For the Higher Forms. By C. HERON-WALL with Introduction by M. Littré. Crown 8vo. 6s.

A SMALLER FRENCH GRAMMAR. For the Middle and Lower Forms. Abridged from the above Work. Crown 8vo. 3s. 6d.

THE TECHNICAL SCHOOL FRENCH GRAMMAR. By Dr. W. KRISCH, sometime Teacher of Latin and Greek at the Birmingham Midland Institute, Examiner in Modern Languages to the Midland Counties' Union of Educational Institutions. Crown 8vo. 2s. 6d.

FRENCH STUMBLING BLOCKS AND ENGLISH STEPPING STONES. By Francis Tarver, M.A., late Senior French Master at Eton College. Fcap. 8vo. 2s. 6d.

Mr. Francis Tarver's skill as a teacher of French to Englishmen is well known. His thorough knowledge of *both* languages, and his thirty years' experience as a master at Eton, have afforded him exceptional opportunities of judging what are the difficulties, pitfalls, and stumbling-blocks which beset the path of an Englishman in his study of French.

Sir Wm. Smith's German Course.

GERMAN PRINCIPIA, Part I. A First German Course. Containing Grammar, Delectus, Exercises, Vocabularies and materials for German Conversation. Cr. 8vo. 3s. 6d.

⁎⁎ *The present Edition has undergone a very careful revision, and various improvements and additions have been introduced.*

This work is on the same plan as the "French Principia," and therefore requires no further description, except in one point. Differing from the ordinary grammars, all German words are printed in Roman, and not in the old German characters. The Roman letters are used by many modern German writers, and also in Grimm's great Dictionary and Grammar; and it is believed that this alteration will facilitate, more than at first might be supposed, the acquisition of the language. But at the same time, as many German books continue to be printed in the German characters, the exercises are printed in both German and Roman letters.

GERMAN PRINCIPIA, Part II. A Reading Book. Containing Fables, Stories, and Anecdotes, Natural History, and Scenes from the History of Germany. With Grammatical Questions, Notes and Dictionary. Cr. 8vo. 3s. 6d.

PRACTICAL GERMAN GRAMMAR. With a Sketch of the Historical Development of the Language and its Principal Dialects. Cr. 8vo. 3s. 6d.

Sir Wm. Smith's Italian Course.

ITALIAN PRINCIPIA, Part I. A First Italian Course. Containing a Grammar, Delectus, Exercise Book, with Vocabularies, &c. Thoroughly revised and in part re-written by C. F. COSCIA, Professor of Italian in the University of Oxford. Crown 8vo. 3s. 6d.

ITALIAN PRINCIPIA, Part II. A First Italian Reading-Book, containing Fables, Anecdotes, History, and Passages from the best Italian Authors, with Questions, Notes, and an Etymological Dictionary. Crown 8vo. 3s. 6d.

Spanish Course.

SPANISH GRAMMAR. With Exercises, Vocabularies, and Materials for Conversation.

Part I.: Nouns, Adjectives, Pronouns, etc.

Part II.: Verbs, etc., with Copious Vocabularies.

By Don FERNANDO DE ARTEAGA, Taylorian Teacher of Spanish in the University of Oxford. Crown 8vo. [*In preparation.*

This book has in the main been formed on the plan of Sir William Smith's well-known and deservedly popular "Principia Latina, Part I." It possesses, however, one new feature which is as novel as it is likely to prove valuable to the student who uses the book. English people, for the most part, who set themselves to learn Spanish, are not children, but either would-be travellers in the country, students of its literature, or persons engaged in commerce with Spain or Spanish-speaking countries. It has therefore been the aim of the Editor throughout to avoid the old-fashioned Ollendorfen sentences in illustration of the grammar, and instead to make use of phrases and expressions which are likely to prove of practical use to the traveller and the man of business.

English Course.

PRIMARY ENGLISH GRAMMAR for Elementary Schools. With 134 Exercises and carefully graduated passing lessons. By T. D. HALL, M.A. 16mo. 1*s.*

This work aims at the clearest and simplest statement possible of the first principles of English Grammar for the use of children from about eight to twelve years of age.

"We doubt whether any grammar of equal size could give an introduction to the English language more clear, concise, and full than this."—*Watchman.*

SCHOOL MANUAL OF ENGLISH GRAMMAR. With Historical Introduction and copious Exercises. By SIR WM. SMITH, D.C.L., and T. D. HALL, M.A. With Appendices. Crown 8vo. 3*s.* 6*d.*

This work has been prepared with a special view to the requirements of Schools in which English, *as a living language,* is systematically taught, and differs from most modern grammars in its thoroughly practical character. A distinguishing feature of the book is the constant appeal for every usage to the authority of Standard English Authors.

"An admirable English Grammar. We cannot give it higher praise than to say that as a school grammar it is the best in this country."—*English Churchman.*

MANUAL OF ENGLISH COMPOSITION. With Copious Illustrations and Practical Exercises. Suited equally for Schools and for Private Students of English. By T. D. HALL, M.A. Crown 8vo. 3*s.* 6*d.*

"Certainly the most sensible and practical book upon English composition that we have lately seen. The great variety of subjects which it suggests as themes for exercising the imagination as well as the literary powers of young students will be found a great assistance to teachers, who must often be sorely puzzled to hit upon subjects sufficiently diversified without being ridiculously beyond the scope of youthful experience."—*Saturday Review.*

Eton College Books.

THE ETON LATIN GRAMMAR. For use in the Higher Forms. By FRANCIS HAY RAWLINS, M.A., Fellow of King's Coll., Cambridge, and Assistant Master at Eton College, and REV. W. R. INGE, M.A., Fellow of Hertford Coll., Oxford. Revised Edition. Crown 8vo. 6*s.*

"The Syntax has the merit of compressing a great deal of matter into a short space, and of avoiding much of the technical terminology which afflicts some of the readers of the Public School Grammar. It is also lucid in arrangement, and clear in its presentation of facts."—Prof. NETTLESHIP in the *Classical Review.*

ETON LATIN SYNTAX AND EXERCISE BOOK. Consisting of pages 97-127 and 152-306 from the Eton Elementary Latin Exercises. Compiled, with sanction of the Head Master, by A. C. AINGER, M.A., Trinity College, Cambridge, and H. G. WINTLE, M.A., Christ Church, Oxford, Assistant Masters at Eton College. Crown 8vo. 5*s.*

Eton College Books—continued.

THE PREPARATORY ETON GRAMMAR. Containing
the Accidence and the Syntax Rules with the sanction of the Head
Master. By A. C. AINGER, M.A., Trinity College, Cambridge, and
H. G. WINTLE, M.A., Christ Church, Oxford, Assistant Masters at
Eton College. Crown 8vo. 2s.

OVID LESSONS: being Easy Passages selected from the Elegiac
Poems of OVID, with Explanatory Notes by A. C. AINGER, M.A.,
and H. F. W. TATHAM, M.A., of Trinity College, Cambridge,
Assistant Masters at Eton College. Crown 8vo. 2s. 6d.

THE ETON HORACE. The Odes, Epodes, and Carmen
Sæculare. With Notes. By F. W. CORNISH, M.A. In Two
Parts. With Maps. Crown 8vo. 6s.

As it is considered desirable that the notes should be used only in the
preparation of the lesson, and not in the class, they are bound up separate
from the text.

"One good feature is that the notes are printed entirely separate from the text
in a separate volume. They are just those that are suited to boys at that stage."
—*Schoolmaster.*

* **ETON EXERCISES IN ALGEBRA.** By E. P. ROUSE
and A. COCKSHOTT, Assistant Masters at Eton College. Crown
8vo. 3s.

* **ETON EXERCISES IN ARITHMETIC.** By REV. T.
DALTON, M.A., Assistant Master at Eton College. Crown 8vo. 3s.

* *Keys may be obtained by* AUTHENTICATED TEACHERS *on application.*

University Manuals.

Edited by PROFESSOR KNIGHT, of St. Andrew's University.

A HISTORY OF ASTRONOMY. By ARTHUR BERRY, M.A.,
Fellow of King's College, Cambridge. With over 100 Illustrations. 6s.

THE PHILOSOPHY OF THE BEAUTIFUL. Parts I.
and II. By PROFESSOR KNIGHT, University of St. Andrew's.
3s. 6d. each part.

CHAPTERS IN MODERN BOTANY. By PATRICK
GEDDES, Professor of Botany, University College, Dundee.
With Illustrations. 3s. 6d.

THE STUDY OF ANIMAL LIFE. By J. ARTHUR
THOMSON, Regius Professor of Natural Science in the University
of Aberdeen. With many Illustrations. 5s.

THE REALM OF NATURE: A MANUAL OF PHYSIOGRAPHY.
By DR. HUGH ROBERT MILL. With 19 Coloured Maps and 68
Illustrations. 5s.

University Manuals—continued.

AN INTRODUCTION TO MODERN GEOLOGY. By R. D. ROBERTS. With Coloured Maps and Illustrations. 5s.

THE PHYSIOLOGY OF THE SENSES. By JOHN M'KENDRICK, Professor of Physiology in the University of Glasgow, and Dr. SNODGRASS, Physiological Laboratory, Glasgow. 4s. 6d.

THE JACOBEAN POETS. By EDMUND GOSSE. 3s. 6d.

THE ENGLISH NOVEL. By PROFESSOR WALTER RALEIGH, Glasgow University. 3s. 6d.

THE FRENCH REVOLUTION. By C. E. MALLET, Balliol College, Oxford. 3s. 6d.

THE RISE OF THE BRITISH DOMINION IN INDIA. By SIR ALFRED LYALL, K.C.B. With Coloured Maps. 4s. 6d.

ENGLISH COLONIZATION AND EMPIRE. By A. CALDECOTT, Fellow of St. John's College, Cambridge. Coloured Maps and Plans. 3s. 6d.

OUTLINES OF ENGLISH LITERATURE. By WILLIAM RENTON. With Illustrative Diagrams. 3s. 6d.

FRENCH LITERATURE. By H. G. KEENE, Wadham College, Oxford, Fellow of the University of Calcutta. 3s.

LATIN LITERATURE. By J. W. MACKAIL, Balliol College, Oxford 3s. 6d.

SHAKSPERE AND HIS PREDECESSORS IN THE ENGLISH DRAMA. By F. S. BOAS, Balliol College, Oxford. 6s.

GREECE IN THE AGE OF PERICLES. By A. J. GRANT, King's College, Cambridge, and Staff Lecturer in History to the University of Cambridge. With Illustrations. 3s. 6d.

THE ELEMENTS OF ETHICS. By JOHN H. MUIRHEAD, Balliol College, Oxford, Lecturer on Moral Science, Royal Holloway College, Examiner in Philosophy to the University of Glasgow. 3s.

LOGIC, INDUCTIVE AND DEDUCTIVE. By WILLIAM MINTO, late Professor of Logic and Literature, University of Aberdeen. 4s. 6d.

THE USE AND ABUSE OF MONEY. By W. CUNNINGHAM, D.D., Fellow of Trinity College, Cambridge, Professor of Economic Science, King's College, London. 3s.

HISTORY OF RELIGION. By ALLAN MENZIES, D.D., Professor of Biblical Criticism University of St. Andrew's. 5s.

ELEMENTS OF PHILOSOPHY AND PSYCHOLOGY. By GEORGE CROOM ROBERTSON, late Grote Professor, University College, London. Edited by MRS. C. A. FOLEY RHYS DAVIDS, M.A., from Notes of Lectures delivered at the College, 1870—1892. 2 Vols. 3s. 6d. each.

Miscellaneous Works for the Young.

EARLY CHAPTERS IN SCIENCE. A First Book of Knowledge of Natural History, Botany, Physiology, Physics and Chemistry for Young People. By Mrs. W. AWDRY (Wife of the Bishop of South Tokyo, Japan). Edited by W. F. Barrett, F.R.S., Professor of Experimental Physics in the Royal College of Science for Ireland. With nearly 200 Illustrations. Crown 8vo. 6s.
> " Deserves a warm welcome from all teachers of the young. . . . The illustrations are models of clear, careful, and unconventional work."—*Literature.*
> " It can be confidently recommended to the young as a sound and pleasantly written introduction to science."—*Guardian.*

ÆSOP'S FABLES. A New Version. Chiefly from the Original Sources. By Rev. THOMAS JAMES. With 100 Woodcuts. Illustrations by John Tenniel. Crown 8vo. 2s. 6d.
> " This work is remarkable for the clearness and conciseness with which each tale is narrated ; and the book has been relieved of those tedious and unprofitable appendages called ' morals,' which used to obscure and disfigure the ancient editions of the work."—*The Examiner.*

THE BIBLE IN THE HOLY LAND. Extracted from Dean Stanley's work on Sinai and Palestine. With Woodcuts. Crown 8vo. 3s. 6d.

SERMONS TO YOUNG BOYS. A New Edition with two New Sermons. By the Rev. F. de W. LUSHINGTON, M.A. (Late Scholar of Clare College, Cambridge, and Assistant Master at Elstree School. 2nd Edition. Crown 8vo. 3s. 6d.

SERMONS FOR CHILDREN PREACHED IN WEST-MINSTER ABBEY. By Dean STANLEY. Post 8vo. 3s. 6d.

Miscellaneous Works for Advanced Students.

GROTE'S HISTORY OF GREECE, from the Earliest Period to the close of Alexander the Great. With Portrait, Maps, and Plans. 10 vols. 5s. each.

THE GREEK THINKERS. A History of Ancient Philosophy. By Professor THEODOR GOMPERZ, of Vienna University. Hon. LL.D., Dublin, Ph.D. Königsberg, &c.

VOL. I.—Translated by LAURIE MAGNUS, M.A., Magdalen College, Oxford. Demy 8vo. 14s. *net.*
> " We are glad to welcome the first instalment of the authorised translation of Professor Gomperz's great history of ancient philosophy. . . . The translation is excellently done and the translator has had the benefit of untiring help from the author. Such an excellent reproduction of so important a foreign work on one of the greatest of themes is an event in its way. . . . We shall look forward with great pleasure to the appearance of the next volume."—*Spectator.*
> " . . . an exceedingly welcome contribution to this subject. This work not only exhibits accuracy of scholarship and critical acumen, but is easily distinguished by lucidity of expression. . . . bright, lucid, free from pedantry, and occasionally epigrammatic. Prof. Gomperz promises us two more volumes ; we have no doubt but that the interest will be equally well sustained."—*Nature.*

VOL. II.—Plato and Aristotle. Translated by G. G. BERRY, M.A., Balliol College, Oxford.   [*In the Press.*

Miscellaneous Works for Advanced Students.
—continued.

CHAPTERS FROM ARISTOTLE'S ETHICS. By J. H. MUIRHEAD, M.A., Professor of Mental and Moral Philosophy, Mason University College, Birmingham. Author of "The Elements of Ethics." Large crown 8vo. 7s. 6d.

"We cannot commend these ' chapters' too highly, not only to teachers, but to all students of Aristotle or of moral philosophy who feel that the problems of the Old Greeks are in any way unreal in these later days, or their solutions out of date."—*Pilot.*

THE GREAT PERSIAN WAR and its Preliminaries. A STUDY OF THE EVIDENCE, LITERARY AND TOPOGRAPHICAL. By G. B. GRUNDY, M.A., Lecturer at Brasenose College, and University Lecturer in Classical Geography. With Maps and Illustrations. Demy 8vo. 21s. *net.*

This book deals in detail with the campaign of Marathon, and with that of the years 480—479 B.C. The author has personally examined the scenes of the great events recorded, and has made surveys of Thermopylæ and Platæa for the purpose of the work. There are introductory chapters on the relation between the Greeks and the Oriental monarchies prior to the year 490 B.C. The book is fully illustrated by maps, photographs, and sketches of the main sites of interest.

"It is but seldom that we have the priviledge of reviewing so excellent a work in Greek history. This book on the great war which freed Greece from the attacks of Persia will long remain the standard work on the subject."— *The Athenæum.*

"Mr. Grundy's book is one which no one working at Greek history can afford to neglect."—*Manchester Guardian.*

THE DAWN OF MODERN GEOGRAPHY. By C. RAYMOND BEAZLEY, M.A., F.R.G.S., late Fellow of Merton College, Oxford. A HISTORY OF EXPLORATION AND GEOGRAPHICAL SCIENCE.

VOL. I.—From the Conversion of the Roman Empire to A.D. 900, with an account of the achievements and writings of the early Christian, Arab and Chinese Travellers and Students. With Reproductions of the Principal Maps of the Time. 8vo. 18s.

"Mr. Beazley is only at the threshold of his great subject, and the manner in which he has dealt with the obscurest part of his theme causes us to look forward with pleasant anticipations to its continuation. It is gratifying to think that the best extant account of the dawn of Geography should emanate from an Englishman."—*Athenæum.*

VOL. II.—From the Opening of the Tenth to the Middle of the Thirteenth Century (A.D. 900—1260). With Maps and Illustrations. Demy 8vo. 18s.   [*Just out.*

This volume includes an account of the Scandinavian Explorers, and the Saga travel-literature ; of the Pilgrims and Religious Travellers, such as Sæwulf and Benjamin of Tudela ; of the Merchant Travellers, such as Elder Polos ; of the Missionary and Diplomatic Travellers, such as William de Rubruquis and John de Plano Carpini ; and of the Scientific Geographers and Map Makers such as Matthew Paris, Henry of Maintz, Lambert of St. Omer, etc. With some notice of the Arab and Chinese Geographers and Travellers of this time, such as Edrisi, etc.

As in the above volume, the object of the present is to give a thoroughly representative and so complete account of geographical progress during a great part of the Middle Ages. Beginning with the changes wrought by the Northmen, this second instalment brings down the narrative to the close of the Crusading era, and the highest point of the Empire of the Mongol Tartars.

Miscellaneous Works for Advanced Students.

—continued.

A TREATISE ON MEDICAL JURISPRUDENCE. Based on Lectures delivered at University College, London. By G. VIVIAN POORE, M.D. With Illustrations. 8vo. 12s. net.

". . . Admirable and interesting treatise . . . the reader can almost hear Dr. Poore's genial and witty voice as he turns these instructive pages. They are marked by a kind of 'golden common-sense,' which is the most valuable lesson that any medical or legal student can lay to heart . . . an ideal handbook of the subject for the young student."—*The Spectator.*

HANDBOOK OF PHYSIOLOGY. By W. D. HALLIBURTON, M.D., F.R.S., Professor of Physiology, King's College, London. Fourth Edition, being the Seventeenth of Kirkes' (see Note below). Again thoroughly revised, with the addition of new matter and new illustrations, and certain alteration of the arrangement in deference to the wishes and advice of numerous teachers. With upwards of Six Hundred Illustrations, including some Coloured Plates. Large Cr. 8vo. 14s.

The LANCET of September 7th, 1901 (The Students' Number), gives to this the position of THE STANDARD WORK FOR STUDENTS.

EXTRACT FROM PUBLISHER'S NOTE TO THIS EDITION.

Three completely revised editions of KIRKES' HANDBOOK have now been published since the editorship was first undertaken by Professor W. D. Halliburton in 1896. So extensive have been the changes made in these years, that but little remains of the original work, and the manual has now obtained a higher reputation and a wider popularity than at any time before.

In these circumstances it has been suggested by several professional men and other readers of the book that it would be well to drop the time-honoured name of "Kirkes'," and to substitute for it that of the real author of the present volume —Professor Halliburton. Whatever prestige attached to the old title has now been rightly transferred to the new, and we have accordingly decided to adopt this suggestion, and to call the book in future "HALLIBURTON'S PHYSIOLOGY."

Works by Sir Henry S. Maine, K.C.S.I.

ANCIENT LAW; its Connections with the Early History of Society, and its Relations to Modern Ideas. Sixteenth Edition. 8vo. 9s.

LECTURES ON THE EARLY HISTORY OF INSTITUTIONS, in continuation of the above work. 8vo. 9s.

VILLAGE - COMMUNITIES IN THE EAST AND WEST, with other Lectures, Addresses, and Essays. Seventh Edition. 8vo. 9s.

DISSERTATIONS ON EARLY LAW AND CUSTOM. 8vo. 9s.

POPULAR GOVERNMENT. Four Essays. I. Prospects of Popular Government.—II. Nature of Democracy.—III. Age of Progress.—IV. Constitution of the United States. Fifth Edition. 8vo. 7s. 6d.

INTERNATIONAL LAW. The Whewell Lectures delivered at Cambridge in 1887. 8vo. 7s. 6d.

THE

PROGRESSIVE SCIENCE SERIES.

Large 8vo, cloth extra, 6s. per volume.

NOW READY.

THE STUDY OF MAN: AN INTRODUCTION TO ETHNOLOGY. By PROFESSOR A. C. HADDON, D.Sc., M.A., M.R.I.A. Illustrated.

THE GROUNDWORK OF SCIENCE. By ST. GEORGE MIVART, M.D., PH.D., F.R.S.

EARTH SCULPTURE. By PROFESSOR GEIKIE, LL.D., F.R.S. Illustrated.

RIVER DEVELOPMENT. As Illustrated by the Rivers of North America. By PROFESSOR I. C. RUSSELL. Illustrated.

VOLCANOES. By PROFESSOR BONNEY, D.Sc., F.R.S. Illustrated.

BACTERIA. ESPECIALLY AS THEY ARE RELATED TO THE ECONOMY OF NATURE, TO INDUSTRIAL PROCESSES, AND TO THE PUBLIC HEALTH. By GEORGE NEWMAN, M.D., F.R.S.E., D.P.H., Demonstrator of Bacteriology in King's College, London. With over 90 other Illustrations.

Corrected Edition, and with an added Chapter on Tropical Diseases, an Account of Malarial Infection by Mosquitoes, and other Subjects.

A BOOK OF WHALES. By the Editor of the Series, F. E. BEDDARD, M.A., F.R.S. With 40 Illustrations by SIDNEY BERRIDGE.

THE COMPARATIVE PHYSIOLOGY of the BRAIN AND COMPARATIVE PSYCHOLOGY. By PROFESSOR JACQUES, LOEB, M.D., Professor of Physiology in the University of Chicago.

THE STARS: A STUDY OF THE UNIVERSE. By PROFESSOR NEWCOMB. Illustrated.

IN COURSE OF PRODUCTION.

HEREDITY. By J. ARTHUR THOMSON, M.A., F.R.S.E. Illustrated. Author of "The Study of Animal Life," and co-Author of "The Evolution of Sex." With numerous Diagrams and Illustrations.

The Progressive Science Series.—continued.

THE ANIMAL OVUM. By F. E. BEDDARD, M.A., F.R.S. (the Editor). Illustrated.

THE REPRODUCTION OF LIVING BEINGS; A Comparative Study. By MARCUS HARTOG, M.A., D.Sc., Professor of Natural History in Queen's College, Cork. Illustrated.

MAN AND THE HIGHER APES. By Dr. KEITH, F.R.C.S. Illustrated.

METEORS AND COMETS. By Professor C. A. YOUNG.

THE MEASUREMENT OF THE EARTH. By President MENDENHALL.

EARTHQUAKES. By Major DUTTON.

PHYSIOGRAPHY; or, The Forms of Land. By Professor DAVIS.

THE HISTORY OF SCIENCE. By C. J. PIERCE.

GENERAL ETHNOGRAPHY. By Professor BRINTON.

RECENT THEORIES OF EVOLUTION. By Professor BALDWIN.

LIFE AREAS OF NORTH AMERICA: A Study in the Distribution of Animals and Plants. By Dr. C. HART MERRIAM.

PLANETARY MOTION. By G. W. HILL, Ph.D.

INFECTION AND IMMUNITY. By GEORGE S. STERNBERG, M.D., Surgeon-General of the U.S. Army.

AGE, GROWTH, SEX, AND DEATH. By Professor CHARLES S. MINOT, Harvard Medical School.

Other Volumes will shortly be announced, and the Series in its entirety will comprise volumes on every branch of Science.

CHARLES DARWIN'S WORKS.

THE ORIGIN OF SPECIES BY MEANS OF NATURAL SELECTION. Library Edition. 2 vols. 12s.—Popular Edition. 6s.—Cheaper Edition. With a Photogravure Portrait of the Author. Large crown 8vo. 2s. 6d. net.

Mr. Murray desires to inform the public that the edition which has just lost copyright is the imperfect edition which was subsequently thoroughly revised by Mr. Darwin. This imperfect edition has been reprinted by other publishers without the consent or authority of Mr. Darwin's representatives.

The only authorised and complete editions are those published by Mr. Murray, and these do not lose copyright for several years to come.

ALSO, JUST PUBLISHED, AN EDITION OF

THE ORIGIN OF SPECIES. In Paper Covers. Price 1s. net.

The Spectator says:—"The publisher very properly points out that this original edition did not contain Darwin's mature convictions his views having been modified by criticism and further observations. . . . If the public can get the revised book for a shilling, there can hardly, we suppose, be much of a market for the unrevised. There is sometimes a not very seemly scramble for a work which goes out of copyright."

DESCENT OF MAN, AND SELECTION IN RELATION TO SEX. Woodcuts. Library Edition. 2 vols. 15s.— 1 Vol. Popular Edition. 7s. 6d.—Cheaper Edition. With Illustrations. Large crown 8vo. 2s. 6d. net.

VARIATION OF ANIMALS AND PLANTS UNDER DOMESTICATION. Woodcuts. 2 vols. 15s.

EXPRESSION OF THE EMOTIONS IN MAN AND ANIMALS. With Illustrations. 12s.

VARIOUS CONTRIVANCES BY WHICH ORCHIDS ARE FERTILIZED BY INSECTS. Woodcuts. 7s. 6d.

MOVEMENTS AND HABITS OF CLIMBING PLANTS. Woodcuts. 6s.

INSECTIVOROUS PLANTS. Woodcuts. 9s.

CROSS AND SELF-FERTILIZATION IN THE VEGETABLE KINGDOM. 9s.

DIFFERENT FORMS OF FLOWERS ON PLANTS OF THE SAME SPECIES. 7s. 6d.

FORMATION OF VEGETABLE MOULD THROUGH THE ACTION OF WORMS. Illustrations. 6s.

JOURNAL OF A NATURALIST DURING A VOYAGE ROUND THE WORLD IN H.M.S. "BEAGLE." With 100 Illustrations. Medium 8vo. 21s.—Popular Edition. With Portrait. 3s. 6d.—Cheaper Edition. With 16 full-page Plates. Large crown 8vo. 2s. 6d. net.

MR. MURRAY'S MUSICAL SERIES.

Crown 8vo. 5s. net each.

SONGS AND SONG WRITERS. By HENRY T. FINCK, Author of "Wagner and his Works," "Chopin and other Musical Essays," etc., etc. With 8 Portraits.

THE ORCHESTRA AND ORCHESTRAL MUSIC. By W. J. HENDERSON, Author of "What is Good Music," etc., etc. With 8 Portraits and other Illustrations.

THE OPERA, PAST AND PRESENT. AN HISTORICAL SKETCH. By WILLIAM FOSTER APTHORP, Author of "Musicians and Music Lovers," etc, With Portraits.

CHOIRS AND CHORAL MUSIC. By ARTHUR MEES. With Portraits.

MUSIC: How IT CAME TO BE WHAT IT IS. By HANNAH SMITH. With Illustrations.

HOW MUSIC DEVELOPED. By W. J. HENDERSON, Author of "What is Good Music."

HOW TO LISTEN TO MUSIC. HINTS AND SUGGESTIONS TO UNTAUGHT LOVERS OF THE ART. By HENRY EDWARD KREHBIEL, Author of "Studies in the Wagnerian Drama," etc., etc. With 11 Portraits.

WHAT IS GOOD MUSIC? SUGGESTIONS TO PERSONS DESIRING TO CULTIVATE A TASTE IN MUSICAL ART. By W. J. HENDERSON.

LONDON: JOHN MURRAY, ALBEMARLE STREET, W.

Boyle, Son & Watchurst,]   [Printers, Warwick Square, E.C.